I0590462

Over and Over

Also by Becky Hunter

One Moment

You Make My Heart Stop

BECKY HUNTER

FOREVER

New York   Boston

This book is a work of fiction. Names, characters, places, and incidents are the product of the author's imagination or are used fictitiously. Any resemblance to actual events, locales, or persons, living or dead, is coincidental.

Copyright © 2026 by Becky Hunter
Reading group guide copyright © 2026 by Becky Hunter and Hachette Book Group, Inc.

Cover design by Caitlin Sacks. Cover illustration by Shutterstock. Cover copyright © 2026 by Hachette Book Group, Inc.

Hachette Book Group supports the right to free expression and the value of copyright. The purpose of copyright is to encourage writers and artists to produce the creative works that enrich our culture.

The scanning, uploading, and distribution of this book without permission is a theft of the author's intellectual property. If you would like permission to use material from the book (other than for review purposes), please contact permissions@hbgusa.com. Thank you for your support of the author's rights.

Forever
Hachette Book Group
1290 Avenue of the Americas, New York, NY 10104
read-forever.com
@readforeverpub

Originally published in trade paperback in Great Britain in 2026 by Corvus, an imprint of Atlantic Books Ltd.
First Forever edition: February 2026

Forever is an imprint of Grand Central Publishing. The Forever name and logo are registered trademarks of Hachette Book Group, Inc.

The publisher is not responsible for websites (or their content) that are not owned by the publisher.

Forever books may be purchased in bulk for business, educational, or promotional use. For information, please contact your local bookseller or the Hachette Book Group Special Markets Department at special.markets@hbgusa.com.

Library of Congress Control Number: 2025948107

ISBNs: 9781538773307 (trade paperback), 9781538773314 (ebook)

Printed in the United States of America

LSC-C

Printing 1, 2025

Prologue

He turns away from her. He can't do it anymore, can't stand here watching her throw this all away. It's over now. Done.

He waits for the relief to hit as the rain grows heavier, sliding down his neck and under his jacket. Maybe even for the excitement—because this means a new start, a new location. Neither comes. Instead, all he feels is flat.

Maybe it was a mistake to come and say goodbye.

"Wait."

Her voice stops him as though his body is physically connected to her. He turns, slowly. Watches her as she takes a step toward him, those hazel eyes level on his in a way they weren't moments before, her blond hair damp and scraggly with the rain.

He can't help it. He mimics her, moving toward her so they are standing opposite each other in the middle of the road.

She tilts her face up to him, rain pouring in sheets around them. "I love you," she says. And his heartbeat stutters.

It's the first time she's said it. The first time, he knows, that she's been brave enough to. He stares at her, waiting to see the doubt that sometimes flickers in her eyes. But this time, there is none of that.

He finds his mouth tugging up into a smile. "Yeah?"

She nods. "Yes." Her voice is steady. Certain. "I'm sorry I didn't say it sooner."

His smile grows. "Better late than never." And *there* it is, the relief. Not at leaving her for good, but at knowing for sure that she feels the same. But still he doesn't reach for her. Because even if she loves him, it doesn't necessarily mean she *wants* him.

"I don't want you to leave me," she murmurs, answering that question. That's the permission he needs to reach for her waist, feeling the heat of her skin under her damp jumper. And then he's kissing her, and he hears her breath catch as he takes her mouth in his, feels her arms come around his neck, pulling him closer. God, he's never been able to get enough of this. Of her.

A car horn sounds somewhere nearby, making him remember that they are still, in fact, in the middle of the road.

They are both laughing as they pull away from one another, as he tugs her to where his car is parked. He lifts her, propping her on the bonnet. He can taste her smile as he kisses her again, the rain beating harder on both of their heads.

"I hate to say it," he says against her mouth, "but I reckon we need to make a break for it." A car passes, proving the point by splashing through a newly formed puddle. He cocks his head, his hands resting on her thighs. "Your place?"

"No," she says, jumping down from the bonnet. "Let's go somewhere." He considers her, then concedes with a nod, fishing out keys and unlocking the car.

Inside, it's all steamed up. And it is tempting, right then, to reach for her again. But he knows that if he does, he won't be able to stop. So instead he starts the engine.

"Where shall we go?" he asks.

She laughs, and it's so *joyful* he feels it like a bolt through his core. "Anywhere!"

He takes her hand as he drives, thumb traveling a small circle over her perfect skin. "You know I love you, right?"

She links her fingers with his, gripping tight. "I have always loved you." Her voice is so beautifully certain. And he knows what she means, because he can't imagine ever not loving her either. Jesus, he really fucking loves this woman. He wonders if this is what everyone experiences when they find the person they're meant to be with. This certainty, the sense of rightness whenever they are near. The sense that their souls were made for one another. Because for him, meeting her made everything slot into place, like there were pieces of him missing he hadn't even known existed.

He glances down at her, sees her looking at their joined hands, a perfect smile on her heart-shaped face.

It's just a fleeting glance, but it's enough that he misses something on the road. So it's only when he looks back out of the windscreen, peering through the rain, that he sees the headlights. Coming toward them through the gray.

Too big, too fast. A lorry, he realizes, almost absent-mindedly. A lorry is skidding over to their side of the road, coming right at them.

It's going to hit them. It's obvious in that moment. It's going to hit them, and there's nothing he can do about it. He has already snatched his hand from her grip. He is already turning the steering wheel, trying to control the car. But they're going too fast, and the road is too wet.

His name comes as a panicked plea as she reaches out to grab the wheel, like that might help. Her eyes turn to his, wide, pupils dark. And in the moment their gazes meet, he sees that she knows it too. That she was right. That this deep sense of dread, of déjà vu that is flooding through them, isn't misplaced.

He's going to die, he knows that.

But it's not this that sends a shock wave running through him. It's the realization that this is not the first time it has happened. It's not the first time he's met her, not the first time they have fallen in love.

It is not the first time he has died.

Chapter One

Lissa is drowning. Icy water surrounds her, pressing down on every part of her, clinging to her clothes, scalding her skin. Everything is a murky black. A weed twists round her foot, holding her in place as she thrashes, trying to reach the surface, even as she can't be sure where the surface is. She mustn't open her mouth. She knows that. But her chest is burning, more pain than she's ever experienced, urging her to breathe, to relieve the pressure.

Distantly she hears someone screaming for her, over and over, but the voice is distorted, the tenor of it weirdly unfamiliar. This is it. She knows it is, even as her heart beats faster, urging her to keep fighting, as her arms try to claw their way through the oppressive cold.

But she can't fight anymore. She opens her mouth, desperate for release. And water floods in.

She wakes drenched in sweat, her duvet kicked off. She is breathing heavily, her body trembling. Autumn rain lashes at the window, the only noise in the dark.

She tries to steady her breathing, placing a hand on her chest and rubbing there. She's used to this nightmare, though that felt rougher than usual. She glances at the red numbers on her alarm clock on the bedside table— a birthday present from her dad a few years ago. A demonstration that he didn't have a clue what to get her, but she likes it all the same.

It's 5:30 a.m. On the 16th of September.

No surprise, really, that the dream was more vivid than usual, today of all days. Twenty years exactly since her little sister drowned. It doesn't seem to get any easier, year on year. Perhaps because she knows by now exactly what the day will bring.

She pushes up out of bed. No point trying to get back to sleep after that.

She walks to the bathroom in her small one-bed flat. This is the first year that she's been able to afford to rent on her own, rather than having to house share, and she loves every tiny inch of it. Being a homeowner is still a distant dream, but the relief of not having to tiptoe around on early mornings or force smiles and chats at the end of the evening is something she welcomes almost daily.

She switches the light on, tries to avoid looking at herself in the mirror. She knows she'll be too pale, the shadows under her eyes too dark. She takes a packet of pills out of the cabinet, swallows one, then cups water from the tap to wash it down. A headache is already pressing down on her, throbbing at her temples, and she knows it'll only get worse, despite the pain relief.

She tells herself it's a response to stress, to tiredness. She reminds herself that plenty of people get headaches, that it's very unlikely to be serious. And this, she thinks, is exactly why her phone is on charge in the living room rather than on her nightstand, far away from where she can start to google symptoms and go down a hole she'll only get stuck in.

It's the 16th of September, she reminds herself. It would be weird if she *didn't* wake with a headache today. All she has to do is put one foot in front of the other, keep going until the day is done. It's only twenty-four hours. Less, really, because she can go to bed at, what, 8 p.m.? So that's only a little more than twelve hours when you think about it.

Twelve hours. She can get through that. She's done it before, after all.

She arrives at her mum's house on the outskirts of Bath at 9 a.m. It's the same house Lissa grew up in, on the northern edge of the city, an area that has grown more desirable over the years—close enough to the center, but on the doorstep of some beautiful countryside a few minutes' drive away. It's probably worth a fortune now, a semi-detached three-bed like this, but her mum will never sell, and Lissa imagines the price of it would be significantly devalued given the state it's in.

She steps through the overgrown garden, along the stone path that leads to the front door, mossy grass pushing its way through the cracks. There is a black gate to one side of the house, leading round to the back. She remembers a time when two bikes used to be propped up behind that gate, one bright blue, the other purple and silver with tassels on the handles. Her sister never outgrew that bike—never had the chance to.

She doesn't go through the gate now, though. Instead, she fumbles in her coat pocket for the spare key, turning it in her fingers as she stares at the front door. The rain has eased off, leaving behind just the odd shower in an otherwise sunny morning, like two sides of the weather arguing with one another about what sort of day it should be.

She taps the key against her palm. She doesn't want to go in. She doesn't know what she'll find. Last year, her mum had been passed out on the sofa, a sick bowl next to her, empty bottles lining the kitchen counter. The year before, Lissa had walked in to see the start of a suicide note in the kitchen, torn into pieces. She remembers the terror as she ran upstairs, screaming for her mum, who didn't answer from where she lay curled in a ball on her bed. Lissa doesn't think she'd actually go through with something like that, but it seems that each year, on this day, her mum gets worse rather than better. Like she sees it as the day to punish herself—and the world—for what happened.

The door swings open as she finally turns the key in the lock, and she calls out, aware of how tentative her voice sounds. No answer.

"Mum?" she tries again, heading farther into the house.

She peers into the kitchen to see unwashed dishes stacked in the sink. She'll do those later. Clutter inhabits the house in a way that makes it impossible to see what it would be like without it, and there's that distant musty smell that comes with neglect, no matter how much bleach you spray or how many times you hoover. The carpet has been the same for the last twenty years, frayed at the corners and stained in various places, with a rug that she thinks might have belonged to her now deceased grandmother taking center stage in the living room. The photos on the mantel above the fireplace are the same as they've always been, depicting a happy family that no longer exists. The whole place is a time capsule, like stepping back to the 1990s, and if ever Lissa suggests they clear some things away, or perhaps get a new carpet, she is met with a vicious tongue, red-rimmed eyes or an attempt at a joke, depending on the day.

Her mum isn't anywhere in the house. It's only when Lissa checks the second bedroom—her old room, which overlooks the back garden—that she sees her. She watches for a moment, one hand on the curtains she chose as a teenager—dark blue with bright, colorful birds on them. She thinks they might have been the last thing her dad bought for the house before he left it. Her mum is standing out there in a nightie and a cardigan, barefoot, staring into nothingness. Lissa's heart twists at the sight, though she already knows there will be nothing she can do to make things better. Not today.

She heads down to the garden anyway. There used to be a swing set, but her dad got rid of it when Lissa was about twelve, in an attempt to start making a change. It's the pond her mum is staring at, Lissa notices when she gets there. It's been left to its own devices over the years, and by rights it probably should've dried up or stagnated by now, but instead it has somehow flourished, with flowers and weeds all around, buzzing insects humming with life. It seems cruel that the site of Chloe's death can be so alive.

"Mum?"

Her mum turns, her hazel eyes, so like Lissa's own, red and swollen. Her skin is dull, gray hair unkempt. It's hard to tell from here if she's been drinking, but she seems steady enough.

"You came." Her voice is raspy. She doesn't usually smoke, but today, anything goes.

"Of course. I always do."

Her mum turns away, tugging her cardigan to her. Lissa wonders if she slept last night. She wonders if she too is plagued by nightmares. They won't talk about it if she is. They never talk about it.

"Come on, let's get you inside. I'll make you some breakfast." She brought bread and eggs with her—food is not always reliable in her mother's house.

"We don't deserve to eat today, Alyssa." The words are small and bitter, and the "we" isn't lost on Lissa.

"Well, we still need to." Her voice is flat, because this is what she dreads. This, she feels sure, is why she can't shake the nightmares, why this day never gets any easier. The blame she hears in her mother's voice, no matter how much time passes. The blame, Lissa knows, that she deserves.

"Come on." She turns back to the house, without looking to see if her mum is following. She will eventually. She always does.

She is exhausted when she leaves her mum's house early evening, and the headache is much worse, despite the copious painkillers she's taken. *Stress and tiredness*, she repeats to herself. It is not a sign of a brain tumor; it is not an aneurysm. It is normal. *She* is normal.

She checks her phone as she walks, late sunlight filtering through gaps in the trees that line the pavement, their leaves turning russet and gold. She could get the bus back to her flat on the opposite side of the city, but she needs to walk, to breathe.

There's a message from Mia waiting for her.

I hope you're doing okay. Thinking of you and here if you need me. Be safe. Xxx

Lissa feels irrational tears prick her eyes as she reads it— a fallout from having spent too long with her mum today. As her only cousin, Mia is probably the one person who understands how difficult this day is. Apart from her dad, of course, but either he's forgotten or he's determinedly refusing to acknowledge it, because she's heard nothing from him.

Be safe.

Lissa bites her lip. It's the only recognition that things don't always go as planned on this date, that sometimes Lissa lets her emotions get the better of her. A reminder that what she should do is go home, shut the curtains, have a peppermint tea and a sleeping pill and fall asleep in front of *Gossip Girl* on Netflix.

But she comes to a stop at the end of her mum's road. She is drained right now, yes, but she also can't be sure that when she sleeps it will be dreamless. And for once, she doesn't want to go back to her empty flat. She doesn't think she can face the quiet, the tumble of anxiety that will fill the space.

Anyway, tonight is not a night for lying alone, hoping nightmares don't plague her. Tonight is not a night for being pathetic and helpless. Her sister died on this day twenty years ago, yes. But Lissa is still here, isn't she? She is still breathing, still living. So she might as well bloody do something with said life.

What she needs is a distraction, something to stop her spiraling. And there's nothing wrong with that, is there? Distractions don't have to be a bad thing; they can be *healthy*.

She scrolls through her contacts, hesitating over his name. Fuck it. She sends a WhatsApp. He starts to type almost immediately—he must already be out. She smiles when she sees the reply come through, something akin to excitement spiking her system. This is perfect. This is exactly what she needs.

She sets off with purpose. It's a thirty-minute walk to the city center, but there are several e-scooter stations en route. She's never ridden one before, always worried about the possibility of getting into an accident, but tonight seems like the moment to try it.

She scoots down the hill, passing a line of Georgian terraces. She hears the city center before she sees it—laughter and chatter and the bell chiming in the abbey. The mood is vibrant, people spilling out from bars onto the cobbled streets, the sky a pink glow above the sandstone buildings. The rain from earlier has been whisked away, but a damp chill remains in the air, so that her fingers feel icy on the handlebars. Wasn't everyone promising an Indian summer this year? Whatever happened to that?

It's a Saturday night, she realizes, as she passes a wine bar with al fresco seating, mimicking a European city. A Saturday on one of the few remaining warm evenings, no doubt, and here everyone is, making the most of it. Here *she* is, making the most of it too.

She's not concentrating when she turns the next corner, leaning in with her scooter. She has a moment to think how she's really getting the hang of this scootering business before she hears the horn. She jumps, the scooter wobbling underneath her. She moves to glare over her shoulder, hears the horn again as she swerves unintentionally toward the middle of the road.

Then there are hands roughly grabbing her. One on her waist, the other taking control of the handlebars, pulling her off the road and toward the pavement. She yells, sees heads turn. The taxi blasts past her without slowing down, its wheels spraying up water.

She doesn't get to see the face of the person who has abducted her, because she's falling, straight onto the pavement. The scooter slides out from under her and she hears a male grunt, just as she flings her hands out, catching herself before her chin hits the concrete.

Pain reverberates through her arms, and she grits her teeth against it before shoving herself up, already scowling.

A man is holding her scooter, the other hand outstretched to help her up, blue eyes—ridiculously bright—creased in concern. Oh, great, so he's *concerned* that he shoved her onto the tarmac now, is he? What a fucking gentleman. She swats his hand away as she scrabbles to her feet, her jeans now coated in dirt.

"Shit," the man says, grimacing in what she assumes is supposed to be solidarity. "Are you okay?"

She pushes her hair back from her face. "What the hell do you think you're doing?"

He raises his eyebrows, the same color as his dark hair. "Er, saving you from getting hit by an angry taxi driver?"

"*Saving* me?" She lets out an incredulous laugh as she checks both palms. Grazes. Shallow, but they still might get infected if she's not careful. "You could have killed me!"

"I don't think so," he says with a shrug. "If that was the plan, I would've just stood back and let the car do the job for me." She's so surprised at that—is it supposed to be a joke?—that she can only stare at him for a second. He runs the hand not holding the scooter across the back of his neck. "Look, I just was trying to help," he says, his voice even. Calm in the face of her storm.

"Oh yes," she says. "Because what I was really looking for was someone to help me onto the pavement face-first. It's actually quite difficult to accomplish that on your own, so thank you *so* much."

He blows out an annoyed breath. She can tell it's annoyed from the way his lips tighten. "Look, I acted on instinct, okay? I didn't mean for you to fall." He jiggles the handlebar of the scooter, like he wants her to take it. Well, screw him.

"You acted on *instinct*? Your instincts need some work in that case, hero." The last word drips with a sarcasm that she's pretty impressed with, if she's being honest.

A flash of something crosses his face, causing his jaw to spasm, before he smooths it out. "Well, given that you're okay and not currently roadkill..." It's actually quite annoying, how unflappable he is. She sort of wants him to rise to it. Instead, he holds the scooter out to her again.

She lifts her chin in the air. "Keep it. You clearly wanted it badly enough."

And with a dramatic flair that would make Darcy proud, she spins away, leaving him staring behind her. She realizes too late that it was a totally stupid thing to say—that and the fact she's supposed to check the e-scooter back in. Well, no chance of that. She's not turning around now; she'll just have to take the hit. Especially as there's a tiny part of her that's beginning to feel a bit embarrassed, because there *was* a car coming toward her, wasn't there? And she wasn't paying as much attention as she should have been. But still. A heroic gesture doesn't usually end with the woman face-planting on the pavement. Besides, right now, a random man with a hero complex is not important. Even if he did have nice eyes.

She heads to the gin bar down one of the alleys, a nearby streetlamp flickering to life as she walks past. Warmth and noise greet her as she steps inside, the smell of citrus and spice lining the air. She does a quick scan of the room. She'll need to wash her hands, which are now stinging, but she wants to check he's here first.

Her eyes travel along the length of the sleek oak bar, every single stool occupied. And there he is, right at the end, an easy smile on his face as he chats to one of the waitresses. Her distraction.

Chapter Two

Lissa sits outside a café on one of her favorite streets in Paris, the back of her neck warm in the late-afternoon sun, her head bent over her sketchbook. She doesn't know how exactly she knows she's in Paris given that a) she's concentrating on what she's drawing rather than on her surroundings, and b) she's never actually been to Paris, but there's no arguing the fact. The smell of coffee and cigarettes lingers in the air, the clinking of metal against porcelain mingling with the low hum of chatter.

She loves this place. It's mere streets away from some of the worst damage from the Blitz, areas that haven't quite recovered despite the fact it's been ten years now. This café opened after the war, she knows, the owners determined to see Paris be all that it had been and contribute toward that in some small way. Every time she comes here—mainly at weekends, since she got the job at the school—she feels hopeful, invested in the idea of new beginnings, of building something out of the ashes.

The face is beginning to take shape in the charcoal as she sketches. It's a face she once must have known so well, but over time she's forgotten the exact texture of her sister's expressions, even as she tries to call them into focus.

She hears a feminine laugh coming from inside the café as the bell on the door jingles. Hears a man's voice calling out a goodbye. She doesn't look up, too lost in her work now. She hears the muttered oath a split second before she feels it—searing-hot liquid seeping through the sleeve of her dress. She yelps, then reacts on instinct, pulling her arm toward her and scrabbling to her feet, her hand coming to cover the spot where the liquid scalded her.

There is a man there, apologizing to her, catching his balance from his stumble and bending to pick up his now empty coffee cup. She doesn't look at him, though. Instead she looks down at her sketchbook, at the drawing of her sister. Coffee stains one side of her sister's face, the charcoal edges blurring into one another. Ruined.

"*Je suis vraiment désolé, excusez-moi, puis-je . . . ?*" The man is reaching toward her sketchbook now, like he might pick it up, try to save it.

"Don't." The word is a harsh snap, and she's alarmed to find that tears are burning the back of her throat. *It doesn't matter*, she tells herself. She has countless of these drawings, tucked away in a drawer in her bedroom, somewhere her mother will never find them. And she has other sketchbooks at home—she doesn't need this one.

So without acknowledging the man—or his stupid apology—she bends to pick her bag up off the floor by her chair, then turns to leave. But she feels a hand on her forearm, pulling her to a stop. She wrenches it from his grip, glaring at him.

"What are you doing?" Her voice is clipped and perhaps—objectively speaking—angrier than the situation warrants. She registers, dimly, that she is speaking French—she didn't even know she *could* speak French, but there you go.

He lifts his hand in apology. "Sorry. I was just trying to stop you making the same mistake I did." When she frowns, he gestures down to the pavement by the café door. To the doorstop there, which he clearly tripped over.

She huffs out a breath, pushes a hand through her curls. "Think it's a bit late to be playing the hero." She raises her arm for emphasis, showing off the coffee stain on her polka-dot dress—the dress that her friend encouraged her to buy with the majority of her salary, and that she thought she should make the most of.

He grimaces. "I really am sorry." He glances down at the table, at her ruined drawing. "It's beautiful."

Her stomach tightens. She doesn't like people seeing her work, especially not things like this, which are only ever for her. "It was," she says shortly. *She* was, is what she really wants to say. But she realizes, even through her temper, that this is the kind of behavior she'd scold her class for. He didn't mean it. He is apologizing. So she sighs. "Look, I'm sorry too. You caught me off guard, that's all. But apology accepted, okay?"

He cocks his head to the side as his gaze travels along her sleeve. He has a nice gaze, she thinks. Hazel eyes, on the edge of brown and green. And though she tells herself she's ridiculous because of it, she feels goose bumps prickle underneath the fabric of her dress, along the line where that gaze travels. "You're not hurt?"

She shakes her head. "I'm fine." It had been a brief flare of pain, but it's gone now. Still, she'll make sure she checks it later, to see there is no lasting damage. Can't be too careful, after all. "And I was finishing up anyway," she lies, "so I'll just..." She gestures to the street before moving toward it.

"Wait." He looks like he might reach for her again, then seems to think better of it, shoving his hands into his pockets. "Can I buy you a coffee to make up for it?"

She hesitates, lingering when she probably shouldn't. *I have somewhere I need to be.* The lie is there, on the tip of her tongue. She doesn't have anywhere to be—would rather, in fact, have an excuse not to head home to her tiny apartment or to her parents' house, where they will inevitably be arguing. Maybe that's what makes her do it. Or maybe it's looking down at the ruined sketch and thinking that, perhaps, when it dries in the sun, it won't be that bad after all. Certainly the rest of the sketchbook will be usable, at least.

She meets that warm brown gaze. "One coffee." She says it sternly, in what has become her teacher voice in the few years since qualifying. "And as long as you promise not to spill the next one on me."

"I can promise to let *you* spill it on *me* if that would make you feel better." She almost gives in to the smile. Almost.

He turns to the door, then glances back at her as she sits back down on the woven rattan chair. "What's your name?"

She makes a show of smoothing out her skirt. Beside her, on a bed, somewhere else entirely, a man's body shifts. "I only give out my name to people who earn it."

She looks up in time to see an almost-smile cross his face, a twitching at the corner of his lips, before it's controlled, like he's not sure how she'll react to it.

She can feel it now, that pull toward consciousness, those moments where you hover between sleeping and waking. But the dream lingers just a moment longer, the sound of his lyrical voice traveling along the outskirts of her subconscious.

"I'll take that as a challenge."

His face blurs in front of her as Lissa blinks into an unfamiliar room. Sunlight filters through the gap in the thick blue curtains, slicing a path right over her eyes. A heavy arm is slung over her waist, too hot on her skin.

Her head feels fuzzy, disoriented, like she drank too much last night, even though she only had a few gin and tonics. It's like part of her is still there, sitting al fresco on the streets of Paris. She didn't know she had it in her to conjure a place up so vividly. Maybe she watched a documentary on post-war Paris recently or something?

Bits of it are already fading away, the way dreams always do. But she can still hear the sound of his voice, speaking French no less—who knew her GCSE French had made such a lasting impact on her? Mrs. Cullen would be so proud.

She supposes it's just another way of her brain processing the anniversary of her sister's death—clearly she still has issues, if she's imagining drawing her like that. She used to do it in real life, though it started to feel sad trying to capture someone who would never show any laugh lines or signs of aging, the things about faces she finds so fascinating in art.

But now is not the time to be thinking of any of this. Now is the time to be figuring out how to extract herself from under the heavy, hot male arm currently pinning her to the bed.

She grimaces as pieces of last night come back to her in a blur. It's often like this, the morning after, if she ever gives way to that reckless side of her that she mostly keeps at bay. She remembers nearly getting run over, yelling at a random man—a man with blue eyes. Then seeing Mark at the bar, that wide smile he gave her as she crossed to him.

She likes that about him—his smile. He has very straight, white teeth. And last night she figured, if that wasn't a reason to sleep with someone, what was? They've been skirting round the edges of it for months at work, and although she's always used the fact that they are colleagues as a reason not to go there, that key piece of information somehow slipped her mind last night. Something she will pay for in the weeks to come, she's sure of it.

She tries to edge out from under him, freezes when he lets out a light snore. Then blows out a breath when he doesn't stir.

She is as quiet as she can be as she shuffles around his bedroom in the half-light, collecting her discarded clothes. His flat is bigger and more modern than hers, and is close enough to the center that they were able to walk back together last night, neither of them questioning whether she'd go home with him, that having been decided the moment she sent the text. He'd stopped to kiss her in the street, under the glow of a streetlamp. It was all very romantic, really.

Now, though, she wants out. She can feel panic spiking her system, and the last thing she wants is to have a full-blown panic attack in front of her one-night stand. And yes, okay, he's heard about her "episode" in the office, but hearing about it and seeing it are two different things. She cringes at the memory, shoves it aside and fumbles on the floor for her phone instead.

She finds it in the pocket of her jeans. Only 10 percent battery. Lucky she knows Bath as well as she does, otherwise she'd be worried about getting home. She bites her lip as she sees two missed calls and a text from Mia, asking if she's okay. Shit, she should have checked in. Mia will be worried, and she hates to be the cause of that. There are also three missed calls from her mum. At that, her heart clenches with something akin to dread. When she'd left, her mum had been tucked under a blanket in front of the TV, seeming settled if not exactly happy. So Lissa had done her duty, hadn't she? She's sure it'll be okay. It'll all be fine. The more you say it, the more you believe it.

23

The wooden floorboards creak as she pulls on her jeans. She tenses and glances at the bed. To where Mark's eyes are opening and he is running a hand through his fair tousled hair.

"Hey, sleepyhead." His voice holds that distinct early-morning rasp. She resists the urge to point out that he, in fact, is the one still sleeping.

"Hey." She bends to pick up her top, slips it on, then casts her eyes around for her jacket.

Mark stretches. "Fancy breakfast?"

"Ah…" He looks up at her, then frowns, as if he's only just noticed that she's been trying to dress herself in the dark. She works up a smile. "I'd love to, but I'm meeting my dad for lunch today." The lie comes easily, and she has the briefest moment of guilt about it. But she can't stay here for breakfast of all things. She can't tell him that it feels too hot in here, despite the fact that it is, objectively speaking, a perfectly normal temperature, or that she didn't think this through, or that she wasn't really intending to have breakfast—or anything—with him after. And given that it's a Sunday, and they're employed at the same company, she can't exactly use work as an excuse. Luckily he doesn't know her well enough to know that seeing her dad—or her half-sister, for that matter—is a rare occurrence.

"Oh." Disappointment flashes across his face. Dark brown Bambi eyes, Darcy calls them, with eyelashes longer than hers. Lissa doesn't like being the cause of anyone's disappointment, but in this case she can't help it.

She hesitates, then leans down to kiss him on the cheek, trying not to breathe out because she hasn't brushed her teeth yet. "Thanks for last night."

He grins then. "No thanks needed."

She slips her jacket on, hating the embarrassment of dressing in her clothes from the night before, like a big red arrow is hovering above her head telling the whole world what she'd been up to.

"I'll walk you out," Mark says, throwing the duvet off.

"No, honestly, it's fine, I..." But he's already up, and she averts her eyes even though it's stupid given that she saw every inch of his body last night. It's an impressive body too—all those hours he spends at the gym before work are clearly worth it.

There is a dreadful second when she thinks he's going to walk her to his front door naked, but he grabs a dressing gown off the back of the bedroom door, fluffy and white like a hotel one.

"Where are you meeting your dad?" he asks as he escorts her down the corridor.

"Oh." She gives what she hopes is a perfectly innocent-seeming shrug. "Just at his house. It's in Frome."

"Nice. Well, have fun, yeah?"

She's relieved when he unlocks the front door and holds it open for her—she can't concentrate enough right now for the obligatory small talk, too distracted by the anxiety of what else she may have said or done last night.

Mark grabs her hand as she steps outside. "I had a really great time, Lissa."

"Me too." Why is her voice squeaky? Why can she not be a bloody grown-up? It was her who initiated things, for fuck's sake.

There's a moment where it looks like he's going to say something more, but thankfully he seems to overcome the urge and kisses her forehead instead. "I'll call you."

That seems a bit redundant, given she'll see him in the office tomorrow, but she manages a bright "Yes, okay." She reaches up, but then isn't sure what to do with her hand, and ends up patting his arm like a bloody imbecile. "Bye, Mark."

And that, she thinks to herself as she walks away from his block of flats, is why she really should have just gone home last night.

Chapter Three

Lissa arrives at the office a full fifteen minutes early on Monday morning, something that's pretty much unheard of for both her and Darcy, but something that Darcy reluctantly agreed to due to the need for an emergency debrief. Lissa waits for her friend to join her in the small kitchen. They are on the fourth floor of a building shared with other offices. Out the window you can see the River Avon and, if you squint, Pulteney Bridge in the distance.

She folds her arms as she watches the kettle boiling, then looks up at the sound of heels on the laminate wooden flooring. Darcy is wearing a pair of blue shoes with small, tasteful white flowers today—Lissa swears she has a new pair every week. Her brunette hair is pinned back in her signature knot, perhaps slightly damper than usual, and her lips are painted the same bright red she always wears, no matter the occasion.

As Darcy crosses the small kitchen to where Lissa is leaning against the counter, Lissa catches a waft of her Chanel perfume. When she asked her once how she afforded Chanel and designer shoes, given they're on very similar salaries at a very average digital marketing agency, Darcy waved her away. *It's aspirational, sweets. Live the life you dream of having and one day it'll catch up to you.* Lissa isn't sure the credit card companies would agree with that, but there's no point in arguing with Darcy—she learned that on day one of working together.

"Good," she says as the kettle clicks off the boil. "You're here. I—"

But Darcy holds up a hand to stop her. "Lissa, I love you, but if you don't give me coffee immediately, I'm not going to be any use to you at all."

Lissa rolls her eyes as she gets down two mugs, puts a teaspoon of instant coffee in each, then fills them with boiling water. Darcy petitioned Liam, their boss, for a proper coffee machine, but he said he considered it an unnecessary expense. At which Darcy launched into an explanation of the definition of unnecessary and why a coffee machine did not qualify as such, which didn't go down *super* well in the team meeting when they were supposed to be discussing the performance of several different Meta adverts for an organic dog food company.

Lissa hands Darcy a mug and they both move to the "break-out" area in the kitchen—which is, in fact, just a plastic table and chairs, but which Liam insists that, outside lunch hours, is to be used only to "brainstorm strategy."

Darcy takes a sip of the coffee, grimaces a little, then sighs. "It's caffeine, I guess. So." She lowers her voice, even though they are currently the only ones in the office. "Is this about the job?"

Lissa frowns. "The job?"

Darcy raises her perfectly shaped eyebrows. "Your interview. On Friday?"

"Oh, right." She'd forgotten about that, truth be told, what with the drama of Saturday. But she'd left work early on Friday under the pretense of a dentist appointment—a classic—for an interview with another marketing agency in Bath, only this time for a specific graphic design role, where she'd be working on the artistic creation of the advertising rather than endlessly monitoring click-through rates.

"I'm pretty sure it's a no-go," she says.

"Why?"

"Well, the interviewer called me Katie throughout the whole interview, then asked me if I had any experience in graphic design specifically, to which I said no, then asked me what I love about digital marketing, to which I drew a complete blank."

Darcy groans. "Lissa, you are supposed to *lie* during these interviews; didn't anyone ever tell you that?"

"I must have missed that key piece of advice on careers day. Anyway, it's fine—given I can't think of a single thing I like about my job, I probably shouldn't be moving to another company that does the exact same thing. And," she adds more loudly, when Darcy opens her mouth to interject, "I don't want to talk about that." She takes a deep breath. "I slept with Mark."

Darcy's eyebrows shoot up practically into her hairline. "*Did* you now?"

"On Saturday night."

She purses those red lips. "Well, good on you. Or good on him, I should say. It's only taken him, what, a year?"

Lissa half laughs, half groans, and slams a palm to her forehead.

"That bad?" Darcy asks, taking another sip of coffee.

"No." Lissa blows out a breath. "Bad" wasn't a word she'd use to describe that night. "No, it's just…" She chews on her lip, fighting a horrible knot of anxiety in her stomach. Darcy doesn't know the significance of Saturday's date, so it's sort of hard to explain why, exactly, she'd come over all "live in the moment." Only people who were around during her childhood know what happened to Chloe, and it's difficult to broach the subject with anyone else, given it happened so long ago. That and the fact that she hates talking about it means that it's easier not to bring it up.

"I don't know if I should have," she finishes. "That's all."

"Well why not? He's good-looking and nice and…"

"…and we work together." Lissa gestures emphatically around the small kitchen.

"Well how do you think couples meet? Over seventy percent meet in the workplace," Darcy adds promptly, without waiting for an answer.

Lissa narrows her eyes. "You just made that up."

Darcy shrugs. "Probably something like that, though, isn't it?"

Couples. Lissa experiences a little spasm of panic, the same feeling she always gets when she imagines any sort of long-term relationship. So far, her longest has been three months, but then he wanted to do stupid things like meet the family and she decided enough was enough.

On her lap, her hand throbs, and she looks down at the graze on her palm. She took the grit out of it at the time, and has used a ton of antiseptic on it since, but still…

"What's up with your hand?"

She wrinkles her nose at how obvious she's being. "Nothing. Just fell over on the pavement the other day." She decides to leave out the exact how, given that causes a flare of embarrassment whenever she thinks about it. "But it feels a bit hot and I'm not sure if…"

"Give it here."

Lissa holds out her hand to Darcy, who takes it gently, twisting it one way then the other. "Looks totally normal." She lets go. "If it was infected, it would be getting more red, not less."

Lissa allows herself a long exhale. "Thanks, Darcy." It's a stupid thing, but it helps, sometimes, having reassurance from someone else, even if they are no more qualified than she is. Maybe all it does is pull her back to the world of the sane, but whatever it is, she's grateful. Grateful, too, that Darcy never makes a big thing of it, and somehow knows the exact line to walk between not dismissing her entirely and reassuring her that everything is okay.

"Just call me Dr. D," Darcy says with a wave of her hand.

"I definitely won't."

"Sounds like a superhero, doesn't it?"

"A super*villain*, more like."

"Hmm. Maybe villain suits me better. They always seem to get the nicer shoes, don't you think?"

Lissa laughs, and feels her body settle a little. Laughing releases endorphins, she reminds herself. Endorphins are good for you. She should definitely try to do more laughing.

"So are you going to go out with Mark again?"

"Umm…" She sips her coffee to buy herself time.

"Maybe you should. It'd be good for you."

"Good for me how?"

"You know, getting out. Dating."

"What if it doesn't work out?"

Darcy shrugs. "What if it does?"

At that moment, the lift doors opposite the kitchen open, spitting out one of their colleagues, who heads straight for her desk, zombie-like. Lissa lets out a long exhale, then smiles a little when she meets Darcy's gaze.

"You know," Darcy says, "we really ought to have had this conversation at a café or something, rather than here."

At the word "café," Lissa experiences a brief tug in a corner of her mind, one that takes her back to her dream the other night, to sitting outside the café in Paris, to the smell of coffee, the color of the man's eyes.

"Lissa?"

She jolts, nearly spilling her coffee over the rim of the mug. Just like he'd spilt his over her at that table. She blinks, looking up at the owner of the voice—not Darcy, but Liam, who is peering down at them. He glances between them, then at their mugs, somehow making the action disapproving.

He strokes a hand down his stupid little beard. "Nice to see you're both on time." The *for once* is left as subtext. He levels a look at Lissa. "How are you feeling?" The question is careful, and she can tell it's less concern for her and more to do with whether she's about to have a negative impact on the "office flow," as he likes to call it.

"Fine, thanks," she says brightly, partly because she knows it will annoy him, partly to curtail the embarrassment that is trying really hard to flare up. "And you? Good weekend?"

He grunts a non-answer. "I'll see you both in the Monday meeting at half nine, yes?"

Darcy gives a salute—honestly, Lissa doesn't know how she gets away with it. "Absolutely," she says. "I've been thinking about those lookalike audiences for that health water company all weekend."

Liam gives her a suspicious look, but clearly decides it's too early to deal with her, and walks away. Darcy and Lissa get to their feet—he'll only keep shooting them looks if they stay sitting here.

"He's such a dick," Darcy mutters as they cross the office floor to their desks.

"Mm," Lissa agrees, though noncommittally enough that she could deny it if overheard. He's never exactly *fun*, Liam, but he's been worse since her panic attack in the office a few weeks ago. She grimaces thinking of it, the way she dropped her glass of water, cut herself when she picked up the smashed pieces. How she saw the blood, so much from just one tiny cut, and spiraled. The dizziness, the way her heart raced, breathing harder and harder until she couldn't breathe at all. Then she was on the floor, curled in a ball under her desk. She can still hear Darcy's voice fighting through the ringing in her ears, before her friend managed to get her to her feet and to the bathroom, while Liam looked on in comical horror.

Darcy gives her a look, like she might bring said incident up.

Lissa shakes her head firmly. "We're not talking about it."

"Oh, is this denial?" Darcy nods musingly. "All right. I can get on board with denial—I've been known to partake of that myself every now and then."

Lissa snorts, just as they reach her desk—and find someone already there. Someone with blond hair and big brown Bambi eyes, who seems to have quite literally popped up out of nowhere.

"Oh hey, Mark," Darcy says brightly.

He smiles that very straight white smile. "Hi, Darcy. Good weekend?"

"Oh, you know. Not as fun as Lissa's."

Lissa feels her cheeks reddening. She cannot *believe* Darcy went there. Actually, who is she kidding, of course she can. She just wishes her friend would show a little restraint.

"Anyway," Darcy continues, before Lissa or Mark has the chance to make any awkward comment, "we were just talking about our horoscopes."

Lissa raises one eyebrow at her, just as Mark says, all gallant politeness, "Were you?"

"Yep. Mine says I'm going to get *shocking* news this month."

"Does it now?" Lissa asks drily, before she can help herself.

"Yep," Darcy says again, smiling breezily. "And Lissa's says it's time to try new things."

Honestly, the woman is shameless. Lissa tries to convey this with her eyes as Darcy moves to sit at the desk next to hers. They'd initially had desks on opposite sides of the office to one another, but Darcy had bribed Jan, the woman who used to sit next to Lissa, with a week's supply of Pret coffee to switch.

With Darcy semi out of the way, Mark turns to Lissa and smiles, and she does her best to smile back, to try not to think of when she last saw him, and how very naked he was. *You are an adult*, she reminds herself. *You can deal with this.* "Hey, Lissa," he says, his voice an octave lower.

Right then, Lissa is actually grateful for Darcy when she pipes up with, "Want to know what yours says, Mark?"

He frowns, glancing at her. "My what?"

"Horoscope."

"Ah, no thanks." He looks back at Lissa, shifts his weight from foot to foot. He's nervous, Lissa realizes. And that makes her just a little less so. "So I was wondering... would you want to get a drink one day after work?"

And just what exactly is she supposed to say to that? "Umm, sure." Because she can't exactly say *no*, can she?

Not to his face. "I mean, it depends on which day, but—"

"She'd love to," Darcy pipes up, clicking on her mouse and not looking at either of them.

Lissa sighs and shakes her head at Mark to convey her apology, which gets a grin out of him. That's something, she supposes.

"Cool. Anyway, I better get going." He gestures to his own desk. "Need to make sure I've got my prep ready for the meeting." And unlike Darcy, he is not being ironic. For some unfathomable reason, he actually seems to like working here—or at least cares enough about it to be angling for a promotion—and finds discussions about search engine optimization downright fascinating. Which, to be fair, is probably what one should look for in a digital marketing specialist.

"Thanks for that," Lissa says to Darcy, once Mark is out of earshot.

"What?" Darcy asks, the picture of innocence. "I was being helpful."

"Yes, well. Maybe the 'new thing' I do this month can be giving you a lesson on just what exactly being helpful usually constitutes."

Darcy grins, in a way that makes it impossible for Lissa to even contemplate being mad at her. "Much as I love your lectures, I can think of *plenty* of other new things that would be far more fun, can't you?"

All things considered, Lissa decides it's best not to reply to that.

Chapter Four

There is a chill bite to the air as Lissa walks down the cobbled street, tall sandstone buildings stretching above her into the pink hues of the sky. A sign that it won't be all that long before winter coats are dusted off, hats found from whatever corner of the drawer they've been lost in.

"So," Mia says down the phone line, "this is the Mark you've been refusing to go out with for a solid eight months, is that right?"

Lissa glances up the street, checking that Mark isn't immediately behind her, before switching her phone into her other hand. "Correct. I decided it might be good for me." Well, technically Darcy decided, but she went along with it, and that's basically the same thing, right? She put it off for a few days, then decided that going for a drink with him couldn't be any worse than the slightly awkward not-quite-flirting dance they've been doing in the office. She opted for a Friday, given they're all allowed to work from home, meaning she wouldn't have to endure the small talk en route from the office to the pub.

"I agree," Mia says. Lissa can hear the sounds of the train in the background, a robotic voice announcing the stops. Although she lives in Bristol, Mia has to go to London twice a week, and Lissa knows she hates it, especially when one of those days falls on a Friday.

"What about you?" Lissa asks as she gets closer to the pub. "How are things going with that American girl?"

"Oh, you know," Mia says vaguely. "We send the occasional GIF, but it's kind of hard given neither of us has any imminent plans to cross the Atlantic." Mia recently had a holiday fling with a woman she met while visiting her parents, who have lived in Denver for the past ten years.

There's a beat of quiet; then she says, "Have you spoken to your mum since…?"

"No," Lissa says, then winces at how hard her voice sounds. "Actually, though, that reminds me. Are we still on for Sunday after next?"

"Of course. You know me, I love my roasts with extra gravy and *just* a side of tension."

Lissa's lips twitch. "Good." It's become a tradition—the first Sunday of every month, Mia and Lissa go to Lissa's mum's for a roast, cooking it themselves, often drinking far too much red wine. Her mum either gets involved or sits in the corner, depending on what mood she's in, but it helps Lissa to feel less guilty—and Mia, she knows, does it for her.

"I have to go," Lissa says, coming to a stop outside the pub. There are a few people spilling out of the front onto the street, the door propped open so that laughter and chatter swells in the air.

"Lover boy in sight?" Mia asks.

"Sure, something like that. Hope the rest of the journey isn't hell."

"I'm just looking forward to a pasty from the train station. Have fun tonight—don't do anything I wouldn't do. Well, apart from the whole sleeping-with-men thing."

Lissa laughs. "Bye, Mia."

She pushes her way into the pub, inhaling a good lungful of hops. There's no immediate sign of Mark, and she bites her lip, checking her phone.

We're out in the garden when you get here x

She frowns down at it. We? What does he mean, we? Shit, did she read this wrong? Is this not a date? She's not an idiot, right? This was arranged following staying over at his—a drink in a pub, possibly dinner. That all definitely signals date. Maybe it's a typo. Then again, is it the worst thing in the world if it's *not* a date? Maybe that's better. Maybe he's with Darcy. Though she dismisses that idea at once—Darcy would have told her.

She works her way through the crowd, heading toward the beer garden. It's packed, everyone trying to make the most of the last light and if not warm, then at least not freezing evenings. The smell of smoke replaces the hops as she steps outside, and she glances around the picnic benches under umbrellas with outdoor heaters. She spots Mark in the far corner, facing her, his fair hair glowing a little orange in the light of the heater. He's in a blue coat, hands in his pockets, leaning across the table and laughing. Laughing because he's very much not alone.

He's talking to a man with his back to her, dark hair the only thing she can see. And okay, maybe she shouldn't assume this based on the back of his head, but she's sure she doesn't know him—he's certainly not anyone from work.

She hesitates, hovering outside the door. He told her to meet him here, but has he changed his mind about a date with her and is too polite to bail? Maybe it was never supposed to be a date—had he always said it would be a group thing and she just missed that? Was *she* supposed to bring a friend, too? And if it's not a date, then she's dressed wrong. Although, actually, maybe she's fine. Black jeans and a nice top—that doesn't necessarily mean date, does it? God, she's so out of practice at this.

She's still standing there like a bloody lemon when Mark does a quick scan of the garden, spots her, and smiles with those very straight teeth. He immediately beckons her over. Well, okay then.

She fixes a smile to her own face as she heads toward him, squeezing by a crowded bench and coming to a stop at his table. He immediately scooches over for her and she takes a seat next to him, opposite mystery man.

Only, as he turns his blue gaze on her, smiling politely over his pint of beer, she feels a jolt of recognition. She knows this man from somewhere, she's sure of it. Where? *Think, Lissa!* She sees his eyebrows pull together as he sweeps his gaze over her face, clearly trying to place her, too.

Then it clicks. She feels a rush of heat flooding her cheeks as she opens her mouth to speak, but he beats her to it.

"You," he says, setting his beer down. She bites her lip as Mark raises his eyebrows.

"You guys know each other?" he asks.

"Know is a bit of a stretch," not-so-mystery-man says mildly. A corner of his mouth pulls up into half a crooked smile as those blue eyes find hers again. "A shared near-death experience is a little closer."

Lissa grimaces. That fucking scooter. She should never have got on it in the first place.

Mark glances between them again. "Right. So . . . you've met?"

Scooter Man picks up his beer, gesturing with it as Lissa does her best not to squirm in her seat. "Remember last weekend, when we were in that gin bar and I left but you hung on to wait for—"

"Me," Lissa pipes up, not sure she wants him to finish that sentence.

"You," the man agrees, and the intense way he focuses in on her makes her wish she hadn't spoken. He laughs again. "Small world."

"Small city," she mutters, a little darkly. Scooter Man's lips twitch.

"So is this a story I'm going to like, or . . . ?" Mark trails off pointedly.

For God's sake, her cheeks are red, aren't they? "It's not—"

"I saved her," Scooter Man—Mark's friend, presumably—interrupts.

Lissa scowls. "You didn't save me, you..." She stops, takes a breath. "I lost control of my scooter slightly and you...pulled me over," she says, as diplomatically as she can.

"There was a taxi behind you."

"Right."

"You would have been hit."

Jesus, she should have turned around as soon as she saw Mark wasn't alone. "Okay, fine." She holds up her hands in a sign of surrender. "You were trying to help, I know."

"And you shouted at me for it," he points out mildly, taking a sip of beer.

"*Did* you?" Mark asks, pulling back as if to get a good look at her. "Now that's interesting."

She closes her eyes, wishing she could turn back time, just five minutes, and not come into this pub. Although actually, if she could turn back time, she could go back to the scooter incident and stop that from happening. And really, if she's turning back time, there's a better date to turn back to, isn't there?

She opens her eyes to see both men still looking at her.

"Right," she says, trying to keep her voice even. "Well, I'm sorry about that. Shouting at you, I mean." She pulls a hand through her hair. "I wasn't quite...myself that day, so maybe I made a mistake or two."

"Is that so?" Mark asks.

If her cheeks were any hotter, she could cook a steak on them, medium rare. "Not you. I didn't mean..." She puts her head in her hands. "I'm going to get a drink. Possibly several."

Mark laughs, puts an arm around her shoulders. It's an easy gesture, though she feels herself stiffen automatically, not used to the casual contact. "Don't worry, I'm only teasing." He gives her a squeeze. "I'll get you one. What'll it be?"

"Ah..." She glances at Scooter Man, still sitting opposite her.

Mark gives her a guilty smile. "I was fifty-fifty whether you'd actually show."

"I was fifty-fifty whether I would too," she admits, coming out with it before she can stop herself. She hears a quiet snort from Scooter Man, one she's not sure was supposed to be audible.

Mark puts a hand to his heart. "Ouch." But he's laughing, thankfully.

"Oh, I see how it is," Scooter Man says, nodding. "I'm the backup date, right?"

"You said one drink after work," Mark points out. "Technically this is one drink, and it is after work."

"Half a drink," Scooter Man says, looking down at his pint—which, to be fair, is indeed still half full.

"You finish it. Lissa, what would you like?"

But she hesitates. He's going to just leave her with a random stranger?

Said stranger's lips twitch, like he knows what she's thinking. "I'm Ash, by the way."

"Saving her life didn't get you on a first-name basis,

huh?" Mark shakes his head mockingly, then gestures between them. "Lissa, Ash, Ash, Lissa. Lissa, Ash doesn't usually hang out much in Bath, but apparently makes a habit of saving random women when he's here. Ash, Lissa is the girl who has finally agreed to go out with me, and who may or may not refuse to ever see me again outside of work after this disaster."

They both laugh—Lissa wonders if Ash is only doing so because it seems expected. She doesn't think so. He has the type of laugh that sounds like it comes easily.

Ash, she thinks. Well, at least he has a name now.

His head is cocked as he studies her. "Lissa." He says her name like he's trying it out, considering whether it fits her. Bizarrely, she wants to know if he thinks it does.

Mark kisses her cheek, another of those easy gestures. "I'll be back."

And she has no choice but to stay, given that he is already clambering his way over the bench, even though she still hasn't said what she wants to drink.

When he's gone, there's a beat of quiet. She gets out her phone, but unhelpfully there are no new messages to answer urgently, so all she does is lay it on the table between them. On the bench next to them, a girl shrieks as one of her friends drops an ice cube down the back of her top. It's a younger crowd than she's used to—she wonders why Mark chose this place.

"So," Ash says, breaking the silence between them. "The famous Lissa."

"Famous?"

Another of those crooked smiles. "Mark may have mentioned you a couple of times."

The idea makes her insides squirm. She can't work out if it's a good feeling or not. She glances to the door, but can't see the bar from here. She looks back at Ash. "And you are...?"

He shakes his head mockingly. "Don't tell me you suffer from short-term memory loss as well as terrible scootering abilities?" He points a thumb to his chest. "Ash."

"Mm," she agrees. "Ash. Saver of lives, stealer of scooters." He grins, and she feels her own lips pulling up in response. "But apart from that...?"

He shrugs. "I'm a friend of Mark's. We went to secondary school together."

"Oh good. He's not just picking up random men in bars while he waits for a date with me."

He smiles again. It's a nice smile, she decides. Not as straight or white as Mark's, but there's something about the crookedness of his mouth that's...endearing? Sexy? No. Not sexy. She probably shouldn't be thinking of Mark's friend's mouth as sexy—she's been out of the dating game a while, but she's almost definitely sure that's against the rules.

"So." He takes a pull on his beer. "Make a habit of falling off scooters in general, or was that just a one-off?"

"Oh, all the time," she says with a wave of her hand. "Not just scooters, though. Bikes. Tricycles. Skateboards. Really anything with wheels. As long as it's something I can throw myself off at the feet of strangers, I'm there."

He laughs, and she notices the way his eyes seem to lighten as he does. "Is that so?"

"Yep," she says lightly. "So don't consider yourself special or anything like that."

"Wouldn't dream of it." He considers her for a moment. Then, "I returned it, by the way."

"What?"

"The scooter. I figured you'd get charged if I didn't."

"Oh." She's momentarily stumped by the kindness of the gesture. "Thank you. That's really..." She sighs. "I am sorry, you know. I didn't mean to shout at you. It was just..."

"A bad day?"

"Yeah. A really bad day."

He's looking at her in a way she recognizes, like he might ask what's wrong. Or what *was* wrong, perhaps. His head is slightly tilted, the weight of his focus heavy on her. She needs to distract him, because she really doesn't want to talk about it. She doesn't want to explain the relevance of that date or why it has a tendency to send her off the deep end. The anniversary of your little sister's death isn't exactly a conversation starter, is it? Besides, Mark himself doesn't even know about it, so she hardly wants to be discussing it when he comes back.

She opens her mouth, but nothing comes out. Why can't she think of a damn thing to say—is she really this terrible at small talk?

Then Ash smiles, and the intensity in his gaze is lost. "So. You work with Mark?"

She lets out a long exhale, grateful for the change of

subject, whether it was intentional or not. She nods, feels like a nodding dog and stops. "Yep."

"Digital marketing, right?"

"Mm-hmm."

"What's that like?"

"Umm, very...digital," she concludes with a nod. He laughs. "And you?" she asks. "What do you do? You don't live in Bath?"

"Nah. I move around a fair bit. I'm in Belgium at the moment—just stopped by for a couple of weeks to visit Mark. And my dad," he adds, almost like an afterthought.

Lissa raises her eyebrows. *Belgium?* He laughs, and she realizes it's probably because she made it sound like she could never imagine anything as unlikely as living in Belgium.

"Yes. Belgium."

"Doing what?"

"I'm a location scout—for music videos, mainly." He takes a sip of his beer as he says it.

"A location scout? I'm pretty sure I have zero idea what that is."

He grins. "It means I try and find the best places to film music videos. I speak to the director and the artist to find out the vibe, then look for somewhere that matches up to it. Then there's a bunch of boring logistical stuff like working out parking and electricity access and so on."

"Wow. That sounds pretty cool."

"Yeah, it is. Means I get to do a lot of traveling, which I like."

Lissa nods, as though she knows exactly what it's like to love traveling, when her last trip abroad was after her A levels with Mia, to Lanzarote of all places.

"The life of a nomad, this one." Lissa jumps as Mark comes up behind Ash, clapping him on the back. She hadn't noticed him crossing the garden. "No responsibility, going wherever the wind takes him." He sighs dramatically. "The life so many of us crave and aren't brave enough to go for."

Ash rolls his eyes good-naturedly as Mark moves round to sit next to Lissa, sliding a gin and tonic over to her. A good guess, she concedes, made easier by the fact that they spent their last date, if you could call it that, in a gin bar.

"So where's the best place you've ever filmed?" she asks Ash.

"God, so many. There was this really cool run-down house in Wales where we did a shoot for an up-and-coming artist. It was all about her letting loose, and it worked so well. We did a great one on some cliffs in Ireland. And there was this big-budget project I was hired for once where they wanted to film on a rooftop overlooking the Paris skyline. That was pretty incredible."

Mark shakes his head. "Paris, mate. Could you be any more clichéd?"

Ash only shrugs and grins, as Mark gets out his phone, frowning at something on the screen.

"Have you ever been?" Ash asks her, saving an awkward silence. "To Paris?"

She's back there then. In that café, on that street, with that man. Only it's not the same day. It's dark outside, and the door to the café is shut, curtains mostly drawn, while live music plays in one corner and one of the owners walks around topping everyone's glasses up. He's there, next to her, his hand pressed lightly into the small of her back as they chat to another couple. She doesn't want to be chatting to them. She wants to be talking to him and only him. His thumb moves, traveling a small circle over her back, and even though she doesn't look at him, trying very hard to nod and smile in the right places, her insides tighten and coil.

"Lissa? You okay?"

She blinks a few times. It's Ash, rather than Mark, asking the question, Mark still looking at his phone. She swallows and nods, taking a sip of her gin. What *was* that? It was so vivid. Was that part of her dream, a piece of it she'd forgotten?

"No," she manages. "I've never been to Paris." She wonders why it feels like a lie.

"Sorry," Mark says, setting his phone down. "Just work." Lissa wonders what can be so important at past 6 p.m. on a Friday, then remembers that Mark, unlike her, has a long-term game plan at the agency.

"You staying for one more, mate?" he asks Ash. Lissa notices, though, that he didn't get another pint for Ash while he was at the bar.

Ash smiles. It's only when he looks at Mark that she realizes he's been holding eye contact with her all this time. "Nah. You were right, I only had time for one anyway."

"Ah, yes. Don't want to be late for abseiling tomorrow morning."

Lissa makes a spluttering noise that is definitely not attractive. "Abseiling?"

"At the Cheddar Gorge caves," Ash says with a nod. "Never done it before and I've got time before my flight, so I thought, why not?"

Lissa can think of plenty of reasons why not, but decides not to voice them right now. Ash drains the rest of his pint, then sets it down and gets to his feet. He smiles. "It was nice to meet you—again—Lissa. Now I know whose life I saved that day, it'll stop the sleepless nights, wondering what happened to her, whether my heroic gesture was all in vain."

She snorts out a laugh before straightening her face. "Now you know," she agrees. "Consider this damsel no longer in distress—all thanks to you."

He gives her a wry look. "You didn't seem very damsel-like when you were yelling at me."

"Let me know when you're visiting again, yeah?" Mark says, perhaps a bit louder than necessary.

"Sure." Ash winks. "You two kids have fun." And with that, he turns, taller and more broad-shouldered than he seemed sitting down, and strides toward the exit.

"So," Mark says, and Lissa pulls her attention back to him. He takes her hand, links her fingers with his. "Tell me about your day."

Oh good. Her favorite question.

Chapter Five

Around her, the world is dark and cold. Water pushes in on her, her eyes sting as she tries to open them. Her arms and legs are frantic, trying to propel her to the surface, only she's not sure she knows which way that is anymore. Her lungs are threatening to explode as she fights that desperate urge to breathe. This is it. She can't think as panic overwhelms her, even as she hears someone just out of reach, calling her name.

She wakes before the sun does, blinking into a new kind of darkness. Cold sweat dampens her back and her breath comes in short, sharp bursts, like she really has just wrenched herself out of a lake. She waits until her breathing settles, until her heart stops beating so loudly against her chest. All this time, since Chloe died, and she still can't shake the nightmares, can't stop herself imagining what her sister went through.

She takes a deep, shuddering breath, does her best to push the nightmare to the corner of her mind, where it belongs. Then she throws off her duvet and resigns herself to another early-morning start.

*

Lissa tries to ignore the headache that is currently pressing in on her temples as she walks from Frome station toward her dad's house. It's a headache born of lack of sleep and staring at her laptop all day while she worked from home, but is made worse, no doubt, by the low-level anxiety she feels whenever she heads out this way. She dodged the last couple of dinner invitations from her dad and stepmum, but was fast running out of excuses when this one rolled around. She thought of inventing a new hobby, but then having to learn all about said new hobby felt like more effort than just saying yes to dinner. Even though she's pretty sure her dad only invites her round because of some kind of residual familial obligation.

She squares her shoulders as she reaches his house—a beautiful period cottage just outside the town center. It's the one he moved to fourteen years ago, just before Elsie, her half-sister, was born. The evening light is drawing in now, casting the nearby fields in an orangey glow, and in the distance she can hear the sound of farm animals. It's like something out of a bloody fairy tale.

She knocks on the door—an ornate iron knocker. It's Nicole, her stepmum, who answers. She beams at Lissa and moves in to air-kiss both her cheeks, then gestures her inside. She's dressed in a chic blouse and slacks, barefoot with toenails painted a bright red. Her long brunette hair is plaited down her back and her deep brown eyes are framed with eyeliner. She is in stark opposition to Lissa's mum, whose gray hair often doesn't look brushed, and whose makeup bag consists of a bareMinerals foundation, one peach lipstick and a tube of mascara from the Middle Ages.

"Come in, come in!" Nicole says—redundantly, given that she is already shutting the door behind her. Lissa can smell her stepmum's perfume as well as the scented candles she always has burning around the place. "Do you mind?" Nicole asks, pointing to Lissa's boots.

"Oh. Sure." She bends down to unzip them.

"It's just we've had the carpets redone."

"Oh, lovely," Lissa says as she straightens. "Well they look great." In fact they look exactly the same as before, from what she can tell—the same slightly impractical cream color.

Nicole smiles. "Thank you. I got a discount through one of the suppliers I work with, and I just thought it'd be a shame to miss the opportunity."

"Absolutely," Lissa says, nodding as Nicole ushers her through to the kitchen. Nicole is an interior designer, and you can tell. Another contrast with Lissa's own childhood home—here, everything manages to hold the aesthetic of a period property while still adding a touch of the modern. It's full of life, with just the right amount of clutter on the shelves, yet not bogged down by the weight of the past. The kitchen was upgraded a few years ago, and is now complete with underfloor heating beneath the large slate tiles, and a breakfast bar where you can sit and chat to whoever is cooking.

"There she is!" Her dad's voice is booming—and just a touch too enthusiastic—as he turns to greet her in the kitchen. Although she supposes that's better than a touch too *un*enthusiastic. He moves toward her, abandoning whatever he was stirring at the counter. He looks for a second like he might hug her, but ends up patting her slightly awkwardly on the arm instead.

"We're making steak with a peppercorn sauce and a few salads—is that okay?" Nicole asks, giving Lissa's dad an easy squeeze on the forearm as she brushes past him.

"Sounds great," Lissa says. She decides not to point out the risks of eating too much red meat.

"Train okay?" her dad asks, rocking back on his heels.

"Yep. All good. I brought some wine." She holds up the bottle of rosé to demonstrate.

"Oh that's so kind of you." Nicole takes the offered bottle. "I've already got some white chilling in the fridge, so we'll have a glass of that to start, shall we?"

Thank God for that—maybe wine will help with the small talk. Lissa sits on one of the high stools at the breakfast bar as her dad gets down the glasses and sets them on the counter for Nicole to pour. His hair is the same salt-and-pepper gray as the last time she saw him, with a few days of stubble growth in the place of the beard he once had—and which Nicole made him shave off before their wedding.

She remembers that—he'd not told her he was doing it, and when she'd seen him before the ceremony it had been like seeing an entirely different person. In hindsight, maybe it wasn't only the lack of beard making him seem different. She'd been a teenager—it was only a year after he'd left her and her mum, and barely two since Chloe had died.

The wedding had been awful. Lissa had been put on a table with her dad's side of the family, who *he* barely spoke to, let alone her. She'd been allowed to bring a friend and she'd brought Mia, though that had been awkward because she was a cousin on her mum's side. Mia had snuck them both champagne, which they'd pretended to enjoy, and after watching the first dance, Lissa had hidden in the loo to cry. It hadn't seemed real until then. And she knew he wouldn't change his mind now he was married. He wouldn't come back.

"Here you go, love," her dad says, handing her a glass of wine.

"Thanks." She takes a grateful gulp. It has that smooth, light taste she's come to associate with expensive wines she can't afford. She glances around the kitchen, through the big French doors that lead to the huge garden. "Where's Elsie?"

"Up in her room," Nicole says, getting out a chopping board. "You know what teenagers are like."

"Can I do anything to help?"

"Oh no." She waves a hand in Lissa's direction. "You just relax, it won't take long."

She'd rather have been set to work—at least when chopping food you can pretend to be busy. Now she has to think of something to bloody *say*. She taps her fingernails on her wineglass. "So, Dad. How's the life of a copywriter treating you?" He was a teacher when she was growing up, teaching history at one of Bath's best secondary schools. But after Chloe died, he quit. She often thinks it's because he couldn't face seeing all those young faces and knowing Chloe would never be one of them. It's how she felt when she saw the younger years of her sister's primary school filtering through the gates, or caught sight of one of Chloe's friends years later. Her mum, on the other hand, still works as a nurse, though admittedly on reduced hours. In her darkest moments, Lissa can't help wondering if she does it as punishment to herself—to save other people's children, when she couldn't save her own.

"Oh, you know," says her dad, picking up his glass. "Much the same as always. Lots of coffee, a bit of staring at a blank screen, a lot of checking for typos. But soon enough it will all be done by AI, won't it? Might as well enjoy it while I can."

"That's the spirit," Lissa says.

"What about you? Still in the same job? Marketing, right?"

"Mm-hmm. Not much new to report there." There's quiet for a beat as he nods along to that. She hates this. When she was growing up, they had such an easy relationship. She used to lean against his office door while he was marking papers, chatting to him, enjoying the peace he brought to the house in contrast to her mum's mood swings, even then. She can remember the smell of that room—like old books, but in a nice way, not a musty

56

way. The smell lingered for a few years after he left but has now faded completely.

She remembers one time hovering outside his office, her hand poised to knock, wanting to tell him that her mum is upstairs, crying again. She can see her own shadow against the door as she wonders whether to ask him what he thinks about the idea of her leaving Paris. And above all, whether he'll even be behind the door, or if he'll be out with another woman.

Only, no. She doesn't remember that. Her dad's office door was never closed when he lived at home with them. She's never wanted to talk to him about leaving, and although there was probably a crossover between her mum and Nicole, he didn't make a habit of staying out late with random women. So where the hell did that come from?

Paris. Paris again.

"And your mum?" her dad asks, forcing Lissa's attention back into the room. She swears Nicole stills, the knife she's using to cut cucumber hovering over the wooden chopping board. "How is Esme?"

For a moment, it hangs in the air around them, even though he asks this every time he sees her. "Oh, she's fine," Lissa says, as she always does.

"Good," her dad says. "That's good." Her parents don't talk anymore—haven't for years, as far as she knows. She wonders how often her dad thinks of Esme, still in the house they bought together in their early twenties—or if, in general, he tries not to think of her at all.

She is saved from having to think of a change of subject by the arrival of her half-sister. Elsie slides into the kitchen wearing an oversized hoodie, dark eyeliner to match her brunette hair—the same color as Nicole's, but curlier—and baggy jeans. She seems to deliberately avoid looking at Lissa as she moves around the breakfast bar and takes a loaf of bread out of the bread bin, only to have it immediately taken out of her hands by Nicole.

"Dinner is two minutes away," Nicole says. She bends to get a stack of plates from one of the cupboards. "Here." She hands them to Elsie. "You can lay the table."

"Gee, thanks," Elsie mutters, turning with the plates.

"Hi, Elsie!" Lissa immediately cringes at how her voice comes out, too bright and over the top. *She is your sister, Lissa, not a puppy.*

"Hey," Elsie says. Or grunts, to be more specific.

"How are you?"

Elsie shrugs. "All right."

That's all she gets before Nicole gestures them through to the table in the adjoining dining area, near the sliding doors. It's fair enough, Lissa supposes, as she helps Nicole carry through the impressively colorful bowls of salad. She's barely around, and although she has Elsie's number, it's not like they text or anything.

Lissa takes a seat next to her dad and opposite Elsie, as Nicole tops up her wine. "So, how's school, Elsie?" she asks—a glutton for punishment, apparently.

"Fine," Elsie says, with a big eye-roll. Right. School—not a great question to ask a young teenage girl. Lissa should know that, shouldn't she? She'll be asking about her grades next. This is another reason she gets so anxious about visiting them—this is her *sister*, for God's sake; how does she not know how to talk to her?

She wonders what Chloe would have been like as a teenager. Would she and Lissa still have got on, even with the six-year age gap? Would she have aced her exams or been a sporty type? She loved playing outdoor games as a six-year-old, but then who doesn't? Would she have gone to university? Maybe she'd have moved to London, as so many of Lissa's friends did, or to Bristol, like Mia. Lissa tries to imagine her sister as an adult but just can't—she's forever six years old in her mind. She wonders if Elsie knows anything about her—if her dad talks about her at all. She doubts it. There are no photos of Chloe in this house, no reminders. He left her behind when he set up this new family. And unlike Lissa, he's managed to forget.

The scrape of cutlery on plates sounds too loud as they all cut into their steaks, and Lissa tries to look like she's concentrating *super* hard on which salad to eat next to disguise the awkwardness.

"Lissa," Nicole says into the quiet, "we're thinking of heading to the Maldives next year for a holiday. It's your dad's sixtieth and we thought we could make it really special."

Lissa chokes on a mouthful of her food, slams a hand on her chest. "That sounds great," she manages to get out, clocking the way Elsie glances at her, a little suspiciously, as she says it.

"It looks amazing," Nicole continues. "A friend of mine—another designer—went last year, and you wouldn't believe the photos. The internet doesn't do it justice, she said. It really is all white sands and clear blue seas. Anyway, I was thinking, maybe you could come?"

Lissa jolts, and from the second look Elsie gives her, she realizes it was noticeable. Nicole, however, continues like it was not. "There's this place I want to stay—it's right on the beach, and each villa has its own pool. I think there's even a swim-up bar at the main pool. Wouldn't that be fun?"

"Lissa doesn't swim," her dad says abruptly, before Lissa has the chance to process that Nicole is inviting her on a family holiday, let alone think of a reply.

Nicole's mouth turns down. "Oh. That's right."

A layer of tension ripples around the room, even as Lissa takes a sip of her wine, pretending she doesn't notice.

"You don't swim?" Elsie frowns. "As in you don't like it, or you can't?"

"Leave it, Elsie," Nicole murmurs.

"I'm just asking. Because it's a bit weird, isn't it? Not being able to swim."

"Not weird if you live in the middle of a desert," Lissa says with a shrug, in an attempt to lighten the mood.

Elsie rolls her eyes. At what age does it stop becoming acceptable to do this so obviously? Definitely by Lissa's age, she reckons. "Yeah, but we don't. We live on an island."

Lissa nods, conceding that with a jab of her fork. "Also not weird if you're allergic to chlorine."

"Are you?"

"No. And I suppose that wouldn't explain not swimming in the sea."

"Unless you were also allergic to salt."

"True. Imagine being allergic to salt. Chips would lose their joy. And it would take all the fun out of tequila shots."

She realizes a bit too late that a fourteen-year-old wouldn't—or at least shouldn't—know anything about tequila shots, and glances to her dad in silent apology. Elsie, however, snorts out a small laugh, and Lissa can't help feeling a little pleased at being the cause of it.

"But why can't you?" Elsie presses. "Did you never want to learn?"

Lissa hesitates. She could tell her the truth, that she's always had a healthy respect for the water and that any hopes of her wanting to learn were dashed when Chloe drowned in the pond in their back garden while Lissa was upstairs talking to a friend on the phone. But she's guessing her dad wouldn't actually want her to explain all this—and that theory is proven right when he says, perhaps a bit more harshly than necessary, "That's enough, Elsie."

Lissa can't help feeling a little sorry for Elsie. It's not her fault, is it? She clearly hasn't ever been told enough to understand why this is taboo.

Nicole must sense this too, because when she changes the subject it's with a deliberately bright tone. "Elsie is on the netball team this year. She made the A team." The smile she follows that up with is pure proud mother, and it's enough to make Lissa smile too.

"Really? That's amazing. Well done, Elsie."

"It's no big deal," Elsie mumbles. Her cheeks have gone a little red, and she's looking down at her plate. "I'm not even sure I *like* netball."

"Of course you do," Nicole says.

Elsie shrugs, pushing a piece of tomato across her plate with her fork. Then she looks up. "Mum, Jess wants to go into Bath next weekend to go shopping. Just the two of us. We'll get the train. That's okay, right?"

Nicole glances at Lissa's dad. "I'm not sure," she says slowly.

"Oh come on." Elsie throws her hands in the air. "This isn't about the train thing again, is it? We're fourteen; we're not going to be harassed."

"You don't know that," Nicole says. "Those teenagers the other week…"

"What, so just because one bad thing happened to one person this one time, now I'm never allowed to get public transport again?"

"Maybe your dad can take you."

"Sure," her dad pipes up. "I can—"

"But Bath is *safe*. It's, like, known for it. It's not like I'm asking to head to a drug den in the middle of Leeds or something." Lissa's lips twitch, but she stops herself from smiling. Elsie seems to sense it, though, and glances in her direction. "It's safe, isn't it, Lissa?"

"I suppose it is considered pretty safe," Lissa hedges.

"*See!*" Elsie gestures emphatically. "Lissa agrees with me."

"Ah…" She's not quite sure how she's been pulled into

the opposing team here—probably not a very safe place to be.

"We'll discuss it later," Nicole says firmly.

Elsie huffs and crosses her arms in protest, shrugging off the hand that Lissa's dad puts on her shoulder. "We're just looking out for you, Else."

Elsie deliberately looks the other way.

"So," her dad says, his tone full of faux brightness, "I was thinking we could invite both neighbors round for dinner at some point in the next couple of weeks."

"Lovely idea," Nicole says. "How about we…"

Lissa allows her mind to drift while her stepmum embarks on a list of various suggestions of what they might cook for the neighbors. Music plays softly in the background—some sort of classical playlist Nicole put on to accompany dinner. Her scented candles still burn around the dining room as the evening light outside fades. The scrape of Elsie's fork on her plate merges with other sounds—the clinking of glasses, laughter, a different sort of music playing in the background, with a husky voice singing in French.

They are sitting in a restaurant, flickering candlelight reflected in his eyes. There are empty plates in front of them, waiting to be cleared. The meal cost more than she could afford on her teaching salary, but he insisted on paying. Beneath the table, their knees almost touch.

"I wish you didn't have to leave," she says on a sigh, picking up her nearly empty wineglass and twirling the stem between her thumb and forefinger.

"I know, I'm sorry." She loves the sound of his voice, soft and lyrical even when he's saying things she doesn't want to hear. "I'll take you to the film premiere, I promise."

She shakes her head. Because yes, it would be something special to go to a premiere—to go shopping for something fabulous to wear, and sit there next to the film composer himself. To listen to the music he'd chosen for each scene and wonder what he'd been thinking when he did so. She wants that—the insight into his world. But more than that, she wants him. And she can't have him when he's away for work. More than that, she can't have him if he chooses to go to America to chase the big league and work in cinema out there, as he so often talks of doing.

"Have you given any more thought to applying for art school?" he asks. She wonders if it's deliberate, the change of subject. Still, she sighs and shakes her head again.

"I can't."

"Why not?"

She rolls her eyes, an attempt to bring playfulness back to the evening. "You know why."

He leans forward to take her free hand over the table, twining his fingers with hers. She feels her pulse hitch as his thumb circles a path on her wrist. She knows he's going to push her on it. Because although she's tried to explain the situation with her family, with her parents, she doesn't know if he fully understands. He'd understand more if he met her mother, maybe, but she'd rather avoid scaring him away just yet.

"What do you think, Lissa?"

She blinks. She's holding the stem of her wineglass, twirling it between her thumb and forefinger. For a moment the two scenes blur. She can feel his knee pressing into hers as they draw closer. Can hear the chatter and laughter of the restaurant humming around her, can feel the echo of his touch on her skin. Then her dad's face comes into focus, peering over at her.

She puts her glass down. "Hmm?"

"About putting a sculpture in the back garden."

Clearly the conversation has moved on from appropriate food to give the neighbors—or is the sculpture being put there to impress said neighbors? "Oh, umm…A sculpture, that's…hmm. Like a big marble naked man or something?" She's trying to think of sculptures she's seen in gardens before, and that, apparently, is all she can come up with. Some artist she is.

Elsie snort-laughs and her dad exchanges a look with Nicole, like she is a second teenager in the house. After that, she tries to stay present—it's the least she can do, given how little she sees them. But all the while, there is a part of her brain trying to pull her back to that restaurant in post-war Paris.

It's the echo of a dream. That's all, surely. A yearning of her subconscious to be somewhere else, somewhere with more glamour, more romance.

But if that's the case, how is she able to conjure up such specific detail? And why does it not feel like a dream at all, but a memory?

Chapter Six

Lissa prods at a lump in her neck as she walks along the high street. It's been there for two days now—just a tiny little thing. It probably isn't anything serious. A cyst, according to Google, is the most likely option.

"What are you doing?" Darcy asks, eyeing her.

"Nothing," Lissa says quickly, dropping her hands to her sides. Misty rain settles around them, tiny droplets clinging to Darcy's hair, tied into its signature knot. It's still light outside, but a gray sort of light, the cloud cover thick and dense above them while a chill holds the air. A week to go until the clocks change, and it's like the weather has accepted its fate, given up the good fight.

"There's nothing there," Darcy says, glancing at Lissa's neck.

"It *feels* like there's something there." She lifts her hand to prod at the lump again.

"Stop it," Darcy says, taking Lissa's hand and lowering it. "You're just nervous."

Lissa frowns. "Why would I be nervous? It's a pub quiz, not the *University Challenge* final."

Darcy goes quiet and Lissa narrows her eyes. "Why would I be nervous, Darcy?" she repeats, more suspiciously now.

The pub comes into view, farther down the high street. It's one of the oldest pubs in Bath, apparently, with rumors that Charles Dickens once stayed there. As they near the blue exterior, nestled into the Georgian buildings either side, Lissa spots Mia waiting underneath the hanging sign, her red hair falling in waves around her heart-shaped face.

Darcy still hasn't answered her. And she knows Darcy. Knows that the casually innocent expression she has fixed in place is a sure sign she's up to something.

"Darcy," she says firmly as Mia waves and comes toward them.

Darcy curls a strand of her glossy dark hair back into place behind her head, then sighs. "All right, but don't hate me."

"No promises."

She faces Lissa. "I invited Mark."

"Mark?"

"Yes, Mark. You don't have to sound so incredulous—you're the one who's been sleeping with him."

"Slept with him," Lissa corrects. "One time." There have been vague promises to do something soon, some overly polite conversations at work—thankfully helped by the fact that Mark is really invested in the project he's currently working on, meaning he doesn't have all that much time for small talk in the kitchen—and some awkward, lingering eye contact across the Monday meeting table. Lissa had just about decided that this was all for the best, that she'd let things fizzle out on their own, and now Darcy has to go and bloody ruin it.

She opens her mouth to ask just what the hell she was thinking, but Mia has closed the distance between them, hoop earrings bouncing in her ears. She's smiling, a light dusting of freckles framing her nose, and Lissa makes herself smile back. She invited her cousin because she's seemed a bit down recently, and Lissa figured an outing might cheer her up.

Darcy bends to give Mia a hug—and she really does have to bend, because Mia is only about five foot tall, whereas Darcy is somewhat of a giant, especially in the heels she insists on wearing. Darcy once told Lissa that she'd put walking in heels on her CV—Lissa still isn't sure whether to believe her.

"So nice to see you!" Darcy says.

"You too." Mia grins back. "I only just got here. I wasn't sure whether to go in—I've never done a pub quiz before. Are there, like, allocated tables?"

"I don't think there's a seating plan," Lissa says, "but it's a good thing you didn't get us a table for three, because Darcy here has invited a plus-one." She tries to keep her voice mild. Doesn't quite succeed.

Mia raises her eyebrows at the tone. "Okay..."

"For me," Lissa adds.

"Ah." Mia purses her lips, then glances at Darcy. "Ohhhh." She draws out the word. "Mark?"

Lissa sighs. "Yes."

"Good idea," Mia says to Darcy.

Darcy gives a gracious little bow. "Thank you."

Lissa throws her hands in the air at the two of them.

"You're not trying hard enough, Lissa," Mia scolds. They're only a few months apart, but Mia has scolding down.

"How do you know? And you've never even met him."

"Well now's the perfect time, isn't it? Come on." She links her arm with Lissa's, steers her toward the pub. Lissa resigns herself to being overruled as she slips her phone out of her coat pocket.

"Looking for an excuse to get out of this?" Mia asks.

Lissa rolls her eyes—okay, so you *can* still do it at her age—and looks down at her screen. "I'm not that immature. I like Mark. I just don't like being ambushed on what's supposed to be a nice quiet Sunday evening." No new messages, no missed calls. "I've done the food shop for Mum," she explains, at Mia's questioning look. "Sometimes they ring me rather than her when they're there, and then she misses the delivery."

Mia raises her eyebrows and Lissa preempts her. "Stop it. I know what you're thinking."

"No you don't."

"I do. You don't think I should still do that for her."

Mia shrugs. "Your words, not mine."

A burst of warmth greets them as they step through the blue oak door and into the little pub with its low timber-beamed ceilings. There's a crackling fire in the main room, its flickering light dancing off the old plaster walls.

"Oh look," Darcy says, indicating a table a few feet from the bar. Lissa follows the direction of her gaze to see Mark on one side of the round table, hand around a pint, talking to...

"Who's the hottie?" Darcy asks.

Lissa frowns. "That's Ash. You invited Ash?" There is no reason her voice should sound this panicked. What's one more person in the grand scheme of things?

"Seeing as I have no idea who Ash is, I'm going with no. I told Mark to bring a friend if he wanted. Thought it might make it seem less weird."

"Did he know I was going to be here?"

Darcy hesitates. "I said it was a group of us."

"Oh for God's sake, Darcy," Lissa snaps. "Bad enough that you set me up, let alone him."

Mark looks over then, and a flicker of surprise crosses his face before he smiles, waves.

"There we go," Darcy says, clapping her hands in satisfaction. "I told you he'd be happy to see you."

"No you didn't," Lissa mutters. Mia gives her a sympathetic pat on the back.

"Well I thought it. Come on. I'll get us drinks."

Mia and Lissa make their way over to the table while Darcy heads to the polished bar. Ash is looking at them too now, and for a second Lissa's gaze snags on his as the corner of his mouth turns up in greeting. She forces herself to focus on Mark instead as they come to a stop. There are pens and paper already in the center of the table, and the smell of beer and fried food fills the air.

Lissa takes a seat next to Mark, smiles as best she can. "Mia, this is Mark and Ash. And this is Mia, my cousin."

"Your cousin?" Mark cocks his head in surprise, then holds his hand out to Mia across the table.

"Doesn't talk about me much then, does she?" Mia asks wryly, shaking Mark's hand.

Mark gives Lissa a small smile. "I take it Darcy played you too?"

Lissa shakes her head. "Don't know why I'm surprised, really. Not that I'm not happy to see you," she adds quickly. Although she'd been all set to start phasing out their interactions at work as of tomorrow, and put the whole one-night-stand thing firmly behind them.

"Well that's something then." His voice is low, his gaze very focused on hers. She wishes she had a drink to distract herself with. Instead, she glances down, sees a motorbike helmet under the table. Very unlikely to be Mark's. And of course Ash is the bloody motorbike-riding type.

"I got us all chips," Darcy announces as she joins them at the table, handing Lissa a white wine and Mia a cider. She takes the remaining seat next to Lissa, forcing her to move up slightly so that her thigh brushes against Mark's under the table.

Darcy pulls the piece of paper over to her. "It's about to start," she says, with enough command in her voice that they all go quiet. Then she smiles at Ash. "I'm Darcy, by the way." She's giving Ash a very direct look— one that Lissa recognizes as, in Darcy's own words, her *come hither* look.

Ash's lips twitch. "Ash. A friend of Mark's." His gaze slides over to Lissa's. God, his eyes are really bloody blue, aren't they? "Also saver of lives, stealer of scooters."

Lissa laughs around a mouthful of her wine, coughs it down in a way that makes her eyes water. *Way to go, Lissa.* She tries to shrug it off. "Or saver of scooters, I suppose, depending on how you look at it."

His lip twitch gives way to a fuller smile. Although is it just her, or does that smile look a bit sad today? "Hi, Lissa."

"Hey, hero." It comes out before she can think better of it, but thankfully she's rewarded with another smile.

"So what do we get if we win?" Mia asks loudly.

"Money behind the bar," Darcy says.

"To spend in here?" Lissa asks.

"No," Darcy says with an eye-roll. "To spend down the road in Pizza Express."

"I better get us another round then," Mark says, placing a hand on Lissa's knee, giving it a gentle squeeze. A pleasant prickling runs up the inside of her leg at the contact—that's a good sign, right? "Don't want to get thirsty halfway through." He nods at Ash's half-empty glass. "Same again?"

"Sure, mate. Thanks."

Mark gets to his feet, leaving a gap between Lissa and Ash, while Mia and Darcy chat about tactics—or Darcy does, while Mia nods. Lissa glances sideways at Ash, finds him looking back her way.

"So. Passing through again?" she asks him.

"Yep."

"How's Belgium?"

"Good."

"Monosyllabic today, I see," she muses. She sips her wine. "Okay, I can take a hint."

"Sorry." He pulls a hand through already messy brown hair. "I'm just having a bit of a..."

"Bad day?"

He gives her a small smile as she provides the same excuse she gave him. "Yeah." He sighs. "Bad day."

And for a moment, she sees it more strongly—the sadness in his eyes. "Anything I can do?" she asks quietly.

He hesitates, glass halfway to his lips. Is he surprised she asked? She's not really sure why she did—what is she planning on doing to help, exactly?

"No," he says, sipping his beer, then lowering the glass. "But thanks. It's why I came along. I could use a distraction."

"Well, I can promise that. Things get pretty rowdy in here."

One eyebrow rises. "Is that so?"

"Oh yes," she says seriously. "Dancing on the tables. Darcy is sure to do a bit of karaoke."

Darcy checks in at the sound of her name. "She's kidding, in case that isn't obvious. Sometimes it's hard to tell, what with her tone and all."

"Shame," Ash says, with an over-the-top sigh. "I love a bit of karaoke."

"Well, sure," Lissa agrees with a nod. "I suppose you'd have to, what with working on music videos and all."

Darcy cocks her head. "You work on music videos?" Hard to ignore the blatant interest in her tone.

"Well sort of," Ash hedges. "Although I have to admit, it's rare that me and the talent head to a karaoke bar when things wrap up."

Lissa snorts quietly—at least she hopes it's quiet—into her wineglass, just as Mark comes back, sliding a pint over to Ash before taking his seat again. He smells pleasant, Lissa thinks—eucalyptus maybe. Pleasant is good, right?

"We need a team name," Darcy announces. "I suggest Darcy and the Diamonds."

Mia laughs. "I'm actually all for that. As long as it's not blood diamonds."

"Darcy and the Ethical Diamonds?"

"The Fellowship of the Quiz?" Mark suggests. Darcy blinks at him.

"*Lord of the Rings*, Darce," Lissa says.

"Ah."

"Ctrl Alt Defeat?" This from Ash, earning a laugh all around.

"Cute," Darcy says, "but it's not optimistic enough. We will not be defeated!" She punches a fist in the air for emphasis.

Mia taps her fingers against her cider glass. "Les Quizérables?"

There are general impressed nods all around, and Darcy writes it at the top of the quiz sheet.

At that point, a man wearing, for reasons best known to himself, a beanie hat propped and tilted to one side on his head gets up and makes his way toward the mic next to the bar. There are now six other tables set up ready to compete, and all eyes turn to beanie-man.

"Hello, everyone! Welcome to our Sunday-night quiz! You know the drill. Three rounds, plenty of drinks on us if you win, anyone seen checking an answer on a phone is banned for life." He says it cheerily enough, though he could be deadly serious—Lissa knows some of them take pub quizzing very seriously around here.

"So without further ado, here is question number one. How many hearts does an octopus have?"

"I know this," Darcy says excitedly, writing the answer down immediately. There is a general hum around the pub as other tables confer.

"Question number two. In what year was the U.S. Constitution ratified?"

"Mia?" Lissa looks across the table at her cousin.

Mia scoffs. "My mum might be American, but that doesn't mean I know all there is to know about the country."

"You're half American?" Darcy asks. "That's cool."

"I think it was the 1700s," Ash says, just as Lissa's phone buzzes in her pocket.

She gets it out, sees a text from her mum. *Food shop arrived. Thank you for sorting.*

She types back quickly. *Great. Thanks for letting me know.*

"Lissa!" Darcy exclaims. "No phones!"

"Right," Lissa says, shoving her phone into her pocket and glancing up at beanie-man, who doesn't seem to have noticed. "Sorry."

Mark tuts teasingly. "Shame on you, Lissa, cheating so early in the game."

"Ah well, you know me. Never trust me to play fair."

He grins, showing off those white teeth, and his hand comes back to her thigh under the table, staying there for the next few questions.

"Question number seven. What is the smallest species of shark in the ocean?"

"Ash?" Mark prompts.

Darcy cocks her head at Ash. "Shark expert?" Lissa isn't sure how she's managing to make *that* sound flirtatious.

"I went cage diving with them once," Ash says. "But the aim was to see the big ones, not the small ones, I'm afraid." He catches sight of Lissa's expression. She's not actually sure *what* her expression is, but he adds quickly, "It was ethical. We went somewhere they don't bait them or anything, and it was about promoting the conservation of sharks."

"Well," Lissa says, "I mean, that's good to know, but I have to admit it wasn't my first thought." She wonders what he'd say if she admitted she's too scared to get into a swimming pool, let alone a cage to deliberately see sharks. Then she wonders why she cares what he thinks.

There are a few more questions that Lissa has absolutely no idea about, before beanie-man announces they'll move on to the medical round. "Where in the body would you find the alveoli?"

There's quiet round their table for a moment. "Sounds like aioli," Darcy pipes up. "Something to do with garlic?"

"It's the lungs," Lissa says. They all turn to look at her. She shrugs, but doesn't offer up more of an explanation as Darcy writes it down.

Mark squeezes her leg. "Impressive."

"Question number twenty-one. What is the common name for the condition 'epistaxis'?"

"Nosebleed," Lissa says promptly. Darcy laughs as she writes it down, well aware why Lissa knows the answer, but Mark gives her a quizzical look. "I, ah, read it somewhere," she says vaguely. She doesn't admit to the Google hole she went through a few years ago when she thought her nosebleed was a sign of something more sinister, or the emergency doctor's appointment she tried to book, quoting "epistaxis" rather than "nosebleed" as the reason in the hope that it would get her seen sooner.

"Question number twenty-two. Which part of the human body has the fastest healing time?"

"Oh I know this," says Ash. "It's the mouth."

Darcy has started to write it down when Lissa pipes up. Usually she wouldn't care—must be the second glass of wine. "No it's not."

Ash looks at her, eyebrows raised.

"It's not the mouth," she insists. "It's the tongue."

"Well the tongue is *in* the mouth," Ash points out.

"Yes. But it's an entirely different body part."

He considers her, tapping a fork against his palm. "Okay. How about we do an experiment. You stab yourself in the mouth and I'll do my tongue, and we'll see who heals faster."

Lissa snorts. "Well, I mean, if you want to do that, go for it. But I'm sure I'm right."

"I'm going with Lissa on this," Darcy says, writing it down. "Sorry, Ash."

Ash, however, is still looking at Lissa, head tilted slightly as if she's an anomaly of some kind. Which, all right, maybe she is, but *he* doesn't know that, does he? "Why am I starting to think you might be a good person to have around in a medical emergency?"

"Trust me, I'm not." She meant to keep it light, but can't stop the tinge of sadness creeping in—and from the way his eyes find hers, he heard it.

Lissa averts her gaze just as Mia stands up abruptly. "I'm going to get a round in before the next, well, round." She jerks her head at Lissa. "Lissa, give me a hand carrying them, will you?"

Lissa raises her eyebrows at the definite command in Mia's voice. "Sure."

She gets to her feet and follows Mia to the bar, where glass bottles glint in the soft glow of the pub. "What are you doing?" Mia demands the moment they get there.

"Ah, coming with you to get drinks...?"

"No." She sweeps her red hair behind her shoulders. "You're flirting with Mark's friend, *that's* what you're doing."

Lissa huffs out a laugh. "No I'm not. I'm *talking* to him."

"No. You're doing that thing you always do."

"What, being polite to acquaintances?"

"You're self-sabotaging."

"Mia. Don't be ridiculous."

"I know you," Mia presses. "You don't want to get hurt. You don't want to believe you deserve a nice healthy relationship, with someone nice and healthy—like Mark."

"How do you know he's nice and healthy? Maybe he's got a dark past. Maybe he's into weird shit or is a secret drug dealer."

"Is he?"

"Well, not as far as I know, but you can never be sure, can you?"

"You're deflecting."

"And you're overreacting."

Mia gives her a long look—long enough to make Lissa wonder if maybe her cousin is right. Maybe she is self-sabotaging.

She shakes her head, pushing her hair back. "Look, I'm not in the best place right now to start something up, okay?" Hasn't been in the right place for quite some time—if ever, arguably.

Mia's expression softens. "And I wouldn't want to push you into something. But, Bissa, I do want you to be happy." The childhood nickname squeezes Lissa's heart. Chloe used to call her Bissa. Her mum, too, used to sing it, rhyming, playful. Mia is the only one who uses it now. "Sometimes I feel like you shoot down the chances that are out there, the things that might *make* you happy. And you never know—what if Mark is one of those things? Because he seems *nice*."

She reaches out, lays a hand on Lissa's arm and squeezes. "Okay. Intervention over." She orders the drinks from the barman, then gets out her phone. Lissa doesn't miss the small smile on Mia's lips when she opens a message.

"Who is it?"

"Oh." Mia looks up. "Just Lottie."

"The American girl?"

"Yep."

"Still sending each other GIFs then?"

"Yep. It's fun." She shoves her phone back in her pocket. "Come on. We'll miss the next round."

Darcy looks over as they head back to the table. Does *she* think what Mia thinks—that Lissa is self-sabotaging?

"Everything okay?" Mark asks as she takes her seat next to him.

She works up a smile. "Everything's great." Ash is talking to Darcy now, Darcy laughing at something he's said. Lissa turns very deliberately to Mark. "So, what did you get up to this weekend?" It's a lame, boring question, but in that moment, she doesn't have anything better. It doesn't matter anyway, because beanie-man returns to his podium, and the quiz starts up once again.

The window behind their table is open a crack, cool night air creeping in to combat the crackling heat from the fire. Lissa can smell smoke through that window, she's sure of it. Can *see* smoke swirling around them, weaving its way through a chandelier while jazz music plays in the background. Only, no, there is no chandelier. There is no jazz music, just the sound of beanie-man's voice. Her subconscious, playing tricks on her again.

"Third place," Darcy announces, loud enough to make Lissa jump, and glances around the table. "Anyone keen for one more?"

Ash pushes his glass away. "Not me. I'm beat."

Lissa takes a steadying breath.

"You seeing Niamh this evening?" Mark asks, a note of playfulness in his voice. Enough playfulness to make Lissa—and Darcy, from the way her eyes sharpen—wonder who this Niamh is exactly.

"Nah," Ash says. "Just going home to bed."

"I have to go too," Mia says. "But this has been fun, thanks for inviting me."

"Where are you headed?" Darcy asks, glancing briefly at Mark and Lissa—the only ones yet to announce their plans.

"To the station."

"I live that way, I'll walk with you."

Lissa just about manages to stop her eye-roll. Real subtle, Darcy.

"What about you?" Mark asks Lissa. "Heading too?"

And she has an excuse ready-made, doesn't she? Everyone else is leaving; they have work tomorrow. But what Mia said at the bar cut a bit too close to home, even if she wants to deny it. She should try, shouldn't she? Mark is nice, and smells pleasant, and doesn't, as far as she can gather, have any deep dark secrets. Maybe Mia is right. Maybe she ought to be trying a bit harder in the present, rather than obsessing over daydreams. After all, if all they're about is meeting a guy, maybe that's just her subconscious's way of telling her that she wants to meet a guy now.

She taps her nails against her empty glass, meets Mark's gaze. "I'll stay for one more, if you will?"

Chapter Seven

She gets home late that night, exhausted from all the trying she had to do with Mark, even though they only stayed for an hour after the others had left. She's thinking of the pub as she falls asleep. Thinking of Mia telling her she shoots down chances to be happy. Of Darcy laughing at something Ash said. Of Ash, and the way his smile didn't reach his eyes. And of smoke coming through the open window, curling its way around a chandelier that wasn't there.

She is moving from a corridor into a drawing room, laughter and music swelling around her. The scent of perfume mixes with coal from a low-burning fire in one corner. A haze of cigarette smoke lingers near the ceiling, snaking around the crystal chandelier. There is a group of men in suits nearby, exchanging cigars, while a cluster of women in flapper dresses congregate by the champagne tower.

She takes off her coat, revealing a gold dress to match her shoes and a long pearl necklace, and gives it to the doorman. Someone passes her a glass of champagne and she takes it with hands that are not her hands—a different color, different texture.

A woman wearing a ruby dress and black heels moves to her, loops an arm through hers and grins, a fun, wicked smile. She clinks her glass with Lissa's and Lissa feels a laugh bubble out of her—at the fact that they're actually here, inside this house they've only ever seen from the outside. Only New York's brightest and best get invited to these parties, and yet here they are, a stroke of luck that one of her sewing clients happens to like her. It's everything she'd dreamt it would be—the smell of it, the sound of the music, the taste of the atmosphere. It's enough that she doesn't care about the looks some of them are giving her, like they know she doesn't belong.

She takes a sip of champagne. She's only tasted it once before, so it's not just the fact that it's illegal that makes it feel like an indulgence. Though technically *she's* not the one doing something illegal here—she's not the one who bought it, after all.

The woman at her side—her friend—takes her hand and drags her toward the center of the room. Lissa laughs again as she follows, feeling the weight of many eyes and not giving a damn. She turns to face her friend, her dress swishing with the music. A dress that took all of her savings to buy.

Her friend kicks out a leg, starting to dance, and Lissa spins, joining in, the champagne already going to her head. She looks over to the band as she dances. It's set up at the side of the room, the saxophone taking its solo as the man with the clarinet waits, poised to join in. She's always admired these bands, the way they don't need sheets of music, the way they listen and work together in harmony. It's joyful, though secretly she wishes it were her up on that stage.

It's then that she sees him. He had his face angled away from the crowd to take a sip of water, but now he turns, nodding to his bandmates. He's wearing a charcoal suit, jacket fitted around his broad shoulders. She can see the glint of his cufflinks under the light of the chandelier as he lifts a hand, sweeping it across his dark brown hair.

The music shifts, changing rhythm, and her friend immediately matches her dance steps. But Lissa slows to a stop, watching as the man draws the mic toward him. As he starts to sing.

His voice is beautiful, husky and lyrical all at once—the type of voice to set your nerve endings alight. The type of voice that leaves you craving more.

It's in the middle of the next note that he shifts position, angling toward her. It's too late to look away, to pretend she's not watching. So she is standing there, still, as his gaze catches hers, those brown eyes warm and deep. For that moment, it's like the breath is stolen from her. Then he smiles, almost like he is smiling in greeting. And her heart stutters.

In her dream, the scene shifts. She's outside the house, at the bottom of grand stone steps, as the last of the partygoers spill out the front door.

She can hear footsteps behind her, the crunch of shoes on gravel. And her subconscious seems to know who it will be before she turns to see him. His bandmates are behind him, carrying their instruments from the house, loading them into a car. His dark eyes are on hers as he crosses to her, hands in his pockets, posture casual.

"I saw you on the dance floor," he says by way of introduction. His accent holds a touch of the South.

She nods, her hand moving to play with her pearls—fake, of course. "I saw you on the stage."

He smiles in acknowledgment. "You all right out here?"

"I'm waiting for my friend."

"The one you were dancing with?" She nods. "She left about twenty minutes ago," he says. "Got a ride with a man—not sure who he was."

Lissa grimaces, even if it's not too surprising. But they were supposed to walk home together, keep each other safe.

"I can take you home," he says, his voice gentle. "If you need?"

She raises her eyebrows. "Doesn't seem all that wise to get into a car with a stranger."

He runs a hand along his chin. "True. But it doesn't seem all that wise to stand out here alone, either."

She glances to the side. His bandmates are watching them curiously, but his eyes remain on her face, waiting.

"You don't have to," she says quietly.

He shrugs. "I know I don't." A corner of his mouth rises in a half-smile. He has a beautiful mouth, she thinks.

Crooked and full at the same time. She wonders if it's only because she's heard him sing that she thinks that.

She lets go of her necklace. "Okay. Thank you." There are witnesses, after all, people who will see her leaving with him. She tells herself that's what makes her agree, rather than this *feeling* she has—like she knows, despite the fact it doesn't make sense, that she can trust him.

Usually when she wakes in the mornings, she can remember only snippets of dreams she might have had. But this time, the image of the 1920s house in New York, the man onstage meeting her gaze as he sang, will not leave her. In fact, like with the dreams of the 1950s, this one only seems to get firmer in her mind as the day progresses, little snippets coming to her out of nowhere as she tries to concentrate on her job. The exact texture of the champagne bubbles on her tongue. The feel of her dress against her skin. The tenor of his voice.

At 5 p.m. on the dot, she pours herself a glass of wine— who cares if it's early—and gives up on the proposal she is working on. She moves from her kitchen table to the sofa and brings up Google. Then she stops, her fingers hovering over her laptop keyboard, realizing she has no idea where she's going with this.

She takes a sip of wine, tapping her index finger on the glass before setting it down again. She starts to type: *Dreams of the 1920s.*

It comes up with a revision site for schoolkids about the American Dream in the jazz age as well as various unhelpful-looking pages. But then what was she expecting exactly? She takes another sip of wine, then rolls her shoulders. *Okay, Lissa.* What is she looking for here?

She tries *Memories of the 1920s and 1950s.* Because that's what they feel like, isn't it? Despite the fact that it makes no sense, when she's lost in one of these dreams, it feels familiar, like she's looking back on an event she'd nearly forgotten, only to be reminded when someone tells a story about it.

The search results are still completely irrelevant, mostly centering around how other people remember those times.

She spends a solid twenty minutes—during which she gets herself a second glass of wine—going down a Google rabbit hole. Only then does she find something that gives her pause, after googling the more vague "memories of another life."

Past life regression.

Past lives. Is that what this is? Ridiculous, surely. Even so, she clicks on it. *A method that uses hypnosis to recover what practitioners believe are memories of past lives or incarnations.* Well, she doesn't need hypnosis, does she? It seems to be happening of its own accord, apparently apropos of nothing.

She stares at the two salient words. *Past lives.* Lives, plural. Is it really possible? That she once lived in the 1920s and 1950s, and that for some reason these memories are coming back to . . . well, not exactly haunt her, but *remind* her?

She continues to click through the search results, scrolling over blog posts about how past life regression changed the writer's life, and a therapist's page offering both regular and "regression" hypnotherapy. She takes another sip of wine—she can already feel it going to her head—and then types out one more search.

Help with past lives—Bath.

And there at the top of the results is the page of a "spiritual counselor" who claims to be clairvoyant and offers a holistic approach that includes tarot reading and past life regression as well as regular therapy—a jack-of-all-trades, apparently. Saskia Arthur is her name. Lissa clicks to her photo to see a woman in her fifties, with light gray hair and a big smile. There's nothing about her that immediately screams a mystical, all-knowing energy, but maybe you have to meet her in person.

She's on the verge of sending an inquiry through when she stops herself. What the hell is she *doing?* The woman is likely a con artist. Lissa doesn't believe in tarot reading, for God's sake. She does not need to sit in some randomer's house listening to her tell her that good fortune is on its way, or try to impose a meaning onto these dreams that does not exist. She is not that desperate. It's the wine making her stupid, that's all.

She'd be better off trying to put the dreams out of her mind and focusing on her present, especially after what Mia said to her at the pub. It's probably nothing—an overactive subconscious. There is no way that a version of her soul once lived in 1920s New York—it's probably just because she fancied Leo in *The Great Gatsby* for a while.

And after finishing her second glass of wine, she's almost convinced herself of that. Almost.

Chapter Eight

There is a light drizzle hitting the windscreen as Lissa drives west out of Bath—an annoying amount of rain because neither the slow nor the fast wiper setting is quite right, so she has to keep changing it every couple of minutes. She clicks the indicator as her sat nav tells her to turn right, past an old stone wall covered in ivy.

She's fifteen minutes away from the restaurant Mark insisted they try, just north of Farmborough, when her phone rings. Mark's voice comes through the Bluetooth speakers as she drives under a canopy of trees, their old, twisted branches knotted and bare.

"Lissa, I'm so sorry, I'm running late."

"Oh. That's okay. How long will you be? I'm halfway there."

"I'm still at work. I got held up."

She resists the urge to point out that she too was at work today—admittedly working from home rather than in the office like him—but that she managed to leave on time. "So you haven't left yet?"

"No. I'm sorry, I've still got a few more things to do."

"Oh," she says again. He'll be ages then. She's not really sure what can possibly be that urgent—she knows he's working on a pitch for a new client, but thought that was basically done. Then again, she doesn't understand why he bothers to go to the office on days when he doesn't have to, either, so perhaps she's missing something here.

"So do you want me to turn around, or...?"

"Ah..." There's a hesitation, and she swears she can hear the click of the keyboard at his end. "Well, you're already on your way, right?"

"Yes," she says slowly.

More clicking. "I know this is a bit weird to ask, but whereabouts exactly are you?"

"On the A39," she says in the same slow voice, because she's not sure what is inherently weird about that.

"Okay. So, look, Ash just called me."

Lissa frowns. "Ash?"

"My friend."

"Right. I know who Ash is." He with the blue eyes and crooked smile and motorbike helmet under the table.

"The thing is, he's broken down."

"Okay..." She's still not totally sure why he's telling her this.

"He was heading into Bath from Bristol airport."

"So...are you going to go and pick him up or something?" In which case, they should just cancel dinner. She's actually a little relieved by that thought—she can grab a takeaway and curl up in front of the TV. Which, she has to admit, isn't a *brilliant* sign, is it?

"Ah, well actually... I was hoping *you* could pick him up. He's stranded not that far from where I figured you'd be, and since I'm still at work..." He trails off.

"You want me to go help Ash?" She's not sure why she's being so slow here—that is very clearly what he's asking. But something keeps snagging. The fact that he's asking her? Or the idea of seeing Ash again?

"If it's too much trouble, don't worry about it," Mark says quickly. "I'm sure he'll be fine. It's just I'm going to be a while, and..."

She taps a finger against the steering wheel. "I mean, I guess I can." She can't think of a good reason why not—she doesn't want to be sitting alone at the restaurant, waiting for Mark for who knows how long. And Ash is nice, isn't he? She's sure she can manage the small talk. Even if those are definitely nerves fizzing in the base of her stomach.

She thinks of the way he looked at the pub, a hint of sadness underneath an easy smile. The way he gives you his whole focus when he's listening.

"Brilliant," Mark says. "You're a lifesaver. I'll send you the location pin."

Approximately thirteen minutes later, she's pulling up on the side of the road behind a small Prius with its hazard lights on. Ash is standing on the passenger side, next to a hedge, his phone out in front of him. He raises one hand above his eyes to protect against the headlights as she stops the car, his whole body in silhouette.

She leaves the engine on, checks her mirrors and waits for a pause in the traffic—cars speeding past without stopping to check if Ash is okay—before getting out of the car. The chill of the air hits her and she pulls her jean jacket—worn because it goes with her dress, rather than for warmth—closer to her. The misty drizzle clings to her hair, her skin.

Ash blinks at her, still bathed in the light from her car. His brow creases, like he doesn't recognize her.

She gives him an awkward wave that she immediately regrets. "Hi."

"Lissa." He's still looking at her in some confusion. She moves closer. He's wearing jeans and a crumpled shirt, his hair is messy and there is day-old stubble grazing his jaw. The stubble suits him, but he looks tired, she thinks. Even with his face still partly obscured by shadows, he looks tired.

"Yep. Mark said you needed some help..."

He blinks again, then looks toward his car, the hazard lights still flashing. "Yes, sorry. He said he would ask you, but I told him not to."

"Right." She has to say, she was expecting a bit more of a welcome, given that she's here with her halo on and everything.

"Not that I'm not glad you're here," he adds.

Way to be obvious, Lissa.

"Okay. Well, just to be clear, I know absolutely nothing about cars, so the help I can offer might be limited."

"I don't know anything either, apart from the go and stop buttons, which I suspect might be the reason I'm in this scenario."

"So…" She pulls her jacket closer as another car zooms past, far too fast on this road that is in effect just a glorified country lane.

"There's a breakdown person coming," Ash says, lifting his phone. "It's a rental and they have it covered."

"Okay. Well that's great." So why did Mark send her?

"Yeah, although they're not going to be here for hours. Some disaster on the M5."

"Soooo…is this a long-winded way of saying yes please, Lissa, I need a lift?"

"If you're sure you don't mind? The breakdown guys said I could leave the keys on the wheel and they'll pick the car up."

"Handy. And of course, a lift I can do."

But still he hesitates.

"Ash," she says firmly, and his gaze meets hers in the dark. "Will you please get in the car so I can stop freezing to death?"

He smiles a little, though it's not quite the easy one from the last couple of times they've met. "Okay. Thank you. Two secs."

He heads back to the rental car, leaving Lissa to get back in hers, shuddering in relief at the warmth. She pulls down the visor, checks her reflection in the little mirror. Her mascara has run in the rain, and water droplets still cling to her hair, which is decidedly more scraggly than when she left the house. She fixes it as best she can, then wonders why exactly she's bothering.

She jumps as the passenger door opens, and snaps

95

the visor back up. "So where to?" she asks brightly as he clambers in, bringing with him the scent of rain, along with something earthier.

He gives her a street name. "Near Combe Down, if you know it? South Bath."

She types it into her sat nav, waits for a space and pulls out. The Prius, she thinks, looks a little lonely abandoned there, hazard lights still flashing, with only an orange cone for company. She refrains from making that comment out loud, though—best to keep the overt sympathy for inanimate objects to a minimum.

She catches Ash glancing at her as they pick up speed, taking in her outfit. Her jean jacket is now hanging loosely off her shoulders, showing off the black dress underneath. It's her signature third- or fourth-date dress—although she's starting to think it's a non-starter with Mark, that agreeing to dinner was a mistake—and it hugs her curves in a way that makes her feel a little self-conscious in this exact moment in time. It's a dress designed for standing up or leaning over a dinner table in candlelight, not for sitting hunched over a steering wheel, illuminated by the artificial light of the dashboard.

She shifts a little self-consciously, and Ash pulls his gaze away, looking straight out the windscreen instead. The way he does it makes heat rise to her cheeks for some reason.

"Where are you off to?" he asks. "Or where *were* you off to, I should say."

"The Pig." Assuming Mark actually leaves the office. And assuming the restaurant holds their table for them. It's bad, isn't it, that she sort of hopes they won't. She doesn't want to spend an evening talking about click-through rates and Liam's ideas for companies they can approach, which she's sure will make up at least 70 percent of the conversation.

"Oh yes. Heard that's good. All organic."

"Exactly."

There is a beat of quiet between them, a weird kind of tension that she didn't notice last time they met, humming in the air.

"So," she says, her voice too loud. "How come you're back again?" Because didn't he say, when they first met, that he wasn't in Bath much? Yet it's only been a couple of weeks since the pub quiz.

He gives a one-shoulder shrug that would look casual if it weren't for the fact it was so stiff. "Got some things I need to sort out."

"Well that's incredibly vague and cryptic. You're not a drug dealer, are you?"

His lips twitch. "My dad lives in Bath," he says. He doesn't seem inclined to offer any further explanation, though—weird for someone who, on first meeting, seems pretty open. Still, none of her business, is it?

"Thank you for doing this," he says, glancing over to her again. "If it's easier to drop me at a bus stop . . ."

"It's fine," she says firmly. "It's not that far out of the way. Besides, maybe this makes up for the scooter incident." He raises his eyebrows in question. "You know, you save my life, I save yours." That near-smile again. "You can even shout at me for it if you want." He gives in to a full-on laugh then, and she feels glad to have coaxed it from him.

"We are definitely even," he agrees.

"Good."

He lapses into silence again, staring out at the rain, which is growing steadily heavier. He looks pale, she thinks, as well as tired.

"You're not hurt, are you?" He looks back at her. "From the accident, I mean," she elaborates.

He raises one eyebrow. "Why, wondering if you can put all that medical knowledge to good use?"

She'll take that as a no, then. She makes a scathing noise at the back of her throat. "Tch. I'm sure you have something you're embarrassingly knowledgeable about."

"Oh, I have plenty to be embarrassed about." The way he says it, voice low, makes her wonder just what he's talking about. "Not sure I'd consider myself knowledgeable about any of it."

Another beat of quiet. She wonders if it's her—does he just not want to talk to her? He seemed so chatty the last few times they met. Something in her stomach twists uncomfortably.

"Do you have a thing, then?" she presses.

"A *thing*?"

The way he says it makes her splutter with laughter. "A pub quiz thing. Like what would be your ideal round."

"Hmm…" The sound he makes when thinking is a little rough, a little raspy. "Does Guess the Intro count?"

She taps a finger against the steering wheel as they wind

down the country road. "Is that where you have to work out what song it is from just the beginning of it?"

"That's the one."

She nods thoughtfully, then uses the buttons on her steering wheel to switch on the last song that was playing through Bluetooth.

" 'Tilted,' " Ash announces almost immediately. "Christine and the Queens. An oldie but a goodie."

Lissa glances at him. "Lucky guess." And only on her Spotify playlist because she'd been looking up French music, trying to understand where this recent Paris obsession had come from. She skips to the next song.

"Shakira," he says confidently as it starts to play. "I'm not sure you need me to expand on that, all things considered." And he's right—if someone *didn't* know this song, she'd wonder what was wrong with them. He slides his gaze over to her. "I'm wondering, though, if we need to introduce you to some modern music, Lissa?"

She laughs, even as the "we," as well as the playful tone, is doing something interesting to her insides. "I'll get right on that. And that's a fun pub quiz skill."

He shrugs. "I like music." He turns to look out the window. "I also like libraries."

As he's looking away from her, she's not sure she heard him right. "Huh?"

"Libraries. That would be my second choice in pub quiz rounds."

"Libraries?"

"You sound surprised." She can hear the smile in his voice.

"Well, sure. I mean, that would be the surprise."

He grins then, turning in his seat. "You don't believe me?"

"Well I don't think you're lying, because it's a weird thing to lie about, but I didn't have you pegged as a library sort of guy."

"Oh? What kind of guy *did* you have me pegged as, exactly?"

"Not sure." She taps the steering wheel again. "Maybe the kind who roams around on his motorbike and likes to drink whisky and could beat anyone at Risk and probably can name every capital city in the world and possibly has a tattoo just because why not."

He nods slowly. "That's quite detailed."

And totally random, Lissa. But Ash is still smiling. She notices the way one corner of his mouth lifts higher than the other, and that, she thinks, gives it away as a real smile.

"I do have a motorbike."

"I know," she says before she can stop herself.

His eyebrows shoot up and she realizes she sounds like a stalker. Coupled with the fact that she showed up to save him moments ago—not a great look.

"I saw the helmet underneath the table at the pub quiz," she explains.

"Aha."

"Let me guess, you like the thrill of it?"

"That, and it's easier to get through traffic."

"But you rented a car," she points out.

"Easier from the airport. Plus harder to rent motorbikes in general. I take it from your disapproving expression," he continues after a beat, "that you don't like motorbikes?"

"I'm not disapproving," she says quickly, trying to even out her expression. Poker, she thinks, would not be her game. "Just easier to get into accidents, that's all." And it is better, isn't it, to play it safe? Given how easily things can go wrong, how easy it is to get hurt.

He gives her a look that she can't quite read.

"So," she says, working up her bright tone. "Libraries."

"I like books," he says with a shrug. "And because I move around a bit, I don't like to buy them. So—libraries."

She nods, taking that in.

"And you?" She glances at him. "I mean, I know you have the whole medical encyclopedia thing going on, but what would be your second choice of quiz topics?" He's watching her with interest now. It makes her wonder if he offered the library intel just so he could ask her the same question in return.

"Art," she says after a moment. "I like art." And thankfully they don't have to drill too much more into the topic of herself, because according to the sat nav, they've arrived. "Where should I drop you?"

"Anywhere on this road is fine," Ash says, already undoing his seat belt. She pulls over next to the curb. It's a very suburban area, all neatly mowed lawns with two-car driveways.

He turns to her before he gets out. Without the distraction of driving, she's not quite sure where to look.

101

"Thank you, Lissa," he says, his voice soft. "This was really kind of you."

"No problem." Her voice, in comparison, is the overly bright one she hates. "Like Mark said, I was in the area." It feels odd saying Mark's name. Almost like she'd forgotten, if only for a second, that he's the reason she's here in the first place. Another great sign.

"Well," Ash hedges, "I'll see you?"

Her gaze darts to his, then away again. "Yep." She wonders if she will. Maybe, she reasons. For someone who said he's not in Bath much, he does seem to be here a lot.

He reaches for the door handle, but still doesn't open it. It's like he's not quite sure how to end this. They don't know each other well enough to hug, do they? He makes the decision, reaching out and placing a hand on her arm instead. His hand is cool and it sends goose bumps up her warm arm. His mouth creases at the corners, and she thinks he looks just a little less tired than when she picked him up. "Bye, Lissa."

And with that, he opens the door and steps out into the night, leaving behind the scent of sandalwood and grass. A scent, she feels sure, that will linger.

Chapter Nine

Lissa sits up straight in the car next to him, conscious not to slouch. His car smells faintly of woodsmoke and leather—not unpleasant at all. Above them, moonlight shines over the New York skyline as they drive toward Manhattan. She's aware of the quiet between them—aware that he is just a stranger and that they are alone together—and clears her throat.

"So you play in these parts often?"

He glances at her. "Just passing through."

For how long? she wonders. It feels inappropriate to ask.

"I've only been with the band for a few months," he elaborates. "I'm just filling in for their regular singer, but let's see where it leads."

"You didn't look like you were only filling in to me," she says.

He smiles. "Thank you. I'll take that as a compliment."

She wants to say more, about how the sound of his voice is that kind of captivating that doesn't come around all that often, but she senses that might be overkill.

He eases the car to a stop outside her house—a narrow brownstone terrace. Behind the tall windows, the lace curtains are pulled shut and all looks dark. Which is good. She doesn't want to deal with her parents.

"Well," she says, one hand on the door handle. "Thanks again for the ride. You're my hero."

His lips quirk a little at the way she flutters her eyelids to accompany the words. Then he reaches out, his fingers gently enclosing her wrist. Where he touches, goose bumps rise.

"Can I see you again? The band is playing tomorrow—I could give you the address?"

Lissa bites a lip that is fuller than the one she's used to. She promised her mum she'd be at home tomorrow, spend the day with her. And even if she's slightly dreading it, a promise is a promise.

"I can't, I'm sorry." She watches the disappointment flickering over his face before he hides it with a small understanding smile. He lets go of her wrist. "But I would really like to see you again," she says quietly.

"Then you will," he replies simply.

And it is said with such confidence that it's impossible not to believe him.

She can feel his gaze on her back as she climbs the steps to her front door—waiting to see her inside safely. She can remember a time when there used to be flower boxes bursting with geraniums on either side of these steps, but now those same pots hold nothing but dirt.

Inside is quiet and dark, as she'd hoped it would be.

She slips off her heels and tries to move through the house without switching a light on, holds her breath when the wooden floorboards of the staircase creak under her bare feet. But the house sleeps on, her parents in separate rooms, no doubt, her father in the sewing room, just so they don't have to share a bed.

She passes her sister's room on the landing. A perfectly good bedroom—small, but certainly more comfortable than the sewing room. But this room has been untouched for years, dust gathering on the shelves, a bed that will never be slept in again. Lissa trails her fingers over the brass door handle but doesn't turn it. She never does.

She can still feel the texture of the brass when she wakes in her own bed, along with the tightness in her heart. In the dark, she curls into a ball under her duvet, wondering if it can be true—if she lived that life. And if so, why a part of it feels so achingly similar to her own.

Mia is waiting for her outside the black gate that leads to her mum's overgrown front garden. It's the first Sunday in November, and although it's still the middle of the day, Lissa swears it already feels darker, the way it always does after the clocks go back.

"I've got the chicken," she says, patting her shopping bag.

"I've got the broccoli," Mia chirps.

"I've got the wine."

"I've got the sedatives." Mia glances at Lissa as they both step through the gate. "Kidding. Mostly."

Lissa snorts but says nothing as she rings the doorbell. Mia looks tired, as she has done the last few times Lissa has seen her, though she insisted when they spoke on the phone earlier this week that it was nothing out of the ordinary—only work stress.

Lissa's mum opens the door, and to Lissa's surprise, her hair is damp, like she's just showered, and she looks fresh. Lissa lets out a silent sigh of relief. "Hi, Mum."

"Lissa." Her mother smiles. "And Mia." She pulls Mia into a hug. "Lovely to see you both. Mia, you look well. You're like me—do better in the cooler months."

"Well, thanks," Mia says. "I think?" she mouths to Lissa behind Esme's back.

"How are your parents, Mia?" Esme continues, leading them into the kitchen. Mia's dad is Esme's brother, but Esme tends to avoid speaking his name out loud as much as possible. "Still living in Denver?" The house has the same musty smell as always, but it does look like Esme has hoovered since last time Lissa was here. So far, so positive.

"Yep," Mia says. "They love it there, for the most part."

"For the most part?"

Mia puts her bag of shopping down on the kitchen counter, which is wiped clean, washing-up all neatly put away. "Well, there are things everywhere that are stressful, aren't there? They don't love the political situation there, for instance."

"Well, here's not too good either, is it?" Esme says lightly, surprising Lissa again, because usually her mum always seems so insular, like she has no idea what is going on in the outside world. "In any case, I'm glad they're happy." And it sounds almost believable.

"I'll tell Dad you say hi when we speak next, if you like?"

The hesitation is so brief, you'd only notice it if you were really paying attention. "Yes. Please do." It's a little stiff, but Lissa has to give her mum credit for trying. Sometimes, when she's really low, Esme can be hostile toward Mia, like she blames her for the fact her parents moved away, even though Mia stayed when they did not.

Her mum had a delicate relationship with her brother even before they lived on opposite sides of the Atlantic. They tried to make sure that their children got to know each other, spent time together as cousins, but Lissa's uncle was exasperated by Esme.

She remembers him coming over, a year after her dad had left, two years after Chloe died. Mia and Lissa were downstairs, curled up under an old gray blanket on the sofa, watching some film or other. Her mum hadn't even come down to greet him, and her uncle headed upstairs, Mia and Lissa exchanging nervous looks as he did.

The shouting came while the opening credits to the film were still rolling.

You're going to have to pull yourself out of this, Esme. David has gone. He's moved on; he's not coming back.

I don't need you to tell me that! That traitor, he left me even after everything that happened.

But you still have a daughter down there, Esme. She's fourteen. She needs you. You're the only thing she has left.

There was a scoff. Was there definitely a scoff, or is

that just something Lissa's brain has imagined, filling in the gaps? *She's got you, hasn't she? Isn't that why you're around all the time? To check up on me? To check I'm doing a good job—that I don't lose another daughter?*

Mia turned the TV up louder, but not loud enough.

He blames me. Her mother's voice wasn't a shout anymore, but still it carried in their too-small house.

What?

David. He blames me for what happened.

Her uncle's voice was gentler now. *Esme...*

But it's not my fault. It's not my fault, you hear me? I wasn't the one who was supposed to be watching her.

Downstairs, Lissa closed her eyes. She'd heard this before, many times.

Mia put an arm around her, saying nothing as Lissa buried her face in her cousin's neck, pretending she was in a reality where her sister had not died.

But she had. She'd drowned because Lissa, who'd been left in charge, had gone inside, just to get lunch, while Chloe had been playing by the pond. Only she'd got distracted, talking to one of her friends on the phone, and hadn't gone back out to the garden until she realized that everything had gone quiet.

She never saw her sister climbing over the fence, put up to stop them getting to the pond, but it was concluded—by the police, and social services—that that was what had happened. That Chloe had thrown her toy, and without an adult to ask for help had been determined to get it back by herself.

Lissa screamed when she saw her sister's body there, face down in the water. She ran to her. But it was too late—*she* was too late.

It doesn't take a lot of water for someone to drown. She heard them tell her mum that. Her mum, who stood in the garden staring at her lifeless daughter until the paramedics arrived. Lissa can still remember the stiff way she held herself as they fixed an oxygen mask to Chloe's little face, her mouth tinged with blue, skin far too pale.

Her mum went in the ambulance with Chloe, while her dad followed in the car with Lissa. She remembers his white knuckles on the steering wheel. How he shouted at her to get out of the car the moment they arrived at the hospital, how he didn't wait for her to undo her seat belt before he was running.

She has only ever imagined what her mum went through on that journey. How she must have sat there holding Chloe's hand, telling herself the doctors would bring her back. How the sirens must have sounded too loud, how the journey time must have seemed endless.

It was pointless, anyway, to go to the hospital. Chloe was dead by the time the paramedics arrived. She'd been drowning while Lissa had been upstairs, giggling over something stupid, unable to hear.

"How's your father, Lissa?" Her mum's voice brings her back to the kitchen, where Mia is unloading groceries onto the counter.

"He's good," Lissa says. Her mum asks about him less than he does about her—a demonstration, perhaps, that today is a good day.

"And your..." Her mum breaks off, clearing her throat. "Elsie?" Still unable to say the word *sister*, fourteen years on from Elsie's birth. "How is she?"

"She's good too, I think." Uncomfortable guilt squirms in Lissa's stomach as she switches the oven on. She should know how Elsie is. She wonders if she got that trip into Bath she'd wanted last time they all met.

Mia claps her hands. "Right. Let's get this show on the road, shall we?"

"Yes, good idea," Lissa says. The quicker they cook, the quicker they can eat, the quicker they can leave. "I'll peel the potatoes."

"I'll help," her mum says.

"Oh. Okay. I mean, great! Do you have two peelers?"

"I could make the cauliflower cheese. Are we having cauliflower cheese?"

"Ah..." Lissa looks at Mia.

"I bought broccoli?" Mia holds up the vegetable in question.

There's a hesitation, then Esme nods. "Broccoli cheese. That will work, won't it?"

"Don't see why not," Lissa says. She will not be the one to ruin the good mood her mum is in.

Her mum switches the radio on, and the three of them set to work on the roast, Lissa rubbing butter over the chicken before sliding it into the oven.

"So," her mum says. "Are you seeing anyone, Lissa?"

"She *is*," Mia says smugly, like she, personally, is the one to thank for that.

"Ah, actually…"

Mia shoots her a look, and Lissa grimaces an apology.

"You didn't go to dinner?" The question is accusatory.

"I did. I tried." She decides not to mention that the highlight of the evening was talking to Ash in the car. "But, Mia, if I'm more interested in the neighboring table's discussion about the merits of keto versus a plant-based diet, then he's definitely not The One."

Mia purses her lips, and for a moment Lissa thinks she's going to push the issue, tell her again that she's not trying. Esme looks between the two of them. "So shall I take that as a no on the seeing-someone front?"

Lissa blows out a breath. "Yes. Definitely a no." Maybe it's the dream-slash-flashbacks she's having that's making her want more? Romance and excitement rather than a date who can't be bothered to leave the office on time to meet her. Then again, she meant what she said to Mia in the pub. If she's having panic attacks in the office, still suffering from nightmares about her sister's death and convincing herself that she's experiencing memories of previous lifetimes, then she's not in the best place to start something, is she?

"And Mia?" Her mum seems determined to keep the bright tone firmly in place. "How's your love life?"

Mia waves a hand in the air. "Oh, all kinds of nonexistent."

"I know that feeling," Esme says, offering a small smile.

Lissa can't help the subtle exchange of glances with Mia. Her mum never talks about her love life—or lack of it. She's been single—and, as far as Lissa can tell, celibate—since her dad left.

Esme glances over at Lissa, frowning like she saw the look. "What about your American girl," Lissa says quickly. "Lottie?"

Mia laughs lightly. "I don't think the odd WhatsApp message counts as a relationship, do you?"

Lissa shrugs. "Some people might disagree."

"You're dating someone in America?" Esme's voice is a touch too sharp.

"Oh no," Mia says. "She's only teasing. I don't have time for dating anyway right now. Work's a bit mental."

"Still in that same job? London, right?"

"That's right," Mia says. Is it just Lissa, or does Mia's voice carry the same forced brightness as her own?

"Something up at work?" she asks. She's always had the impression that Mia enjoys her job as an engineer, even if not the commute.

"Nope. Just busy." Mia catches Lissa's gaze, gives a subtle shake of her head. Lissa lets it drop. If she doesn't want to talk about it here, that's fair enough.

"What about you, Mum?" she asks, a little tentatively. "How have you been?"

"Oh, I tick along. I've cut back my hours at the hospital, but even part-time it's still a lot. Still, it gives me purpose, and that's something to be thankful for, isn't it?"

"Sure," Lissa says as neutrally as she can. It's a line to walk with her mum—you never quite know when she's going to turn. And Esme hasn't really talked about *purpose* before, so much as *punishment*. Still, Lissa supposes it's true —nice to have something to keep you moving forward. She wishes her job had the same effect on her. So far, she's not heard back from a single one of the latest round of job applications.

"You are looking after yourself, aren't you, Lissa?" her mum asks abruptly. "You're exercising, eating right?"

"Yes, Mum."

"And those headaches you were having—you went to see the doctor about them?"

Lissa hesitates. She should never have told her mum about the headaches—she was tired and stressed and Esme had caught her off guard. "Yes," she lies. She actually managed to stop herself going to the doctor, remembering what had happened the last time she'd demanded an appointment for a headache, and how they'd sent her on her way with instructions to take paracetamol, along with the distinct feeling that she was wasting valuable resources. "It was just tiredness, that's all."

Mia glances between the two of them, but says nothing. Perhaps she knows there's no point—Lissa will always be inclined to worry about the little things, and her mum, when she remembers, will always be inclined to feed that worry.

"Good," Esme says, nodding. "That's all right, then. But good to check, in any case. Can't be too careful, can you?"

And although it's not a dig, not this time, Lissa feels the words like a punch to the gut. It's an echo of what's been said too many times before. That what happened over twenty years ago could have been avoided, if only she'd been a little more careful.

Chapter Ten

Lissa meets Darcy at their favorite coffee shop in the center of Bath on Friday early afternoon, having got an *I'm bored* WhatsApp about an hour before. They'd spent the morning in a "brainstorm" meeting, discussing ideas for the creative for a homeware company they'd just won the account on. And Lissa uses quotation marks because it was very much Liam talking *at* them, with the occasional input from Mark. She had a moment during the meeting to remember that she'd once thought marketing might be fun, a way to use her creative skills, before Liam killed any and all hope of that.

"Do you think we should feel guilty?" she asks as she and Darcy carry their cappuccinos to a table by the window—oat milk, because since finding out how many antibiotics they pump into the poor cows, she's decided to steer well clear of dairy for health reasons.

Darcy frowns as she takes a seat in a squishy chair. "Guilty?"

"About not working right now."

"Oh." Darcy waves a hand in the air, fingernails painted purple, and makes a *pff* noise. "After the meeting this morning, we deserve a coffee break. Plus Liam had me working in the office until gone eight the other evening because there was a mess-up with the Facebook advertising—honestly, that kind of behavior is something that's only okay for the likes of Mark." She takes a pointed sip of her coffee. "Speaking of which, I'm guessing the incredibly awkward dance you and he did in the kitchen on Wednesday means that things are not going well?"

"Things are not going at all, in fact."

"Hmm."

"Hmm? Is that supposed to mean you disapprove? Because you're the one who keeps saying you'll magically just *know* when you meet The One, so why should that not apply to me too?"

Darcy raises her eyebrows. She's wearing a red roll-neck jumper today, to go with her signature red lipstick. "No, I just meant, hmm, too bad."

"Oh." Lissa sips her coffee in an effort to detract from the wave of embarrassment. It's Mia getting to her, telling her she should try harder. "Well, all right then."

Darcy snorts a laugh. "Sore subject, I see."

Lissa sighs. "I think I'm just regretting going there in the first place—it's made the office even more unbearable."

"Well not for long, right?" Darcy says. "How's the job hunting going?"

"I mean, not great. This week I've had rejections from a museum, Bath City Council, and that posh hotel, you know the one by the Baths, for a trainee chef position."

Darcy bursts out laughing. "A chef? Seriously? Why on *earth* did you think you could be a chef?"

"A *trainee* chef," Lissa says pointedly, then laughs too. "I don't know, I was getting desperate and I thought it might be fun. It's creative, and I like to cook, and feeding people is purposeful, isn't it?"

"Purposeful?"

"It's just something my mum said, about her job giving her purpose, and I thought…" She shakes her head. "I don't know. I'm being stupid."

"No, you're not. You're trying to figure out what you want to do with the rest of your life; that's not stupid." Darcy hesitates, then, "A museum?"

"Art curator," Lissa says with a shrug. "But they want someone with a degree in art history."

"Ah. And what did you do again?"

"Fine art."

Darcy nods thoughtfully, coffee cup halfway to her lips. Around them there is the sound of coffee beans grinding, along with the screams of a toddler at a nearby table. "You know," she says musingly, "I'm not totally sure I know what fine art actually is."

"Well exactly."

"Is it, like, in opposition to *un*fine art?" Lissa snorts. "Maybe you should just become an artist?"

Lissa wrinkles her nose at that suggestion. She loves sketching, and she can paint pretty well, but she can't imagine anything worse than sitting alone with nothing but your thoughts for company and all that pressure to create. She admires people who can do it, but she knows categorically that she could not. She just wishes she could find a way to honor the passion somehow while still having a sensible job that she can rely on to pay the bills.

"A teacher?" Darcy suggests. "You could teach art? That's purposeful."

She didn't love it when she *was* a teacher, though, so why would she love it now? The thought comes without conscious effort, and Lissa frowns to herself. She's never been a teacher. But she can see it, standing in front of a class, a chalkboard behind her, looking at a class of children who must be aged around five or six. Speaking to them in French.

"I reckon you need to be more targeted," Darcy continues, apparently not needing Lissa's input. "Then you can tailor your CV better."

"Maybe," Lissa says, trying to shake off the weirdness of her thoughts just now. "Or maybe I just go back to marketing. Maybe it's not the job I hate. Maybe it's just Liam."

"That is too many 'maybes' for me to believe you. *Maybe* you should just quit. Then you'll have The Fear and it'll encourage you to really go for it."

"Is that a *Friends* reference?"

Darcy puts a hand to her heart. "You know me too well."

Lissa shakes her head. "I'm not quitting without another job to go to. I have rent and bills and..." And a mother who depends on her. "And stuff," she finishes lamely. "Anyway, why are we only talking about me? You hate it there too."

"I don't *hate* it. I just don't like being treated like I'm an idiot for most of the working week. But that's not the point. *I* am saving to go traveling. I'm going to quit when I have enough money to fund said travels; then I'm going to go off and figure out the meaning of life and everything."

Lissa nods sagely. "Forty-two, I heard."

Darcy grins. "What about if you try further afield? You could apply for a job anywhere, right?"

Lissa shakes her head. "I want to stay here." Not exactly true, but she *needs* to stay here. She can't leave her mum alone. Besides, she could never just up and leave—she is nowhere near brave enough to do something like that.

"All right then. Maybe you should try making your CV more interesting. Lie a bit. You know, like those actors who say they can horse-ride to get parts in films."

"Yes, and that famously goes really well when they have to get on a horse for the first time." But there might be something in that—not the lying part, but bulking up her CV. All she has on it is her degree, a stint as a receptionist at a hotel, a few temp jobs and the three years at Liam's company. Not exactly inspiring to prospective employers.

She says goodbye to Darcy outside the coffee shop and they head off in different directions. Sunlight has broken through the clouds now, brightening up the sandstone buildings. She shoves her hands in her pockets as she walks, watches her breath steam out in front of her. It's so cold now, it won't be long until the Christmas drinks are on the menu—something to look forward to, given that she loves a good gingerbread latte.

She turns off the main high street, weaving her way home the long way. And perhaps it's because Darcy's comment about her CV is still playing on her mind that she notices it. The sign in the charity shop window. She slows to a stop, staring at it.

Help wanted.

Okay, it's unpaid, and only a few hours a week, but it would help pad out her CV, wouldn't it? Who doesn't look favorably on someone who does a bit of charity work? Besides, maybe this is what she needs—something to make her feel like she is giving back, having some kind of purpose.

She takes a photo of the poster—with instructions to apply online—and finds she is smiling as she strides on. On impulse, she heads down Wood Street, then turns left, past a tapas bar and toward her favorite bookshop. Bath is great when it comes to bookshops, but Mr. B's Emporium is the best, in her opinion. Inside, it's a labyrinth of shelves, filled floor to ceiling, and there are seats to curl up on and peruse the books, with staff who don't make you feel judged for doing exactly that.

She smiles at the assistant behind the counter as she pushes the door open, inhaling that brilliant smell of new books, then moves past the other few customers browsing, toward non-fiction. She finds what she's looking for— a small section about dreams—and runs a finger over the spines. Given that her Google search led her nowhere useful, maybe she ought to try reading a book about the subject instead?

She settles on *What Your Dreams Are Telling You*, which sounds nice and obvious. She's opening the book, looking down at the first page, as she heads out of the shop, meaning it's totally her fault when she walks straight into someone.

A tall, broad-shouldered someone, who smells faintly of sandalwood and is looking down at her out of very blue eyes. She takes a step back, attempting to hide her book behind her. A hand comes up to steady her, resting lightly against her forearm, and for a moment their gazes hold, a small smile playing around his lips, like somehow he isn't surprised to see her.

"What are you doing here?" she blurts out.

The smile spreads. "Stopping you from falling over, apparently. And also—hi, Lissa. Nice to see you again."

"Sorry. I mean hi." She moves back ever so slightly, enough that his hand drops away from her arm. "Back in Bath again?" She wonders what the chances are of randomly bumping into him. She supposes Bath isn't *that* big. And he said he liked books, didn't he? Though she feels the urge to point out this is a bookshop, not a library.

Ash hesitates a beat too long. "Oh, well. I'm actually staying for a bit. I'm needed here for now." His voice has a tone she knows well—one that means he doesn't want to talk about it.

"That's nice," she says brightly. God, is she really this much of an idiot? *That's nice?* She rocks back on her heels, not quite sure where to look. Is it awkward? Why is it awkward? She should leave, shouldn't she?

"So how's Mark?" he asks, before she can make her excuses. Out of the corner of her eye, she can see the bookseller behind the counter eyeing them a little curiously.

"You haven't seen him?"

He shrugs. "Not for a while."

"Right. Well, umm, me neither. I mean," she continues quickly, "I've seen him at work, obviously. I just...We sort of...broke up." Not the right phrase, really, given they were never in a relationship, but at least it's universally understood.

"Ah." He shoves his hands into his pockets. "I'm sorry."

"Thanks. Well, I mean, it wasn't..." She blows out a breath, feeling heat creep up the back of her neck. Why is she making such a fool of herself? "Thanks," she repeats. "Anyway, I'll just..." She gestures past him, to the door, with her book. He glances down at the title before she can hide it again.

"Sure." He pauses, like he might say something else, then moves aside for her. "Good to see you, Lissa."

"You too."

She closes her eyes, shaking her head at herself as she steps out of the bookshop. She can hear Ash giving his name to the bookseller, saying he's here to collect an order. Her stomach is jumping uncomfortably, like it's annoyed with her for being so socially awkward. She hears the beep of a horn, opens her eyes to see a motorbike whizzing down the one-way street. Coming right toward her as she steps into the road in front of it.

Her heart lurches as she scrabbles backward, and the motorcyclist beeps his horn again as he swerves past her. She hears the bell of the shop door, then feels someone grabbing her, pulling her back onto the pavement.

Ash steps around her, into the road, and she reaches for his arm automatically, even though the danger has passed, the motorbike now way past them. But he is out on the street, shouting at the motorcyclist. She doesn't hear what he's saying, though, because over the top of his voice is the screeching of brakes somewhere up ahead.

The idiot on the bike is going to hit someone, isn't he? People shouldn't drive that fast—that's the way to kill someone. And it could have been her. It could have been *Ash*, when he'd run into the street like that.

Her ears are ringing as Ash turns to her, and his brow furrows.

"Lissa? Are you okay? He didn't hit you, did he?"

She is breathing too heavily, she realizes. Where she grips her book, her fingertips prickle.

She's not okay. She's not okay but she doesn't know why. Her head is spinning. Her breath comes more quickly. Only she's not got enough oxygen. She's not got enough, and she can't breathe, and now it's not her head spinning but the whole street tilting around her.

Her book falls to the ground with a heavy thump. She can feel pins and needles in her feet, her hands. Her throat is closing, and she can't do anything about it.

No. Not here.

But she is already falling, and an arm is coming out to support her, one hand around her waist, guiding her to the ground. She blinks, but it does nothing to help, so she sticks her head between her knees, hearing the harsh rasping sound of her own breath. Someone is saying her name, telling her to breathe. But that's what she's doing. That's what she's doing, only it's not enough—she's going to pass out, she can feel it.

It didn't happen, she tells herself. No one got hit. No one got hurt. But she can feel it like it happened to *her*. The sting of the tarmac raw against her knees. The sound of someone screaming over the hiss of brakes. A man's head—*Ash's* head—cracked and bleeding.

Come on, Lissa. Don't do this.

A hand is on her back, stroking gently. "It's okay. You're okay." The same words, over and over.

You're okay.

She's okay. She's okay, she's okay, she's okay. She didn't get hit. No one was hurt.

Slowly her breathing calms. She feels the world around her steady, as the ringing in her ears subsides. She stays where she is, head between her knees, for a few more moments, the air cooling inside her mouth. There is a hand on her back, soothing her.

Ash's hand. Ash's voice. He's sitting next to her on the pavement.

She lifts her head, humiliation already creeping in. He is right there, inches from her. He saw the whole thing. Another witness to just how mad she is. It's like Liam at the office all over again.

He holds out a cup of water. Oh God, where did he get that? She glances over her shoulder, sees the bookseller hovering.

"Here," Ash insists. "Drink." He presses the cup into her hand. When she lifts it to her lips, the contents tremble. But she's not the only one shaking, she realizes. Because Ash's hand is not steady either as he moves it away from her.

"Is she okay?" the bookseller asks behind them.

"I'm fine," Lissa says, as firmly as she can manage. It doesn't help that her voice is hoarse, like she's coming round from a cold. For fuck's sake, she didn't even get hurt this time; what is wrong with her? It was the idea that she *could* have been hurt. Or that Ash could have been—that he could have been hit pulling her back like that, charging into the street with the same hero complex she'd seen on the day she met him.

Then it would have been another person dead because of her.

But it all feels so stupid now. Of course he wouldn't have died. There was no real danger.

"Are you injured?" he asks, the question brisk, efficient. Her head feels too heavy as she shakes it. "No. I'm just..." But she can't find the right word. Embarrassed. Mortified. Pathetic. "I'm fine. I'm sorry. I was..." She blows out a breath. "I'm sorry," she says again.

"No need to apologize," he says, though his voice is tight. God. What must he think?

She tries to get to her feet, but he grips her arm, holding

her in place. "I don't think you should move yet," he says, still in that same tight tone.

His face is a little pale, she sees now. And that tone—maybe it's not fear that she's a lunatic, but another kind of fear? She watches him for a moment, considering. Then, "I scared you," she states.

He puffs out his cheeks. "Nah. I mean, sure, I was seconds away from calling an ambulance and trying to remember a CPR course I went on once, but apart from that..."

Lissa snort-laughs, the sound tired. "Thank you for resisting. And I'm sorry for scaring you."

He nods slowly. "So that was..."

She grimaces. "A panic attack. Anxiety attack. Whatever."

"Right. But you're okay now?" His gaze travels over her, as if looking for signs of damage. "I mean, is there anything I should—could—do?"

"No. I mean, if you happen to be on the brink of inventing a time machine, then if you wouldn't mind letting me borrow it, that would be great."

He laughs that easy laugh of his. The color is coming back to his face now. "That might be a bit beyond my technical skills. I suppose I could give it a go," he muses. "I reckon I could get it to *look* really cool."

"Well that's something. We don't want to go back in time in something that looks a bit shit."

"Yeah, especially if it doesn't work."

"Especially then, yeah."

He's still eyeing her critically, like he's expecting her to collapse again. Like she's a broken, fragile thing. She reaches behind her for the book she dropped, partly so she doesn't have to look at him, but he beats her to it, handing it to her.

"Dreams, huh?" he asks as she takes it.

She doesn't have it in her to be embarrassed about that, after what he just saw. "Yep," she says easily. "Pretty sure I'm psychic." Even if the visions she's having are definitely of the past, not the future.

He laughs again, picking up his own book. A language primer. She raises her eyebrows. "Portuguese?"

"Yep. Thinking I might take a bit of a break from the scouting, go to Brazil." He frowns. "After I'm done in Bath."

She cocks her head. "Got a thing for the Bs, have you?"

He grins, then runs another assessing glance over her, top to bottom. "Are you sure there's nothing you need?"

She sighs. "Thank you, but I'll be okay. Honestly. This isn't... I just need to get home."

"Okay. Come on, I'll walk with you."

"You don't have to," she says quietly.

"I know I don't."

There's the edge of a memory there, just out of reach. Turned to smoke before she can fully grasp it.

He gets to his feet, holding out a hand to help her up. After a brief hesitation, she takes it. He keeps hold of it for a moment, his long fingers light and cool around hers. She feels an echo of another man's hand encircling her wrist. An echo of those goose bumps, traveling up her arm underneath her layers. Her breath catches as she lifts her gaze to meet Ash's. As eyes darker than his look back at her.

Then he drops her hand, smiles an easy smile. He jerks his head. "Come on. Lead the way." And that moment, that feeling, is gone.

Chapter Eleven

That evening, Lissa curls up on the sofa in her small flat, heating on, the blanket Mia bought her for Christmas last year draped over her knees. She's taken two paracetamol and is on her second glass of mint tea, but a headache still presses at her temples, the way it often does after an anxiety attack. She feels wrung out, like she's spent the day crying, her body aching as if she's run a marathon. Although since she's never run a marathon, she supposes she wouldn't know.

She hates that it happened again. Hates that someone was there to see it. Hates more than she thinks she should that it was Ash, of all people, who was there with her. If it had been Darcy or Mia, she could've coped, but the way he looked at her out of kind, careful eyes when he said goodbye at her door... She doesn't want to think of the impression she must've given.

When she can't concentrate on the dream book she bought, she heads to the bathroom and switches the shower on as hot as it will go. She doesn't have a bath, but she hates them anyway, hates the feeling of being submerged, surrounded by water. She steps into the shower, the water like needles, stinging her skin. She closes her eyes, breathes in the steam.

There's the sound of screeching brakes as someone pushes her out of the way. The thud of tarmac reverberating through her knees as she hits the ground. The sound of someone's body slamming into a windscreen, the sickening crack of a head hitting the road.

She opens her eyes, scowling at herself.

Stop it, Lissa.

No one got hurt. No one's head hit the tarmac. It was a motorbike, not a car.

The water continues to pour around her, and although it's draining away, she feels as if the water level is rising, can already feel the burn of her lungs, like she's being submerged.

She's running into the garden, desperate to get to Chloe before she drowns, not to be too late this time. Only she's not running through the garden at all. She's running through a city that has turned to rubble, and the screams she can hear are not her sister's, but coming from all around, as the sound of planes above grows steadily quieter.

No. Her heart beats the warning, nausea swells as she runs. To her house—to what *should* be her house—where she left her sister only moments ago. She was supposed to be safe there, but now there is a small, limp hand sticking out from the rubble. It can't be hers, it *can't* be.

Lissa knows, though, that it is. It's her sister's hand, stretching for help as the street was bombed around her. The warning came too late, when Lissa was already out—and her mother isn't home, her dad away fighting. Which leaves only her. She was left in charge and she was supposed to be there to protect her sister, but she wasn't.

She's scrambling over the rubble, ears ringing, people shouting. At her? She isn't sure. She feels a rough grip on her arm, shakes it off as she bends down to reach for the hand. It's her sister's, she knows that, even if she can't see the rest of her yet. She checks the pulse first.

Nothing. Not even a flicker of life.

She is sobbing as she tries to clear the rubble. She shouldn't have left. This is all her fault, she shouldn't have left.

The water is running cold. It's that, she thinks, that pulls her back to reality. She is shivering as she reaches to turn the tap off. And she realizes, when the water stops, that she is crying.

Is that what this is all about—Chloe? Is it a way of trying to process what happened to her, by imagining different ways she could have died? Are the flashbacks she's seeing some weird kind of PTSD? It's so many years after it happened, but trauma can do that to a person, can't it? Or maybe she's just going mad. Maybe she needs a doctor, pills of some kind.

She is exhausted when she climbs into bed, and it doesn't take her long to fall asleep. When she does, she's greeted by the sound of water; soft waves lapping against the shoreline. It's oddly soothing, given that she can't swim.

She is sitting by a loch, her feet bare, just on the edge of the glittering dark blue water. It's as warm as it ever gets this far north, though a cool breeze whisks across her cheeks as she sketches, the movement of charcoal over paper something that never fails to calm her. Around her, heather-clad hills roll into the distance, while ancient pines guard her back.

It feels like another memory, another lifetime. Only it is somehow more blurred than the other flashbacks, like an out-of-focus photo.

She looks up at the scene she's drawing. A man is rowing toward her. *Her* man, one with chestnut hair and pale green eyes. Even from here, she can see him smiling at her behind his beard. Or she can't really *see* it, because there is still that strange blurred quality to the dream, but she can imagine it.

It's become her favorite thing to do, to come and sit here with him. He only came back to this part of Scotland because of his father, she knows. Because when his father returned from the Crimean War, he wasn't the same. But she hopes he'll stay.

He is singing out there on the lake, a beautiful, comforting sound, the Gaelic words tumbling into one another. He's tried to convince her to come out on the water with him before, but she doesn't know how to swim, so it doesn't seem sensible.

She is finishing the sketch when he pulls to the shoreline, jumps out into the water and strides toward her. She tilts her head back, smiles up at him. He asked her once what she wanted from life. She wasn't able to answer, because *want* seemed like such a foreign concept. She had things she needed to do, parents she needed to take care of, things she needed to atone for. But really, when he asked, all she wanted to say was: *You. I want you.* And that just didn't seem like the type of thing it was wise to say to someone before you knew if they were staying. Before you knew if they wanted you back.

From the way he's looking at her now, though, his face framed in sunlight, she hopes he might like her just as much as she likes him.

The shrill ring of her phone jolts her awake. She fumbles for it in the dark as it rings again, feeling disoriented, still groggy from sleep.

She doesn't even check the screen before she answers. There's only one person who can be calling her this time of night. "Mum?"

There is no answer, only the sound of sobbing.

"Shit," she mutters. Then, more loudly, "Mum?" Sobbing again. "I'm coming round, okay? Do you hear me, Mum? It'll be all right. I'll be there soon."

The lights are on in her childhood home as she lets herself in, and the house is cold. She finds her mum in the living room, half passed out on the sofa, paper cut up all around her, like a weird version of the mess a child would make. There's a near-empty bottle of gin on the coffee table, next to a glass still beaded with condensation.

"Mum?" Lissa speaks softly as she moves into the room with practiced quiet.

Her mum half opens one eye, struggles to sit up. Then she opens her eyes more fully and looks at Lissa in a way that makes her insides twist. In a way she recognizes. "You." The word drips with loathing, and even though Lissa has heard this tone before, even though she knows to expect it, that does not stop it hurting.

"Hi, Mum," she says, as calmly as she can. "Let's get you upstairs, shall we? I can make you some—"

"Get away from me," her mum spits as Lissa approaches the sofa. "I don't want you here."

Lissa takes a slow breath of stale air. "You called me, Mum," she says quietly. "Remember?"

"I didn't *call* you." She snatches her hand away when Lissa reaches down to take it. And Lissa sees now what the pieces of paper are—shredded photos. There is an album on Esme's lap, with one photo pulled out on top. She shoves it in front of Lissa's face.

Chloe smiles out at her, missing a front tooth. Her hair, a darker blond than Lissa's at that age, is plaited down her back, tufts of it sticking out. She's wearing dungarees with grass stains on both knees, and holding a chocolate ice cream that is melting in the sun. Lissa doesn't even know when this was taken. Chloe looks around five, so it can't have been long before she died. It's not in their back garden, but the background is generic, some park or other. She hates that she doesn't remember it. She hates that she can't tell which day of Chloe's too-short life this was taken.

"When was the last time you went to see your sister, hmm?" Her mum's voice is scathing, her hand shaking as she reaches for the empty glass on the coffee table. "I bet you never even visit her anymore. I bet you've forgotten all about her, haven't you?"

"No, Mum." Lissa keeps her voice quiet, a familiar dread wrapping around her.

"She was six years old, Alyssa," her mum says, her tone awful and biting.

"I know that," Lissa murmurs, her voice still calm even as her throat tightens. She has to stay calm. One of them needs to be calm.

"Six years old," her mum repeats. "And you left her."

"I know," Lissa says again.

"You left her alone. You were supposed to be watching her, and you left her alone."

Lissa looks back down at Chloe's face, her bright eyes, that toothy grin. So little. So innocent. Let down by the people who were supposed to take care of her—her mother out at the shops, her sister upstairs, talking to a friend. The lump in her throat presses on her airway, constricting it.

"You should have been there!" her mum screams now, snatching the photo from her. She throws it aside like she can't bear to look at it and takes her head in her hands. The sound of her sobs rakes through Lissa. "Why are you here now when you weren't there then?"

"I'm sorry," Lissa whispers. It's all she can think to say—all she's ever been able to say. "I'm sorry, Mum."

Her mum drops her hands, looks up at her with red eyes. "Get out."

"Mum, let's just get you—"

"Get out!" she screeches again. "I don't want you! You're the reason she's gone! *Get out, get out, get out!*" The words tear from her, high, frantic.

"Okay," Lissa says, her voice hitching. *Calm*, she tells herself again. She has to stay calm. "Okay, Mum." And she turns on her heel, turns her back to the broken woman behind her.

"No, wait." Esme's voice is different now, a small, weak plea. "Don't leave me. Please don't leave me. You're all I have." Lissa turns back, hesitating in the doorway. Her mum's eyes meet hers and the anger, the loathing is gone. She shakes her head, the tears slowing. "You're all I have, Lissa."

Lissa closes her eyes, counts a single beat of her heart. Then steps back into the room, bends down by the sofa. "It's okay, Mum. I'm here." She strokes her mum's hair carefully back from her face.

"You're here," her mum repeats, letting her breath out on a slow exhale.

"That's right," Lissa murmurs. "I'll always be here. I won't leave."

Esme presses Lissa's hand against her own cheek, holding it there. "You promise?"

Lissa smiles as best she can, banishes her tears for later, when there is no one around to see. "I promise."

Chapter Twelve

When Lissa wakes in her bed, she is not alone. Mia is next to her, curled in on herself, seeming even smaller than usual in one of Lissa's nightshirts. Lissa listens to the sound of her cousin's deep breathing, scrunching her own eyes closed at the memory of last night.

Of calling Mia when she left her mum's house, gone 2 a.m. Calling in tears because she didn't know what else to do—because she was tired and wrung out and neglected to remember that it was a stupid idea to call her cousin in the middle of the night, a cousin who had a job and a life of her own, and who didn't need to drive over from Bristol past witching hour.

She tries to make as little noise as possible as she pushes off the duvet. She can at least make Mia breakfast as a thank-you. But Mia is a light sleeper—always has been—and blinks heavy eyelids as Lissa moves.

"Hey." Her voice is croaky. "How are you feeling?"

Lissa feels her face crumple. "I'm so sorry, Mia. I shouldn't have called you."

Mia blinks slowly again, clearly forcing herself into

full wakefulness. "Of course you should have. That's what I'm here for. But now that you're up, I'd kill for some coffee."

"You got it," Lissa says, as brightly as she can. "No murder necessary."

She pulls on some socks and heads to her little kitchen, scraping her hair back into a bun. Her head is hurting again, pressure at her temples. It's because she's tired and stressed after last night, she tells herself firmly.

Mia comes into the kitchen, phone in the palm of one hand, as Lissa is pouring out the coffee from the cafetière. She's already dressed in her work clothes, freckly face a little paler than usual. Lissa hands her a mug of coffee, after putting in an extra teaspoon of sugar, like she's trying to emulate Mary fucking Poppins or something.

"Can I make you breakfast?" she asks. "I can do toast. I think I've got some eggs. And I've got—"

"Lissa," Mia says firmly. "It's fine. As long as you're okay."

Lissa swallows, nods. "I'm okay."

Mia smiles a little sadly over her mug. "I wish I could make it better."

"I know," Lissa whispers.

Mia moves across the kitchen, puts one slim arm around Lissa's shoulders. "I know I've said this a thousand times, but it's not your fault. What happened to Chloe, what is happening to your mum. You know that, right?" Lissa says nothing, because Mia is wrong, but she doesn't want to argue the fact, not after Mia has been here for her, the way she always is.

Still with her arm around Lissa, Mia lifts her phone, smiles at something. Because she's standing so close, Lissa can see the message—a long one, from *Lottie, NYC*. She averts her eyes as Mia takes another sip of coffee.

But she can't stop herself from commenting. "That looks like more than the occasional GIF to me." Mia frowns up at her. "I didn't read it," Lissa adds. "Just an observation, that's all."

"Yeah, well. We talk a lot." It's said like an admission, like Mia has something to feel guilty about. "I thought it would peter out, but we just, I don't know…" She taps her index finger against her phone. "She might come over here. To see me."

"That's exciting! Isn't it?" Lissa adds, because Mia doesn't look particularly enamored with the idea. "Or do you not really like her—are you just talking to be polite or something?"

"No," Mia says slowly. "I like her, it's just…" She shakes her head. "Nothing. It'll be fun if she comes. I'm overthinking it."

"Well, tell me if she does. I'd love to meet her—if that's not too intense."

"Of course. We'll go to the pub or something." Mia lifts her phone again, clearly to check the time.

"Please don't feel you have to stay," Lissa says quickly. "I know you have work."

Mia bites her lip. "I would stay. It's just, today is a London day and—"

"You don't need to explain. I shouldn't have even—"

She holds up a hand to cut Lissa off. "Stop." She sets her mug down on the counter. "So look, maybe we could do a spa day soon. Invite Darcy if you want too."

"A spa day?"

"Sure. I thought it might be good for us. They're supposed to be relaxing, right?"

"So I've heard." Lissa contemplates Mia, picking up her own mug and cupping it in her hands. She has a suspicion that by "us" she means Lissa specifically. Emotion clogs her throat, but she manages to smile. "I'd love that. Thank you."

She sees her own phone light up on the counter and picks it up automatically, her stomach tightening with dread at the thought that it might be her mum again. It's a Facebook message, though, which makes her frown. She has a Facebook account, but she hasn't posted on there in about five years. Some kind of scam, maybe?

When she sees the name, her heart does a funny kind of nervous spasm. Ash Hawthorne.

Hey. I hope it's not weird to track you down like this. I just wanted to check you were okay after yesterday.

Then a follow-up message: *It's Ash btw. Mark's friend.*

She stares down at it for a moment. He's checking she's okay. She can't work out whether to be embarrassed or pleased by that.

"Who is it?" Mia asks.

"Oh, no one." She's not sure why she lies, only she didn't mention she'd bumped into Ash yesterday, and now it seems odd to bring it up.

Mia gives her a funny look. "Okay." She casts her eyes around, locates her shoes and slips them on. "I don't have time to push you on that, because I really do have to go." She gives Lissa a quick, hard hug. "I'll text you later."

Lissa hugs her back. "Have a good day, yes?"

When she's alone in her flat, she picks her phone back up.

Well hello, hero. The nickname seems even more fitting given what happened yesterday. *I'm good, v nice of you to check. Hope you're okay too?*

Oh I'm just great. So I think I said—I'm stuck in Bath for the foreseeable at the moment.

She doesn't miss the word "stuck"—as in, not somewhere he wants to be.

Right, she types back, *I remember.* Though he didn't say why exactly that's the case.

So that means I have lots of time on my hands. Do you fancy a coffee later in the week?

Again that nervous spasm in her chest. Her finger hovers over the screen. She should say no. She doesn't need any more complications in her life. She clearly unnerved him enough that he felt the need to check up on her, and that's probably all this is. But he's helped her twice now, and she owes him.

She tells herself that's the reason she agrees—that she'll make it her treat, as a thank-you. That it's not because some inexplicable part of her—the part that felt the echo of something as he took her hand in his—wants to see him again.

*

It was stupid to agree to this. Is she even allowed to see him, given he's Mark's friend? Are there rules here?

It's not a date, Lissa, she tells herself firmly as she makes her way to the café she always goes to with Darcy. It's a thank-you coffee, that's all.

She sees him as she reaches the café, coming from the opposite direction, just as the abbey bells announce the arrival of a new hour across the city. Her stomach twists with nerves—what is she supposed to say to him?—but he greets her with a smile and a wave.

"You look better," he says as he approaches, his breath misting out in the cold. His eyes are impossibly blue today, against the backdrop of the clear sky.

"Than when I was collapsed on the street?" She flicks back her hair, makes her voice faux-coy. "Why, thanks."

He laughs, and the sound of it makes her relax a little. As does the relief that he's happy for her to joke about it, that he's not going to make it weird, the way so many people would. "So this place does great coffee," she says, gesturing behind her.

He nods, rocking back on his heels. "Sounds good. Or …"

"Or?"

"Well, as I was walking through town, I saw the Christmas market is up."

"Right. It goes up at the end of November every year."

He shrug-nods. "Could be fun."

She raises her eyebrows. "You want to go to the Christmas market?" It doesn't seem very on-brand for him, somehow, though maybe that's a little unfair. She doesn't know him, does she? Maybe he's into collecting tiny porcelain Santas or something.

"Sure," he says easily. "Why not? I've not actually been to one before and I like to try everything at least once."

He bounces on his feet a little as he talks, a kind of restless energy coming from him. She wonders if maybe he just doesn't want to sit still.

"Okay," she says. "Sure. Why not?" She repeats his words back to him, and he grins.

They walk side by side, both of them hunched against the cold as they head to the part of the city that has been cordoned off for the market. They pass the charity shop where Lissa applied for the weekend volunteer shift—she is still waiting to hear back, and is beginning to worry that she can't even get a new *unpaid* job—then the abbey, the honey-colored stone illuminated in the sunlight.

When they reach the market, they turn left onto one of the cobblestoned streets. There are wooden stalls set up on both sides, decorated with festive lights that she's sure will look gorgeous come dark. The smell of cinnamon and mulled wine laces the air, and there's a busker nearby singing Christmas tunes, his voice merging with the general chatter around them.

She remembers going to a Christmas market when she was little, though it can't have been this one, as it's only been running for the last few years. But she can recall eating warm roasted chestnuts, can remember her dad sweeping her into his arms, even though she was far too big for that really. Her dad. So it must have been before Chloe died. Chloe must have been there, but she can't recall her sister's voice, or the sound of her laugh. Can't remember what they did at that market—if she and Chloe played together, as they sometimes did when Lissa's friends weren't around and the age gap managed to melt away.

She thinks briefly of the most recent waking-dream she had, standing in the shower a few days ago. The one in Paris during the war, when a different little girl—but still her sister—was killed, again because of a decision she'd made, because she wasn't around to save her. She wonders again if that's what this is about—her brain processing trauma in some weird way, years and years after the fact. Although that doesn't explain the other images she gets, does it?

"Look!" Ash's voice jolts her back to the present. "They have jalapeño hot chocolate there, Lissa." He sounds totally delighted, pointing at a stall selling hot drinks. "We have to try it." He marches on over, leaving her to follow him.

"I'm definitely not trying that," Lissa says firmly. She looks at the menu. "I'll have an ordinary hot chocolate."

He shakes his head mockingly. "Way to be adventurous."

"Yes, because I show all signs of being the adventurous type."

"Ah, come on," he insists. "What do you have to lose? Worst case, it's awful and we throw them away. But good to try something new, right?"

Lissa isn't totally sure she agrees with that philosophy—new can often have catastrophic consequences, after all—but he seems so enamored with the idea it's hard to argue. "Fine," she says on a sigh. "But I'm buying them—my treat to say thank you, remember?"

He frowns as they edge closer to the front of the queue. "Thank you for what?"

"For the other day," she says, really hoping that the heat doesn't show in her cheeks.

"Oh." His frown deepens. "Why do you need to say thank you?"

"Because..." But he's at the front of the queue now, ordering the two spicy hot chocolates and not giving her the chance to finish. And she has to admit, as she sips it, that it's really not as bad as she thought it would be.

They pass various stalls selling an array of gifts, which makes Lissa wonder whether she ought to start thinking of Christmas presents for this year. Maybe there's something here she can buy for Nicole—she never knows what to get her.

Ash exclaims in delight at a stall selling hats and scarves, as if the concept of a hat is entirely new to him. "What do you think?" he asks, jamming one on his head—a particularly garish one, with a rabbit riding a reindeer stitched into the front.

"I don't believe you'll ever wear that," she says, trying not to laugh at how ridiculous he looks.

"Sure I will. Goes with everything. And here..." He does a quick sweep of the hats on offer, pulls out one that is clearly meant to be gold but is more of a sickening yellow color, and which she is pretty sure is supposed to be in the shape of a star. Something that, by the look of things, is hard to pull off in a hat. He plonks it on her head, then grins. "Perfect. Definitely suits you."

She rolls her eyes and pulls it part way off, but he just shoves it back down again and tucks a stray strand of her hair underneath it. The nape of her neck prickles with awareness.

He turns a beaming smile on the saleswoman. "I'll take both," he announces.

"Oh no," Lissa says quickly, "don't get one for me. I—"

He holds up a finger as he slides his card out his pocket. "You wouldn't buy it if I didn't."

And that logic is kind of hard to argue with.

"So do you reckon there's a roller coaster around here somewhere?" he asks as they start walking again. And now it feels rude to take the yellow star hat off, even though it will definitely be clashing with her hair.

"A roller coaster?"

"Sure. Don't some of these markets have like a mini fairground?"

"Ah, if they do, I think it's more like the odd Ferris wheel rather than a full-on roller coaster."

"Hmm." He looks unsure whether to believe her—like she could be lying about the lack of roller coaster.

"Though I can tell you right now, I'm not getting on any sort of fairground ride. They're not safe."

"They probably are."

"They're definitely not."

He glances down at her. "Would you have a panic attack again?"

She's taken aback at the direct question, though there is nothing more than genuine curiosity in his voice. But no one usually asks directly, at least not people who've only just met her. And not even people who have known her for years—look at Liam, who is still eyeing her almost suspiciously whenever she's in the office, as if he's expecting her to collapse again, but who hasn't actually addressed the subject head-on since it happened.

"No," she says after a beat. "Probably not." But she bites her lip, because can she be sure of that, after the motorbike incident? "I mean, maybe. Usually they only happen when I'm actually hurt—like if I cut myself badly or something." She can't quite look at him as she speaks.

"You fell over the day we met," he points out. "You fell off the scooter."

She hesitates. "Yes." She can't quite explain that she was in a different headspace then. That when that part of her takes over—albeit very occasionally—her brain doesn't work in quite the same way. And that it's not *every* time she hurts herself, only sometimes, which makes it all the harder to predict, to manage.

"I thought you were a bit of a daredevil, given the way we met for the first time." She looks up at him then. Somehow he still manages to be attractive, even wearing that stupid hat.

"Trust me, I'm anything but a daredevil. Sorry to disappoint."

"I'm not disappointed," he says mildly. "Just curious."

Inside her coat pocket, she twiddles her house key between her fingers. "It's just, that day..."

But she breaks off, catching sight of two teenage girls up ahead. She doesn't recognize one of them—the blonde—but she *does* recognize the brunette, who's wearing a hoodie underneath her jacket along with baggy jeans.

Lissa comes to a stop, wondering what to do. She barely hears Ash asking if she's okay. Should she go over and say hi? Would Elsie want her to—maybe it'd be embarrassing? And, God, is she really this bloody out of touch?

The decision ends up being taken from her, because Elsie looks over, sees her. Her eyes go a little wide, and she nudges her friend, clearly muttering something to her. The friend glances over too, gives Lissa what is undoubtedly an appraising look up and down.

"Who's that?" Ash asks at her side.

"It's... She's my sister." She fixes a smile to her face as she walks past a stall selling cheese, closing the gap between them. "Hey, Elsie."

Elsie gives her a jerking nod. "Hey."

Lissa smiles at Elsie's friend, and Elsie jerks her head again. "This is Jess."

"Hi, Jess." Jess gives her another scrutinizing look. Lissa can feel Ash coming up behind her, catches the way Elsie looks over at him. The way she looks at them *both*, taking in the ridiculous hats.

Lissa takes hers off, runs a hand through her hair. Then feels utterly ridiculous. Why does it matter if Elsie sees her in a stupid hat?

"This is Ash," she says. "We're just, ah, shopping."

"Us too," says Elsie.

"That's nice." Lissa smiles again. "Is Dad here? Or your mum?" She's wondering if she'll have to see them—she really doesn't want to go through that kind of small talk in front of Ash. And would she have to suggest a coffee all together or something? She cringes at the thought of it.

"Nope," Elsie says. "Just us." She must have won the argument about coming into Bath alone, then.

"Are you having fun?"

"Sure."

"What have you bought?"

She shrugs. "Not much. Don't really have much money."

"Right. Have you, ah, seen anything you like?"

Elsie gives her a narrow-eyed look, like there is something inherently suspicious about the question, rather than just Lissa fishing for present ideas.

"I personally like the hats," Ash pipes up, pointing at the one on his head. Elsie looks like she might be about to laugh, then presses her lips together, thinking better of it. Jess glances curiously between Lissa and Ash, then Lissa and Elsie. Lissa wonders what—if anything—Elsie has said about her.

"Well," Elsie says. "We're going to get some food."

"Right," Lissa says brightly. "Right, of course. Have fun!"

Elsie nods, hesitates, then shrugs again. "See ya."

There's a beat of quiet after the two girls leave, linking arms as they walk away. Lissa feels a pang of sadness— that Elsie so clearly would rather be anywhere than here, talking to her. Then again, whose fault is that?

"So that's your sister?" Ash asks. "The curly-haired one, right?"

"Half-sister." She immediately winces at the correction— the almost-justification. "Not that it matters," she says quickly. "I just . . . I had a sister. Another sister. She, well, she died."

It's out before she can think better of it, like she needs to explain that she's not a terrible person, that there is a reason for the type of relationship she and Elsie have. But she regrets the words almost instantly, because of the sympathy that flashes across his face. This is why she never says it—because she doesn't want the conversation that follows.

He lifts his hand, looking for a second like he might reach for her. Then he drops it to his side. "I'm so sorry."

It's funny, isn't it, how no one has come up with anything better to say in all the centuries of experiencing loss. Sorry. She's lost track of the number of times she's heard that word—the number of times she's said it herself.

She chooses to focus on the cheese stall instead of Ash. "It's why I'm more 'daredevil-esque' on the sixteenth of September. The day you met me. It's the day she died."

He balks. "She died the day you—"

"No," she says quickly. "No." She lets out a long breath. "It was a really long time ago." She hesitates. "I was twelve."

Sometimes it helps for people to know that—it makes the grief seem less immediate, more manageable. It means they don't worry as much about what to say. "I just...I still think about it every year. On that day."

He nods, and although she doesn't look, she can feel his gaze on her face. "Of course you do." It's said sincerely, but she doesn't think he can understand the full extent of it. She wonders, too, if he has the same assumption everyone else does—that because it was so long ago, she should have got over it by now.

And she finds herself opening her mouth, wanting to explain, to justify, before he can ask. "It's not all the time or anything. I just, sometimes I remember her and I—"

"Lissa." Her name is an interruption. "You don't need to explain it to me. That kind of grief...it never really leaves you. I get it. Trust me." She finally looks back at him, his gaze waiting for her. And the way he is looking at her—she believes him. She wants to ask who he lost, because he is so clearly speaking from experience. But he doesn't seem to want to elaborate, and she is not one to pry.

"So," she says, "have you spoken to Mark recently?" As far as changes of subject go, it's not great, but it's all she can come up with on the spur of the moment.

"We speak every now and then, yeah." He looks down at her. "Have you?"

"Well, I mean we work together, so..."

He nods thoughtfully. "Still broken up?"

She wrinkles her nose. "Yes. I mean, I'm not sure we had anything to break up, but still." She bites her lip.

"What?" he asks.

"Nothing. I just... Did you tell him you were meeting me?"

"It hasn't come up." His tone is easy, but there was enough of a hesitation that she feels sure he knows what she's saying. "You're wondering if I asked his permission," he states, confirming her theory.

"No, I... Well, yes." Although *permission* feels a bit strong to her. Permission for what, exactly?

"I'm not deliberately not telling him," he says, pulling his hat off his head and rumpling up his hair. "I know there was something between you, I know he liked you—and I'm not trying to be a dick or anything."

Not trying to be a dick. Permission.

She has to ask, she realizes. "Ash, this isn't a... date, is it? Because I'm not... I don't think I..." She's trying to find a way to explain just what a bad idea it would be to go there, Mark or no Mark. That she has issues, that she needs to figure things out before she thinks about getting involved with another person. "It's just I—"

He places a hand lightly on her arm to stop her talking. "Lissa, relax. It's not a date. I just wanted to check you were all right, that's all."

"Okay." She lets her breath out on a whoosh, though she can't quite name the feeling coiling inside her. It should be relief, right? "Okay," she repeats. "Good."

"Ash?" They both look around at the sound of a woman's slightly high-pitched and definitely very loud voice. "It *is* you!" The woman—blond hair a shade darker than Lissa's, wearing a hat that is *definitely* a lot more chic than the star hat, and heeled boots that would make Darcy drool—launches herself at Ash, pulling him into a hug, which he returns, patting her on the back.

"Hey, Niamh."

Lissa takes a moment to realize why she recognizes the name, then remembers. Mark mentioned it at the pub quiz. She doesn't know *why* she remembers, but the fact that she does makes her a little uncomfortable. Or maybe it's more to do with the way Niamh is looking at Ash, kind of like she wants to eat him, and hasn't yet acknowledged Lissa with so much as a glance.

"It's been too long," Niamh says, squeezing Ash's arm for emphasis. Lissa feels that clearing her throat pointedly is a bit beneath her, but she's tempted to do it anyway.

"Niamh, this is Lissa." Ash's voice, however, is definitely pointed, and it makes the corners of Niamh's mouth turn down. She acknowledges Lissa with a semi-polite nod.

"So you're back?" she asks, turning back to Ash. Someone calls her name behind her—one of a group of women—and she waves a hand vaguely in their direction. "Look, I have to go," she continues, without waiting for Ash to answer—and as if it had been him who interrupted her, not the other way around. "But if you're back in town, we should go out. Call me, yeah?" Another squeeze of his arm and she's gone.

Lissa stares after her, then turns slowly to raise her eyebrows at Ash. He laughs at her expression. "Ex-girlfriend?" she guesses. Although maybe not so ex.

Maybe it's more of a continuous thing. The thought makes her gut squirm uncomfortably. If she'd known about this before, she wouldn't have awkwardly brought up the date thing.

"Ex-hookup," he corrects.

"Ah. Not a relationship sort of guy?" She shouldn't be asking this. Besides, she can hardly judge, can she? If anyone's not the relationship type, it's her.

He shrugs. "Only if it's right. And it was always casual between us."

"She definitely still wants to be with you," Lissa says as they start walking again.

"Nah. She's more of a grass-is-always-greener kind of gal. Which, to be fair to her, she actually admitted while we were . . ." He trails off.

"Hooking up?"

"Right. Well, anyway, she sees me with a hot girl, assumes we're together, immediately wonders if there's something she's missing. Hence the, you know . . ." He waves a hand behind him, presumably to indicate whatever it was Niamh did.

Hot girl. Something sparks inside her at the idea that he thinks she's hot, enough that she has to stop herself from smiling. Then she frowns at herself. *Get a bloody grip, Lissa. Are you fourteen?*

"Something up?" he asks.

"Nope," she says, in what she hopes is an easy tone. "So are you all Christmassed out yet?"

"Oh, I don't know. I reckon we've got time for a

mulled cider or two." He cocks his head, still wearing that ridiculous hat, as he waits for her answer.

He's being friendly, Lissa. Nothing more. "Sure," she says, in her best impression of a breezy tone. "I'm game if you are."

Chapter Thirteen

The night air is warm as they walk hand in hand through the streets of Paris. The champagne from the party after the film premiere has gone to her head, and she feels pleasantly buzzed. They snuck away after a couple of hours, because although she was starstruck—the actors were right there in the same room as them—when it came down to it, it was him she wanted to spend the night with.

"*C'était incroyable*," she says, for what must be the millionth time.

He laughs. She loves the sound of his laugh, how light, how joyful it always is. Even though she knows he has reason not to be as joyful as he always makes out. She's seen the darkness there, lurking out of sight. She knows it's been hard for him, with his father. Knows his father was supposed to come to the premiere this evening, to see the film—his first big film where he was the lead composer. But he found it impossible to leave the house, after promising he would. He's been like that since the war, apparently, too haunted by memories, unable to live in the real world anymore. He wouldn't be the only one, she supposes.

His smile softens as he looks down at her, his face illuminated in the dusky late-night glow of the city. "Thank you for coming with me," he murmurs, his voice a caress.

She shakes her head. "You don't need to thank me. It wasn't exactly a hardship."

"Oh, you mean you actually *like* drinking champagne with famous film stars?"

She gives a one-shouldered shrug. "I mean, it's not perfect, especially compared to my usual life of instilling a lifelong hatred of maths into young minds, but I suppose I could put up with it every now and then."

He laughs again, then squeezes her hand. "Seriously, though. It meant a lot to me to have you there."

He was nervous. He hasn't told her this, not explicitly, but she realizes it now. She should have noticed before, but she was too caught up in seeing him again, and then in the glamour of it all.

She stops walking, takes both his hands in hers. "The music was perfect. That scene where Jeanne Moreau was crying in the attic—the music was what made it." She means it, too. Because what is a film without music? What is *life* without music, really, when you think about it? Although, she's not totally sure if that's the champagne talking.

He squeezes her hand again. "Thank you."

"So. How long are you staying this time?" She's been trying all evening not to ask, not to dampen the mood. But they're nearing her apartment now, having taken the longest route possible back, and she needs to know.

He lets go of her hand. "Well. I'll be around a little bit, for my dad. To make sure he's, you know, okay." It's said lightly enough, but she can hear the pain, the worry behind it. He's told her how, like so many others, his father didn't come back from the war the same as when he left.

Outside her apartment door, he turns her to face him. "But I was thinking, when I go, you could come with me." His eyes travel over her face—one that she spent hours perfecting in front of the mirror earlier. "They have art schools in Los Angeles, after all."

She laughs. "Los Angeles? Why on earth...Oh." She gets it then. Hollywood. He wants to chase the big films, the big orchestras, the big money. He wants to make a name for himself. Which she's not surprised by. He's always had this kind of restless energy about him, the need to keep moving, to find the next thing. It's like he's never content just to sit in one place. Even for her.

She offers a smile she hopes doesn't look forced. "I'm not really sure Hollywood is for me."

"Why not?"

She gestures down at herself. "Do I seem like the adventurous type to you?"

Although she has been thinking of it. Not Hollywood, obviously, but art school. And on nights like tonight, when art—because film is art—moves her to emotion, it makes her think about how she wants to do something more than teach finger-painting to five-year-olds. Not that she doesn't love the children—she does, and a part of her feels content with it. But maybe it's him, and his need to experience everything life has to offer, that's making her want more.

He takes a step toward her, her back against the door, and reaches out to tuck a stray strand of hair behind her ear. Where he touches, goose bumps prickle. "I don't know," he says, his voice soft. "I think you might have more adventure in you than you give yourself credit for."

Their gazes meet, the streetlamps of Paris flickering in his eyes. She stretches on her toes to press her mouth to his, feels the curve of his lips as he smiles against hers. He edges closer, one hand coming to her hip, over her dress, the other cupping her neck. Her skin turns hot and needy under his touch, and her breath hitches as he moves his mouth to her jawline.

Her head tips back, her eyelids flutter closed as he kisses a path down her neck. She wants him. She's not supposed to have men inside her apartment, not with the landlady downstairs, but it's getting harder each time to say goodbye.

He pulls back, the weight of his focus heavy on her, and the darkness between them hums.

Later, when she lets herself into her small apartment, she reaches for the drawer in her bedside table, pulls out the application forms she has stored there. One for a school in Paris, because where better to study art than here? But the thing is, although she's never imagined America, other than a strange sense that she might like to visit New York one day, she *has* imagined leaving Paris, escaping this city where her sister died, where her parents are, where, despite all the richness it has to offer, she feels trapped sometimes.

There's a good school in Lyon, and she's even thought about learning Italian, trying Florence.

It's a silly dream, so unlikely to ever happen, for so many reasons. Even without the barriers she's sure she'll face, she couldn't just *leave*. She'd be abandoning her mother for one, her father spending most nights out with one of his many mistresses. The two of them are married only in name, and her father is too chicken to divorce her mother, worried about how it might look, especially after the loss of a child. And her mother might not want her here, given that she still blames her for what happened the day of the bombing, but she definitely *needs* her.

Still, it can't hurt to apply, can it? If she doesn't get in, then that's the decision made for her.

When Lissa comes to, on the sofa in her flat, Netflix still playing, she presses her hands to her temples. Enough. That's enough of this now. She needs to figure out what it means, why it's happening.

The dream book she bought was useless. She thinks of the Google search she did several weeks ago, of therapists claiming they could help people uncover their past lives. Well then. Maybe it's time to look up this Saskia Arthur's number and see if she really is as clairvoyant as she claims to be. After all, what has she got to lose?

She's having second thoughts by the time she parks up outside the little cottage over a week later. If it's possible to have third thoughts, then she's having those as she gets out of the car and crunches across the gravel driveway.

She could just not go in. Turn around, call and say she got stuck somewhere. But she's here now. She's paid for the session already. And worst case, it'll be a funny story to tell Darcy.

Saskia Arthur, when she opens the door, is a little older than she appeared in her photo, a few more creases around her eyes and mouth. Her smile is the same, though—warm and inviting. Her gray hair is pulled back into a rather severe bun, small diamond studs winking out of her ears in the evening sunlight, and she's wearing a jumper and jeans combo that can only be described as practical. Where is the flowing skirt and hoop earrings and mystical energy?

She beckons Lissa inside, then leads her through the cottage into a small back room, where there is a therapy couch opposite two armchairs. The walls are painted light blue, and landscape paintings make up the majority of the decoration. She gestures for her to take a seat in one of the armchairs, and Lissa does so, trying not to fidget.

"So," Saskia says, taking a seat in the other armchair. She folds her hands in her lap like a schoolteacher, the gold ring on her little finger glinting as she does so. "Tell me what brings you here today."

"Ah..." Lissa feels her neck heat as she tries to think of an acceptable answer to this.

"You said you were interested in past lives; is that right?" Saskia prods. Lissa nods. "So were you hoping for me to help with some past life regression?"

"No." The firmness in her voice makes Saskia's eyebrows rise, just a fraction. "Sorry," Lissa says, biting her lip. "It's more...I wanted to ask you some questions, if that's okay."

The eyebrows creep up even farther. "Questions?"

"It's just...I know you do the hypnotherapy and stuff, but on your site it says you're also..." She gestures into space, trying to remember the word.

"Clairvoyant?"

"Right. Exactly. Well, I was wondering if you could use that to help me out a little."

"Help you out?" Saskia repeats, sounding genuinely baffled.

"I just..." Lissa realizes she's twisting her hands in her lap. She makes herself stop and blows out a breath. "Look, this is going to sound crazy, but—"

Saskia holds up a hand. "There is no judgment here. And I don't believe in the word 'crazy.'"

"Right." Lissa shifts her weight in the armchair. "Well I think I might have had a past life." Saying it out loud sounds totally insane—and yet not at all. Because giving voice to the idea seems to settle something in her. "Or, well, multiple past lives. Is it possible to have multiple past lives?" And yes, she is going there. She is having this conversation with a so-called holistic psychic therapist. She's just thankful that no one is around to see her doing it.

"Of course," Saskia says, matter-of-fact. "Most people do. I, for one, feel confident that I have lived a life in Egypt, though I'm sincerely hoping I wasn't mummified, and I'm sure that at one point I knew how to start a fire with nothing more than wood and stone—something my partner is adamant can't be true, based on my barbecuing skills."

This gets a surprised snort of laughter from Lissa, and Saskia smiles in response. She seems *nice*. So maybe, if she's a con artist, she doesn't know she is.

Lissa leans forward, placing her hands on her thighs. "The thing is, I've been having these flashbacks. That's what they are, I'm sure of it—like memories. From another lifetime. Three lifetimes, to be exact."

"Three," Saskia repeats. Is it just Lissa, or does she sound a little careful? Despite what she said, maybe she thinks Lissa's mad. To be fair, maybe she is.

"You said most people have multiple past lives?"

"Yes, but—"

"Well I have three." Possibly more, but her current working theory is that Scotland in the 1800s is the first one, based on the fact that she's only had one memory of that, and it was blurred.

"Okay..." Saskia's gaze is very direct on Lissa's. "Well if you're sure about that, what do you need help with?"

Lissa feels a spike of something—excitement maybe, at finally getting to the point, at being able to talk it through with someone. "I want to know *why*."

"Why? You mean why souls are reincarnated?" Saskia purses her lips, painted a pale pink. "I'm not sure I can answer that for you—there are plenty of different theories, many centered on the fact that energy doesn't just disappear when someone dies, but—"

"No," Lissa interrupts. "Not why they are reincarnated, why *I* am."

She gets another raised-eyebrow look at that—because she's being egotistical?

"Or," she continues, trying to make up for it, "not, like, why I'm reincarnated in the grand scheme of things, but more why I'm having these...visions."

Saskia cocks her head. Her diamond stud earrings glint in the sliver of sunlight through the window at her back. "Well, maybe you're a little clairvoyant yourself?"

Lissa frowns. "But I've never experienced anything like this before. So why now all of a sudden?"

Saskia hesitates for a beat, uncrossing and recrossing her ankles. Lissa wonders if she doesn't believe her. Then she wonders if it matters all that much if she believes her if she can still give her some answers. After all, she's paying for the whole session, isn't she?

"How long have you been experiencing the memories?" Saskia asks, apparently coming to some internal decision.

"I don't know. A few months, maybe?"

"Can you think of when they started, specifically? Did something happen, perhaps, to trigger the first one?"

Lissa leans back in the armchair, tapping her fingers against her thigh. She remembers waking up disoriented after the first one. Waking up in a bed that wasn't her own. And if she was in Mark's bed, that means it was the day after the anniversary of Chloe's death—the day after her reckless, stupid decision. So does that mean it really *is* all about her sister?

Saskia smiles, the skin around her eyes creasing. "You're figuring something out, I can see."

Lissa shakes her head. "I'm not so sure about that." Because why would it happen *now*, twenty years after the fact? Is she trying too hard to understand something that arguably doesn't make sense at all?

"In each of them, I lose a sister," she says slowly, thinking as she speaks. She's not totally sure of that statement—she knows it happened in the 1940s, but she had a hint of it in the 1920s, too, walking along the corridor of her house, trailing her fingers over the brass doorknob, behind which lay an untouched room—her sister's bedroom. So it would follow, wouldn't it, given when the flashbacks started, that that's what connects them all?

She blinks over at Saskia, who is watching her, waiting. "Why would that happen again and again?"

"Well," Saskia begins, her tone even, "there are some theories that people create similar responses in others whenever they meet over the course of a lifetime. That because we react to our parents, our friends, love interests in similar ways, we make a sort of pattern. Until our souls are able to learn and grow, that is."

Lissa's heart rate spikes uncomfortably. "So you're saying it's my fault—in every life?"

"No," Saskia says quickly, "no, that's not what I mean at all. I just mean that often there are similarities between lifetimes, not in what we might have been doing or where we were living or even the gender we were, but on some basic core level." She takes a breath, her chest rising and falling with the motion. "But the other thing that could be happening, Lissa, is that your sister's death in the past lives that you think you're seeing could be a metaphor for something else entirely—or it could be you simply processing the trauma of her death in *this* lifetime."

Lissa doesn't think she's told Saskia about Chloe—but then it's not exactly a leap, is it? "Yeah," she mumbles, "I did wonder that." But she keeps coming back to the fact that if that's what it is, why wouldn't she *only* see her sister's death—why would she be experiencing glamorous parties, for instance?

"Is it..." She hesitates, knowing how this will sound. "Could it be punishment?"

"Punishment?" Right, yes, she sounds insane, based on Saskia's reaction.

But Chloe died because she left her by the pond. And her sister in the 1940s died because of her too. She doesn't know yet if it's the same for all of them, but if it is...

Saskia is frowning at her now. She has a very expressive face, Lissa is finding. "Do you think you deserve punishment, Lissa?"

"No," she says automatically, even as her brain thinks: *Yes.* "I'm just curious."

"Hmm. Well, either way, I don't think that can be it. I'm not qualified to explain life's mysteries—far from it—but I can say that I don't think the universe sets out to punish or reward people, however much some might wish that were the case."

166

Lissa is quiet for a moment. She hopes Saskia is right about that. She hopes it's not about experiencing the grief of many lifetimes in order to pay for what she did.

"Perhaps it's more about you learning something," Saskia says, after a beat of quiet.

Lissa's eyes refocus on the woman in front of her. "But what?"

Saskia smiles a little, shakes her head. "I can't tell you that. You're the one experiencing this."

Lissa frowns—that's not overly helpful, is it?

As if she can hear Lissa's thoughts, Saskia chuckles quietly. "Often with these things it's not about the specifics, but about something much more general. And I have found that sometimes it seems as if a present life is giving us a chance to right the wrongs of the past. I'm not saying that's always the case—though it would be nice if it was—but I had a client once who had a traumatic past life, from what she could remember after her regression. A house being burnt down, children torn from her, forced to flee her home. In the present, she's a happily married mother of three who has been in the same home for twenty years. So it was like she'd had the chance to have the life she wanted—or at least she wanted those things because of what had happened to her."

Lissa stares at Saskia, trying to keep up. Then, "I don't know how that applies to me," she says bluntly. After all, Chloe has already died. And it's far too late to rectify that, isn't it? Unless it's about her learning something now to take into a future life. So that next time, she doesn't leave her sister alone—so that she can prevent her death.

Which leads her to realize..."I don't know how I died." She finishes the thought out loud. "In any of the lives, I mean. I'm only getting flashes of particular moments—and I don't know how I died." Her sister, and romance, that's all she's seeing. And she doesn't know what the romance is teaching her, unless it's trying to encourage her to find the love of her life in this lifetime too. But she doesn't seem to be much older than she is now, in any of the flashbacks. And if she lived in both the 1920s and the 1950s, she must have died young in at least one of her lives.

Saskia offers another of her sympathetic smiles. "I know better than anyone that we can't control what we see or don't see, and that things are often confusing, out of order. Our minds are trying to make sense of a bigger picture, but we're unequipped to do so."

Lissa huffs out an impatient breath. "I just... I feel like there's something I'm supposed to be understanding from all this, but it's like my mind just won't catch up."

Saskia contemplates her for a moment. "It may be you're thinking too hard about it. There's not necessarily a reason behind everything—and even if there is, sometimes by staring directly at something it becomes harder to see what that reason is." She lets that sink in, then adds, "For what it's worth, when I do regression sessions, I often tell my clients that the experience is less about trying to pinpoint what exactly happened in the past—because we rarely get concrete answers about that—and more about what we might be able to uncover about ourselves in the present, to help with our future."

Lissa wrinkles her nose at that—it's not the answer she came here for. Saskia smiles a little, like she can see her thoughts. "I do also think there's a danger that by focusing obsessively on the past, we let our present lives pass us by. That's the same with any past—I'm not just talking about past lives here."

But how is she supposed to *not* focus on her past, when it seems intent on haunting her?

"I wonder, Lissa," Saskia continues, "would you consent to letting me read your cards for you?"

Lissa frowns. She seems to have done a lot of that this session. "Cards?"

"Tarot. It might help us figure out what you need to reframe in order to move past this and learn whatever it is you feel you need to learn."

"Tarot cards?" She can't quite keep the skepticism out of her voice.

Saskia laughs, a big, booming sound. Lissa finds she likes it. "So you're willing to believe in past lives, but you don't believe in tarot?" Lissa wrinkles her nose, unable to answer that one. "Well," Saskia says, "there's no pressure. But if you decide you want to give it a go, let me know. It would be free of charge, given that I don't think today really counts as a session."

"Oh. Well, thank you." It's a kind gesture, one that leads Lissa to think she was right in her assessment of Saskia the first time around—if she's faking her clairvoyant skills, she's not doing it intentionally. "I'll think about it."

"Do," Saskia says as they both get to their feet. "Because I'd say it sounds like you're a little stuck in the past, and maybe you ought to start thinking a bit about your future."

Chapter Fourteen

"This is glorious," Darcy says, resting her head back against the wall of the sauna. The air is hot and dry, and sweat coats the back of Lissa's thighs, despite the fact they've only been in here a matter of minutes.

"Mm," Mia agrees, closing her eyes and taking a breath.

To Lissa, it feels way too hot, but she knows there are plenty of benefits to a sauna. She recites them in her head as she tries to adjust to the temperature and relax. Improved circulation. Detoxification. Good for the skin. *Hot, hot, hot.*

"So what do you think?" she asks out loud, needing to talk to distract herself from thinking her insides might be about to boil. Luckily, it's just the three of them in the sauna, and she doesn't have to worry about being overheard. "Am I crazy?" She's told both of them that she thinks she's getting memories from her past lives, figuring that if she can't tell Mia and Darcy, she can't tell anyone.

"Probably," Darcy says on a yawn.

"It's just . . . You don't think it could be a tumor, do

you?" The idea had come to her in the middle of the night, when she'd been unable to sleep.

To their credit, they both keep their attention firmly on her, rather than exchanging rolled-eye looks with each other as she thought they might.

"A tumor?" Mia asks carefully.

"A brain tumor. Because you get hallucinations when you have a brain tumor, don't you?"

"What are you basing this on?" Darcy asks skeptically. "*Grey's Anatomy?*"

"No. I'm basing it on the very real fact that tumors can cause auditory or visual hallucinations."

"Right. Sorry. I don't think it's very likely, though. Wouldn't you have other symptoms?"

"I get headaches."

"Everyone gets headaches, Bissa," Mia says gently.

Lissa nods, though she's not wholly convinced. She knows logically that it probably *isn't* a brain tumor. She tries to take a deep breath—the last thing she needs is another panic attack—but that's easier said than done in a sauna.

"I wish I knew what *I* was in my past lives," Darcy says with a yawn. Mia snorts her general disbelief at the whole idea. "Although what if it was something terrible. What if I was lost at sea or trapped in a lighthouse or—"

"I think that's a film," Mia says musingly.

"Hmm." Darcy taps her nails against her thigh. "Quite possibly."

"Saskia says she can read my tarot," Lissa says.

"Right." Mia pushes her red hair away from her face. "And Saskia is...?"

"The psychic," Darcy pipes up.

"Of course," Mia says—and you have to hand it to her, she has the long-suffering tone down. "Lissa, why don't you go to an *actual* therapist? I'm sure these dreams you're having—"

"They're not dreams," Lissa interrupts. "Well, I mean, sometimes they are, but they're not *only* dreams."

"Fine. I'm sure these *visions* you're having are a response to stress, or trying to figure out what you want to do with your life, or dealing with past issues, that kind of thing. Honestly, Freud would have a field day."

"I don't need a therapist," Lissa insists. "I just need to figure out what they're trying to tell me."

"They?" Mia laughs, the sound slightly high-pitched. "Lissa, it's *your* mind. The only one trying to tell you something is you."

Lissa turns to Darcy. "So—tarot? Yay or nay?" Mia mutters something incoherent under her breath.

"Well, I tried one of those fortune-teller hotlines once," Darcy muses. "You know, where they give you more detail on your horoscope. He told me I would get a pay raise, which Liam did not agree with. He did get a few things right, though, to be fair."

"Like what?" Mia asks skeptically.

"Like the fact that a secret would come to light."

"A secret?" Lissa repeats.

"Yep. And that very month, my mum told me she'd been

learning to belly-dance for years, and keeping it secret from the whole family."

Lissa laughs, and Mia grins, then shakes her head. "I'm going to change the subject now, before the two of you start telling me you can see shapes in the steam like a crystal ball or something."

"You're a Capricorn, aren't you?" Darcy asks. "Classic skeptic."

"How's the job hunt, Lissa?" Mia asks loudly, ignoring Darcy.

"Oh. I sort of...stopped on that. But," she adds quickly, before Mia can criticize, "I did get a job at a charity shop."

"Woo-hoo!" Darcy punches the air. "Now you can quit!"

Lissa laughs again. "Not quite. It's a volunteer thing, and only a few hours every Saturday."

"Oh." Darcy frowns. "And the point of that is...?" Mia prods her lightly on the shoulder in admonishment.

"The *point*," Lissa says emphatically, "is to give something back, do something useful. That kind of thing. Plus, you're the one who said getting some different experience would look good on my CV."

"Did I?" Darcy cocks her head, then nods decisively. "Sounds smart and wise, and I am both of those things, to be fair." She stretches her legs out in front of her as far as they'll go. "So, Mia, what are you doing for Christmas?" she asks, an abrupt change of subject that makes Lissa throw her a look.

"Spending it with this one," Mia says, jerking her head at Lissa.

"Weren't you thinking of heading out to see your parents this year?" Lissa asks.

"Couldn't afford it. They said they'll come over here next year."

Well thank God for that. It's selfish of her, but she is so grateful Mia will be there. Christmas with just her mum would've been awful—the holidays are always a possible trigger time.

"Is Lottie still planning on coming to visit in the new year?" Lissa asks.

"Lottie?" Darcy pipes up. "Who's Lottie?"

"Mia's girl," Lissa says.

"She's not my girl." Mia's tone is a little harsh, enough to make Lissa sit up a bit straighter, wondering if she's said something wrong. "Sorry," she huffs. "I just… Sorry. Yes, she wants to come."

"Still not sure about it?" Lissa asks tentatively.

Mia bites her lip. "What if we don't get on in person?"

"Well," Lissa says evenly, "I suppose there's only one way to find out." Although really who is she to be giving out relationship advice? Without meaning to, her mind jumps straight to Ash. To the short message exchange they had after spending the day together at the Christmas market.

She'd agonized over whether to message, over what to say, and ended up texting: *Thanks for the hat, hero.*

She got a reply instantly. *Thank you for spending the day with me. Next time I see you, you better be wearing that hat.*

Next time. As if he thought there would—should—be a next time. Or did he mean nothing by it?

She's kept the bloody hat, just in case. *And now is not the time to be thinking about it, Lissa.* Especially not with Mia still talking about Lottie.

"Or what if we *do* get on and..."

"And?" Lissa prompts.

Mia tucks her hair behind her ear, shakes her head again. "Nothing. Guess I'm just nervous, that's all."

"Well I think it's romantic," Darcy says. "I'd love it if someone flew all the way over from America to see me." Mia smiles a little at that. Darcy glances out the steam door. "I think we might have to go for our floating pool session in a minute."

Lissa feels a sudden spike of nerves, palpable even over the heat in here. As if she can sense it, Mia glances at her. Lissa has never told Darcy that she can't swim. It would open up a whole host of questions that she hasn't wanted to answer, and somehow, years into the friendship, it felt odd to bring it up.

"When you say floating..." Mia begins slowly.

"It's supposed to be like the Dead Sea," Darcy says. "They put loads of salt in it or something, and you just lie there and float around and have a little nap."

Mia looks back at Lissa. "You don't have to do it if you don't want," she says. "We can stay here. Or, well, maybe not *here*, because I'm sweating an indecent amount, but, you know."

Darcy frowns between them, looking confused.

"No," Lissa says, getting to her feet to punctuate the point. "It's okay. I'll come." It's just the same as a bath, right? And all right, she doesn't *love* baths, but she is also very unlikely to drown in one because she can't swim.

The "celestial flotation pool" is located in a softly lit room at the back of the spa. Lissa tries not to look at the shallow water as the spa technician explains the mechanics of the pool, and how it's best to just lie still and let yourself gently float around. She offers up pool noodles, which Lissa takes, grateful she's not the only one.

She tells herself to stay calm as she follows Mia and Darcy into the warm water. She grips the edge of the pool as she reaches waist deep, which seems to be as deep as it gets. She is safe, she tells herself firmly, willing her heart to stay steady. She doesn't need to be able to swim. She can stand up any time she wants to.

"All right," the spa technician says brightly from the sidelines. "Relax, enjoy, no talking—and have fun! I'll be back when the thirty minutes are up."

The lights dim as she leaves the room, and on the ceiling, stars flicker to life. Lissa takes a deep breath as she lies down. She feels a moment of panic at the feeling of the water underneath her, even with the pool noodle behind her head. But she forces herself to stay calm, stay still. And hey, she really *is* floating. No swimming needed.

Her heart rate is still too fast, and she can feel a prickling in the tips of her fingers, an early warning if she lets it escalate, but she's okay. She can do this—she is not about to have a panic attack in a bloody spa, for fuck's sake. She stares up at the fake starry sky, breathes in the smell of lavender. She can hear the distinctive spa-like music softly chiming in the background. This is okay, she tells herself again. She's here, she's fine, she's doing this.

She closes her eyes, flexing her fingers on top of the water. She's in control. She's safe.

She's back there, at that same loch in the Scottish Highlands. Like before, the edges of this memory are a little blurred, shifting in and out of focus. But she notices one key difference to last time. She is not *by* the loch—she is on it. In the boat. With him.

His sleeves are rolled up, showing tanned forearms. His pale green eyes watch her, reflecting the glistening surface of the water, the rolling heather-clad hills a brighter green in the background.

"What?" she asks. "Why are you looking at me like that?"

He shakes his head. "Sorry. I just . . . I know this isn't an easy day for you. I suppose I'm just trying to work out if you're all right."

Her stomach squirms at the reminder of what happened all those years ago—of the fall that could so easily have been prevented. But she doesn't want to think about it. She doesn't want to be sad. Because yes, this date is always a reminder of something terrible, a reminder of who she and her parents lost. But they are not the only ones who have lost someone, are they? She wishes she could change it, is sure she'll never let go of the guilt she feels at what happened. But today she wants to forget about that. She wants instead to make the most of the fact that she is still here, the way she so often forgets to. She wants to do things that make her feel alive.

Which is why she's out here, on this boat. Because today felt like the day to say yes—to not let herself be controlled by fear, but to take chances instead.

"I'm fine," she tells him firmly.

He nods slowly, contemplating her as though he's not sure whether to believe her. Then he lets go of the oars, allowing the boat to drift to a stop. He reaches out, across the small distance between them. The boat sways beneath her, but she's not afraid—not today, not with him. His fingertips brush lightly against her cheek, pushing aside a wisp of hair. His eyes are locked on hers, and her breath hitches. She knows that look. He's going to kiss her.

Instead he eases back, and she fights to control the disappointment. "I've been thinking," he says slowly.

"Oh?"

"I know I have less reason to be here since my father died, but I do still have the estate."

"That's true," she says slowly, wondering where he's going with this, and trying not to get her hopes up.

"So maybe I could stay, try my hand at running it."

"Maybe you could," she agrees.

"And maybe..." He reaches out, takes her hand in his. "Maybe you'd want to help me with that?"

There it is, that spike of excitement. She cocks her head. "Help you how?"

His thumb traces a circle on her wrist. "Marry me," he says—and she feels it, that tilting of an axis. This—this was the reason to come here today, this was the reason to say yes to going out on the boat. Her life has led her to exactly where she's meant to be, she's sure of it.

She meets his gaze, and knows from the way his smile grows that he can see her answer in her eyes. "Yes," she says, leaning forward to kiss him. "Of course yes."

She laughs, and he joins in. He is pulling her to him now, both of them needing to touch. "And maybe we could build a room where you could paint, if that's what you—"

She kisses him again, tasting woodsmoke and salt. "I don't care about any of that," she says as she breaks away. "I only want you." Because with him she'll be complete, she knows it. And what is today, the anniversary of her sister's death, if not a reminder of the fragility of life, a reminder to grasp the things you want with both hands, because you don't know how long you'll be around to take them.

The boat wobbles again, and he eases back, pressing his forehead against hers. Need is coiling low in her stomach as she hooks her arms around his neck, and she sees from the way his eyes have darkened that it is a reflection of his.

"Later," he murmurs against her lips. A promise.

But she can't sit still, not now, not with this excitement coursing around her system, this hope for the future. She gets to her feet right there in the middle of the rowing boat and laughs as she lifts her arms to the sky.

He laughs too, though when he speaks, it's with a note of caution. "Be careful. I thought you said you couldn't swim?"

But she can't be careful, not today. She grabs his hand, tries to pull him to his feet alongside her. He holds her wrist firmly, anchoring her in place. He murmurs a name—her name, but one she doesn't recognize.

"Come on," he says in that lilting Scottish accent. "I'll row us back to shore."

She's still trying to pull him to her, to get him to join in her celebration—because that's what this should be, a celebration. His grip loosens slightly on her wrist as she pulls again, and she stumbles. It's barely anything, no more than half a step. But the tiny boat rocks, and she knows, in the split second before it happens, that she will fall.

Icy water surrounds her as she plummets, and though she reaches for the edge of the boat, she can't find it. She tries to scream, but there is water flooding into her, choking her. She kicks out, but there is something around her ankle, pulling her down, and the sunlight above the surface of the lake looks so very far away.

Her name again—he is screaming her name. She hears it distantly, the splash of water, feels the ripple around her, then an arm trying to tug her away from the weeds and to safety, even as her muscles seize with the cold.

It's not just her who will drown now. She doesn't know how she knows that, not with everything turning dark, not when the memory becomes even more out of focus. But she feels with a certainty like a lead weight in her stomach that neither of them will make it out of the lake today.

She's coughing, spluttering, warm salty water coating her tongue.

"Lissa!" Someone is shouting her name—not a deep male voice but a high-pitched female one. "Lissa, stop it, you're okay!"

She is thrashing, she realizes. She is thrashing in the pool, kicking her legs, even as her feet make contact with the stone bottom. She is sobbing. There is the sound of someone nearby, slipping on wet tiles.

"What's happening?" A young, petrified-sounding voice.

"She's scared of water." A voice she recognizes this time.

"What! Why is she in here then? I'm going to get my manager."

"She's scared of water?" A murmured question, accompanied by pressure on her arm.

"Yes. Because of what happened to Chloe."

"Chloe? Who's Chloe?"

"Breathe, Lissa, you're okay. Look, we're nearly out now, okay?"

Lissa heaves in a breath, tries to calm down as she blinks her surroundings into focus. The pool. Darcy and Mia looking at her, each holding one of her arms, like they're trying to drag her from the water. She is at the edge, a few feet away from the steps. Everyone else is out of the pool, some hovering, staring at her.

"It's okay, Bissa," Mia says again, voice soft, soothing.

A wave of embarrassment floods her as she looks down at the pool steps, grasping the edge to ground herself. "I'm okay," she repeats back to them, and sees the worried look they give one another. She doesn't know why she keeps telling everyone this—clearly she is not okay. Clearly she is a fucking headcase.

But she wonders for the first time, as she leaves the pool on shaky legs, Darcy rushing to get her a towel, whether she's had it right all these years. If the reason she is scared of water, the reason for the drowning nightmares, is not because of what happened to Chloe, but because of what happened to *her*.

Chapter Fifteen

Lissa leans against the shop counter, checking her email on her phone for the millionth time. There have been barely any customers today—she supposes the start of January marks the beginning of work for most people. She's waiting on an update on her most recent job application—a receptionist at a law firm, because maybe she needs to go more mainstream—but so far, nothing. She only applied a few days ago, she reasons. Part of the whole new-year-new-you philosophy—though Mia made a face when she told her about the job, saying a law firm didn't sound very *her*. But how is she supposed to know if it's her or not if she doesn't give it a go, right?

She glances around, looking for something to do, but there are no new items to sort through, and everything is where it should be on the racks. Emily, the woman who oversees the running of the shop, is super organized, and though she's promised that there will be an influx of new donations in the first few weeks of the year—people giving away unwanted Christmas presents—for now, everything is quiet. Which is probably for the best—Lissa has been left alone in the shop for the first time, and she's not sure what she'd do if there was a massive queue of people wanting to buy things or ask questions. But she is starting to get a bit bored. She spent the first hour cleaning—wiping down the counter and working her way to the corners that might have been missed in the morning, trying to get rid of that slightly musty smell that seems to linger no matter what they do about it.

She checks her email again. Nothing. There is, however, a WhatsApp from Ash.

My head is still sore from NYE and I think I might never recover. Send help.

She feels her lips pull into a smile, her stomach doing that light little flutter it's started to do whenever she sees his name pop up. He'd headed out of town for New Year, spending it in Edinburgh with some friends, while she was curled up on the sofa with Mia and fell asleep before midnight. She then had to lie about that when he asked what she'd done, because it seemed so incredibly lame in comparison to his story of being pulled up onto a Celtic salsa stage at one of the street parties in Edinburgh, followed by a wild night of antics with people he'd only just met. He's staying on in Scotland for a few days, checking out some castle as a possible filming location.

She scrolls through the GIFs on her phone, finds one of a cat batting someone's face and sends it.

Thanks, he replies. *I feel much better now. Also I want a cat. Please don't let me buy one—I don't trust my decision-making right now.*

No promises. Time for some New Year's resolutions then?!

Lissa. Resolutions are only for lame people who want to change how they do things. I, however, am perfectly happy in that regard and will continue to carry on exactly as I always do.

He quickly follows that up with *Unless you are the resolution-making type. In which case, resolutions are great and very worthwhile and not at all lame.*

She finds another meme on her phone that says, *Can't break your New Year's resolutions if you don't make any.*

She gets a strong-arm emoji back. *Attagirl.*

Although she probably *should* make some resolutions, shouldn't she? Other than random job applications. Maybe *that* should be her resolution: figure out ideal job. Darcy insisted last year that they write their resolutions down and stick them above their computer screens at work, because according to her, you're four times more likely to make a positive change if you make a resolution than if you don't. Though she didn't exactly prove this point herself when she changed her resolution from *buy fewer shoes* to *buy more shoes* at some point in February.

The bell above the shop door rings and in comes a woman around Lissa's age, holding the hand of a little girl who can't be more than about six, her hair in lopsided pigtails, cheeks rosy from the cold. Lissa smiles politely at the woman but leaves it at that—different people like different levels of engagement, she's learning, and best to let them lead the way on that.

The little girl makes a beeline for the big teddy bear—

almost brand new—that is displayed in the window. "I want this," she announces.

"We're just here for clothes today, honeybee," says the woman, placing a gentle hand on top of the girl's head.

On the glass counter, Lissa's phone lights up, and this time it is the email she's been waiting for.

Dear Lissa, Many thanks for your application. Unfortunately, on this occasion...

She doesn't bother to read the rest. All these rejection emails say some version of the same thing. But really—she didn't even get an interview? She's heard the job market is tough at the moment, but still. Or is it just her? She wants to text Darcy, to lament and to be reassured that it's *not* her, but she doesn't. Things have been slightly off between them since the spa incident. It hasn't been terrible—they still had Christmas drinks together, exchanged presents—just...off.

"Come on then, Rosy," the customer is saying, heading to the counter with a selection of children's clothes. She smiles a little awkwardly at Lissa. "They just grow out of them so fast," she says, her voice almost apologetic.

Lissa smiles as she puts them through the till. Some of the other people who work here seem to be able to strike up a conversation with anyone who comes in, but Lissa hasn't mastered this skill yet, not quite sure where the line between friendly and annoying is.

"But I want the bear," the little girl—Rosy—says, stopping just short of a foot stomp.

"We can't get the bear too, love, not today. Maybe next month."

"It might not be here next month. I want it for Eddy."

The woman visibly winces, then glances at Lissa from under long eyelashes. "Her brother," she explains in an undertone.

"Ah," Lissa says with another smile, picking up a small vest top and ringing it through.

"He's not..." The woman swallows. "He was a baby and he didn't..." She trails off, seeming to catch herself, as though she's realized that she doesn't need to explain. And the awfulness of what she is saying hits Lissa.

"I'm so sorry," she says, looking up and pausing what she's doing. There it is again, that word. Sorry.

The woman places a hand on Rosy's head again, like she might somehow protect her from the conversation. "My sister, she...Well. I just don't know if the bear is a good idea." Lissa can think of nothing to say, so she only nods, folding the clothes into a brown paper bag.

The woman smiles down at the girl. "Come on then," she says brightly.

But Rosy doesn't leave. Instead she looks up at Lissa out of big eyes. "The bear would be for Eddy," she says again, like she is trying to plead her cause with Lissa now instead. "He isn't here," she adds. "He's in heaven."

Oh God. Lissa's throat tightens as Rosy blinks up at her. "Mummy says we can take flowers to him, but I think he'll like this better." She turns to the woman now. "*Please*, Auntie Cece."

Cece's eyes are shining, and Lissa can tell from her expression that she is only just keeping it together. Lissa swallows, trying to dislodge the lump in her throat. This little girl has lost her brother. And she's got to be about the same age Chloe was when she died. She wonders if Cece doesn't want to buy the bear because of what it would remind Rosy's mother of—the future that could have been. She remembers that feeling well—saw it in both her parents in the months and years after Chloe died.

"Come on, Rosy," Cece says again, and Lissa can hear the effort it takes her not to let her voice break. "We're going to go to Tesco next—how about we get some chocolate for you and Mummy?"

Rosy hesitates, then nods, looking down at the floor. "Okay." It's a deflated little sound, one that makes Lissa's heart break. She wonders if the girl understands what happened exactly. Wonders if she ever met her brother. But thinking about it makes it even sadder, because it's such an awful thing to have happened.

She watches them leave the shop, the bell chiming happily again as they do so. They are just out of the door when she grabs her purse, stuffs a ten-pound note in the till and snatches the bear from the window. She doesn't think through what she's doing as she runs after them.

"Wait!"

They both turn around, and she holds out the bear. "Here. I've paid for it."

Cece looks at her, expression guarded, and Lissa wonders if she's crossed a line. But Rosy's eyes light up and she lifts her arms to take the bear.

"It's not for me," she says.

Lissa nods. "I know."

"We'll take it to Eddy."

She works up a smile. "I'm sure he'll like that."

Rosy smooths the bear's head, the way Cece smoothed her hair. "I suppose we won't know, will we? Because he's not here to ask."

"You can talk to him, though," Lissa murmurs. "Tell him about the bear when you take it to him."

Rosy looks up at her out of those big eyes. "Really?"

"Sure." She bends down so she is at eye level with the little girl. "My sister died too," she tells her, like a secret. "I used to talk to her all the time when I was younger."

"Do you think she heard you?"

Lissa hesitates. She doesn't know what to say to someone this young, this innocent. In the end, she settles on the truth. "I hope so."

Rosy blinks at her. "How come you don't talk to her anymore?"

Cece's hand tightens its grip on her niece's.

"Well," Lissa says, holding her voice steady, "it was a long time ago." Rosy nods, like that is explanation enough.

Lissa straightens, and Cece smiles. It is a little stiff, but Lissa thinks it's sincere.

"Thank you," she says quietly.

Lissa nods as they turn to go, Rosy gripping the bear tightly. She tries very hard not to succumb to tears as she heads back into the shop.

There's a message from Ash waiting for her on her phone.

Meet me for a drink next week?

And because she's feeling sad, and vulnerable, she types her answer without thinking, because it's honest, because she wants to know.

Why?

The three dots indicating that he's typing start and stop a few times. She wonders if he'll send another GIF, make it into a joke. She wonders if it's made him question that very fact himself—why, exactly, they are still talking to one another.

Then, finally, the message comes through.

Because I want to see you.

The gravel path crunches under Lissa's boots as she makes her way from the car park into the graveyard. Ivy creeps up one side of the church building, and there's a nod to the end of the season in the form of a Christmas tree outside, modestly decorated with white fairy lights. She passes crumbling gravestones commemorating people who have long since been forgotten, and moves onto the grass, feeling its dampness seep through the toes of her boots.

It's been years since she's been here, but she could never forget the exact route to her sister's grave. She stopped coming because it became easier not to. Because she had reminders enough of what had happened, because she didn't want to see it, all the graves, with their loved ones left to grieve. Because, she always told herself, it happened so long ago.

Now she bends down at the rose and black granite headstone, traces her sister's name in faded gold lettering, then the dates, painfully close together.

"Hey, Chlo-bear," she whispers. It has always felt odd to bring flowers to her grave. She was too young to really understand the gesture of flowers, and in any case, flowers wither, they die. She planted a plant a few years ago, and wonders if it will still flower come spring. And this time, there's a wreath on the grave, which can only have been put here by her mum.

It was little Rosy in the shop who reminded Lissa of what she used to do. Bring tokens to Chloe—things her mum would sometimes tell her off for leaving on the ground because they weren't suitable for a graveyard. But now she places a wooden reindeer, one she picked up at the Christmas market because she liked the look of it, by the corner of the headstone.

She kneels, cold water seeping through her jeans. "I'm sorry I haven't been to visit in a while," she whispers. "I'm glad Mum has, though." She takes a breath, watches it dissolve into the graying mist around her. She used to come here as a teenager without her mum. Used to find it so easy to talk to Chloe—as long as there was no one else here.

"So I went to this spa before Christmas," she says. "It was a bit of a disaster." She can still feel it, water flooding her lungs, the panic at being sucked under. When, of course, in reality she was perfectly safe. All these years she's thought the drowning nightmares were because of

Chloe, but what if it was a memory of a past life straining to get through? A memory of the first time she died.

She sighs. "What do you think, Chloe? Am I mad?" She tries to imagine what her sister would say, but can't quite conjure it up. Because she's only ever known a six-year-old Chloe, and they would never have had this kind of conversation.

She sits in silence, aware of people coming and going around her, the distant sound of a sob. But also the sound of a child laughing. It's unfair, so terribly unfair, that Chloe lost her life so young. Lost. Like she misplaced it, rather than it being ripped from her because the people who loved her, the people who were supposed to take care of her, didn't do their job.

She blinks away tears, her vision blurring. And as she does, she sees the grave in front of her morph into another —a simple wooden cross under a cold gray sky. The scene shimmers, so that she's unable to fully grasp it. She can feel grass under her knees and a hand resting lightly on her back, comforting her. A man's hand, one she knows, one she hopes will always be there.

It disappears before she can delve any deeper, and she takes a shaky breath as she gets to her feet, traces her sister's name one last time. "I'm sorry, Chloe," she says as she leaves, even as she knows that no matter how many times she says it, it will never be enough.

When she gets back to her car, she sees she has a missed call. A sense of panic spikes her system when she sees who it was. Because Elsie never rings her.

She calls her back immediately. "Elsie?" she says.

"Finally! I've been trying to get hold of you for ages."

Lissa switches the car engine on so she can get some heat, wondering what exactly "ages" constitutes for Elsie, given the missed call was only five minutes ago, tops.

"Where are you?" her half-sister asks.

"I'm...I'm over at the church. St. Michael's."

"The church?" Lissa can hear the frown in her voice. "What, are you religious or something?"

Lissa laughs, the sound a little tired, and sad. Because Elsie has to ask the question, because she doesn't know enough about her to be sure. "No, I'm not religious. I'm just visiting someone."

"Visiting s— Oh."

The line goes quiet.

"Are you okay, Elsie?" Lissa prompts. "Do you need something?"

"We-ell," Elsie drags the word out, "I'm sort of... stuck."

"Stuck?"

"Yeah. See, I came into Bath again with Jess, but she got picked up early and there was no room in the car, and I was going to get the train but it's like another hour or something until the next one, and Dad has already texted asking where I am."

It is a lot of information given very quickly, and way more than she's used to getting from Elsie. "Right. And reading between the lines, Dad doesn't actually know where you are?"

"Well, no, not exactly. I sort of said we were in town, but I let him think it was Frome."

"Aha." Lissa taps her free hand against the steering wheel. She's not sure what to do here—what is the big sister role in all this? Should she immediately call her dad—or Nicole—to tell them about it?

"So, like, do you have a car or something?" Elsie prompts.

"A car?"

"Yeah."

"You want me to drive you home?" Lissa finally cottons on.

"Yes."

She hesitates again. She should almost definitely tell her dad. But Elsie is barely fourteen, alone in Bath, and it's getting dark. She can deal with the family politics later. "Where are you?" she asks.

"Near Anthropologie."

"Okay—if you walk to the end of the high street, I'll meet you there. Give me about twenty minutes, okay? I'll be as quick as I can."

When Lissa picks Elsie up on the corner of the street, her sister looks a bit sheepish. And a bit cold, Lissa thinks—her nose red, hair windswept. Lissa dials the heating up.

"Thanks," Elsie mutters, looking down at her knees as Lissa turns the car around.

"No problem."

"Are you going to tell Dad?" It's blurted out immediately, like she can't stop herself.

Lissa glances across at the passenger seat. "I don't know. I probably should." Elsie's lip juts out in response to that.

"So they said no?" she prompts. "To you coming to Bath by train?"

"Yep." Elsie scowls. Lissa notices that she's wearing mascara, and that it's run a little. "They won't let me do anything; it's totally ridiculous. I mean, I'm allowed to babysit by my age—surely that's responsible enough to get a half-hour train?"

"I guess they're just worried about you," Lissa says diplomatically. As she says it, it occurs to her that the reason they might be so worried is because they know how easily a child can be lost. Her dad must have talked to Nicole about what happened to Chloe. And all right, maybe it has nothing to do with that—maybe Nicole just doesn't like trains. But it gives her a twinge of guilt that she'd not thought of the possibility before.

"I guess they'll know anyway, when you drop me off," Elsie says, sounding resigned.

"I guess so. Though I suppose I could drop you at the end of the street."

Elsie brightens at this. "Yeah. Could you?"

Lissa doesn't answer. As the big sister, she should take Elsie all the way to her front door, shouldn't she? And come to think of it, she absolutely cannot be responsible for something bad happening to another sister, even if the possibility is slim.

"No," she says. "I'm sorry. I really should drop you at your house—it's dark out. But I'll let you tell Dad what happened. I won't say anything." Because she decides in that moment that it's better that Elsie knows she can rely on her if she needs to, rather than her being someone who will dob her in.

There's quiet for a moment as Elsie fiddles with the radio, switching it to Radio 1. Then she sits back in her seat. "So do you go there often?" she asks. "To her grave?"

Lissa brakes a little too hard at the next set of lights. She wasn't expecting the direct question. "No," she says. "Not as often as I should."

Elsie purses her lips at this, then gives a one-shouldered shrug. "I suppose you don't have to go there to think about her. You can do that anywhere."

Lissa stares at her, so that a car behind beeps when she doesn't immediately pull away at the green light.

"What?" Elsie asks, frowning. "Why are you looking at me like that?"

"Nothing. I just...You're right." Lissa hadn't expected her to be so insightful about it. Though she doesn't know why—as Elsie pointed out, she's fourteen, almost a mini adult.

Elsie nods, like that's obvious.

"So how was Christmas?" Lissa asks.

"Oh, all right. My grandparents came round." Which would be Nicole's parents, given that their dad's parents died a long time ago. "Thanks for the hoodie," she adds, like an afterthought.

"You're welcome."

"I didn't get you anything." It's not exactly an apology, but somehow it reads like one.

"That's okay. You didn't have to."

"So what did you do?" Elsie asks, fidgeting slightly.

"Spent it with my mum and my cousin." And actually, it wasn't as bad as it could have been—her mum retired early, and she and Mia stayed up drinking far too much red wine.

"Huh. Maybe you should have come to ours. We had way too much food." Lissa glances across at her, trying to work out if that is Elsie's version of an invitation.

"What was she like?" Elsie asks abruptly. She looks out the window as she says it.

"Who?"

"Chloe. Dad never talks about her."

Lissa thinks about this for a moment. "She was . . . young." She bites her lip, knowing that is not enough. So she makes herself carry on. "She was adventurous. Like, she was always trying to go off and find things when we went on walks and stuff like that. She loved the swing set. Her favorite flavor of ice cream was vanilla. She could touch her nose with her tongue, something I could never do." She attempts it now in the car, making Elsie snort a laugh. It sounds a little like her own laugh, she reckons.

"It's weird. To think I had a sister I'll never meet."

Lissa is taken aback at this—but of course, Chloe would have been Elsie's sister, too.

"Well, thanks for the lift," Elsie says as they pull up outside her house.

"Elsie?" Lissa says as her sister reaches for the door

handle, ready to jump out. "If you're ever in Bath and need anything, you know you can call me, right?"

"I know," Elsie says, her tone suggesting Lissa is somewhat dim-witted. "I just did."

And she did, didn't she? Which is better than nothing. So maybe there's hope for the two of them after all.

Chapter Sixteen

On the first day back in the office after Christmas, Lissa feels her stomach twisting with nerves as she exits the lift on the fourth floor and heads to her desk. She doesn't know why. Or, well, she *does*, but it's stupid. She and Darcy have been messaging loads; it's not going to be awkward. But they still haven't directly addressed it, what happened at the spa.

Darcy is already at her desk, scowling at something on her computer. Lissa is concentrating so hard on her friend, trying to work up the perfect "hey" for when she sits down next to her, that she doesn't notice Liam walking straight at her, holding a mug in one hand and his phone in the other. She yelps as they nearly collide, and he swears loudly as the liquid in his mug—black coffee—spills down her arm. She hisses in her breath, pulling her arm back toward her as she has a brief flash of another time this happened, in a much more romantic setting.

"Why weren't you looking where you're going?" Liam demands, rescuing what remains of his coffee and rocking back on his heels. She resists the urge to point out that *he* wasn't looking where he was going either, and examines the damage to her blouse. Well, at least it isn't white.

She can feel multiple gazes from around the office on her and tries to swallow down the embarrassment as she looks back up at Liam. She tries to get out a "sorry," but it doesn't quite come.

His expression twists into a different type of frown. "Are you okay?" he asks stiffly. "I mean, you're not going to..." He gestures down at her arm, then vaguely around. She has no idea what he's referring to.

"Umm, no?" That seems the right answer, if she's taking bets.

"Good." He lets out what is clearly a relieved breath. "Because after last time, HR coming down on me, can't be having another of those in the office, can we?"

It clicks, then. He's talking about her panic attack. She feels heat flush her cheeks, and really hopes no one is near enough to hear this.

"I'm fine," she says stiffly, and turns on her heel before he can ask anything else.

Darcy looks up at her as she slides into her chair, humiliation still burning her face. "Are you okay?" she murmurs.

Lissa swallows. "Yeah. He just wanted to know if I was going to cause problems for him with HR by having another panic attack in the office."

Darcy makes a hissing sound. "Dick."

Lissa nods her agreement, then blows out a breath, glancing at her friend. "How was Nottingham?" Darcy went home over Christmas to see her family.

"It was good. We all drank far too much, of course, so I'm in need of a massive detox, but it was nice to see everyone."

"Good, good."

"And you?" Darcy asks as Lissa switches on her computer. "How are you?"

"Oh, fine, you know. January blues, et cetera."

"Mm," Darcy agrees with a nod. Are things awkward? They feel awkward.

"New shoes?" Lissa asks, pointing down at Darcy's feet, which are crossed at the ankles and encased in low-heeled snakeskin boots.

"Naturally. Christmas present to myself."

And that, Lissa thinks, was a terrible effort to get things back on track. She takes a breath. "Darcy? Are we...okay?"

"What do you mean?" But Darcy's tone is noticeably too light.

"Since the spa," Lissa elaborates, glancing around to check no one is within earshot. "I mean—did I completely freak you out? Because I know I looked crazy, but I promise I'm not really. Or if I am, I'm not *completely* crazy and I'm not any different to the person I was when we—"

"Lissa. I don't think you're crazy. Well, no crazier than the rest of us."

"Maybe a little bit more," Lissa says on a sigh. Given that her friends don't tend to have meltdowns at the spa and scare everyone so much that the manager insists on giving you complimentary juice for the rest of the day. At the time, Darcy said it was a great way to get free drinks and maybe if Lissa had thrashed around *just* a little more they could have got champagne instead. But since then...

"Yeah, well, okay," Darcy says. "Maybe a little bit more. But whoever said crazy was a bad thing? The word needs a PR overhaul in my opinion."

Lissa snorts quietly.

"You didn't freak me out," Darcy says after a beat.

"Okay. Well, good." But things still feel off.

"I just..." Darcy bites her lip, swiveling her chair to face Lissa head-on. "I didn't know you didn't like water—or couldn't swim, or whatever. I never would've booked the session if I'd known."

"I know," Lissa says quietly. "I'm sorry. I thought maybe it would be okay." And it would have been, wouldn't it, if her mind hadn't decided to go elsewhere.

"I didn't even know you had a sister," Darcy says after another beat. And Lissa knows this is the crux of it.

"I'm sorry," she says again. "It's just...it's all a little..."

"Complicated?" Darcy guesses. "Yeah. Mia said. I just figured it would've come up, something like that. That's all."

"I should have told you," Lissa says, resisting the urge to look around again as she hears footsteps behind her, someone else on their way to their desk. "I guess I just didn't want you to think differently of me." She pulls a hand through her hair, matted slightly from the January wind outside. "Everything with Chloe...it defines so much of who I am. I suppose I didn't want it to define who I was with you, too."

203

Darcy studies her for a moment, in a very direct, Darcy way. Then she purses her red lips and nods. "Yeah. I think I can understand that."

Lissa feels her chest relax a little. "So we're good?"

Darcy smiles. "We're good, sweets."

They both turn back to their computers, waking up the screens. They had a company-wide office closure for two blissful weeks, and now Lissa is dreading the daily slog again. She's decided to stop her job hunt for now— the countless rejections are starting to make it seem a bit pointless. She's feeling a little lost on that front.

"So," Darcy begins, "still convinced you're seeing visions of your past lives?"

Lissa wrinkles her nose as she clicks on a company-wide email from Liam. "I know you don't believe me."

"I never said that."

"Right, but I know you think reliving memories from previous lives is unlikely."

"We-ll," Darcy says, drawing out the word, "on the scale of likeliness, most likely being I'll drink wine this weekend and least likely being one of us will sleep with Liam…"

Lissa snorts, and automatically glances around to check that Liam is in his glass office—the only one of them to have his own office, with the rumor being that he designed it deliberately so he could spy on the rest of them. Seems unlikely, given that it was built before the company moved in, but she wouldn't put it past him.

"But you can try to convince me over a drink if you like.

Maybe I should go and see this Saskia person myself, as long as she'll only tell me the good stuff and not the bad."

"Well, I mean, she doesn't really *tell* you about it, it's a whole trance thing, and also, I was having the memories before I went to see her, but..." Lissa catches the way Darcy is looking at her, one eyebrow arched, a slight smirk around her lips. "Never mind," she says on a sigh. "But yes to a drink."

"Fab, I need something to get me through this month. Friday?"

"Yes. No, wait. Shit, I can't do Friday. But any other day, I'm yours."

"Thursday, then. Why can't you do Friday?"

She hesitates. Her instinct is to lie about it—to say she's seeing her dad or something. But given the conversation they've just had... "I'm seeing Ash."

"Ash?" Darcy's voice rises an octave. She glances behind her to where Mark is sitting, right at the back of the office, then drops her voice. "Ash as in the hot friend of Mark who came to the pub quiz with us and completely ignored my attempts to flirt? *That* Ash?"

"Er, yes."

"What? How?"

"I don't know. We bumped into each other and I guess we're sort of... friends?" She's not sure why she says that like a question. "Or potential friends, at least." Darcy lets out a low whistle. "Please don't tell Mark," Lissa adds. She's not sure if Ash will have already mentioned it, but if not, she doesn't want Mark to hear it from Darcy, like office gossip.

"Come on, would I?"

"I'm not sure I should answer that."

Darcy makes a *pff* sound and waves her hand in the air. Then she rests her hand on her chin, leaning toward Lissa. "So this thing with Ash..."

"It's not a thing," Lissa says quickly.

That message she got from him, though. *Because I want to see you.* It could be innocent—she wants to see Darcy, doesn't she? Admittedly, her insides don't fizz if Darcy tells her she wants to see her, but that's her problem. It isn't Ash's fault.

"Hmm. Okay. Well we can add it to the agenda for Thursday. Item one."

Both of them straighten as Liam opens his office door, heads their way. They make a very obvious show of answering emails as he approaches.

"Raring to go after a good break, I hope, ladies?" he asks, running his thumb and forefinger over that stupid beard.

"Oh absolutely," Darcy says brightly. "I've got all kinds of ideas for companies we might be able to pitch for."

"Well that's great. I look forward to hearing about them all in the meeting." He walks away, over to Mark's desk.

"You know," Lissa mutters, "if you keep that up, he may very well fire you before you have enough saved for traveling."

"Nah, I'm too good at my job." Said with a confidence that Lissa envies. "Besides, I can definitely come up with some ideas of companies to approach. How long do we have until the meeting?"

Lissa checks the time on her phone—tries not to be disappointed when there's no message from Ash waiting for her. It's Monday morning, for Christ's sake.

"Ten minutes," she says.

Darcy grins and rubs her hands together. "Easy."

Lissa laughs, shaking her head. And selfishly wonders how the hell she'll survive in the office if Darcy leaves before she does.

Lissa moves through the crowded bar, spots Ash in the corner waiting for her. Or, it seems, not exactly waiting for her, but chatting to a tall woman in a skin-tight black dress. He laughs at something the woman says—the easy laugh that she's starting to know so well. The woman is twirling a strand of chestnut hair around her finger, leaning toward him over the table in a way that makes Lissa grit her teeth.

She catches herself as she takes another step forward, under the low concrete ceiling of the cellar bar that Ash suggested they try. Is she *jealous*? She's not allowed to be jealous. Ash is perfectly entitled to hit on beautiful chestnut-haired women if he wants to. Her insides don't seem to quite agree with her on that front, though, because as the woman gives him a big flirtatious smile, Lissa's shoulders tense, and she has to fight a strong urge to shove her away from the table that Ash has quite *clearly* reserved for him and someone else.

"Hey," she says loudly as she reaches him, needing to project her voice over the chatter.

"You're here!" He sounds delighted, enough to make her shoulders relax a little. He reaches over the table to give her a kiss on the cheek, her skin prickling where his lips make contact.

"I'm here," she agrees as the other woman slinks off back to the bar, wearing a disappointed expression. "Made a friend?" Lissa asks as she sits down.

"Steph," Ash says with a nod. "Visiting from Texas."

"She's American?"

"Yep. Got the accent and everything."

Lissa hesitates. She should probably ask—it's what a friend would do, right? "Do you want to...call her back?"

Ash raises his eyebrows. "Not particularly. Do *you*?"

"No, I just meant..." Her cheeks are heating now. "Nothing. Forget about it."

He grins, clearly finding something amusing in her embarrassment. "Okay." He pushes a gin and tonic across the table toward her.

"Thanks," she says with a smile. "So how was the castle in Scotland?" A sentence you don't say every day.

"Oh, it actually wasn't quite right," Ash says. "But I think I've found the perfect one in Sussex, so I'm off to check that out next week."

She leans toward him to hear him better over the noise of the bar, and as she does, their knees bump together under the table. Heat immediately flares up her thigh, just from that small point of contact. She shifts away as subtly as she can. *Stop it, Lissa.*

"So you can do a lot of your work from the UK?"

"Yep," he says easily, taking a sip of his beer. She nods thoughtfully, and his eyes travel the lines of her face in a way that feels intimate. The corner of his mouth crooks up. "You're wondering why I don't stay put if I can work from anywhere."

"Well, I mean I wasn't going to put it quite like that, but yes. If you're scouting locations in Scotland and Sussex, why would you choose to live in Belgium?"

He shrugs. "Why not?" An answer he gives a lot, it seems. "I'm freelance, so I can pick projects depending on where I am at the time. The pay isn't mega, but it's decent, so it allows me to be flexible—and it's not like I have a mortgage to pay. I hate the idea of being stuck in one place for too long, you know?"

She nods, even though she doesn't know, because she has no choice but to stick around in Bath. And she doesn't like it, the thought that he can so easily pick up and move, even though she knows she shouldn't feel as strongly about that as she does.

"How do you choose a location?" she asks, changing the subject to something that feels a little safer. "How do you know if something is right? Or do you ever think it is and then the singer disagrees?"

It's a lot of questions all at once, but he doesn't seem to mind. "I don't know, it's like a feeling? Which sounds incredibly wanky, I know. But I listen to the song on repeat before I even chat to the artist and the director; then I have my own ideas going in, and usually we're on the same page. Where we're not, we talk it out and get there. I try to really understand what the artist wants, and some of them are brilliant and happy to chat it through for ages, usually the ones just starting out. So then I have the idea of the type of place we're looking for, and then it's a case of going there and *feeling* it. I play the music through my headphones and imagine it there and... I don't know. You can either see it or you can't." He shakes his head. "Sorry. I'm rambling."

"No. It's interesting. I didn't even know it was a real job until I met you, to be honest."

"I didn't know it existed either. I sort of stumbled on it."

"Because you love music?"

"Yeah. I met someone who did the same thing when we were both auditioning to be in a band. I didn't get the gig, but I did get a new career goal."

Lissa's eyebrows shoot up. "A band?"

He laughs. "I play the guitar—a bit. Sort of thought I should give being in a band a go, but really I think maybe it wasn't for me."

"So do you love it? What you do now?"

"I do," he says slowly.

"But?" Lissa prompts.

He smiles a little. "But I sometimes feel like I'm, I don't know, a step away from the music. Like there's something else out there I could be doing." He shakes his head. "I think that's just what everyone goes through, though, you know, wondering if they're in the right career, wondering if there's something better."

"Yeah," she says on a sigh. "I think I know that feeling."

He twists the neck of his beer bottle, watching her. "You don't love your job?"

She grimaces a little, realizes what she's doing and straightens her face. "I don't *hate* it. I don't love my boss, that's for sure, and I get a bit bored. But it's not terrible. It's just not..."

"Inspiring?"

She smiles at him. "Yeah. It's just not inspiring. I've been applying for a ton of other things, but I'm having no luck, so..." She breaks off with a shrug.

"If you could do anything, what would it be?"

She blinks at him. It's such an obvious question. It's what you get asked as a child, or at a job interview when they ask you where you see yourself in five years' time. "I don't know," she says, feeling stupid for it. But the thing is, she doesn't feel like she has the luxury of only going after her dream job, because she needs something that enables her to pay her bills, and some of her mum's, and to be on call in Bath when she's needed. She's the reason her mum is the way she is, after all. "Something to do with art, I guess," she finishes lamely.

"You're an artist? That's cool."

"I'm not really an artist. I mean, I *can* paint, but that's not what I want to do. It would just be nice to, I don't know, use it somehow." But there's been another thought playing around her mind since meeting little Rosy at the charity shop. There must be so many kids out there like Rosy, like Lissa herself, who have lost siblings. So many kids whose parents might be struggling, unable to give them what they need, because of their own grief—because losing a child, it's unlike anything else, isn't it? And what if she could do something to help those kids? But she has no idea just what form that help would take. She doesn't think she has it in her to be a therapist, because don't you need to have your own shit together for that? So she doesn't say any of it out loud.

Under the table, his knee bumps against hers again, and this time she doesn't move away. His gaze meets hers across the table, a spark of something flying between them.

"So how's your dad?" she asks, determined to keep the flow going. He doesn't talk about him much. Then again, she doesn't talk about her family, either, but she's curious about the reason he came back to Bath. And after his declaration that he hates being stuck in one place, she wants to try and understand how long he's planning to stay here.

"Oh, he's fine," Ash says, in that same noncommittal way he always does. "So, Facebook tells me it's your birthday in a few weeks. March the fifth, right?"

Lissa cocks her head. A wave of laughter carries over to them from somewhere in the cellar. "Facebook-stalking me, are we?"

"It's how I spend all my free time, Liss."

She laughs, and tries not to notice the way the blue in his eyes sparks.

"So what are you doing?" he prods. He leans toward her, and his knee presses closer against hers. "For your birthday?"

"Oh, probably just having drinks with Darcy and Mia or something." He nods serenely and she narrows her eyes. "Why?"

"No reason. Just wondering." He grins, getting to his feet before she can press him on it. He gestures at their empty glasses. "Another round?"

She nods, and as he heads to the bar, she takes a slow breath, trying to ignore the way her leg immediately feels less warm without his pressed against it. Trying to remind herself of all the reasons it would be a bad idea to go there with Ash.

Trying—and coming up blank.

Chapter Seventeen

Lissa is so lost in the conversation with Ash that it surprises her when last orders are called at the bar.

"I guess that's our cue," she says, hooking her jacket off the back of her chair.

He moves behind her as they weave through the crowd to the door, his hand hovering just behind the small of her back. She's aware of it being there, not quite touching. Aware of how easy it would be to move back into it. Of how much she wants to do that.

She welcomes the cold air as they climb the steps back onto the street, where the atmosphere is still buzzing, students out in force. They meander down the street, heading vaguely in the direction of Lissa's flat but without any real purpose. Then Ash stops, looking over at a pub on the other side of the road where people are spilling out onto the street, the door propped open so they have a view of a band playing inside.

"Hey, come on," he says, grabbing her hand. "That looks like fun."

He pulls her across the road, not seeming to bother to

check for traffic, and she laughs a little breathlessly as she goes with him. He doesn't drop her hand as they reach the doorway, and she tries not to notice the way goose bumps are rising up her arm, grateful they are hidden by her jacket. Tries not to think about how all her attention goes right to that point of contact between them.

It's the alcohol, she tells herself firmly. It's making her light-headed and silly. But still, she extracts her hand with the excuse of looking in her bag for something. Safer, all things considered, not to touch.

The pub is warm and loud, with a makeshift dance floor cleared at the front where the band is playing. The female singer's voice is low and sultry, the hoops in her ears dancing as she moves. Low lighting flickers from the corners of the room, candles on tables burnt down to their wicks. It reminds her of somewhere...

Somewhere underground, with dim lighting and flickering candlelight. Somewhere with a jazz band playing in one corner of the room, trumpets blaring, the singer's voice rising over the hum of chatter. Where women spin in sequinned dresses and men lean against the bar in tailored suits and shiny shoes. Where the air is thick with sweat, perfume and liquor and the laughter feels slightly too loud, almost frantic—a tension that no one wants to look directly at.

A speakeasy, she knows. One she's not supposed to be at. But she couldn't resist the opportunity to see him again, to dance with him—not when she doesn't know when he'll be leaving this time.

Lissa blinks, the memory fading as Ash comes to a halt, his body, just for a second, held oddly stiff before he visibly relaxes, like it's a conscious effort. Lissa realizes why a moment later, and her stomach does a horrible, awkward squirm. Because that's Mark walking toward them, his arm around a girl—petite, well dressed. Smiling up at him like she's more than a little loved up.

He jerks to a stop a few feet from them, late to notice. He looks to Lissa first, and the smile fades from his face a little. Then he clocks Ash right next to her, seems to do a double-take. "Oh," he says, the smile now gone completely.

It's ridiculous. They haven't been on a date in months, and they see each other all the time in the office. Although they might *see* each other, but they've fallen into a pattern of tactfully not talking, haven't they?

"Hi, mate," Ash says breezily. He smiles at Mark's date. "Hey, Jen."

She smiles back. "Hey." Jen, okay. She has a name, and Ash has met her, so she's clearly not too recent.

Ash clears his throat. "Ah, Jen, Lissa. Lissa, Jen." He gestures between them at the introduction.

"Hi, Lissa." Lissa does a sort of awkward wave back. Jen cocks her head. She's wearing blue studs in her ears, and they glint a little in the dim lighting. "I'm missing something, aren't I?"

A flash of a grimace passes over Mark's face. "Lissa and I used to…" He wafts a hand in the air and Lissa feels her cheeks flush. "I mean, not seriously," he adds quickly. "And not for a while."

"Right," Lissa agrees, making her voice both firm and upbeat. "Not for a long time. And not seriously." For fuck's sake, why does this city have to be so bloody small?

Mark glances between Ash and Lissa. His arm is still around Jen, though he has loosened his grip. "So are you guys hanging out now?"

Ash shoves his hands into his pockets, rocks back on his heels. "Depends what you mean by hanging out. I mean, we are currently hanging out, but we're not 'hanging out.' " He lifts his hands to do the air quotes.

"Right," Mark says, nodding slowly.

"Well, this is brilliantly awkward," Jen says brightly. Lissa decides she quite likes her. "So I reckon either we all do tequila shots together, or else we leave these two to it. Mark, what do you think?"

"Yes." Mark's hand moves to her waist, squeezes lightly. He nods at Ash and Lissa. "You guys have fun."

Ash moves to the side to allow them to pass. "Catch up later?" he asks, sounding a little sheepish.

"Yeah," Mark says. "Sure."

He and Jen step through the doorway, and when they are definitely out of earshot, Lissa thumps Ash in the ribs.

"Ouch," he says drily.

"You didn't tell him," Lissa hisses.

"No. Sorry. Although, to be fair, you didn't either." She wrinkles her nose at that. "I was going to," Ash continues, "but I wasn't sure what exactly there was to tell him." He looks at her then, his blue eyes intense, so that it feels like a question. One she doesn't think it's best to answer.

Instead she jerks her head toward the bar. "Drink?"

"Good idea."

Lissa's skin feels itchy as she stands next to him at the bar, like something has changed between the doorway and here. Like Mark seeing them *means* something, when really it shouldn't. The music, some sort of jazz fusion, thrums inside her, and she feels too hot even as she strips off her jacket.

Ash downs his drink in one, sets the glass on the bar. His knee is moving, like he's trying to siphon off some energy. "Let's dance," he announces.

"Er, why?"

"Why not?" He takes her hand and pulls her onto the dance floor without waiting on an answer.

He keeps hold of one of her hands, places his other on her waist. Beneath her top, her skin heats, and when she looks up, feeling the weight of his focus on her, she thinks he can tell. Thinks he can feel it. He moves her across the limited space, lifts one arm for her to twirl under, and she obliges.

"You can dance," he states.

She grins. "Why, surprised?" She's never exactly loved dancing in public, what with the whole being-the-center-of-attention thing, but she's always been able to do it.

His fingers skim lightly down her spine, and it's all she can do not to shiver. The space between them feels flimsy, and not just because they're so close. He's watching her, his gaze holding hers. She should look away. But she doesn't want to. She moves her hand from his shoulder to rest on the side of his neck instead, sees the pulse in his throat jump. His hand slides back to her waist, his fingers curling there, and heat flares between her thighs. Her heart is beating fast, a warning drum that she doesn't want to listen to.

The pub blurs around them as they dance, colors swirling in a way that doesn't feel real. She's back there in that speakeasy with him. Music swirls around them, urging them on—not his band this time, but another one.

"Did you think any more about it?" he asks, his voice low, meant only for her. She knows what he's talking about. He wants her to move out of the city, to take her art more seriously.

You could be the next Augusta Savage, he told her the last time she saw him, as they walked through Central Park hand in hand.

"I'm still thinking," she hedges, not wanting to let him down. "But I'm needed here, for now." And it's a stupid dream anyway, to paint, to do something with that. She knows she is destined to stay here in New York. She only wishes he would stay too.

A slight crease furrows his brow—he knows a little, about her sister, the way her parents are broken because of it. She takes her hand from his, places it on his chest. "Let's not talk about it now, okay? Let's just enjoy tonight." Because he's leaving in the morning, off with his band to the next city.

He smiles a little, nods. At her waist, his hand moves in a slow circle, and she tries not to shiver. She can almost taste the subtle edge of his cologne, and she breathes in the smell of him, deeper than that. His fingers move to the small of her back, tightening their grip, and she sees the way his Adam's apple bobs as she holds his dark gaze.

I love you. She wants to say it then. Wants to let the words loose, to taste them on her tongue. But she can't—not yet. Because he is only ever passing through. Because, as much as she'd like to pretend otherwise, she can't leave until her mother is better.

He bends his head toward her, his mouth a hair's breadth from hers. She closes her eyes, waiting for the kiss. Only it doesn't come.

She can still feel his hand pressed to her lower back, holding her in place. Can smell sandalwood and grass. Only it's not *his* hand. It's Ash's. It's Ash's thumb rubbing a light circle over her knuckles. A soft, subtle gesture—one that shouldn't make her breath catch as it does. She knows he hears the sound, because his fingers curl at her back, tightening their hold, and his eyes darken in the flickering light. His gaze drops to her mouth and her breathing stutters.

Jesus. She should have stopped at one gin and tonic. It's making her light-headed.

He moves closer, close enough that she has to tilt her head up to look at him. Until this moment, she hasn't let herself realize just how attracted she is to him. She tries to remind herself of the reasons not to go there. He's Mark's friend. She's not ready for a relationship. He's only here temporarily, and she doesn't want to fall for someone who will leave her. But right now, there is a buzzing in her mind, eclipsing those thoughts.

So when he leans in, closing the distance between them, she meets him there, so that she's not sure who it is who kisses who. She feels that first shock to her system as his mouth captures hers, hears the sound she makes as he tugs her hips flush to his. She grips his forearms tightly, nails biting gently into flesh. Her lips part for his, and she can taste the alcohol and something deeper, something that is distinctly *him*, both electrifying in its newness and somehow comforting in its familiarity.

Her outline feels like it's dissolving, her whole body turning to liquid. She knows that if she were to open her eyes now, it would be impossible to tell where she is. Her hands are hooked behind his neck, holding him to her. She doesn't remember moving them, but she must have. She scrapes them through his messy hair and he lets out a quiet hum of appreciation.

Somewhere very far away—or that's how it feels—there is the sound of a glass shattering. The sound of cheering and whooping. They move apart, and Ash glances over in the direction of the noise. Lissa blinks, coming to her senses. What is she *doing*?

She lets go of his neck, backing away. His hands fall away from her at once.

"I need some air," she mutters, unable to meet his gaze. She grabs her jacket off the stool where she left it and practically runs out of the pub.

Only once the cold air hits her does she realize how hot her skin has become. She takes a steadying breath, then another, needing to chase away whatever she felt in there. She shouldn't have done that. She shouldn't have kissed him.

She hears his footsteps behind her. He's followed her, as she knew he would. She can't turn to look at him, though—not yet. Her emotions still feel rocky, out of control, and she knows what happens when they get like that. Drinking with him was not a good idea, she realizes in hindsight.

"Do you want to head home?" he asks, and his voice is neutral, no hint that he's embarrassed or hurt.

She bites her lip, glances back at where he's standing a careful distance away from her. "Yeah. I think so."

"I'll walk you." She hesitates, then nods, falling into step alongside him.

For a moment they walk in silence, away from the buzz of the last few open bars and toward the quiet residential streets.

"Lissa, I…" She thinks, from his tone, that he's about to say something about what happened and finds herself tensing automatically. But he doesn't. "You want to do something tomorrow?" he asks instead, tone easy once more. "Lunch, maybe?"

"I can't." He gives her a critical look at this. "I'm not evading, I promise." He keeps looking at her, and she lets out a small laugh. God, her head still feels unsteady. Her skin still feels too tight. "Well, okay, maybe partly that."

His lips twitch. "At least you're honest."

"It's just I have to take my mum to the garage—her car needs fixing." She leaves out the part about her saying she'd pay for the repairs. She knows how that will sound.

"Fair enough."

He says it casually enough, but she can't help thinking of the look she gets from Mia every time she does something for her mum. And even though it's a perfectly legitimate excuse, she can't help wondering if he thinks she's making it up to avoid dealing with what happened. So she tries to explain. "It's just, it's important that I look after her. You know, after what happened."

"Okay."

"Okay?" They are nearing her street now. "What's that supposed to mean?"

He raises his eyebrows. "Umm...okay?"

She pushes her hair back from her face impatiently. "You don't get it."

"Oh? What don't I get, exactly?" His voice is still calm, but now there's a touch of her own impatience reflected back at her.

And with her emotions in flux like this, with the alcohol fueling her, she finds herself spitting it out. "I left Chloe alone. Okay?" She turns to him in the middle of the street, a few doors down from her flat. "I left her playing by the pond, and because of that, she died."

He steps toward her, reaching for her. "Lissa—"

"Don't." She swipes him away. "I'm just trying to...No one gets it, why I have to do things for my mum, why she needs me. But it's my fault." Angry tears spark her eyes—

God, what is wrong with her this evening? "It's my fault my sister died."

He looks at her for a long moment, and she thinks this is it—this is when he realizes just what kind of person she is. This is why she never tells people exactly what happened. And maybe, if he knows, then he'll go, leave her alone. Maybe it'll drive him away, and she won't have to deal with this anymore, whatever *this* is.

But he doesn't leave. Instead, he moves closer to her, slowly. Then he reaches out and takes her in his arms. She's so surprised that she doesn't push him away, holding herself stiff as he rests his chin on top of her head.

"You were only a child, Lissa." She can feel the vibration of his voice against her chest.

She shakes her head as best she can. "I was twelve."

"A child," he repeats firmly. "You can't blame yourself."

"I can." Her voice is bitter. "I do."

He pulls back just a little, so he can see her face. "How did she die?"

She hesitates. "She drowned."

"An accident?"

Lissa frowns, shakes her head again. "No."

He looks like he might contradict her on that, but instead he reaches out, brushes a strand of her hair back from her face. "I'm so sorry it happened to you, Lissa. I'm so sorry that it happened to your mum, too. But it's not your fault." He repeats it like that's all that's needed for her to believe it. Like all he needs to do is say that, and it will magically be better.

"You don't get it," she repeats. She pushes him away, then starts to walk again, heading toward her building.

"Maybe not," he says evenly. "But I lost someone too." She looks around at that—she can't help it. "My mum," he continues. "She died when I was a teenager."

She turns all the way round, and it's her turn now to step toward him. This is why he speaks of loss like he knows it. "Ash—"

He holds up a hand to stop her. "My dad didn't ever recover from it. That's why I'm here, in Bath. Because he needs me. Because he's not okay—he hasn't ever been, not really—and I've been trying to run away from that. So I do get it," he says, with a self-deprecating smile. "The guilt. It's not the same, but I think I do get it."

Her heart twists for him, but she doesn't know what to say. She doesn't know how to take back what she spat at him. For a moment, they just stare at each other. Then Lissa swallows.

"We shouldn't have . . ." She sighs. "This can't go anywhere, Ash," she murmurs, keeping her gaze on his. "Between us. You don't . . . When you look at me, I don't think you see just how broken I am. I think you see a version of me that doesn't exist." And it's best, isn't it, to admit that now, before anyone gets hurt. Before he realizes how damaged she is and takes off, or before *she* does something to hurt him because, as Saskia pointed out to her, she is so lost in the past.

He looks at her for another long moment, and she feels her pulse beating against her wrist. She tenses as he moves

225

toward her, but all he does is lean down and press a chaste kiss to her cheek. There's a whisper of his breath against her ear as he pulls away, and her muscles tighten and quiver.

It feels like a goodbye, she realizes. She doesn't know why that should hurt quite so much.

"It doesn't have to go anywhere," he says. "Not if you don't want it to." He backs away, ready to turn, to leave. "But, Lissa? Just so you know, I'm pretty sure that when I look at you, I do see the broken parts." Her breath hitches just a little as he holds her gaze. "I'm pretty sure that when I look at you, I see all of you."

Chapter Eighteen

Esme sits awkwardly on Lissa's sofa, looking out of place in the flat. She hardly ever comes here—in fact, Lissa is pretty sure she can only remember her coming for the obligatory look around when she first moved in, years ago. She's aware of the damp in the corner of the living room, the stain on the rug from spilling something or other. Not that she should worry about that, probably, given the state her mum's house is so often in, but still.

She crosses to the sofa, holding two mugs, and hands her mum the milky tea, keeping the mint for herself. Esme smiles as she takes it, and Lissa props herself awkwardly on the other side of the sofa. Her mum is still in her blue nursing uniform, carrying with her the faint smell of antiseptic. She looks tired, dark circles under the hazel eyes she shares with Lissa, her gray hair just a little greasy. Lissa wonders sometimes which side of her mum the patients get to meet—whether she is a welcome presence on the ward. Then tells herself that's an awful thing to think.

"Here," her mum says, reaching into her bag and producing a birthday card, along with a small wrapped present. "I wanted to get you a cupcake, too, you know, from the nice place next to the hospital, but they were all out."

Lissa glances from the card to her mum's pale face and back again. "That's so nice, thanks, Mum." She takes the card and present, hesitating slightly before opening them. They don't usually do this—exchange gifts on birthdays. The card is a simple balloon birthday card, with *To Lissa, From Mum* written inside. The present is a selection of bracelets from Accessorize, gold and blue. Blue like the color of Ash's eyes.

No, Lissa.

"These are so pretty." She slips them onto her wrist. "Thank you," she says again.

Her mum gives a little shrug of acknowledgment, takes a sip of her tea.

"So how was work?" Lissa asks.

"Oh, you know. Tiring." Esme shifts on the sofa, angling toward her. "But on the subject of work...Mia told me you're not very happy in your job."

Bloody Mia. She'll have to have a word. "Did she now? And what else did she say?"

"Oh, not much really. But I just, I wanted to check... are you okay?"

The mug in Lissa's hands stops partway to her lips. She doesn't really know how to answer that question. Her mum has asked about her health a lot in the past, insisting on doctors' appointments for every little thing when she was a teenager. Lissa knows that even if she blames her for Chloe, her mum also worries about losing the only daughter she has left.

"Yeah, Mum," she says slowly. "I'm okay."

She decides not to bring up the past-life thing—her mum would have her straight to a psychiatrist.

"And are you...happy?" Just what exactly has Mia been saying to make her ask these questions?

"I'm..." But she doesn't know how to finish that sentence. Is she happy? She doesn't think she's *un*happy. And there are moments, of course, that are filled with joy—laughing with Darcy about something stupid, curled up on the sofa with Mia. Dancing with Ash in the middle of some random pub. No. Not Ash. *Stop thinking about him, Lissa.*

She settles with, "I'm fine, Mum. Do you want a biscuit to go with the tea?" She gets to her feet before Esme can answer, heading for the cupboard and the spare pack of digestives she has in case of emergency.

She holds out the packet to her mum, who takes one, staring down at it. "Lissa? Why did you stay in Bath?"

Lissa frowns as she comes back to the sofa. "What do you mean?"

"Well, you could have got a job anywhere. Moved to London or something. Or even gone traveling, like all you young people. So why didn't you?"

"Because..." She sighs, unable to think of an excuse quickly enough. "Because you need me, Mum."

Her mum peers over at her. Her eyes seem very clear, very focused today. "You know, I don't remember much

229

of what I said before...before Christmas." It's not very specific, but Lissa knows she's talking about the latest "episode," or whatever you want to call it. When she told Lissa to get out, then begged her not to leave. "But I...I know you came to help me. So thank you for that." The words are a little stilted, but Lissa thinks they're sincere.

She opens her mouth, shuts it again. Shoves a biscuit in her mouth so she doesn't have to talk. They never usually address these things directly. Never usually talk about what happens when her mum gets lost like that. They put it behind them, move on. It's the only way they know how to function.

"I...I'm talking to someone," her mum continues. "Someone at work suggested it, and, you know, because I work for the NHS, I was able to get an appointment."

Lissa is about to ask what appointment she means when she realizes—therapy. Her mum is getting some kind of therapy.

"I suppose what I'm trying to say is that, well, I'm trying. To get better. To work on it. And that I'm sorry. For not trying sooner. Anyway," she says abruptly, getting to her feet and effectively stopping—or saving—Lissa from responding to that, "I just popped round to give you your gift. And I'm sure you have plans this evening, don't you?"

Lissa nods. "I'm seeing Darcy and Mia for drinks."

"Well then." Esme sets her tea and uneaten biscuit down on the coffee table. Hesitates, then reaches over to give Lissa an awkward pat on the back. "Happy birthday. I'll see you soon, okay?"

"Okay. Thanks, Mum." And she watches her mum leave the flat, wondering what it means that she's tried to talk to her, in even a small way, about this. If there's a chance, maybe, that she'll get better. Or if it's only a matter of time before she spirals again.

"She's here!" Darcy gets up from the corner table in the pub, where she's sitting with Mia and a woman Lissa doesn't recognize, with short platinum-blond hair, high cheekbones and expertly applied gold eyeliner. Lottie, she realizes—this must be Lottie. She told Mia to invite her, given that Lottie is only over from New York for the week, but Mia was very noncommittal about the whole thing.

"Happy birthday, sweets," Darcy says, pulling her into a hug before dragging her over to the table, where there are already three packets of crisps and a bottle of white wine chilling in a cooler.

Mia hugs her too as she slides into the booth. "Happy birthday, Bissa." She pulls back, then gestures toward a smiling Lottie. "Lottie, this is Lissa."

"Lissa!" Lottie has a brilliant New York accent, and she sounds totally delighted. "I'm so pleased to meet you! Thank you for letting me crash your birthday drinks."

"Of course. I'm so happy you came." Under the table, Lissa catches Mia taking Lottie's hand in hers and squeezing.

Darcy fills the spare glass with wine, slides it over across the water-stained wooden table. "So...no Ash?"

"Nope," Lissa says lightly, taking a sip of the Sauvignon. "Just us girls."

"Didn't fancy inviting him, then?"

She chews the inside of her lip. "Ash and I . . . we're taking a bit of a break."

"A break?" Mia asks, while Lottie tears the crisp packets open so they lie flat on the table for everyone to help themselves to. "A break from what, exactly?"

"I don't know. Our friendship? It was just getting a little . . ." Lissa gestures with her wineglass. "Intense." Mia and Darcy exchange a look at that, though they say nothing.

She hasn't really spoken to him since the night at the bar. The night they kissed. She feels awful for the way she treated him, telling him he didn't understand, when he's clearly got his own stuff going on. But it's for the best, she's sure of it. She doesn't want to get in deep with anyone, especially someone who might leave at any moment. And it's not like she can pick up and leave with him, is it?

Still, she woke to a message from him this morning. One that she's already reread several times over the course of the day, despite the fact that it only consists of three words.

Happy birthday Lissa. X

"So," she says, "I thought you'd both like to know that I am officially on the job hunt again."

"Excellent," Darcy says.

"About bloody time," says Mia.

"And I'm thinking—I'm going to start applying in the charity sector." It was talking to Ash on their night out that reaffirmed it for her. Listening to his passion for music, for what he does, and realizing that she'd not spent enough time figuring out what she wanted. And okay, this has nothing to do with art, but it's a step toward her idea about helping kids like Rosy, like the kid she herself was.

Darcy cocks her head. "Like, more volunteering?"

"No. Well, I mean, I'm going to keep doing the charity shop thing because it's actually quite fun, but I mean more like switching to working in marketing for a charity." A charity that deals with bereavement, preferably, but any step in that direction would feel like a positive one as far as she's concerned. And okay, she can't jet off too far away, but she could do a commutable distance, couldn't she, and still have her base here?

"Well I think that's an excellent idea," Mia says.

"Much better than becoming a chef," Darcy agrees.

"What's wrong with chefs?" Lottie asks.

Mia grins at her, and in that moment, she looks so damn happy that it makes Lissa want to hug them both. "Nothing," she says. "Only, Lissa can't cook."

Lissa makes a fake-offended sound. "I can. My pesto pasta is to die for."

"What do you do?" Darcy asks Lottie.

"Work at a magazine, basically writing fluff pieces. Probably be out of a job in five years." It makes Lissa think of her dad's claim that soon his job will be lost to AI, and she smiles a little.

Darcy holds up the empty wine bottle, makes a face.

"I'll order another one," Lissa says, getting to her feet.

She's halfway to the bar when Mia sidles up next to her. "You don't think I'm going to let you pay for drinks on your birthday, do you?" She links her arm with Lissa's, and they head the rest of the way to the bar together.

"What about *your* job?" Lissa asks after they've ordered the wine. Her cousin frowns at her in question. "A while ago it seemed like you might not be totally happy with it."

Mia taps her fingers on the wooden bar. "It's not the job I don't like. It's just going up and back to London all the time, it's a bit tiring. And I..." She glances back at Lottie, who has her head bent toward Darcy, already in easy conversation.

"You want to have time to visit her?" Lissa guesses.

"Yeah," Mia mutters. "Something like that."

At some point in the evening, possibly after the third bottle of wine, Darcy orders four tequila shots.

"To birthdays!"

"To job hunting!"

"To airplanes!" Everyone looks at Mia at that one, and she shrugs. Lottie, however, grins at her.

"Another round of shots?" Darcy asks.

"Absolutely not," Lissa says. "We're too old for all that."

"Speak for yourself," Lottie says brightly. "I'm not even thirty—I've got at least four more rounds in me."

"Regardless, I'm out," Lissa says. She hugs them all goodbye, whispering, "I like her," to Mia as she does. She opts to get an Uber home, figuring she's too tipsy and it's too late to manage the walk solo.

As she gets into bed, she reads the message from Ash

one last time. A message that from anyone else would be disregarded as one of many. But because it's from him, it makes her smile as she drifts into sleep.

Happy birthday Lissa. X

In her dream, she's on Coney Island beach, the smell of salt water merging with that of hot dogs. Laughter rises around them, along with the sound of children screaming as they run through the waves. The air shimmers with heat, and the back of her neck pricks with sweat.

"Sure I can't tempt you into the water?" he asks, grinning down at her from where he is propped on one elbow.

"I told you, I don't swim." *Don't* sounds better than *can't*—and best not to mention anything about the drowning nightmares. She doesn't want him to start worrying about her sanity, after all. She flips onto her belly, the towel coarse on her exposed shins, and props herself up, tracing patterns in the sand.

"So I was thinking," he says, and the tone of his voice makes her glance up at him. "Maybe I could stick around for a while."

Her heart does a funny little spasm. "Stick around?"

"In New York. I've got a bit of a name going for myself in the band now. I think I could find work here. And my dad—maybe it would be good for me to be around a bit more often for him."

She nods slowly. He doesn't talk much about his dad, but she knows he's struggled since coming back from France.

"What do you think?" he prompts.

"What do *I* think?" She laughs, shakes her head. "Well of course I'd like you around more." Maybe that would mean things could progress between them. And if he stays, that would make it easier for her to stay too, wouldn't it?

He grins, gets to his feet and holds out a hand. "Come on. Let's walk."

She allows him to pull her up, and the two of them walk barefoot along the shoreline. She's not looking where she's going, too caught up in wondering if he means it, if he'll really stay this time, so she doesn't notice the sharp shell on the sand until she steps on it.

She feels a slice of pain across her foot. Sees the blood. And feels the telltale ringing in her ears.

Not here, she thinks. *Not now.*

But her breathing is coming too fast. The blood is swelling from her foot, and she sinks to the ground, stretching it out in front of her to get a better look.

"Ouch," he says. His hands on her calf. "It doesn't look deep. I can find something to wrap it with. Hang on."

But the words don't register, and in front of her, the sea blurs on the horizon. She can't breathe. There is a tingling sensation in her hands, her feet, and no matter how much air she sucks in, it's not enough.

"Hey. It's okay," he's saying, a hand on her back. "You're okay."

She's breathing heavily as she wakes, her spine slick with sweat. Her heart is beating fast, like she really did have the panic attack.

She huffs out an impatient breath as she sits up in bed. How is she supposed to move forward with her life if she keeps getting drawn to memories of the past, memories that she doesn't even understand? She still feels sure that there must be a reason she's seeing all this. A reason it's happening now. But if it was triggered by the anniversary of Chloe's death, why does she keep reliving her previous romances?

Maybe Saskia is right. Maybe it's time to stop obsessing over the past and start thinking about her future.

Chapter Nineteen

Lissa checks her phone as she parks outside Saskia's house once again. She thinks she's partly looking for an excuse not to go through with this—because does she really think that tarot cards are going to help her?—but all she has is a message from Darcy wishing her luck and asking her to ask Saskia when she—Darcy—is likely to find her soulmate.

As she walks to the front door, though, one more message pops up. Her heart does that familiar little skip as she opens it.

Are you free next Saturday? There's somewhere I'd like to take you.

Straight to the point, without so much as a *how are you.* Without reference to the fact that apart from her birthday message, they haven't spoken since the night they kissed.

Where? she types back, figuring that if he is being abrupt, she can be too.

You'll have to meet me to find out.

She bites her lip as she rings the doorbell. She's decided, in the space she's had from him, that perhaps she's overthinking things. Yes, they kissed, but that didn't mean

238

he wanted to move in together and get a golden retriever, did it? And maybe she wasn't even that attracted to him. They'd been drinking that night, after all, and it's easy, under the influence, to think you really fancy someone—she's made that mistake plenty of times before.

She looks up as the front door opens. Saskia's gray hair is down today, her eyes creased in a smile.

"I'm glad you came," she says, gesturing Lissa inside.

Lissa tries not to think too hard about it as she follows Saskia to her back room. It's not going to *hurt*, is it? And a distant part of her can't help wondering if it might actually help—given that she believes she's experiencing memories of past lives, is it really such a stretch to think some people may be able to see the future?

"So," Saskia says as they take seats opposite one another. The couch, Lissa is guessing, will go unused again today. "How this usually works is that the querent—that would be you—asks a question, and we use the cards to help answer it." Lissa sees them now—the deck of cards, sitting on Saskia's desk.

"Er, right." She didn't realize she'd be expected to come up with a question. She frowns, trying to think of what she wants to know most. Why is she getting these memories? Or, are the memories real? Or, what is she supposed to be learning from them?

Saskia smiles a little at whatever passes over Lissa's face. "I got the impression last time that you were a little confused about things in the past, and what they might mean."

"Right," Lissa agrees, thankful that Saskia is taking charge. "Yes."

"So perhaps we could do a general reading to give you an idea of where you are now and a sense of what's to come? I'm hoping it might clear up some things, and help direct you."

"Okay. Yes. That sounds good."

"We'll do the Celtic Cross." Saskia picks up the cards and shuffles with quick, practiced fingers. Lissa nods, because what else is she supposed to do?

She feels her nerves spike as Saskia begins to lay the cards out on the desk in front of them, forming an uneven cross. She doesn't say anything as she does, doesn't give away anything with her expression, but to Lissa's untrained eye, some of them look pretty damn alarming. A man dead on the ground, swords coming out of his back. A woman blindfolded and all tortured-looking. A creature labeled *The Devil*.

Saskia studies the cards for a moment, then sits back, placing her hands in her lap. "Now, forgive me if I'm wrong, but I'm assuming you don't know much about tarot."

"You'd be right," Lissa says drily.

Saskia smiles a little, then nods. "Well, the first thing I'd say is that there are quite a lot of swords in this reading, which can be an indication of challenges and difficulties in your life."

Lissa glances at the various sword cards on the desk. Does that mean the challenge of figuring out what these memories are about? Or does it mean more practical things—her anxiety, her mum, her search for a job?

"We begin with things as they are now." Saskia points to a card directly in front of her, in the middle of a column of three, partly obscured by another card lying horizontally across it. This is the blindfolded woman, a tower looming ominously behind her. It doesn't look *great*, Lissa has to say.

"I'd say this is indicating that you feel trapped or restricted by something," Saskia continues, looking to her for confirmation.

She gives a half-shrug. "I suppose so." Trapped by needing to stay put, by her mum. But she's trying to do something about that, isn't she? She's trying to apply for different jobs, looking at cities she can commute to.

"Well, what I'd always say with this card is that although it may feel bad at the moment, remember that you are less trapped than you think. It's within your power to change your situation, but only if you recognize what you've done to create it."

Lissa frowns. "What *I've* done?"

Saskia gives her another of those creased smiles. "It can be a state of mind rather than something you're actively doing. Something you need to reflect on in order to break free of it."

"I think I'm already doing that." It's hard not to sound defensive. But that's the whole reason she's here, isn't it? To *reflect*.

"Well, that's good then," Saskia says neutrally. "So now we move to current challenges or obstacles." She indicates the card lying horizontally over the trapped woman. The Devil. A winged creature setting fire to people in chains and collars beneath him. Fabulous.

"This can make some people panic," Saskia says, "but it's often more about something dark in your own psyche rather than an external force out to get you." She hesitates for a beat, then adds, "The Devil is also often seen as the lord of patterns—of circles and cycles that go round and round. A pattern you might be trapped in." She indicates the first card—the trapped, blindfolded woman.

"So I'm trapped by a pattern?" Lissa asks, frowning. She thinks of the memories she's having. A sister who died in all of her past lives. A romance that is still unfolding in every one of them. A death. Because although she's only seen one of her deaths, she knows there has to be more.

Is that what this means? A certain pattern repeating over and over? A sister who dies because of something she does. A mother who hates her because of that. A romance, someone she falls for completely.

Ash. Her mind goes there even when she doesn't want it to. But is he part of this—part of the pattern repeating itself? And if so, is that a good thing or a bad thing?

"I can see you thinking it through," Saskia says gently. "And what I would say is that it feels to me like there is a danger of this cycle—whatever it is—repeating endlessly. But," she adds forcefully, when Lissa makes a face, "you do have the power to break free of it if you make a change."

Lissa bites her lip. "What change, though?"

Saskia shakes her head. "I wish I could tell you that."

Lissa hesitates, then decides what the hell—in for a penny, right? "I think it might be about the past lives. The ones I told you about last time. I think there might be a pattern to all of them—a similar thing happening again and again. Could that be it?"

"It could," Saskia says, and Lissa reckons that's about as much agreement as she's going to get.

"So does this mean I need to do something different in *this* life?" Or is it too late—is it that she needs to do something in the next life, to save Chloe?

"Maybe. Let's see if the cards can help, shall we? We now look to something in the past that might still be influencing you now." Saskia points to the card the farthest to the left. A heart being pierced by three swords. "The Three of Swords. This is usually grief or trauma." She pauses, then asks, "I think you mentioned a sister who died?"

Lissa's throat bobs as she swallows. "Yes. And yes, that does still influence me."

Saskia nods slowly. "Well, maybe it's about coming to terms with something to do with her death. It might be that it's only by doing so that you're able to break the pattern."

Lissa nods, but she's frowning. There's only so much coming to terms with it she can do—she's accepted it, hasn't she? She isn't still lost to grief like her mum. And how would that help across multiple lifetimes? It does add credence to her theory that it might all be about Chloe, though.

"Looking ahead now," Saskia says, "to a possible future. And I emphasize *possible* here, because the future is never set in stone." Lissa wonders if she emphasizes that so strongly because of how bleak the next card looks. The Ten of Swords. The man lying face-down in the grass, alone, swords sticking out of his back.

"Is it a death?" Lissa can't help asking.

"Not necessarily," Saskia says slowly. *Necessarily.* Well, that's a brilliant comfort. "But it's definitely the end of something."

"My job?" That would be a good thing, right?

Saskia's eyebrows pull together. "Maybe. But I think it's more linked to this pattern you're in." She indicates the Devil, and under him, the trapped woman.

"So I break free of it? End the pattern?"

"Perhaps," Saskia says.

It's not very definite is it, this whole tarot thing? Or maybe Saskia just doesn't want to tell her the truth, because could this be another death, another of *her* deaths? Could it mean that this life is going to end, only to repeat the pattern all over again? Because she hasn't learned what she needs to learn?

"I think it's a warning," Saskia says, after what feels like several minutes. "As with all tarot cards, things aren't wholly black or white. There is hope on the horizon—a new dawn after the end of something. But I don't think that new dawn will come unless you make different choices to the ones you always make."

"But *what* choices do I always make?"

A sympathetic smile. "Only you can answer that."

Lissa frowns, staring at the cards, trying to think of what they might mean—and realizing distantly that she is getting caught up in all of this. She doesn't know what choices she always makes, though. Choosing to stay in Bath? Well, she can't do anything about that, can she? And that's more one continuous choice, rather than multiple ones. Leaving Chloe alone—leaving her sister alone in previous lifetimes? But then she would need another chance to put that right. She grimaces as she looks back at the Ten of Swords. Does she need to die in order to fix it?

"Now," Saskia picks up, "we look to things that are influencing you now. The Page of Wands here I'd assume is a reference to your sister again—something about her death that still affects you."

Lissa can't help thinking of her mum, whispering bitter words. *You're the reason she's gone.*

"But there's also the High Priestess." The card Saskia points at depicts a grand-looking woman dressed all in white. "She is often related to mysticism, and represents something you aren't consciously aware of yet. There are things being hidden from you, but soon you will be able to peer beyond the veil, so to speak."

At this, Lissa's heart beats a little faster. Does this mean she'll learn why this is happening to her? Does it mean she'll figure out what she needs to do next?

"In terms of where you go from here, the Six of Swords would indicate that there are more positive times ahead." This card is someone being rowed in a boat by a figure with a black hood—why do they all have to be so bloody ominous? "This is a move toward more peaceful times. If, that is"—and here a note of caution creeps into Saskia's voice—"you heed the cards. If you come to terms with the things that are affecting you, and if, perhaps, you uncover the secrets that have previously been hidden from you."

Right, thinks Lissa. Brilliant. No big deal—simply figure out what the memories are trying to tell her and she'll be just dandy. But that's a good thing, right? Because if it's something in her future she can change, it's not about fixing something that has already gone wrong.

"Now, this is a nice card." It's the first time Saskia has said that, and Lissa wonders if that's relief she's hearing. She points to the Knight of Cups—a man on a gray horse. "To me, this would suggest that there is a person about to enter your life, someone who will bring energy and change."

Ash. She knows Saskia is talking about Ash. The energy she feels whenever she's around him.

"Could this person already be in my life?" she asks as casually as she can.

Saskia purses her lips, painted the same pale pink as last time. "Yes. Perhaps. If they are, then I'd say there is going to be a change in the type of relationship you have."

Nerves crawl around Lissa's stomach. "A good change or a bad change?" She thinks of the message she got from him just now—the one waiting for an answer. She thinks of the kiss, and the way she shut things down.

"I think that'll be up to you. I think this person is a chance to make things better. But it's also someone who is ruled by their heart rather than their head. And that's something to be mindful of."

Definitely Ash, she thinks.

"Is that another warning?" she asks.

Saskia smiles. "Advice, Lissa, not warnings." She looks down at the card again. "I think, with the Knight of Cups, there will be an invitation of some sort—not necessarily literal—but remember that it is always up to you whether to accept. Either way, this person has the capacity to change your life in one way or another."

Nerves flutter again at that. So is it already too late? Is it pointless to try to stay away from him because she doesn't feel ready? Because she's trying to protect him from her baggage? Or is this encouragement—that it's okay to go for it? That it's okay to want the kind of love she thinks she had in each of her past lives.

"The Star"—Saskia points to a naked woman pouring water into a pond, with a big star shining over her—"is a reminder to hold on to hope." She offers Lissa one of her kind smiles. "Your experiences have made you who you are, but I think you need to try to accept that you can't change what's happened. Take the time to heal, if you need it. But don't be afraid to take a leap of faith when the time comes."

A leap of faith—with Ash?

"The final card..." She points to the Fool. Lissa grimaces and Saskia laughs lightly. "It's not an indication that *you* are a fool. This card—another of the Major Arcana—indicates new beginnings. It can often be a new job, or a new partner. But for you, I think it is even bigger. I'm getting the sense that it will all come together to offer you a chance to leave the past behind and embark on a new journey, one where you are free of the cycle you're currently trapped in."

It feels out of reach, the idea that she could leave the past behind, even figuratively. How can she do that with her mum constantly around to remind her? But maybe this is about the past lives. Maybe it's about leaving *those* behind. Which is what she wants, isn't it?

Saskia clasps her hands together in her lap and leans toward her. "I think this all means there are some big choices coming up, Lissa. The cards are here for guidance only, but if it feels right to you, if you identify with this cycle you're stuck in, then I would say think about the choices you make. Because maybe it's only by making a different choice to the one you've made in the past that you can get to where you need to be for your future."

And that's all very well, Lissa thinks, but how is she supposed to know what the right choice is if she doesn't understand the wrong one?

Chapter Twenty

Lissa parks the car as close as she can to the address Ash gave her. It's a house right at the southern edges of Bath, trees leafier and greener than they must have been just weeks ago lining each side of the street. She checks the address again on her phone. It's near to where she dropped him after his car broke down.

She glances up and down the street and sees him leaning against a small stone wall, eyes on his phone screen. He's wearing a black jacket, jeans. His dark hair is messed up in that way teenage boys in her secondary school used to try to emulate. And just seeing him, for the first time in weeks, causes an inadvisable prickle of anticipation across her forearms, down the back of her neck. So no. Maybe it wasn't only the alcohol making her want him.

She gets out of the car. She has no idea what she's doing here—he insisted on being cryptic throughout the message exchange, enough that it made her agree just to see what he was planning. That and the tarot reading. The Knight of Cups and a leap of faith. Does it matter, really, if tarot is "real"? If she identified with what was being said, then maybe it's just a different kind of therapy.

She walks along the street to the cottage—gray stone like the wall, with a front garden that looks a little overgrown but still loved, daffodils coming to the end of their lives in one corner. Ash notices her before she reaches him, lifting his head like he can hear her footsteps. She worries for a moment that it will be awkward, given the last time they saw each other, and given the fact that she's so clearly pulled back from him afterward.

But his crooked mouth softens into a smile when he sees her. "Hey. Glad you came."

She smiles back, because it's impossible not to. "I said I would."

Ash jerks his head toward the front door, bright red against the green of the garden. She frowns as she follows him. She's gone through various theories in her mind—none of them involved a small cottage in a pretty suburban area. Her frown deepens when he fishes a key out of his jeans pocket, lets himself right on in. Does he *live* here? Somehow she can't imagine him somewhere like this. And if it really is his house, then why meet her outside?

"Ash, what are we—"

He holds up a hand to silence her as he shuts the door behind them. "Dad?" he calls, and Lissa's stomach does an uncomfortable backflip. He brought her to meet his *father*? Without telling her? "We're here!"

"Ash." She hisses it this time, her voice full of warning. He only glances at her, the picture of innocence.

And she can't say anything more, because there is a man now limping into view from the room on the right. He is older than she would have imagined Ash's father to be, what little hair there is left turned stone gray on his head. He walks with a stick, his left leg seeming to drag behind him, and his skin is tinged with yellow. His eyes, though—she can see Ash in his eyes. A paler blue, but the same shape, somehow the same texture. And his smile, she thinks, as his eyes crease. He has that same easy smile.

Ash walks toward his dad, clapping him lightly—carefully, Lissa thinks—on the back. His dad is wearing slippers, and a checked shirt over fraying jeans. He is clean-shaven, though Lissa can see several nicks there. Despite the stick, he stands very straight.

"Dad, this is Lissa," Ash says. "A friend of mine." He gestures to where she is standing in the doorway, unsure what to do with herself. "Lissa, this is Jack."

"Hi, Jack." Her voice comes out embarrassingly squeaky. But parents are not her thing. She can't even manage a successful relationship with her own, let alone someone else's. Should she shake his hand? Hug him? She settles for an incredibly awkward wave. And sees the way Ash's lips twitch, finding her *amusing* of all things.

"Well come in, come in," Jack says, his voice a pleasant rumble. "Can't stay loitering around in the hallway, not with this bloody leg."

They follow him into the living room, because obviously Lissa has no choice but to go along with it now that she's here. It's clean and tidy, with a neat stack of books on the coffee table—a combination of crime novels and nonfiction from what she can tell. There is a faintly musty smell, though, like a window hasn't been opened in too long. Lissa takes a seat on a blue armchair, while Jack sits on the sofa, where the cushion is indented, like he always sits in the same spot. Over on the mantel above the fireplace, framed photographs smile out at them.

"So, Dad," Ash says, perching on the arm of the sofa. "Did you go to the doctor's today as planned?"

"Can you believe this one?" Jack asks Lissa, jerking his head in his son's direction. "Always checking up on me."

"Dad," Ash says, voice firm. Lissa notices his knee is doing that bouncing thing it sometimes does, like he doesn't want to be sitting still.

"I'll go tomorrow," Jack says, waving it off with a hand. "Or maybe you could see if you could pick the prescription up for me?"

"It's not only the prescription, though, is it? Didn't you have an appointment?"

"I'll go tomorrow," Jack repeats, just as firmly. "Now, let's not get hung up on it," he adds, speaking over Ash's protest. He smiles at Lissa. "We've got company."

Ash hesitates, like he might be about to push the point. Lissa wonders what the appointment was for. She wonders why he didn't go. "All right," he says eventually. He stands up. "I'll go make us some tea, shall I?"

"Good idea," Jack says with a nod. "I'll take butter in mine."

Lissa laughs, assuming it's a joke, but Jack looks at her oddly. She glances at Ash, whose expression flickers, a muscle contracting in his jaw. He catches her looking at him and smiles a little sadly. And Lissa feels a slow sinking sensation inside her.

"So," Jack says, propping his stick between his knees and leaning forward on it, spine still very straight. "Are you a friend or a *friend*?"

Lissa laughs again, surer of the intent this time, and his eyes light with it, the way Ash's do sometimes. "Just a friend," she says firmly. "The regular kind."

"Hmm." It's the same "hmm" that Ash sometimes gives—an inherited sound, apparently.

"Hmm?"

"He doesn't really bring girls to meet me," Jack says, scratching his chin. "Or boys, for that matter. Doesn't seem to be able to make anything stick." Lissa glances in the direction Ash headed in, wondering if he would mind his father telling her this. "There was someone at university," Jack muses. "Missy? Maisie? Can't for the life of me remember. But no one since then. I suppose he moves around too much to settle down."

"I suppose," Lissa hedges. At least they have one thing in common—an inability to commit, form a long-term relationship. Though she imagines Ash finds it easier than her to form short-term ones.

"He mentions you a lot," Jack says, voice a little sly. She decides she likes him more for that slyness.

She also decides to play it innocent. "What's that?"

"Ash. He talks about you. Nothing major," he adds, while she works to keep her face carefully neutral. "I barely know the first thing about you, but he throws your name in every now and then. I remember that. I used to do it with Nicola when we first met. Try to think of ways to bring her into the conversation, just so I could say her name."

Lissa feels her cheeks warm at that, and can think of absolutely nothing to say. She glances around the room by way of distraction, catches sight of a photo above the fireplace of someone who can only be Ash's mum. A wide smile, curly hair, slightly crooked teeth.

"That's her," Jack says, following the direction of Lissa's gaze. "That's my Nicola." He sighs. "It was such a long time ago really, but I still miss her every time I look at her. You ever get that?"

"Yeah," Lissa murmurs. "I get that."

He nods somberly. "Yeah. Fact of life, loss. But it's not a fun one. She was brilliant. Nicola, I mean. Vivacious, no-nonsense. You would've liked her." Lissa wonders how he can possibly know that, having only just met her, but he waves a hand in the air like he can guess her thoughts. "Everyone liked her, but more than that, Ash likes you, so you would've liked her." There's a logic in there, she's sure of it.

Ash likes you. She hates what that does to her insides, making them all fluttery. *Get a bloody grip, Lissa.*

"Things haven't ever been the same since she died," Jack continues, and Lissa looks again at the photo. She thinks of Ash losing his mum. A teenager, he said he was. She feels suddenly, impossibly sad about that. "I thought,

maybe I'll get back to my old self one day. But I haven't."
He sighs again. "I was a bad parent."

"I'm sure you weren't," Lissa says automatically. Because she can feel the love, the warmth coming from him.

"That's kind of you, but I was. I wouldn't leave the house. That's when it started. Well, I suppose it started before then, but it used to be manageable. Nicola made it manageable. But after... Well, Ash had to do everything for me. I couldn't even go out and get milk for a while."

Lissa watches him as he talks, sees the way he twists his walking stick. She wants to ask what he means exactly. Was he depressed? Was it like her mum after Chloe died?

"I think that's what made him, you know," Jack continues, his voice shrewd.

"What do you mean?"

"Ash. He's always so restless, isn't he?"

He seems to want an answer to that. "I guess?" But he just likes to do things, doesn't he? Keep busy, make the most of life. The total opposite of her.

"He is," Jack says, nodding. "He always used to do stupid things that I told him not to. Took part in some car rally when he was a teenager. And did you know he went skydiving when he lived in Morocco?"

Lissa feels her mouth quirk into a smile at the total incredulity in Jack's voice—like no one sane could possibly want to go skydiving. And true, she herself wouldn't want to do it—definitely not—but lots of people enjoy it, don't they? It's not that far-fetched.

"No, I didn't," she says. She didn't even know he'd lived in Morocco. It makes her realize how little she knows about him. It makes her want to ask him about it.

"Yes," Jack says with a sigh. "I think he's seen just how fragile life can be, and he's seen, from me, how fear can eat you up. He fights against that. And that's good," he continues, nodding. "I don't want him to end up like me either."

His mouth thins then, a hard line. And Lissa's heart twists a little at the self-judgment there. She wants to say something, to offer comfort. She starts to open her mouth, not totally sure what she's going to say but hoping it'll come to her, when Jack beats her to it.

"He's been a while, hasn't he?" His voice is different now, a little brighter. But she feels, because she's done it so many times herself, the effort it takes for that brightness to come. Still, he clearly doesn't want to talk about it anymore, and that's fair enough. She's not totally sure how they ended up in such a deep conversation so quickly anyway.

"Maybe he's forgotten where the tea is," Jack says, and he pushes down hard on his stick, making an attempt to get up. He loses his balance as he's rising, rocks back onto the sofa. Lissa jumps to her feet.

"Let me," she says, and he concedes with a nod.

She heads out of the living room, and as she does, she hears a high-pitched incessant beeping. She follows the noise to the kitchen.

Ash is standing there, staring into the fridge. One hand holds a carton of milk, index finger hooked through the handle, the other rests on the open fridge door. He is still—frozen, almost—and doesn't seem to notice the beeping.

"Ash?" Lissa asks hesitantly. He jumps and spins to her. His expression is tight, and his gaze flickers past her, down the corridor. He turns back slowly, reaches for something inside the fridge, then shuts the door. The beeping stops.

He faces her again, and this time he holds something up in his free hand. A set of keys. Lissa frowns at them. "What...?"

"He put them in here," Ash says, his voice hoarse. "My dad."

"Oh." For a moment, she doesn't know what to say. She wonders if she should brush it off, say that everyone misplaces things sometimes, that we can all be absent-minded. That she herself has been known to store keys in the fruit bowl and then forget about them.

Instead, she crosses to him, lays a hand on his rigid arm. She feels his muscles relax, just a little, under her touch. Their gazes hold, and she squeezes his arm. He blows out a breath, nods. And just like that, the right thing to say is nothing at all.

Chapter Twenty-One

Thankfully, there are no more deep conversations about love and loss during the rest of the visit with Ash's dad, but rather general chatter about everything ranging from what the new tax rate will mean for small businesses to whether they'll have another cold snap before summer.

Jack hugs Lissa goodbye when it's time to leave, his checked shirt soft, his arms surprisingly strong. "I hope I see you again," he says, pulling back with a wink.

"I'll see you tomorrow for the doctor's appointment," Ash says, clapping his dad on the back as he did when they got here.

Jack waves a hand in a way that is clearly supposed to say, *yeah, yeah*, but Lissa can tell, from the way he offers her a small, apologetic smile, that he's not actually brushing it off so lightly. Maybe this is why he talked to her about losing his wife—because he wanted her to understand a little about what exists between him and his son. She doesn't know why, exactly, he thought she needed to understand, but she thinks she gets it. She feels that way sometimes—the need to explain why her mum is how she is.

He mentions you a lot.

She supposes that could also be the reason he opened up. She tries hard to control the fizzing in her stomach when she thinks about that.

"He's not well," Ash says as they leave the front garden. Lissa slows her steps. She could see that, of course, but she glances at him, waiting.

"He used to be a military man, you know," he says, and Lissa frowns a little at the change in subject. She tries to picture it—Jack in the army. He seemed so...soft. Not the hard edges she'd expect, which shows how much she knows. Ash looks toward her car, a few meters ahead of them. "You need to head off?"

She hesitates. "I can walk for a bit, if you want?"

"Better idea," he says, heading for her car. "You drive." She raises her eyebrows as he gets out his phone, then shows her his maps app, set to directions for somewhere five minutes away.

Deciding it's easier to go along with it, Lissa follows the directions to Prior Park, a National Trust landscape garden. Ash pays for them both to go in, and leads them into an oasis of green, with views overlooking the stone spires of Bath in the distance.

"Why here?" Lissa asks.

He shrugs. "Why not?" He tugs his hand through his hair. "I guess that's why I'm so used to living in different places," he says, like they're continuing a conversation without a massive detour.

"Huh?"

"Because we moved a lot when I was a kid," he explains. "When my dad was in the army. We settled here once he left, but I suppose it's in my bones, all the traveling about."

"Here?" Lissa asks, gesturing around to the park, with its open meadows and ancient trees. "Fancy place to settle."

Ash laughs, and she's glad to take a little of that sad edge away, one that has lingered since she caught him in the kitchen, staring into the fridge. They're quiet as they walk through the garden, and Lissa waits, not sure if he wants to keep talking.

She gets her answer when he says, "He fought in the Falklands, believe it or not. He met my mum later—she used to work for an NGO, and they met while he was on a posting. He never really talks about it much, so it took me a while to figure out that he had PTSD. Although I suppose I didn't even know what that was, and by the time I understood, he was just Dad and that was the way he was. He always dealt. But when Mum died, it was like . . . I don't know. Like the thing that was holding him together just snapped."

He leads them down to a serpentine lake with a stone bridge reflected in the water underneath. The bridge is two stories high, a mini temple-like structure on top of it.

"How did she die?" Lissa asks. "Your mum."

He glances at her. "Aneurysm." She sucks in a breath and he shakes his head. "No way we could have known. Happens like that sometimes, the doctors said. She had a bad headache and Dad insisted on driving her to hospital, but she died on the way."

Lissa feels sick. "That is awful. I'm so sorry you had to go through it." She realizes it's the same thing he said to her about her sister. This shared language between people who have experienced grief. A club no one wants to be a part of.

Ash steps onto the bridge, running one hand along the stone railing. "He just broke after that," he continues, not really acknowledging her words, staring into the water, his reflection merging with that of the bridge. It's getting late, a cool breeze whisking across the lake, the blue sky slowly muting into subtle orange and pinks. "He used to be able to force himself to leave the house, even when he was stressed. Or, I don't know, maybe Mum forced him. But when she died, he didn't set foot outside for weeks. And he never really got better."

"Agoraphobia," Lissa murmurs.

He gives her a funny look, and she wonders if she's said the wrong thing, giving it a name like that. But then he nods. "Yeah. I guess. He's not well," he repeats. "Physically too, I mean. And he gets confused, and that doesn't help." She thinks again of the keys in the fridge. But maybe talking about that is a step too far just now. Maybe Ash needs time to come to terms with what it might mean.

"He needs to be somewhere with more support, really," he says, running a hand over his face. Tired, she realizes. He looks tired. "He has a cleaner, and he gets food shopping delivered, but it's not enough, and if I'm not here..."

"It's why you came back," she says quietly, and he nods.

"Yeah. He had a fall. The stairs are getting a bit much now, with his leg, and he got up in the middle of the night and...He called me when it happened. He called me, and I wasn't there."

"It wasn't your fault that he fell, Ash," she says, keeping her gaze on his face even if he doesn't look back. He shakes his head, and she knows that look. She knows it's pointless trying to argue. "But he was okay?" she asks instead.

"Yeah," he mutters, and there is a trace of bitterness to his voice now. "Yeah, he was okay. But he might not have been." The guilt, she remembers. He'd said he understood the guilt. "I tried to take him to look around a care home a while back. It was actually really nice—assisted living more than anything, nice gardens, people seemed friendly. But he couldn't get out the car when we got there. And I just couldn't do it to him. I couldn't force him to leave his home."

You don't get it, she'd told him. How wrong she was.

They are quiet for a moment, then Lissa leans back against the railings. "Why did you ask me to meet you today?"

"Because..." He runs a hand down the back of his neck. "Because I meant what I said, about seeing the whole you." Something inside her tightens at that. At the way he holds her gaze as he says it. "I can't quite explain it, but I *feel* it. So I suppose I want you to know the whole me, too. And this"—he gestures around, not at the park but at something bigger—"my dad, is part of it." The part hiding, she thinks, beneath the smiles and easy laugh. She wonders if that's the part she feels drawn to.

"I also..." He leans both hands on the railing next to her. "I know you don't like that I've seen you when things get too much." It's a kind way of phrasing it—*seen you at your worst* would be more accurate. "But I thought maybe you'd understand that I'm not ignoring it. That I do get it." Because he's lived with it, she thinks. Or a version of it.

But Lissa isn't that bad. It's a horrible thought, but it comes before she can stop it, the way thoughts often do. She can leave the house, she can function. She doesn't ever fall apart completely. But would that happen if she let it get worse? She wants to think not, but how can she be sure? She wonders briefly if that's another reason Ash brought her here—as some kind of warning. Somehow, though, she doesn't think so.

"Also," he says, and his tone is a touch lighter, "I wanted you to meet my dad."

She laughs—and she loves how he can make her laugh after all that. He grins down at her, then, without warning, pushes himself up onto the stone railing and starts walking along the edge of the bridge toward the mini temple-like structure.

Lissa's heart lurches. "What are you doing?" It's a harsh snap. She didn't mean it to be. Her throat is dry as she looks down at the water. Imagines him falling. Imagines him hitting his head, the way the blood would gush…

He doesn't seem to hear her. She follows him on the main walkway. "Ash," she says, trying to level out her voice.

He glances down at her, raising one eyebrow. "You know, I've got pretty good balance."

She bites her lip, looking at the water again. It's not that far, she tells herself. He'd be fine.

She can still see it, though. Him falling. Bleeding.

Water surrounding her. Pulling her under.

Snap out of it, Lissa.

He's looking at her curiously. "You okay?"

"Yes." She manages a smile. "Just thinking, it would be a shame if you got all wet."

He grins, slow and sure. "*Would* it now?" She can feel heat rising to her cheeks, even as there's a pulse of something right through her core just from the way he's looking at her. He jumps down next to her. "Not a fan of bridges, huh?"

"Bridges are fine. I'm less of a fan of falling off them."

He makes a tutting noise. "One of only four Palladian bridges, this. You shouldn't be scared of it, you should be *admiring* it."

She rolls her eyes. "I'm not *scared* of it." *I'm scared for you,* she adds silently, knowing that it would make her sound like a total lunatic if she said it out loud.

Ash comes to a stop underneath the temple structure, looking like something out of a painting with the lake as his backdrop. A scene she'd like to draw herself if she had the time, the space.

She thinks about what Jack said—about how Ash is the way he is because he is so desperate not to be like him. She wonders if there's any truth in that. The past defines the two of them, she supposes, no matter how much they might fight against it. Maybe that's her problem too—maybe it's her past lives defining her. Experiencing the same grief over and over. And if that's the pattern she's stuck in, how is she supposed to break free of it? How is she supposed to let go of a past that stretches back not just in her lifetime, but in multiple others?

She watches Ash, the low sunlight filtering through a gap in the structure falling over one side of his face. He glances over at her, raises her eyebrows when he sees she's still standing there staring.

Only by making a different choice can she have the future she's meant to have. She doesn't know what that means. But she does know that she's made the choice before to walk away from him.

A leap of faith. That's what Saskia said.

Her skin is buzzing as she moves very deliberately toward him. Tiny currents of electricity spark her skin—that feeling she usually only gets once a year, when the need to act, to prove that she is still alive, becomes overpowering. Her eyes are level on his, and a slight crease forms between his brows—not a frown, exactly, but like he is trying to figure out what she's going to do next.

She stops in front of him, and he goes very still as she reaches out, places her palms on his chest. On the railings, she sees his fingers flex, though he doesn't move his hands, like he's being careful to stay exactly as he is.

"Thank you," she says, tilting her chin up. His eyes are even bluer out here, with the sunlight bouncing off the water. "For bringing me to meet your dad."

Her pulse is spiking against her wrist as she pushes up on her tiptoes, lightly pressing her lips to his. It's nothing.

Barely a whisper of a kiss. But she feels the curve of his smile against her lips. Hears the soft, gentle exhale, the sound something akin to relief. Feels that same sensation course through her body, uncertainty chased away as something tightens in her. Something that makes her want to sink deeper. It alarms her a little—the intensity of it. Alarms her enough that she eases back.

Only then do his arms come out, fingers gently skimming down her sides, then taking her hands gently, holding her in place. He encircles her wrists, thumbs moving to the underside—almost like he's reading her pulse. At his touch, it jumps, giving her away, and the corner of his mouth lifts. His eyes are darker now, a deep, inky blue.

Neither of them moves. Neither of them takes it any further. They stay still, Lissa's heart thrumming against her ribs, an awareness she's never felt before running down her spine. Just from the way he's looking at her. Just from the lightest touch, the tiniest point of contact, skin against skin.

Nothing else happens. But still, it feels like something has changed.

It feels like a choice has been made.

Chapter Twenty-Two

She is clutching her sketchbook as she arrives at the café, breathing in the scent of coffee and croissants. It's hot, even though it's early. Soon shimmering heat will sweep across the city, surrounding the landmarks with a haze.

He's waiting for her at their usual table, the one where they first met. Her stomach twists and rolls when she sees him—a combination of nerves, excitement and dread. His face, that beautiful, angular face, breaks into a smile as he spots her. Her heart flares in the same way it always does whenever she sees that smile, and for a brief moment, she wishes she didn't feel like this. Then it would be so much easier to leave him.

Because this is it—she got in. An art school in Florence, something that still feels surreal. She didn't really expect to be accepted. She hasn't even told her parents yet, because she knows what the reaction will be. But she's going. She has to give it a chance, has to try to break free. She doesn't want to think too hard about what will happen to her mother once she's left, or of the blame that will be thrown her way for abandoning her.

How ironic, that she received the letter today of all days. On the anniversary of the bomb that killed her sister. She's been to see her mother this morning, and it was awful. Her father didn't come home last night—she doesn't know what time he'll be back, or if he'll stay away, unable to deal with his wife's spiraling grief, her inability to move on even after all these years.

It wasn't the right time to tell her mother about Florence this morning. She'll break the news in a few days. But before that, she has to tell *him*. Has to tell him she won't be coming to Hollywood with him. That was never her dream anyway. And she can't wait around for these moments in Paris, can't sit here hoping for something more between them when he is so desperate to chase all that life has to offer.

She reaches the table, and he kisses her on the cheek, lightly, respecting the fact that they are in public.

"I have something to tell you," he announces without preamble, that smooth velvet voice that she loves.

She sets the sketchbook on her lap. He doesn't comment on it. She always carries one around with her, after all. Only this time, the letter is inside it. "Well that's a coincidence, because I have something to tell you too."

He grins, then gestures. "You first."

"No, you," she insists. Because she thinks she knows what it is he wants to say—she thinks he's finally going to tell her that this is it, that he's leaving for America, chasing the bigger-budget films, with bigger orchestras.

He cocks his head. "Should we argue about it a bit, do

you think? Just for show?" She laughs, but waits. It'll be easier to tell him if she already knows he's leaving her.

He leans forward, sunlight bouncing off his pale gaze. She's tried countless times to get the exact shade of his eyes in her drawings—somehow, she never can.

"I'm staying in Paris," he says, and his voice is soft, almost a caress.

She blinks. "You're . . . staying? As in permanently?"

He nods. "Permanently. What happened with my dad . . ." He trails off, and she reaches for his hand automatically, wanting to comfort him. His father died a few months ago, and she knows it's been awful for him. Not just the loss itself, but because he wasn't there when it happened—he was with her instead. He doesn't blame her for it. But she knows he blames himself.

He shakes his head, like he's shaking himself out of something. "It made me realize—I've been chasing the idea of something better since before I can remember." He watches their joined hands as he talks. "Chasing excitement, like I only have so long to experience it. But my dad and you have made me realize that I don't want that. I don't want to be chasing an idea. Maybe it would be good to sit still, to appreciate everything I have." He lifts his gaze to hers. "And with you, I know I already have everything I need."

Something tightens within her as she swallows. "I don't think I know what you mean," she says slowly, not sure whether to believe him and not sure, with everything so tight inside her, how she feels about it.

His thumb circles against her wrist. "I want to be with

you," he murmurs. "I want to stay here with you. I know America isn't what you want—but Paris, that could be for both of us." He takes a breath, and she watches the movement of his chest. "I want you to marry me—if you want that too."

For a second, she can only stare at him, her body not catching up with what her brain is hearing. She sees the doubt flicker over his face, feels the way his thumb stills against her pulse. "Only if you—"

"Of course I do!" The words burst from her, eclipsing all thought of the letter, of art school and Florence. "Of course I want that." She takes his face in her hands, not caring about the disapproval emanating from the lady at the table next to them. She kisses him, brief and hard. And feels the sense of rightness as she does. Because there are other art schools, aren't there? There will be other chances.

And what is today, the significance of the date, if not a reminder to take the things you want, because you don't know how long you'll be alive to experience them? It was meant to happen today, she knows. She was meant to face this choice, on this date, to remind her to live for the moment. And in this moment, what she wants, above anything else, is him.

A laugh bubbles from her and she gets to her feet. She pulls him up, hearing his laugh merge with hers. "Come on," she demands. "We need to go somewhere. We need to celebrate."

"We *are* somewhere," he says, still laughing. "And trust me, I've got ideas on how we can celebrate." The way he says it, voice dropping low, his gaze holding hers, sends a bolt of something right through her. Then she laughs again, because this is good, this is perfect. This is exactly what was supposed to happen.

She links her fingers with his, drags him from the table, away from the café and down the street. She doesn't know where exactly she's heading, only that she needs to go *somewhere*.

"Wait, what did you want to tell me?" he asks. But she just shakes her head in answer. She doesn't want to mention it, because she knows it'll make him question his decision, knows he'll worry about holding her back, and she doesn't want that.

She's not concentrating as she charges across the next road. He's speaking, but her head is too light and his words blend into something she can't quite understand. She doesn't hear it until it's too late. The car horn. The screeching of brakes. When she turns to see it, it's in slow motion, like it is happening to someone else, someone onscreen, someone far away.

A car, coming toward her in the street. She's paralyzed, her mind moving far too slowly for the urgency of the situation. She hears her name screamed from what sounds like a long way away. Then she feels him pushing her out of the road. Trying to save her.

But it's not enough. She feels the impact of the bonnet, feels her skull cracking against tarmac. Another blast of the horn, people screaming. Her ears ringing. Only this isn't a panic attack. This isn't her body thinking it's been hurt—she really has been.

Her movements are slow. She can taste blood in her mouth as she rolls on the tarmac. She doesn't think she can feel her legs, doesn't think she can stand.

She tries to blink through the pain, tries to think. She can see shattered glass on the tarmac, and there are people running toward her, blocking her view.

But through the chaos, she can see him, farther down the road. He tried to push her out of the way and took most of the impact in the process. There is blood seeping from a crack in his skull, his neck crooked at an impossible angle.

She knows he's dead. Even as she tries to crawl toward him, she knows. And she knows with a certainty she can't explain that she will die today too.

To Nicole's credit, she only does the smallest of double-takes when she opens her front door to see not just Lissa, but Ash too, standing on her doorstep. Her gaze sweeps over him, taking in the black jacket slung over one arm, the messy dark hair, the stubble that Lissa is learning he lets grow out because he can't be bothered to shave. Then she smiles.

"Lissa. And Ash? Come in!"

It's impressive, really, how she immediately treats Ash like a part of the family—or at least a good, well-known friend of Lissa's—when in reality it was only a few days ago that Lissa asked her dad if it was okay to bring Ash to his birthday barbecue. After all, he took her to meet *his* dad, so it's only polite to return the favor. Plus, she thought it might make the barbecue easier to bear—someone to share the small talk with.

Nicole takes the bottle of damson gin (a more interesting offering than wine, according to Ash) with a smile of thanks, then gestures toward the back garden. "Come on. Everyone's out here—we got so lucky with the weather, didn't we?"

She's right—it's only May, and already it feels like summer has arrived, warm enough that Nicole is wearing a sleeveless dress, white with blue flowers on, complete with fancy sandals that Lissa is sure Darcy would covet. It makes her glad she spent time picking out the playsuit she herself is wearing, rubbing fake tan into her legs. Even if the outfit choice wasn't really with Nicole in mind. And if the way Ash's eyes dropped straight to her legs when she met him outside is anything to go by, it's already had the desired effect.

"So you decided against the Maldives then?" Lissa asks as they head through the house.

"Hmm?" Nicole is wearing butterfly earrings, which jangle as she walks.

"The Maldives. You were going to go there on holiday. For Dad's birthday."

"Oh, yes. Well I looked into it and turns out it's rather more expensive than I thought. So it's shelved for the future—definitely one for the bucket list, though." So it wasn't that they changed their minds about inviting her, Lissa thinks.

"The Maldives," Ash says with a low whistle. "Fancy."

Lissa glances at him. "Surprised you've never been. Didn't fancy working from there for a year, then?"

He grins. "Well, sure. If I could find a way to stay there without selling my spleen."

"Bone marrow would probably get you more on the black market," she says, offhand.

He huffs out a laugh. "It's scary that you know that."

There's an array of bottles and little cans of Fever Tree on the table as they reach the kitchen, and Nicole adds the damson gin to the selection. The sliding door is open to the patio, where several dozen people mill around. Lissa had no idea her dad had this many friends—she recognizes literally none of them.

"Apparently they have great diving," Ash says, and Lissa frowns at him, not following the thread. "In the Maldives," he expands.

Nicole's smile immediately becomes more sincere. "Oh, you dive?"

"Yep. Learned on my gap year."

"Of course you had a gap year," Lissa mutters. From the way his mouth crooks up, she knows he heard her.

"It's wonderful, isn't it?" Nicole says.

"*You* dive?" Lissa can't help the incredulity, something that causes both Ash and Nicole to look at her. "Sorry," she says quickly. "I mean...you dive?" She tries to make it more casual, sees Ash give her a sarcastic thumbs-up behind Nicole's back.

"Oh yes. It's why I wanted to go. Your dad doesn't, but he could do a DSD, and I think Elsie would *love* it."

Lissa has no idea what a DSD is—and she can't really imagine anything worse than being trapped underwater in a neoprene suit—but she nods along as Ash and Nicole start exchanging stories of their best dives. She squints at Nicole, trying to picture her in a mask. But she just can't imagine her tidy interior-designer stepmum in all the scuba gear.

"Sorry, Lissa," Nicole says, when several minutes have passed with Lissa attempting to look politely interested.

"No," she says quickly. "It sounds very…fishtastic."

Ash's lips twitch at her lame attempt at a joke. "You should try it. I'll take you." The way he says it, like it's the most natural thing in the world, does something interesting—and a little unnerving—to her insides.

She sees the way Nicole's eyes flick to her, then away, down to the kitchen tiles, like she doesn't want to look directly at her.

"Not my thing," she says lightly. "I don't really swim." He gives her one of those looks—like he understands more than what she's saying—and Nicole, thankfully, clears her throat.

"Well, what can I get you both to drink?"

"She seems nice," Ash says, when they are outside with drinks in their hands, hovering at the edge of the patio.

"Yeah." Lissa takes a sip of her Prosecco—it's a party after all. "I guess she is."

"You guess?"

"I don't know her all that well."

"Have you tried to get to know her?"

It's a genuine question, no judgment in his tone, but still, it pulls her up short. She's not used to people asking her stuff like that so directly. "I guess not," she says after a beat.

"There she is!" Lissa turns at the sound of her dad's voice to see him crossing the patio toward them, beaming. He switches the spatula he's holding to his left hand, holds out his right as he nears. "And you must be Asher." And of course, he has extended Ash's name for absolutely no reason at all.

Ash raises one eyebrow at Lissa, who shrugs, trying to convey that it has nothing to do with her.

"Thanks for letting me gatecrash," Ash says as they shake hands.

"No! Thrilled to have you here!" Dad does in fact sound thrilled—over the top, maybe, but still thrilled. "Maybe don't crash the actual gate, though, Nicole will have a fit."

"Happy birthday, Dad," Lissa says, rising on tiptoes to kiss his cheek. She hands over her present—a card with gift vouchers inside, dinner for two at a fancy restaurant-slash-wine bar in Bath.

"This is wonderful!" he exclaims. "Let me know when you're free and I'll book it in."

It takes Lissa a moment to realize what he's getting at—he thinks it's supposed to be a meal out with *her*. "Well actually," she begins, but the rest of her sentence—*it's for you and Nicole*—gets swallowed up by the way he's beaming at her.

"David!" someone calls from next to the smoking barbecue. "How burnt do you want these sausages?"

Her dad leaves them with a promise to catch up later, and Lissa and Ash find a spot on the garden steps, next to a bed of tulips and peonies. Lissa sees Elsie down the end of the garden with her friend Jess and waves. She considers it a win when Elsie waves back. She wondered what the fallout was from their unauthorized trip into Bath—no one ever called her about it, so she figured it couldn't have been *that* bad.

She shifts on the step, the concrete warm against her calves. Her knee knocks against Ash's as she does so. Neither of them moves away. She glances up at him, finds him watching her.

"So how's your dad doing?" she asks.

"He's okay. Not great, but okay. The doctors have him on new medication, which seems to be helping." Lissa nods, and Ash sighs. "I'm thinking I might need to move in with him for a bit, actually. He keeps telling me not to, but..." He trails off, but she gets it. She found it hard to move out of her mum's house, even when space was definitely what they both needed.

"How's your mum?" he asks, and she frowns. Is he reading her thoughts now? He shrugs in explanation. "You don't talk about her much, so I'm reading between the lines a bit here."

"She's... It's complicated."

"Complicated how?"

She chews her lip, thinking of how to explain. "So on the

one hand I think she might struggle a bit with depression, or a version of it." She never really voices this thought out loud, but seeing Ash with his dad makes it easier. "And on the... well, on the same hand, I guess, we don't have the best relationship." She looks away from him, toward the stepping stones making their way down a perfectly mown lawn toward a decorative fountain. "She sort of blames me for what happened," she admits. "To Chloe."

She wonders if he'll say that he's sure she doesn't—everyone says that, quick to jump in and offer reassurance. Only it's not reassuring, because they don't know, do they? But he doesn't. Instead he takes a moment, then says slowly, "I imagine something like that... it can either tear you apart or bring you together."

She lets out a low exhale. "Right. Exactly that."

She can feel his gaze on the side of her face. "You ever think maybe she blames herself, too?"

She frowns at that. On some level, she supposes it must be there, but it is always eclipsed by the blame placed on Lissa.

"So how did the interview go?" Ash asks, changing the subject. Which is good, because her dad's birthday barbecue is not the time for an in-depth conversation about her mother. "Marketing for Mind, right?"

She smiles. "It went well, I think." The interviewer remembered her name, Lissa had a genuine answer for why she wanted to work there, and she didn't feel like she'd babbled *too* much. "I find out if I make it to second interview next week."

"That's great. Well, fingers crossed and all that. I'm sure you impressed them."

She rolls her eyes. "Because you were spying on me in the interview?"

"Yep," he says easily. "Got you bugged, hope that's okay."

She laughs and shifts as subtly as she can to try to put space between their thighs. She's too aware of how close they are. It's distracting.

He gives her a friendly nudge with his shoulder. "I'm sure because you're impressive."

The compliment is given so easily, she doesn't really know how to take it. She glances at him, finds his eyes right there, waiting for her. She can't help her gaze being drawn to his lower lip. They've not talked about it—the fact they've kissed not once, but twice now. That *she* kissed him. Things seem easy between them, the same as always. But there is an awareness humming around her body, a kind of *what if.* What if he kisses her, this time? What if he *doesn't?*

She realizes what she's doing and looks away, taking a swallowed breath. She glances at him again, and he smiles— easy, natural.

She drums her fingers on her thigh, over her playsuit. "Ash?"

"Hmm?"

"Do you believe in past lives?"

He raises his eyebrows. "I suppose I've never really thought about it."

"If you did think about it, though," she presses, "would you believe in it?"

"I don't know. Maybe. I think there's a lot of stuff out there that we don't understand—that maybe at some point science will shed light on things we haven't even got close to figuring out. Like the near-death experiences people claim to have, and people who swear they can feel the energy of a ghost in their house. Maybe there's an explanation for all of that. I mean, people used to believe the world is flat, right? So maybe there will be a time in the future where everyone's like, oh my God, I can't believe they didn't believe in ghosts back then, when there is all this evidence." He glances at her. "Or past lives, I suppose."

She nods, pursing her lips. Now it's his gaze that drops to her mouth, just briefly. She feels the echo of a tingle in her lips.

"Why?" he asks.

She hesitates. "No reason." She doesn't want him to think she's *totally* insane, after all, not when she might just be getting away with the endearing side of crazy for now.

"Hmm," he says, making that familiar noise in the back of his throat.

"What?"

"Well, that's the kind of 'no reason' that definitely doesn't mean no reason."

She laughs, lifts one hand to brush her hair away from her face. "I just…"

"You think you had a past life?"

"Maybe," she hedges. *Or several. And something bad happened in all of them.*

She can still feel it, the impact of the car in her dream last night. Can still taste the blood, see his broken body lying on the tarmac, too far away for her to reach.

"Lissa?" She blinks Ash's face back into focus. "You okay?"

She smiles. "Sorry. Yes, I'm okay."

She feels colder than she did a second ago, though, even as she tries to shake it off. She always knew she must have died before—because how would she have past lives if not? But last night she woke up crying and was unable to stop. It had happened on the anniversary of her sister's death. She'd died on that day. Which might mean there was something in her punishment theory after all.

"The swimming thing," Ash says.

"Huh?"

"Earlier, when you said you didn't swim." Right. And she'd been careful—using the word *don't* rather than *can't*. "Is that because of your sister? Because she drowned?"

She hesitates, then sighs. "Astute, aren't you?" Because she can hardly tell him that no, she doesn't think it is—she thinks it's because *she* drowned once. It's too easy to go back there, to feel the water flooding her lungs. Can still feel a hand grasping hers, trying to pull her to safety. Only the water didn't want to let her go.

So he didn't pull her to safety, did he? Instead, he drowned too.

"Nah," Ash says with a smile. "I just pay attention."

She glances sideways at him. "Anyone ever tell you that's slightly annoying?"

He laughs, just as a head-shaped shadow falls over his

face. Lissa glances up, then jumps to her feet. "Dad!" She didn't realize he was lurking there.

"Just came to see if you guys need a top-up," he says with a smile.

"I'll come with you," Ash offers, standing up.

Lissa sits back down, watching him strike up an easy conversation with her dad as they head to the kitchen—he really is good at that, isn't he? Almost immediately, Elsie takes the spot on the step next to her. "So is that your boyfriend?" she asks without preamble.

Lissa laughs. "No." Does she want him to be, though?

"Huh. Jess and I had a bet he was."

"I'm not sure that's how bets work," Lissa says drily.

"Whatever. Anyway, Jess had to go and now I'm bored."

"Ah."

"So do you think you could convince Dad to let me go into town? There's a bunch of people meeting there."

"I think my powers of persuasion with him might be pretty limited. Plus it's his birthday—don't you want to hang around?"

Elsie makes a face, making her look younger than fourteen, just as Ash comes back with a glass of Prosecco for Lissa, a bottle of Corona for him. "What's up?" he asks, handing her the glass.

"Elsie is bored." Elsie gives her a look at that, and she wonders if she wasn't supposed to divulge said boredom.

"Well we can't have that," Ash says. "We could play a game?" Elsie gives him a cynical look that makes Lissa want to laugh.

"Pictionary?" Lissa suggests. Elsie huffs.

There's a beat of quiet.

"I've got it," Ash says, clicking his fingers. "We could build the Eiffel Tower out of beer bottles."

Both Lissa and Elsie stare at him, making Lissa sure she's not the only one wondering where the hell that came from. But Elsie shrugs. "Okay." And that, apparently, is as enthusiastic as they're going to get.

Ash and Elsie hunt down empty beer bottles together, and Ash draws a diagram on a napkin—Lissa is sure that Mia, with her engineer brain, would have plenty to say about his efforts. She leaves them to it while they're still on the planning phase, and goes to get herself a burger.

At the barbecue, her dad swings an arm around her in the way he only does when he's had a few drinks. "It's nice to see you and Elsie hanging out together."

"Yeah. It's nice to hang out with her." He takes his arm away from her to slide a burger onto a plate. "Dad?"

"Hmm?"

She hesitates. "Did you ever try to teach me to swim?"

He glances at her, something flickering over his face, gone too quickly to read. Then he shakes his head. "No. You were always too scared of the water to try."

She nods slowly. Well, that would make sense, wouldn't it?

"Your mum tried to do those mother–baby swimming classes with you," he continues, "but you cried so much on the first one that she didn't take you back. We tried a few times when you were older, but you still hated it. Then, after Chloe..."

"Yeah," Lissa agrees, pulling a hand through her hair. After that, no one would have wanted to make her.

"Dad, I'm..." She doesn't quite know what she's going to say—sorry for bringing this up on your birthday?—but she doesn't get to finish anyway, because there is the sound of glass smashing against the patio. Lissa turns just as the Eiffel Tower collapses. Elsie lets out a wail of despair. Ash swears, loudly. And Lissa sees it—a glint of red in the sun. Blood.

Her heart lurches, and she drops her burger, already running.

"Who's hurt?" she demands when she reaches them. She scans Elsie first—her sister.

"We're fine," Elsie says with an easy wave. "Ash just..."

But Ash is holding out his hand, palm up, and she can see the cut now, deep, blood flowing far too quickly. Her head spins, nausea swells.

"Lissa?" Elsie asks. "You look a bit pale. Do you not like blood or something?"

"I'm fine," Lissa says shortly. She breathes through it, grabs Ash's hand to look at it. "You're hurt."

"It's only a—"

"You're *hurt*," she repeats.

"I'll get the first-aid kit." This from Nicole, somewhere nearby.

Lissa drags Ash into the kitchen and over to the sink, turning on the tap and thrusting his hand under it. The water turns from clear to murky pink. Blood coating the pavement. Only they're not on the pavement, and there is not much blood, not anymore.

Get a fucking grip, Lissa.

She keeps it together as she takes the first-aid kit from Nicole, bandages Ash's hand. He holds very still, saying nothing. Like he knows she needs to do it, to reassure herself. He only speaks when she backs away.

"You're shaking," he murmurs, taking one of her hands in his uninjured one.

She swallows. "I told you—I'm not that great in medical emergencies."

"You did okay. Hey." He tightens his grip on her hand, because alarmingly, horribly, tears are stinging her eyes. "I'm okay, Liss," he says gently.

But is she? She can hear ringing in her ears, a warning sign of an anxiety attack. And who can blame her for those? Of course she has a bloody health anxiety complex—she's died several times before.

Her breathing is getting faster as Ash moves to her, then slowly wraps both his arms around her. She lets out a shuddering breath as he runs a hand down her back, and inhales the earthy, woody scent of him.

"I'm okay," he murmurs again. "You're okay." Because he doesn't let go, she allows her head to rest on his shoulder, allows herself to close her eyes. And feels her heartbeat settle to the rhythm of his.

He eases back, just a few centimeters. His fingers come up to trail a path down her face. Her breathing hitches for an entirely different reason when they reach her jaw, and he notices the sound, his gaze flashing to her mouth again, this time with more intent.

Her arms have come around him too, she notices, and she moves them up his back to rest on his lovely broad shoulders. She tips her head back, waits for his gaze to meet hers. And feels that pleasant pull inside her as his pupils darken.

Then Nicole comes into the kitchen, making them jump apart like they've been caught in the act rather than, really, standing here completely innocently.

"All okay in here?" Nicole asks. "Do I need to drive anyone to A&E?"

"All good," Lissa says, looking away from Ash. "Thank you."

"Yes, thank you," Ash repeats. "And I'm sorry. Maybe playing with glass bottles is a bad idea."

Lissa wonders if Nicole will be cross—it could have been her daughter who was injured, after all. But she's smiling. "Mm. Think I heard that somewhere. There's a burger outside for both of you when you're ready." And with that, she steps back through the sliding doors.

Lissa clears her throat. "Well, I suppose we'd better get back out there..."

He grabs her hand when she turns to leave. "Come away with me."

"What?"

"Next month. Let's go somewhere for a weekend."

Her pulse skitters. "Why?" she asks, before she can think better of it.

He laughs a little. "Because I like you." So easy. "Because we get on. Because it'll be fun."

She stares at him, feeling her heart drum against her rib cage, a prickle of something—nerves? Anticipation? Warning?—running down her spine.

"Come on, Liss," he says, and his fingers move from her hand to trail up her forearm, leaving goose bumps in their wake. "What have you got to lose?"

Is this what Saskia saw in her cards? The Knight of Cups issuing an invitation. A choice she'll have to make. And a leap of faith.

She takes a deep breath. "Okay."

She loves it, the way light flares in his eyes. "Okay? Really?"

She laughs, squeezes his hand. "Yes. Really."

Chapter Twenty-Three

Lissa wakes as Ash pulls the car onto a gravel driveway, and surreptitiously tries to wipe the drool off the corner of her mouth. She blinks, feeling disoriented as she glances around. Ahead of them is a gray stone cottage that looks to her like it's standing right on top of a cliff. Close enough to make her wonder if it will still be here in a few years' time, or if it will fall, piece by piece, into the ocean below, as waves and wind and salt eat away at it. The definition of living on the edge.

Beyond the cottage she can see the ocean, stretching out to the horizon over the gray and green cliff, a beautiful turquoise blue under the clear sky and shining sun. In the distance, a few white boats bob on the waves, a picture-perfect image of the Cornish coastline.

She glances at Ash as he switches off the engine—and with it, the air conditioning. "Sorry I fell asleep."

One corner of his mouth lifts in a smile. "No problem. You're cute when you sleep." His gaze slides to her, a teasing light in his eye. "Even when you drool."

She laughs. So much for surreptitious. They get out

of the car, the hot air immediately clinging to her skin. A heat wave, according to the radio—one that they are either encouraged to make the most of or hide inside from, depending on who you ask. She can feel sweat start to prick the backs of her thighs as she lifts her small suitcase out of the car.

She ties her hair into a bun, sees Ash watching her as her vest top lifts, showing the barest hint of her stomach above her shorts. Her skin prickles in awareness, even as he moves away. She went for casual for the drive down, trying not to look—or dress—like she'd spent actual hours agonizing over her wardrobe. Agonizing over the whole bloody trip, in reality, wondering whether to make some excuse and bail. They haven't even slept together. What the fuck does she thinks she's playing at, coming on a weekend away?

It was Darcy, via voice note, who convinced her to stick with the plan. *You've been friend-dating for like six months. I don't think it's that inappropriate to go away together. I went to Berlin on a long weekend with someone I met in a club once. Admittedly he turned out to be completely obsessed with his cousin, but don't let that put you off.*

She follows Ash into the cottage. There is a definite sense of isolation here. Ash found the place, but she looked it up before they left—the nearest town is over forty minutes away, hence her insistence that they stop for supplies en route.

The interior is gorgeous. Abandoning her suitcase by the front door, Lissa immediately heads left, into a kitchen with gray slate flooring and beautiful teal cupboards. A coffee machine stands on one of the wooden counters, and a full fruit basket sits center on the kitchen table, next to brochures for activities in the area.

Ash opens one of the cupboards, somehow finding glasses on the first attempt. He fills one with water, offers it to her. Because she can't think of what else to do, she takes it.

"Thanks," she says, taking a sip while he gets himself one too. "This place is amazing."

He nods in agreement, moving to the window, which looks out over a small garden fenced by an old stone wall. "It really is."

There is quiet between them, Lissa leaning against the counter, Ash with his back to her, facing the window. You can hear the waves even through the closed window, but apart from that, it feels so still. She is very aware, in all this quiet, that it is just the two of them. That they have come away for the weekend with no discussion over what it means. She knows, from her Google search, that there are two bedrooms. She doesn't think he'd hold her to any kind of expectation, but what is he thinking? What is he hoping for?

He turns from the window, looks at her. And she feels it between them—the unsteadiness in the air.

"We should go for a walk," she blurts out. Her voice is too loud, and she sees him attempt to control a smile. Is that a knowing glint in his eye? Of course it bloody is.

"Sure," he says easily. "Let's do that."

They find a path that takes them over the cliffs and along the coastline. She can see a way down to the sandy beach below, but right now, they opt for walking rather than sunbathing, and although it's hot, it feels easier to be moving. Easier not to wonder what will happen later, at the cottage, or what it means that he asked her to come away with him. What it means that she said yes.

"You know, I think I've been to Cornwall once before," she says musingly as her legs loosen, stretching to cover more ground and fall into step with his long stride.

He crooks an eyebrow at her. "You *think?*"

"I must've only been about eight or something, so I can't be totally sure it was Cornwall. But I remember sitting in the car for what felt like a lifetime, playing all the car games with my mum." It makes her smile a little to think of it. She can remember her mum's face as she turned to smile at her in the back seat, rounder, younger and happier than it is now.

She remembers, too, sitting with a bucket and spade, collecting shells and presenting them to her dad. Remembers watching her mum splashing in the waves in her swimming costume, holding a toddler in a blue hat.

"Chloe was there," she murmurs. "She was at the beach with us." And Chloe hadn't inherited Lissa's fear of water, because Lissa can hear her giggling as their mum took her a little deeper, holding her so she could dip her toes in the ocean.

"Do you remember much about her?" Ash asks, and though she's looking out at the ocean, not at him, she can feel his eyes tracing her face, like he's checking she's okay to talk about it.

"I remember bits," she says. "But it's like, I don't know..." She bites her lip. "This might sound awful," she begins slowly. But she can tell him, she thinks. She can tell him, even though she never talks about it with anyone else. "It's like she doesn't feel like a real person, in my mind. She exists as my little sister, but only as I knew her then. I was twelve and she was six, and when she died we all just...stopped talking about her." She swallows. "They never wanted to say her name. My parents. Or when my mum did, it was when she was...struggling. It was never about Chloe, but rather the loss of her. So it feels like I never really knew her. Like I didn't appreciate her for *her*.

"I do remember some stuff, though," she goes on quickly, feeling the need to justify. "I remember she was learning the recorder at school. I remember that she was *terrible* at it." She laughs a little at that, and Ash smiles, his features softening. "I remember her being in the nativity play. I was so annoyed that I got dragged along to watch, but she played a shepherd and she was so cute. She used to force me to play Barbies with her when I was trying to convince myself I was way too old for that. She used to let me paint her nails, to practice. She had the *best* smile."

She can feel tears pricking the backs of her eyes, but she smiles. It's nice, she realizes, to talk about Chloe. To remember that she existed, despite the tragic fleetingness of her life, that she was loved. To have *proof* of that in her memories, even buried as they are. She'll have to tell Elsie, she thinks. Share bits of the sister she lost with the sister she still has.

"What about you?" she asks. "Do you remember your mum? Or, I mean, of course you do." He was sixteen when she died, so he had nearly as long with her as he's now had without. "I just mean…"

He takes her hand, squeezes. Then links his fingers with hers as they walk. "I know what you mean. And I get what you said about not thinking of Chloe as a person, too. I was older when Mum died, sure, but I feel like I'd only just started to think of her as someone with her own thoughts and feelings, rather than simply my mother. I wish I'd had the chance to get to know her in her own right. She was great, though. Very strict on no shoes in the house." Lissa laughs. "But great. She cooked the best lasagne, but for some reason burnt chips literally every time she put them in the oven. She made herself go to the gym most days, but claimed it was only so she could drink as much red wine as she wanted. She always had time to talk, no matter what she was doing, and I didn't always make the most of that."

"You were a teenager," she says. "Talking to parents isn't exactly par for the course."

"Yeah. I wonder, though, if I'd taken the time…" He trails off as they start heading down to a lower part of the cliff. "And I also can't help wondering…"

Again he doesn't finish, but she can guess. "Your dad?"

He looks at her, offers her a reflection of that slightly sad smile she knows she was wearing moments ago. "Yeah.

I wonder if he might not have got so bad if she'd still been around."

She can't think of what to say to that, because there is no way of knowing, is there? He comes to a stop, then lets go of her hand and heads toward the edge, peering over it. She goes with him, but a little cautiously. It's not like she's particularly scared of heights, but it doesn't exactly seem sensible for someone who can't swim to be right on the brink of a cliff. She wonders why there aren't barriers to stop people getting too close.

They've wound their way down the path, so that they're now only twenty meters or so up, waves crashing white against rock on either side of them. The ocean is a glistening blue, and if Lissa didn't know how dangerous it could be, she'd say it looked almost inviting.

"You know," Ash says contemplatively, "I'm pretty sure this is a spot I read about when I looked the place up. You can jump from here."

Lissa laughs, sure it's a joke, but he grins at her, completely misreading her response. Grins at her in a way that for a moment makes her heart stutter with something that can only be fear.

He kicks off his shoes. He's kidding. He's *got* to be kidding. His eyes are alight as he looks down at the water. "You only live once, right?"

And he jumps. He actually fucking dives off the cliff edge and into the sea below.

Lissa doesn't even scream. Because already she is running, adrenaline flooding her system in a way that makes her feel sick. She looks frantically one way, then the other, searching for a path down to the beach.

Shit. Shit! What if he gets knocked unconscious? What if he needs help? She can't swim. What the fuck is she supposed to do? She fumbles for her phone as she sees a narrow overgrown path and sprints for it. She stumbles, skidding down a few feet.

Her vision is blurring. She can feel the water as if it's pouring into her own lungs.

Not again, not again, not again.

She reaches the shoreline to see him surfacing. He whoops, as if it's a fucking game. There are rocks ten meters or so either side of him. He could have hit his head. He could have *died.*

She's breathing heavily, her hands literally shaking, while he strikes out in a front crawl toward her. He's still wearing his clothes. He didn't even bother to take the time to think of what might have happened.

He stands up, shaking his head like a dog. She is still trembling. But it's not from fear anymore.

Hot anger surges through her, so forceful it's almost painful. She can feel her heartbeat pounding, urging her to do something. To *smash* something. Her muscles quiver as he *grins* at her. Then that grin falters, at whatever he sees in her expression.

"What the fuck do you think you're doing?" She doesn't shout. She's beyond that. Instead the words are tight, lethal. She doesn't think she's ever heard herself speak like this before.

"I—"

But there is no justification he can give, so she holds her hand up. "If you ever do something like that again, Ash, I swear to God, I'm done with whatever the fuck this is."

He moves a little closer to her, now only ankle-deep in the waves, his shorts sopping wet. She hopes it fucking hurts, walking on the pebbles barefoot.

"It was safe, Liss," he says. His voice is soothing—it's almost like he thinks she's overreacting. Like he thinks it's totally acceptable to quite literally jump off a fucking cliff.

"You can't possibly know that." She plants her legs wide, to stop her doing something stupid. What, she's not quite sure. "And *you* might not put any value on your life, but *I* do."

He moves closer to her, but she backs away. "I'm sorry. I didn't mean to upset—"

"Upset?" She lets out a hysterical laugh. "I'm not upset. I am *livid*." And it feels *good* to feel this anger. To direct it outward. Because, she realizes, she is so fucking angry. Angry at him, angry at herself. Angry at Chloe for climbing over the fence, for going into the pond that day.

Her breath is hot between her teeth, her skin crawling, adrenaline surging again. She turns, needing to work off the excess energy. He reaches for her hand, and she snatches it away. She can hear the crunch of pebbles beneath her trainers.

"Lissa…" His voice is placating.

"Don't," she snaps. She turns back to see him watching

her. His skin is glistening, his eyes the color of the ocean behind him.

She is still so angry. Still has all this energy, with nowhere to direct it. So she does the only thing she can think of. She strides toward him, fists her hands into the front of his T-shirt. And kisses him.

Chapter Twenty-Four

It is not a gentle brush of lips this time. This time, when she kisses him, he captures her mouth with his, hot and hard and certain, his hands moving to her waist, fingers digging in. He tastes of salt and sea and *him*, and God, the relief to finally have his mouth on hers. She moves her hands to his hair, angling his head down toward her. She is not cautious, not this time. She only wants *more*.

He mutters a soft oath against her lips as she pushes against him, feeling the wet of his clothes clinging to her. It's not enough. She runs her hands down his back, nails lightly scraping against his shirt. His mouth moves to glide down her throat. She lets out a moan as she tilts her head to give him better access to her neck, her fingers tightening their hold on his back.

And then he lifts her, quite literally hoists her up, and she doesn't even have time to gasp with the shock of it, because as she hooks her legs around his waist, he is kissing her again, moving to press her back against the rock. The feeling of him between her thighs sends a rush of heat to her core. She is practically clawing at him, hands coming to his front to run up under his T-shirt, feeling smooth, hard muscle. He shudders at her touch, bites her bottom lip softly and presses her back further against the cliff.

She can taste it, the same urgency in him, and wonders if that feeling is why he jumped in the first place. If this has been simmering underneath the whole time. Need stretches out in every direction as his tongue sweeps hers. She doesn't think she's ever felt like this—it's overpowering, all-consuming.

His hands are on her waist, still holding her up, but his thumb sweeps a taunting circle just under her top. Her world narrows to that point of contact.

"Ash," she murmurs a plea against his mouth.

His grip tightens still further—hard enough to bruise. But the sound of his name on her lips seems to remind him of something. He eases back, just a little, so he can look at her. His eyes are almost black.

He swallows. "Maybe we should...take a beat."

She nods, although taking a beat is not what she wants to do right now. Not what he wants to do, either, from what she can feel pressing against her. He leans in, kisses her again, slower this time. Kisses her jaw, her throat. She can feel the throbbing between her thighs, and her legs tighten their hold on him. Her skin is too hot, too needy. She shudders as he bites, gently, where his mouth travels.

"You taste like I dreamed you would," he murmurs against her skin.

Everything inside her twists and tightens. "Dreaming about me, are you?" The wry tone is somewhat ruined by the fact that she gasps when he kisses the spot between her collarbone and neck.

"Oh, you have no idea." His voice is low, strumming a too-tight string in her core. He stops what he's doing, his gaze finding hers again.

"We should..." She gestures in the vague direction of the cottage. Because he's right—they probably do need to think this through.

"Yeah." His gaze drops to her mouth, returns to her eyes. "Yeah, okay."

He lets go of her, allowing her to get her feet on the ground again. His own feet are still bare, shoes long since forgotten about. Her clothes are almost as wet as his now.

They don't touch as they make their way back to the cottage. She's not sure if he doesn't reach for her for the same reason she's walking a careful distance away from him. Because she's not certain she'll be able to stop this time if she touches him again.

When they get back, they take it in turns to shower, and she says she'll make dinner. She needs something to do to distract herself, and they are too far away from anything to contemplate eating out. She chops asparagus and starts to fry onions and garlic, preparing to make a light pasta dish.

It is cooler now, a slight breeze drifting through the open back door. She's half watching the sunset from the window, the sky changing from blue to orange and reds, when she hears footsteps coming into the kitchen. The back of her neck prickles in anticipation, even before she turns to see Ash in the doorway. His hair is damp and he's clean-shaven. He's barefoot, dressed in jeans and a fresh top. The corner of his mouth crooks up when their gazes meet.

"Hey." Her pulse skitters at the sound of his voice.

Get a bloody grip, Lissa. She focuses on the pan, figuring that's safer.

"So I got you a birthday present," he says.

She frowns, looking around again as he moves toward her. "You do know my birthday was months ago, right?"

Though of course he knows. *Happy birthday, Lissa.*

"I do," he confirms. "But you were being all weird then. So I've been saving it."

"Until I'm good?" The words are out before she can sense-check them, and she inwardly cringes at how it sounds. Like she might be trying to flirt. *Is* she trying to flirt? Is she really this bad at it?

But he only smirks, radiating confidence. "Something like that."

He holds up a small box, which she hadn't noticed before now—too distracted by, well, him. She turns down the hob, then takes the box with slightly hesitant fingers. She was a total bitch to him, cutting him off like she did. And still he bought her a present. Still he thought of her.

She opens it, feeling his gaze on her face, watching. She swallows in the moment before she sees what it is, worried about showing the wrong kind of reaction. But then all she can do is stare. At the earrings inside the box. Not her usual style, which is studs, with the occasional hoop if she's feeling out there, but huge dangling earrings, gold, with big blue spheres giving way to red at the bottom. They are nothing like anything she would buy for herself. And for that very reason, they are totally perfect.

"Thank you," she murmurs.

"They're how I see you." He shrugs. "Bright and full of color."

And oh God, how is she supposed to stop herself when he says things like that? She lifts on her toes to press a kiss to his cheek. She inhales the scent of him. Earthen, grounded, despite his somewhat erratic behavior at times. As she eases away, he takes hold of her arms, gently holding her in place.

"I'm sorry about earlier."

She cocks her head. "Which part?"

His lips curve in a smile that makes her toes curl. "Which do you think?" His voice has dropped to that low tone, the one that makes her insides shiver.

She shakes her head. She's not sure she wants to think about it again, the feeling she had as he went over the cliff. The certainty that something awful was about to happen.

"I didn't really think it through," he continues.

"No," she agrees. "I got that." Then again, she wasn't thinking too clearly when she kissed him, either. She bites her lip. "Your dad said…" She trails off, not sure if she's crossing some sort of line here. But they've always been able to talk to each other, haven't they? "He said that maybe you do all this stuff because you don't want to be like him."

He contemplates her. "Maybe that's true." She doesn't know why she's surprised how easily he admits it to her. He's not exactly a half-truths kind of guy, is he?

He lets go of her arms, lifting a hand to run it through his towel-dried hair. As he does, his shirt rides up, exposing a sliver of hard, toned muscle beneath. She tries not to look. Tries not to remember what it was like to have her hands there earlier today.

"It's just," he says, "do you ever get the feeling that life is...I don't know. Fragile? Like it could be taken from you at any moment?" She nods slowly. "Right, so I guess I'm just trying to make sure I have all the best experiences before that happens."

She hesitates, then nods again. "I think I get that." She's carried it with her, that innate feeling he's talking about, since Chloe. Maybe even before that, because of something on a far more subconscious level. Because a part of her remembers death in her previous lives. For her, it presents differently—as the need to be cautious, protect herself, stay healthy. So she doesn't necessarily agree with how he deals with it, that feeling. But she does understand it.

He's watching her as he places his hands either side of the counter and leans in slowly—a question. It is a slow sinking this time, when he kisses her. His nose skates down hers, one hand moves to cup her neck, his thumb tracing a small circle there. Her skin goes hot and needy from the brush of his tongue against hers. A stupid gasp escapes her as his teeth catch her bottom lip, and he moves closer to her at the sound, pressing her against the counter. Her spine arches, every muscle in her stomach trying to draw closer to his.

He moves his attention to her throat, and she groans, her fingers digging into his back. With the sound of it, he hoists her up again, sitting her on the kitchen counter in a move that sends a breathless laugh through her. A laugh that is cut off as his hands travel up her calves, to her thighs, underneath the dress she's wearing. His gaze meets hers, sparking as he bends down to kiss behind her knee, higher up on her thigh. Her breath is uneven, her mind on fire.

But still she manages to think. "Wait," she says, her breath hitching. He pauses, but keeps his hands on her legs, like he's about to spread them. The space between her thighs heats. But she doesn't feel embarrassed. His eyes are practically black, and the sight of that—of knowing he wants this just as much as she does—sends a thrill tumbling through her.

"Wait?" he asks. And he would, she knows. He'd stop.

"I just mean...We can't have sex in the kitchen."

His mouth pulls up into that crooked smile she loves. "Why not?"

"Well, it's not our kitchen for one."

His smile deepens and he steps in closer, right between her thighs. She slams her hands up to his chest to stop him. He places his own hands over them. "And what about dinner?" she asks, almost a squeak.

His smile changes, becomes something different. Hungrier. He reaches around her to switch off the stove. And despite the fact that his arm barely brushes her side, her nipples pinch in anticipation.

"Later," he murmurs. A promise of some kind.

Then he lifts her, as easily as he did on the beach, and quite literally *carries* her to the bedroom.

"How are you doing this?" she laughs. "I'm not that light."

He grins. "You're not that heavy, either."

She doesn't even notice which bedroom they're in, couldn't tell you if the walls were blue or green, if the decor was modern or old-fashioned. All she can concentrate on is the feeling of his hands on her thighs, and the way he is looking at her—a way that makes her want to touch him.

He sets her gently on the end of the king-sized bed, and draws down the strap of her dress, kissing her shoulder. Her whole body buzzes at the feeling of his lips on her bare skin.

She drags her fingers through his hair as his own hands travel up, under her dress, bunching it at the waist. She moves her hands to his long, lean torso, tugs at his T-shirt. He's grinning as he helps her take it off. She acts on instinct, leaning in to lick a column up his core, over muscles that feel tight enough to snap. He shudders, and she loves it, the feeling of power that flows through her.

"Fuck, Lissa," he hisses out. And he is pushing her back, lifting her dress up and off her, his thumb sweeping the outside curve of her breast. Every nerve ending in her body lights up. She raises her hips, grinding them against his while her heart pounds into his urgent touch.

She hears the hiss of his belt buckle and sits, helping him out of his jeans. There is no awkward fumbling, no hesitation. She knows dimly that this is not how the first time with someone is supposed to feel, but she closes her eyes, giving in to sensation as he pushes her back onto the bed, his fingers traveling up her inner thighs, electricity pulsing in their wake.

Because tonight, she doesn't want worry and the what-ifs to eat away at her until there is nothing left. She wants to feel strong and needed and powerful—and she does, with him.

"Fuck, Lissa," he says again, slipping one finger inside her. "You have no idea how long I've wanted this."

Her hips move against him even as she reaches between them, thrilling at the feeling of him in her hand. His head bows into her shoulder and he kisses her collarbone as his fingers move inside her, thumb circling around her clit. She whimpers as the pressure inside her builds, her muscles clenching. And when his thumb presses down, she cries out as pleasure skitters down her spine, the first wave of release tearing through her.

His eyes are on hers, black, as he watches her. She breathes his name, not sure what she means by it, as she takes him and guides him into her, groaning at the weight of him on her. She runs her hands down his back, and as he begins to move inside her, it's like her edges seem to blur.

"Look at me, Liss," he murmurs.

She didn't realize her eyes were closed again, but she opens them to find him staring right back at her. The sight of him looking at her like that is enough to send another pulse running straight through her, even as she bows up, meeting his rhythm.

You, she thinks. *Always you.*

She says his name as she comes again, almost like it's a spell. He captures her final cry with his mouth, linking their fingers together above her head. And together, they shatter.

Chapter Twenty-Five

Ash is curled around her when she wakes, his arm holding her in place, his heartbeat a steady rhythm against her back. The duvet has been kicked to the end of the bed, far too warm to need it. Maybe that's what woke her—the heat. The window is open, but the breeze it's trying to tempt is nonexistent.

She has no idea what time they fell asleep, or what time it is now. She blinks into the dark, moonlight filtering through a gap in the curtains. She shifts a little, easing away from him. She feels sore, in a good way. But she also feels restless, like she's only got more energy after last night, not less.

It takes her all of about a minute to decide she can't stay here pretending to sleep. She's never been very good at sharing a bed with someone—always feels too vulnerable. And while it's different with Ash, she figures she'll go for a walk—cool down, work off a bit of the energy—and be back before he wakes.

She dresses in whatever clothes she can find and heads out of the cottage. The night air is pleasantly cool on her sticky skin. Pieces of last night come back to her, making her smile—and making her glad she is alone. The sound of his name on her lips. The way he looked at her when he was inside her.

The feeling she had, a kind of certainty. *You. Always you.*

She feels it again, a restless jump inside her. Something crawling under her skin, like it's waiting to be set free.

The ocean seems restless, too. It's calm on the surface, but as she weaves her way down the cliff path toward the shoreline under the bright moonlight, it's like she can sense something underneath it. It seems silly to think that. What does she know about the sea?

But still. It feels like something is happening. Like something has changed. She supposes it has, because there's no going back after last night, is there? A choice, Saskia said. Is this it? Has she already made it?

She stops when she reaches the beach, waves coming up to the tips of her trainers. She can remember what it felt like to drown. Can imagine it now, the water sucking her under.

She was in water when she figured it out, saw the first time she died. And that's what she needs now. She needs to see beyond the veil, or however Saskia phrased it. Because there's got to be something else she's missing.

She slips off her shoes, dips a toe into the water. It's not exactly warm, but it's not freezing. She's not really thinking as she strips off down to her underwear. She's letting whatever is inside her drive her on. Because of last night. Because she can't be with Ash—really be with him—if she doesn't understand, if she's still lost in the past.

She wades deeper. Her heart is hammering fast, but it's the usual fear she's feeling. She thinks of Ash's comment right before he jumped. *You only live once.*

But she hasn't only lived once, has she?

The water is cold around her as she reaches shoulder-deep. Her lungs feel tight, like they're preparing for something, and she can feel her heart in the base of her throat.

It's so easy to relive the memories. The manor house from the 1920s. The jazz band, the champagne, the laughter. The sound of his voice caressing her skin. His gaze meeting hers. Dancing. A hand sliding up her thigh underneath a table, somewhere no one can see. The sleeve of her dress pushed off one shoulder, a kiss pressed there as her back arches.

Him driving her home. *Thanks for the ride. You're my hero.*

Hero. *Hey, hero.*

Walking through Paris hand in hand. Knowing it had been hard for him, his first big premiere, without his father there. His father too afraid to leave the house.

Agoraphobia.

Yeah. I guess.

Him singing on the lake, rowing his way toward her. Drawing him in charcoal. His dad hasn't been the same since the war.

A film composer. A location scout. A singer.

Dimly, Lissa can feel the water bobbing around her, the tips of her fingers turning numb. But she's only partially here. Because now she's back there again, a different body of water around her as she falls into the loch, pain as her lungs threaten to explode. The certainty that it's not just her who will die, because she's pulling him under with her.

A car speeding toward her. Too slow—she's too slow to move out of the way, so he comes for her, trying to save her.

And now a new memory, the final piece. A feeling of utter joy as she moves hand in hand with him through New York. Because she's chosen him, because he's found a gig in a band right here in the city, because he wants to stay with her.

Dragging him down an alley, desperate to touch him. Laughter.

Then a gunshot. Wrong place, wrong time. An alley that she didn't think to look down, because all she could think of was him. Him shoving her out of the way, again. Trying to save her, again. His shirt stained red as the bullet goes through him.

Screaming. Her screams. Useless, because she can feel it, sharp pain, then the sound of the gun once more.

It's not just her who dies over and over. And it's not lots of different men—it's the same one. The same soul. She's drawn to him again and again. An endless loop. Every time, he chooses her. Every time, she leads him into danger.

Water pulling her under.

Blood coating her hands.

The smell of burning rubber.

He dies every time because of her.

It's real. She's not crazy. This has all happened before. The Devil, lord of patterns. Circles that go round and round. An endless, tragic loop. This is the pattern she needs to break. It's not about her sister—it's about *him*.

Of course it is. Because when did the flashbacks start? When she met him. On the anniversary of her sister's death, she met him.

She can hear it still, the screaming inside her head.

Only it's not her screaming.

"Lissa!" An agonized, cracked sound.

His hands on her shoulders, pulling her from the water, toward land. Carrying her, because she can't stand, because her legs have given way, like they can't support her through this realization.

She is choking as she tries to blink Ash into focus, tries to bring herself back to the here and now. Choking, sobbing, gasping. Her lungs are burning, her head is spinning. She is soaking wet, tendrils of hair clinging to her face.

He sets her down when they are out of the water. He's topless, but wearing jeans—like he didn't stop to strip before wading in after her. She wonders how he found her. Did she scream out loud? Did she call for him?

"What the *fuck* do you think you're doing?" His words are laced with anger—exactly like she shouted at him yesterday. Because he is allowed to be reckless, but she is not.

She is shivering, but she's not sure it's from cold. She hitches in a breath, then another, as she stares up at him bathed in moonlight.

"Lissa?" His voice is more uncertain now.

She could have drowned. She knows that. It was stupid to go in like that. Reckless. She did it like she was possessed—and he came in after her. Because that's what happens. They are drawn together as though it is fate, over and over. He dies because he tries to save her.

And it's so obvious. She doesn't know how she didn't see it before. It was like a mental block, an unwillingness to believe what isn't logical.

She feels her eyes sparking with tears, even as he's reaching for her, trying to make sure she's okay.

She only just manages to get the words out through numb lips. They are words she doesn't want to say—words she doesn't want to believe. But they are words she knows with utter certainty are true.

"It's you."

Chapter Twenty-Six

Ash is frowning at her. "What do you mean? Of course it's me. Who else is going to drag you out of the bloody ocean? And by the way, I thought you couldn't swim." He is gripping her shoulders, hard. "Why the hell did you go out there, Lissa? In the middle of the fucking night." His voice changes, cracking at the end, like he can't quite hold it together.

She can only stare at him, moonlight bouncing off his bare muscled chest, dark hair merging with the shadows. A chill that has nothing to do with the air skates over her skin, and a sob rakes through her.

It's him. It shouldn't be possible. None of this should be happening. But it is. She's met Ash before. A different name, a different body—but the same soul. Not just her repeating the pattern over multiple lifetimes. Somehow she is dragging him down with her too.

"I'm sorry," he's saying now. "Shit, I'm sorry, Lissa." His grip changes, becomes more soothing as he rubs down her arms. He looks around, searching for something, then reaches down and grabs her clothes, which are covered in sand. When she doesn't take them, still numb with shock, he wraps his arms around her and she breathes in his scent. It's why it's always seemed so easy between them—because they already know each other. Because they've already fallen in love.

The knowledge burns the inside of her head, leaving black scorch marks. She pushes away from him, tears stinging her eyes. His gaze searches her face, something flickering across his expression. "Lissa..."

She shakes her head. She can't look at him. Can't bear to. "We... This has happened before, Ash." Her voice is a rasp, like the salt water has burned her throat.

"*What* has happened before?"

"Us."

He stares at her. "I'm pretty sure I'd remember if we'd slept together before now, Liss." She can hear it, the attempt to lighten things, as he's so good at doing.

"That's not what I mean."

"What *do* you mean?" He pulls a hand through his hair, exasperated.

She tries to find the words—opens and closes her mouth a few times, watches the way his brow creases further, trying to figure her out. But she can't do it. If he doesn't already see it, doesn't remember, there is no way he'll believe her. It will sound crazy, she knows that. Because it *is* crazy.

But that doesn't mean it's not true.

Punishment. She thinks it again, even if Saskia told her the universe doesn't work like this. But why else? In each life, she is responsible for the death of a sibling. In each life, she falls in love with Ash. In each life, she loses him.

Why else would this be happening?

He's already looking at her like he's more than a little alarmed, and she wonders if he might, finally, decide she's more hassle than she's worth and leave her. And that would be for the best, wouldn't it? Because that's what needs to happen. Because she's realized, this time, before it's too late. Because that's what she needed to learn. The universe, trying to tell her something. Each time they fall in love, it only ends in tragedy. So that only leaves one answer, doesn't it?

She takes a breath, squares her shoulders and finally looks him right in the eye. "We can't be together, Ash."

He's still holding her clothes out to her as he scans her face, searching for answers. "Did you have a...an anxiety attack or something? Let's go up to the house and—"

"No."

"No? No you didn't or no you won't go to the house?"

"Both. Either." She takes her clothes from him, puts them on, the sand coarse against her sticky skin. "We..." She pauses as she pulls her top over her head. "It's not going to end well if we keep going down this road."

"*What* road?" He's losing patience, she can tell. Good. That will make it easier.

"Us." She gestures between them. "If we keep doing... whatever it is we're doing."

What would have happened if she hadn't figured this

out? Would they have repeated the loop? Fall in love, choose each other. Only to pay for it with their lives.

It won't happen, she tells herself firmly. The future isn't set in stone—and now she has the chance to change it.

"What, and you just know that, do you?" His anger, even subtle as it is, spikes the air. "You've had an epiphany in the middle of the night?"

She bends down to pick up her shoes, hesitates before straightening. "You know when I asked you," she begins tentatively, "if you believed in past lives?"

"What the hell does that have to do with anything?"

And there it is—her answer. She closes her eyes, breathes in the smell of the sea. He might not feel it the way she does, but it's affecting him regardless. He's only drawn to her because of who they were to each other in the past. And it's why he is the way he is, isn't it? Of course he wants to take risks, experience new things, enjoy things while they last, because some part of him must remember just how short life can be.

"I'm sorry," she whispers. "I can't do this."

She moves to step away, but he grabs her arm. "Can't do *what*, Lissa? You're making no sense."

She shakes her head again. She won't do it. She won't continue down the path she's on with him. She thinks of what Saskia said at the tarot reading.

It's only by making a different choice to the one you've made in the past that you can get to where you need to be for your future.

Well this is it, isn't it? *This* is the different choice she needs to make in order to stop the past repeating itself.

She yanks her arm from his grip, and he lets her go. The sand is rough under her feet as she walks away from him.

She hears her name called behind her. "Lissa!"

But she knows now what she needs to do. So she doesn't look back.

Chapter Twenty-Seven

On the first Sunday in July, Mia is waiting for her outside her mum's house. She's dressed in denim dungarees, her freckles more prominent, the way they always are in the sun. She smiles at Lissa, lifting her free hand, the other holding a bag of groceries. It's too hot, really, for a roast today, but tradition prevails.

"You look awful," Mia says by way of greeting when Lissa reaches the front door.

"Why thanks, great to see you too." She actually tried to make herself look *less* awful this morning—put on a nice dress, dabbed concealer under her eyes. No fooling her cousin, apparently.

Mia looks her up and down. "I take it the weekend away did not go well."

Lissa grimaces despite herself. She got back from Cornwall nearly two weeks ago now. Ash had come after her on the beach, but she'd insisted on driving home first thing in the morning. Bar the journey to the hospital, following the ambulance, all those years ago, it had been the worst car journey of her life. She kept nearly crying, he kept asking what was wrong, she kept being unable to explain. It ended with a stiff goodbye—and she hasn't heard from him since. As much as she's told herself that that's for the best, that she's done the right thing, she hasn't been able to make herself *feel* it.

She's not been sleeping well since, either—she keeps being dragged into nightmares every time she closes her eyes, worse than they've ever been before. And they're not just about drowning this time. She sees her deaths—and his—on repeat each time she closes her eyes. She's called in sick at work for over a week, sending Darcy vague explanations.

She misses him. They've gone longer than this without speaking, but she misses the *idea* of him, misses texting him, misses wondering when she might be able to see him again. Maybe that shows that she caught it just in time to stop the mistakes of the past repeating themselves.

Although there's still a part of her wondering why. Why are they destined to meet, to fall in love, to die, over and over? Is this really about punishment? Or is the universe trying to tell them something?

"Shall we?" Lissa asks, gesturing at the house. Mia scrutinizes her, then nods, apparently accepting that she doesn't want to talk about it.

The house smells different as they head inside. Something lemony lingers on the air. It seems tidier, too—like there is less clutter.

They find Esme in the kitchen. She smells of that same lemon scent. She's been cleaning, Lissa realizes. And outside the back door, the garden is different too. The lawn seems, if not freshly mown, then at least mown in the last few weeks.

"Girls!" she exclaims. "Lovely to see you!" Like it's a surprise that they're here as opposed to a long-standing arrangement.

Lissa clocks fresh brushstrokes of paint on a section of the kitchen wall. Teal, light blue, green, over the old whitewash. Is her mum thinking of *redecorating*? She sees Mia notice it too, though after a quick exchange of glances they both look away, like it's something wild they don't want to confront directly, for fear of scaring it.

They cover the usual bases as they cook—their jobs, the nice weather. As they are getting everything together, Esme announces that they ought to eat outside.

"It's such a nice day. And I've bought a new garden table." She gestures out the back door to where there is indeed a new patio table, complete with chairs. It's simple— white plastic—but still, this has got to be the first new thing she has bought for the house in years.

"Sure," Lissa says. It's a little odd, perhaps, to eat a roast outdoors in summer, but what the hell? She thinks of Ash—maybe she's inherited a bit of his *why not* attitude. Then she forces herself *not* to think of him, because it only makes her sad. And leads her back to the question of why—why does she find him in every lifetime, only to lose him?

"Fab." *Fab?* Lissa can't stop another exchange of looks with Mia at this. She doesn't think she's heard her mum say *fab* in her entire life. "Mia, do you mind taking the plates out?"

"Of course." Mia takes the offered plates before stepping out into the garden.

Lissa goes to get cutlery, but her mum stops her. "Lissa, wait. I..." She bites her lip, her gaze darting out to the garden and back again. She lifts her hands to flatten her hair. Nerves, Lissa realizes—and feels her own coil in her gut at whatever she's about to say.

"Lissa," Esme begins again, her tone almost formal. "I need to apologize to you."

"For what, exactly?" Lissa asks.

Esme shifts from foot to foot, smooths down the front of her skirt with her palms. "I..." She swallows. "I shouldn't have blamed you." Her words are quiet but steady.

Lissa stills—and it's as if the kitchen itself stills with her. This is not supposed to happen on these visits. They never talk about it. She tries to think of something to say, comes up blank. All she can remember is the last time her mum had a bad turn.

It's your fault.

"I couldn't cope," her mum continues, looking down at her feet, encased in white pumps. "You know that, of course. But I...I couldn't face the fact that it was *my* fault. I was the mother, the responsible one. But I..." She sucks in a breath. "You were there."

"I know." Lissa's throat is tight as she gets the words out.

"No, that's not what I..." Esme blows out an audible breath. "Your dad, he blamed me. And I couldn't take it.

I couldn't face it." Her eyes, so like Lissa's, flick up now. "But I shouldn't have done that to you. I shouldn't have made you live with it. I should have been the parent." She closes her eyes briefly. "I suppose, losing Chloe, it was like I lost that part of me too."

She's practiced this. It doesn't have the polished air of most rehearsed speeches, but Lissa can tell she's been building up to it. For how long? she wonders. And still she can think of nothing to say.

It's your fault.

"You must blame me too," her mum says, pulling at her skirt now.

"I don't . . ." But Lissa trails off. *Know what you mean* was how she was going to finish the sentence. But she does know, of course she does. Because there have been times over the years, haven't there, when she's hated her mum. Hated that she'd left Lissa in charge. Because if she hadn't done that, it wouldn't have happened. Social services deemed it an accident, after the investigation. But it was an accident that could have been avoided.

And worse than that, darker than that, are the thoughts she has tried to repress about Chloe. Because in her desperation not to blame herself, a part of her sometimes blames her sister. For climbing over the fence, getting into the pond. She hates that part of her. But no matter how much she hates it, she can't stop it creeping in when she is at her most vulnerable.

"But you never said it," her mum continues. "You never told me it was my fault. And that made it easier to convince myself it wasn't. I've been so horrible," she whispers, and there are tears in her eyes. "I know that, Lissa. I don't know why you stuck around." Lissa watches her mum's throat bob. "But I wanted to tell you—I'm grateful that you did."

There is quiet between them. Lissa's hands are clammy on the cutlery she's holding. She blows out a breath, tries to relieve the pressure in her chest. "Therapy going well, then?" she asks, because it is literally all she can think to say.

Her mum, thankfully, laughs. "Well, I'm trying."

"I suppose that's all any of us can do," Lissa says. "Try." But is it really enough? She wonders if her mum is expecting her to accept the apology—she wonders if she *wants* to accept it. But you can't just change years and years of blame and guilt in one conversation, can you? And she wonders, too, if her mum will turn, the next time it all gets too much.

Thankfully, her mum claps her hands, abruptly ending the conversation. "Let's eat, shall we?" It's a good attempt at a bright tone, though Lissa can still see the tears shimmering there.

"Yeah," Lissa says. "Yeah, okay."

"I'll join you outside in a min. I just need the loo." Esme turns then, walking from the kitchen, and Lissa hears the creak of the stairs. She suspects her mum is going to pull herself together, and is glad of the breathing space.

She heads to the garden, where Mia is sitting on one of the chairs, table partially laid.

"All okay?" Mia asks a little cautiously. "I sensed a moment and thought it best to keep my distance."

Lissa snorts her agreement at that. In a nearby lavender bush, left to its own devices over the years, honeybees go about their work. "Yeah," she says. She rakes her hand through her hair. "I mean"—she glances over her shoulder to check they're still alone—"she sort of . . . apologized. For Chloe, I mean. Or not *for* it, but for, well, blaming me." She chews on her lip as she says it, not totally sure how to process that conversation.

"About time." It's muttered, almost under Mia's breath, and the words sound a little bitter. More bitter than Lissa herself feels. She scans her cousin's face, noticing the purpling circles under her eyes. Tired. Mia has brushed it off before, saying it's a result of too many transatlantic phone calls with Lottie, but . . .

"Mia, are *you* okay?"

She taps her fingers on the plastic table. "I'm just pissed off that it took her so long."

"Well," Lissa says, in her best diplomatic voice, "she had—"

"Oh for God's sake, Lissa," Mia snaps. "You don't need to keep defending her."

Lissa's eyebrows shoot up. "I'm not defending her. I'm—"

"You are. You're defending her and you're punishing yourself, the way you always do."

"Mia, I was the one who—"

"It was an accident!" Mia gets to her feet at this, like she can't stay still. She crosses to Lissa, takes her hands. "An accident, Bissa. And Esme . . . she's put all this weight on you, blamed you because she couldn't stand to blame herself—and you have *let* her." She practically spits the last few words.

Lissa pulls her hands away, feeling it like a gut punch, because Mia is supposed to be the one who understands. She shakes her head, not really a denial, but enough of one that Mia says, "You have. You've let it define you. You don't let yourself be happy because you don't think you deserve to be. You've done it your whole life—and you're doing it again, with Ash."

His name is like a spear to the heart. "How do you know what—"

"I don't need to. I don't need you to explain, because I *know* you, Lissa. Because it's so fucking predictable. It's what you do, again and again." A pattern, Lissa thinks, despite herself. A different sort of cycle she's stuck in.

"You said this with Mark." She is trying, so hard, to keep her voice level.

"Okay, fine, I was wrong about Mark. He wasn't for you. But maybe Ash is. Maybe he's your bloody soulmate or whatever, but even if he is, you won't open yourself up to it."

The word *soulmate* reverberates through her. Mia has no idea just how right she is.

"You don't believe in all that," she says instead. Which is part of the reason she can't explain. "Do you?"

"I don't." Mia sighs. "But the basic facts remain." She still sounds bitter. Angry.

"Why are you so mad at me?" Lissa asks, in more of a snap than she intended.

"Because you never change!" Mia finally explodes completely, throwing her hands into the air. "Because I sit here watching it all happen!" She turns from Lissa, like she can't bear to look at her.

"No one asked you to sit watching," Lissa says stiffly.

"Oh for fuck's sake, Lissa." Mia turns back. "Why do you think I'm still here?" Lissa's insides churn. "Why do you think I've stayed nearby all these years? Why do you think I'm worried about what will happen with Lottie? Because I can't *leave* you. I can't leave until you get your fucking act together, and you just *won't*." Her voice is on the verge of a sob now.

Lissa stares at her cousin—the person who has been there for her her whole life—and something like nausea swells. She thinks of how she herself has felt trapped in Bath because of her mum. Is that how Mia feels? Trapped—because of her?

"I'm not stopping you leaving," she says quietly. "If you want to go, be with Lottie, then you should."

She doesn't mean it argumentatively, but she knows her tone is off. And when Mia scoffs, she knows it was the wrong thing to say.

"Fine," Mia says, voice tight. "Maybe I will." With that, she storms out, leaving Lissa staring after her.

Chapter Twenty-Eight

Lissa stares at the clock on her work computer. Still five minutes until she's technically allowed to leave for the day. She picks up her phone, gets up the WhatsApp chat with Mia. Stares at it, then closes it again as she keeps doing. They haven't spoken, haven't even messaged, since last Sunday and she doesn't know what to say. They never usually fight, so there's not exactly a template for this. She hates knowing Mia is angry at her. Hates knowing that she might be the reason her cousin has been stressed and unhappy recently. But she doesn't know how to fix it.

She can feel Liam watching her from his glass office, pretends to be clicking something with her mouse. He's been like this since she rang in sick. She doesn't care as much as she probably should. It feels bizarre that she's supposed to carry on as normal, as if she hasn't figured out that she and Ash have lived a version of this life before. As if she isn't questioning why it keeps happening, and whether she is doing the right thing staying away from him.

A message on the internal office chat pops up on her computer screen.

Ready to go?

Darcy. Thank God.

"So?" Darcy prompts as they reach the lift.

It takes Lissa a second to realize what she is asking about. "The interview?" she asks.

"Of course. What else? How did it go?"

She had her second—and final—interview for the marketing job at the charity yesterday. "It was . . . fine," she finishes lamely.

"Fine?" Darcy's eyebrows pull together. "What do you mean, fine?"

"I mean . . . it was okay." But it wasn't brilliant. She was unable to drum up the enthusiasm she'd felt at the first interview, and she knows the interviewer noticed. She tried to stay focused, answer the questions in the right way, but her mind kept going back to Ash, to the night in Cornwall. She still wants a different job, still wants to make a change in her life. But how is she supposed to carry on as if she doesn't know Ash is, for want of a better word, her soulmate?

"This is about Ash, isn't it?" Darcy says, astute as ever.

Lissa sighs. "No comment." She hasn't told Darcy about what actually happened—how can she? Telling someone you think you have a past life, fine, most people can make a joke out of that, but telling them that you are *sure* that you and someone else are destined to meet, and to die together, in every lifetime? Well, that's something else entirely.

Darcy checks her handbag as Lissa pushes the button for the lift. "Shit," she mutters. "I forgot my lipstick. Give me two secs. I'll meet you on the ground floor. And then I want to know exactly what happened—both with Ash and at the interview."

"Do you really need—" But already Darcy has turned, heading back to her desk.

Lissa steps into the lift, and an arm comes out just as the door is closing. Mark gives her a polite nod as he joins her.

"Hey," he says, pressing the button for the ground floor, which Lissa has already pressed.

"Hey." Her voice sounds flat, she knows it does. "How are you?"

He nods, overenthusiastically. "Great."

She nods too. "Good." Is the lift always this slow? she wonders. "Ah...how's Jen?"

He smiles. "She's good. We're going to Cyprus in a couple of weeks."

"Oh, that's cool."

"Yeah?" It seems meant as a question.

"Sure. I've heard it's lovely there."

He looks at her a little curiously, then just nods again. The pair of them, bloody nodding dogs. "Yeah," he agrees, as the lift door opens. "Supposed to be."

They step out together. "Well," he says, gesturing to the exit.

"Yep," she says. But as he moves away, toward the sunlight beckoning outside the doors, she calls out behind him. "Mark?"

He turns back to her, and she bites her lip. She's not sure how to say what she wants to say. He's looking at her, expectant. She takes a breath. If her mother, of all people, can apologize, she can too.

"I'm sorry, you know. If I hurt you," she explains, when he looks a little quizzical.

He seems to hesitate, then gives a little shrug-nod combo. "You didn't. I was confused more than anything."

"Yeah, well," she says a little bitterly. "I've been told I can be quite confusing."

There's another moment of quiet between them; then Mark gestures again to the outside. "All right. Well, I better…"

"Sure," Lissa says quickly.

"I suppose I'll see you at the funeral?"

Lissa frowns. "What funeral?"

Something flashes across his face, before it's carefully controlled. "Oh. I assumed you'd…" He clears his throat. "Ash's dad. He, well, he died a couple of weeks ago. The funeral is on Saturday." Lissa can only stare at him, horror mounting inside her. Jack? Jack is dead?

"You and Ash aren't…?" Mark trails off as Lissa shakes her head.

"I didn't know," she whispers.

He grimaces. "Maybe I shouldn't have told you."

"No, it's fine," Lissa says quickly. "I'm sure he would have told me. I just—"

Darcy chooses that moment to come up behind her, putting her hands on her shoulders and making her jump. "Ready to go? You coming for dinner too, Mark?"

"Ah, no," Mark says, shifting awkwardly. "I think I'll pass this time. Thanks, though."

"Well," Darcy says as Mark leaves the building ahead of them, "you two sure know how to drag the awkward post-dating phase out."

Lissa turns to her and Darcy's expression changes. "What's happened?" she asks immediately.

Lissa can only get out one word. "Ash."

"Oh my God." There must be something in her expression, her voice, that lets Darcy know it's something bad.

"He's fine," Lissa says quickly. "It's just...his dad." Her eyes spring with tears. "His dad died."

"Oh shit," Darcy murmurs, while Lissa gestures at the door.

"I need to..."

"Yes," Darcy agrees.

But Lissa hesitates. "But wait—should I?"

"Yes," Darcy says again, emphatically.

Lissa gives her a look. "You don't even know what I'm going to say."

"Call him," Darcy says pointedly. "And yes. You should."

But Lissa bites her lip. "I think I'm bad for him, Darcy," she whispers. "I think I'm going to..." She cuts herself off in time. *Try not to sound insane, Lissa.* "It'll only end badly," she says instead.

"So do a lot of things, one way or another."

"That's very pessimistic. And here I was thinking you were an optimist."

"I'm a realist." Darcy reaches out, squeezes Lissa's arm. "You can't control everything, Lissa."

And she can't not call him, can she? Because something like this... She can imagine a little of what he's feeling. And regardless of what she knows, she wants to be there for him if she can.

"I don't want to make it worse," she murmurs.

"You definitely won't make it worse. Think about what you'd want if you were him."

Lissa takes a shaky breath. "Okay. Okay, I have to... Wait, but we're going for dinner!"

"Yeah, about that... I was actually going to ask if you'd hate me if I bailed."

"Bailed? Why?"

"I... Well I think I may have a date."

"A date?" Lissa's voice hikes up a notch. "Why didn't you tell me?"

"Because I wasn't sure there was anything to tell." Darcy pauses. "And because with everything happening with Ash..."

"I still want to know," Lissa says firmly. "Of course I do."

"Okay, but not now." Darcy squeezes her arm again.

"No, maybe not now." Lissa pulls her in for a hug. "I hope it goes well tonight. He's obviously an idiot if it doesn't."

Darcy laughs, patting Lissa's back. "I hope Ash is okay," she says into her neck.

"Me too."

She's already calling him as she leaves the building, stepping out into a warm summer evening. The phone rings for so long, she's not sure if he's going to answer—if maybe he just doesn't want to talk to her. Which would be totally fair enough. She's about to hang up, respect his decision, when he answers.

"Hello?" And despite the awfulness of what has happened, a part of her leaps at the sound of his voice.

"Ash. I heard. I'm so sorry."

There is quiet down the line. "Yeah," he says, his voice a little raspy. "It's been a bit rough."

She hates hearing it—the suppressed pain there. "Is there anything I can do? I mean, I know there's probably not, but…"

"It's okay. I'm just… I'm sorting out his things and just waiting to get through the funeral. I haven't really thought beyond that, to be honest."

"Do you need food? I could cook? Or bring takeaway? Or I can—"

"That's okay. I think I need some time to process."

"Of course," Lissa says quickly. And oh God, *has* she made it worse? "I'm so sorry," she says again. "I shouldn't have called."

"No. I'm glad you did. I wasn't sure whether to tell you—whether you'd want to know."

"Of course I'd want to know," she murmurs. "This is your dad we're talking about, Ash. Why would you think I wouldn't?"

He gives a low, tired sigh. "I don't know, Liss. We sleep together and then you bolt." She winces, slowing down as she reaches a road she has to cross. "Not exactly a good sign, is it?"

"That wasn't about you." She whispers it. "I was just trying to . . ." But she doesn't know how to finish. *Keep you safe. Stop the past from repeating itself.*

There's another moment of quiet. Then, "It happened the night we were together. In Cornwall."

She closes her eyes briefly. "Oh God. Ash." It feels like an awful sign—that the night she figured out what was going on was the same night his dad lost his life. Another indication that they shouldn't be together. And now he'll be blaming himself for not being there. "I'm so sorry." Why can't she think of anything else to say? Why can't she do anything to make him feel better? She hates it, this powerlessness.

"In some ways, I think he would have preferred it this way," Ash says, in a flat tone she's never heard him use before. "He was dreading it. You know, the slow descent. The idea that he might have to move somewhere with more help. And I've been dreading that too, I guess." He doesn't say anything more, but she knows him well enough to guess what's going unsaid here—that because he was dreading it, he is somehow to blame.

"This isn't your fault, Ash," she says as gently as she can. But she thinks of people telling her that very same thing—of how hard it is to believe.

"Yeah," Ash says. "Well."

Lissa thinks of Jack, of the kind smile, the wry tone. A life that had become smaller, fighting mental and physical battles on every front. She can't cry. It's Ash who should be allowed to cry, not her. But still she finds herself welling up. "Mark said the funeral is on Saturday?" She manages to keep her voice steady as she asks.

"Yeah," Ash says again.

"Do you want me to..." She takes a breath. "I'd like to come. Be there for you. But only if you want me."

He hesitates for enough time to make her question the offer, wonder if she shouldn't have put him on the spot like that.

Then his voice comes down the phone, soft, quiet, sad. But not quite as flat. "I'll always want you, Lissa."

Chapter Twenty-Nine

Two days before Jack's funeral, Lissa sits opposite Saskia in her little back room. Saskia's head is cocked as she studies her, sunlight sparking off her silver stud earrings.

"I don't quite understand what you're asking," she says. "You want to do another tarot reading?"

"No," Lissa says, bouncing her knee. "I just want to know if I'm making the right decisions. If I've figured things out the way I'm supposed to have."

Saskia nods slowly, and Lissa can tell she's thinking. Maybe thinking that Lissa is a madwoman? She supposes it doesn't really matter—she just wants someone to talk it through with, and since she can hardly do that with Mia or Darcy, Saskia is sort of her only option.

"You said I was trapped," she says. "In the reading last time. That I was trapped in a cycle. Well, I've figured out what the cycle is." She goes on to explain, what happens. That in each life, she loses a sibling. In each life, she falls in love—with the same person. And each time, it ends in tragedy.

"You said I could only move to a more positive future if I started making a different choice," she continues, ignoring the way Saskia's brow furrows deeper and deeper as she listens. "So I want to know—am I doing the right thing by staying away from him?"

Is she doing the right thing by going to the funeral? And after that, should she hold firm? Is that the only way to keep him safe? Because they always die when they are together, don't they? So maybe by not being together it won't happen.

But despite all that, a part of her wants to be told the opposite. That she's got this wrong somehow. That she doesn't need to stay away from him.

Saskia studies her for a long moment, but Lissa can think of nothing more to say. She feels exhausted, wrung out. She just wants someone to give her the answers.

Then Saskia leans forward on her armchair, clasping her hands in her lap. "Okay, well first things first here, Lissa. I cannot give you a straightforward answer about this. I believe that *you* believe this pattern is happening, and I can understand your desire to figure out why. But I can't say for certain whether you're right about that—I'm not sure anyone can. If it *is* happening the way you think it is, then I also can't give you an easy answer as to why. But what I will say is that just because the past *has* repeated itself doesn't mean it is destined to keep doing so. After all, we can learn, can't we, from the mistakes of our past?"

Lissa lifts her fingers to her temples and massages. "Yes," she says, and tries to keep the impatience from her voice, "but I don't know which mistake I'm supposed to be fixing. There must be something I do in each lifetime to cause this."

Saskia cocks her head. "Why do you assume it's something *you're* doing?"

Lissa huffs out a breath—because isn't that obvious? "What else would it be?" Unless it really is punishment, in which case it wouldn't matter what she did.

Saskia straightens and reaches for the pack of cards on her desk. "I know you said you didn't want another reading, but I'm going to do a simple one to try to help you here. Three cards," she says as she shuffles, "past, present, future."

She lays the first card down. The Three of Swords, the same as last time. A death in the past. Chloe. But also maybe Lissa herself—her previous deaths.

She points at the second card. "The Ace of Swords," she says. "I'd say this means you are on the verge of a breakthrough. That you're close to freeing yourself from whatever is trapping you."

Something in Lissa's gut rolls. "Does that mean I haven't yet?"

"I don't think so," Saskia says. "But it could mean you're on the right track."

Right track? Does that mean that walking away from Ash is the right thing to do? Or that it's the right thing to see him again at the funeral?

Saskia lays out the third card, a figure with angelic wings, the sun as its backdrop. "Temperance," she says. "This card can often mean that things are out of balance, reversed as it is like this. But I'd say this is also about timing."

Lissa frowns at the three cards, not sure how they help her all that much. "So," she says slowly, "does this mean the timing is right for me to be with him?" She can't help it—her heart leaps a little. Because maybe she's wrong. Maybe this life will be different.

"Maybe not right now," Saskia says. "You need to have patience. Someday soon, things will get back into balance, and then maybe the time will be right." She bites her lip as she looks at the cards. "I think there's something you need to do first."

Lissa makes an impatient noise. "But *what*?" Honestly, what's the use of being a bloody fortune teller if you don't have all the answers?

Saskia taps at the past card, the Three of Swords. "I still feel this is something to do with your sister."

Lissa frowns. "You mean I need to learn to stop her dying?" That was one of her earlier theories, after all—that there is something she needs to learn in this life so that she can stop her sister dying in the next.

"No," Saskia says gently. "I don't think you're supposed to stop that, Lissa."

"Why not?" It's hard to keep the accusation out of her voice.

"Because it's in the past, and we can't change the past. We can accept it, learn from it and grow, but we can never go back in time. And from the sounds of things, in each of your lives it was an accident. You'll never be able to stop accidents from happening—and you'll never be able to change what was."

"Then I don't know what it has to do with Chloe." She used to think it was all about her sister, but she knows it's about Ash now. And more importantly, Ash is still alive. She might not be able to change what happened to Chloe, but she *can* change what happens to him.

"I don't think it's only about her. I think it's about you. Often we need to come to terms with what's in our past"—Saskia taps the card again for emphasis—"in order to make the timing right in our future." She taps the future card.

Lissa stares at the three cards again, then shakes her head. "So *do* I need to stay away from him?" That's all she needs to know right now. The why of it all she might be able to figure out in the future—she just needs to stay alive in order to get there.

Saskia smiles that gentle smile of hers. "I can't answer that for you. You're the one who has to make the choice, Lissa."

Lissa swallows. "But what if I make the wrong one?"

"Then that too becomes the past—and at some point, there will be another choice to make."

Lissa stands next to Mark at the funeral, surrounded by twenty or so people, all dressed in black. They are in a woodland, sunlight filtering through the gaps in the trees. A cool breeze rustles the leaves, and in the distance she can hear birdsong, a musical backdrop to the celebrant's words.

When it's Ash's turn to speak, he talks about how he chose this place so his dad could be at peace somewhere outdoors, without too many people nearby. That because he spent so long trapped within four walls, he doesn't want him trapped inside a coffin. He talks about his dad's life. How he joined the army because he wanted to do something for his country but never fully recovered from what he'd experienced there. He talks a little of his mum, and the fact that his parents always said how lucky they were to find someone they loved so completely. He tells a joke about his father bashing a screw right into the neighbor's house on a botched DIY job. He somehow keeps it together the whole time.

Lissa tries not to cry. She doesn't think she has earned the right to cry, having only met Jack once. But it's Ash she wants to cry for. Ash who has lost the last of his family. Another reminder of how fleeting life is.

It is only at the end that he breaks, just a little. A crack in his voice, the shimmer of a tear as he says the final words. "Goodbye, Dad."

Lissa's vision briefly blurs as a tear breaks through. She has a fleeting image then of another funeral, in a churchyard, with a man who looks different to Ash, but is still the same person, speaking in front of a small crowd. Is Ash's dad's death another of those things they can't change—something else that is destined to keep happening? She supposes death comes for them all in the end.

After his speech, Lissa goes to Ash without thinking, without wondering if it's her place. She takes his hand in hers, standing next to him. She doesn't speak. She's just there.

At the end of the ceremony, she goes to the wake, in a café at the edge of the woods. She makes small talk with a few friends of Ash's from school. She watches as Ash smiles at everyone who comes up to him offering condolences. About forty minutes in, she sees him heading back outside. She tells Mark she'll see him later, gets a vague nod in reply.

Ash is out the front of the café, bracing his hands on the wooden gate and staring out at the woodland.

She comes up behind him, pulling her jacket on as she does. It's early August, but it's getting later in the day now, and a slight chill coats the air.

"Are you okay?" she murmurs. Then she shakes her head. "Sorry. Stupid question."

He turns to her. "I'm just..." He scrapes a hand over his jaw. There are dark shadows under his eyes.

"Tired?" she suggests. She doesn't remember much of Chloe's funeral, only little snippets. She remembers her mum, unable to get through it, sobbing as she fled the room. She remembers her dad trying to give a speech, having to be supported by the celebrant, who finished it for him. She remembers the looks she got, people feeling sorry for her. Kids her age not knowing what to say to her. Mostly she remembers feeling so, so tired.

"Yeah," Ash agrees. "I'm knackered."

"Want to take a break? Go for a walk or something?"

He glances back to the café, to the people still milling around in there, eating sausage rolls, the ultimate comfort food.

"I think they'll manage," she says. "Everyone should be giving you what you need today, not the other way around."

He blows out a breath. "Yeah. Yeah, okay."

They walk away from the café and along one of the woodland paths. She sees a squirrel scurrying up a nearby tree, listens to the crunch of gravel under their feet.

"It was a beautiful ceremony," she says quietly.

He glances down at her. "Yeah?"

"Yeah."

"I don't know what he would've wanted," he admits. "But I figured outside, in amongst the trees...I didn't want him shut away somewhere," he says again.

"I get that," Lissa says quietly. "And it's a lovely place."

"I should have asked everyone to wear bright colors," he says with a frown. "He would have liked that."

Lissa shakes her head. "I don't think there are any shoulds with something like this."

But Ash says, "We should have talked about it." For the first time today, she hears a trace of bitterness. "But I think we were both pretending it wasn't happening. And I just assumed I'd have years left with him. Even though I should have known, after Mum..." He swallows that sentence, looking away from Lissa as if to hide his face.

She takes his hand, squeezes it. He keeps hold of it as they walk.

They find a fallen tree trunk in a clearing, and Ash moves to it, perching there. Still holding his hand, Lissa sits next to him. In the distance, she can hear a dog barking, a child squealing with laughter.

"Will you talk to me about something else?" Ash asks abruptly. "Distract me for a bit? All day I've been talking about him and I just...My head hurts," he admits.

She can see the effort it's taking to hold it together. She wonders if he's let himself cry, and whether he's done that alone, behind closed doors. She wishes she could have been there for him—wishes she hadn't closed him off so completely.

"Sure," she says. "What do you want to talk about?"

"Anything. What have you been up to since we..."

She does her best not to wince. She knew this would come up, but was hoping not to talk about it right after his dad's funeral. But there's no way of ignoring it now that it has. "I'm so sorry," she murmurs, "about the way I ran out on you."

"Yeah." He scrapes a hand over the stubble on his jaw. "I mean, it wasn't ideal. Was it... That night, I thought you..."

"I did," Lissa says firmly, guessing enough. "Ash, no, it was nothing to do with you. I wanted that night. I wanted *you*." She still thinks about it. On the nights she's not plagued by nightmares, she wakes craving him.

"I know it doesn't make sense," she says. "I know I'm acting crazy. But can you try to believe me when I say it has nothing to do with my feelings for you?" She frowns. "Or rather, it's *because* of my feelings for you. Because I don't want you to get hurt."

He looks at her then, eyes reflecting the sunlight. "Surely that's my decision to make?"

She bites her lip. "You can only make a decision with all the facts." And he doesn't have them, does he? He *can't* have them—not unless he somehow remembers too. And if he remembered, he would get it without her needing to tell him.

He looks at her for a long moment, then sighs. "I don't think I can do this, Liss."

"Do what?"

"Us. This." He raises their joined hands, then unlinks their fingers. "I don't want to have you here one minute and not the next. I'll try to believe you when you say you didn't mean to hurt me. And I saw you that night— I know something scared you." He hesitates, seeming to try to choose the right words. "You asked if I wasn't a relationship kind of guy before, and I guess I haven't been. But things are different with you. I get that you're scared to commit. And I get why. I could try to convince you, promise not to hurt you, but I don't think making promises like that is smart." He shakes his head sadly. "We both know you can never be sure what the future will hold." He sighs again, closes his eyes briefly. "But I don't want to keep doing this maybe-almost-nearly thing we're doing."

She swallows and nods, because that's totally fair, isn't it? And because maybe this way he is taking the choice out of her hands, so she doesn't have to be responsible for making the wrong one.

"I'm leaving," he says abruptly, but makes no move to get up. And slowly she realizes what he means.

"Leaving? As in leaving Bath?"

"Yeah. I'm not sure where yet. Maybe Brazil."

"Brazil?"

"Yeah. Or, I don't know, somewhere. I just...I don't want to hang around, waiting. The only reason I came back to stay was because of Dad. And now..."

Something horrible takes hold of her insides. But... "I get it," she says, trying to keep her voice even. Trying not to let on how her throat is closing at the thought that he won't be around anymore.

His gaze slides to hers, and she wonders if he can hear it anyway. "Do you?"

She pushes the heels of her hands to her eyes. "I...I'm not being like this to hurt you," she says again, needing him to understand that. "Part of me wants so much to give it a go, but..."

"That's the thing, Liss," he says gently. "I don't want to be a 'but.'"

She swallows. "It's just...I know this doesn't make sense, but I..." How the hell is she supposed to explain? "Sometimes," she continues, a little hurriedly, "I get these flashbacks. Like stuff from another life. And I think they're showing me..." She breaks off, because she can see the way he's looking at her. Not like this resonates, but like he's ever so slightly alarmed. She tries a different tack. "I went to see a...well, a psychic, I guess you could call her, and—"

"Lissa. If you're trying to think of a way to let me down gently, this isn't it."

"I'm not trying to let you down at all." Her voice is small, pleading. "I'm just trying to be careful."

He smiles, a little sadly. "I know you are. But, Liss, there's a whole world waiting out there." He brushes his knuckles lightly across her chin. "Let me know when you decide you want to live in it, okay?"

He gets to his feet, and she immediately does too. "I'll walk back with you," she says.

"No." He smiles again, though it doesn't reach his eyes. "I am so glad you came. And I know my dad would have been happy about it too. But I need a beat, if that's okay."

She wants to protest, to tell him she'll stick with him, but he's right, she can't keep being there for him one moment and not the next. It's not fair. So she nods.

He walks a few steps away, then glances back over his shoulder to where she's still standing by the dead tree. His gaze holds hers, and the corner of his mouth crooks up ever so slightly. "I love you, Lissa." Her breath hitches and something inside her catapults at those words. "I know the timing sucks, but...I guess I just thought you should know that, before I go."

Her whole body prickles. She can feel her pulse thrumming at her throat. He hands the words out so easily. Perhaps because he knows instinctively just how little time there is to say how you feel.

She wants to say it back. She wants to—but she can't. She hovers there in indecision while he waits. A choice. She needs to make a choice.

In the end, all she can get out is "Will I see you before you go?"

He levels a look at her. He must see it. Surely he must see what she can't bring herself to say. But she worries from the way his eyes shutter that he can't. "Yeah," he says. "I'll come say goodbye when everything's packed up."

She nods, swallows. When she speaks, her voice is barely a whisper. "Okay."

And this time, it is him, walking away from her.

Chapter Thirty

Lissa sits at her desk at work, staring at the email.

Dear Lissa, Thank you so much for your time last week. Unfortunately, on this occasion, we've decided to go ahead with another candidate. We very much enjoyed meeting you and...

She doesn't care about the rest. She knew the second interview hadn't gone well, but still, it's hard to stop the sinking feeling in her stomach. Ash is leaving. She didn't get the job she wanted—and she *did* want it. It felt positive to think about doing something different. So now what? She doesn't think she can face going back to the job hunt. She doesn't think she can face being here without Ash.

"Lissa?" Darcy whispers. "What's up?"

But Lissa doesn't answer. Because at that moment she gets an internal message from Liam, asking to see her in his office. She doesn't have it in her to feel nervous. She just gets to her feet a little numbly, tells Darcy she'll be back.

Liam waves her inside when she knocks, then braces his fingers on his desk as she takes a seat opposite him. "So, Lissa. How are you getting on?"

She stares at him, no idea where he's going with this. "I'm good. Thanks."

"Good, good. And how are you finding things?"

She raises her eyebrows. "Things?"

"Your work. Your accounts. Do you feel you're on top of it all?"

"Yes," she says slowly. "Why—has someone complained?"

"No, no," he says quickly. "Nothing like that. It's only, after what happened last summer, and then you've been off sick quite a lot recently...I wanted to make sure things are as they should be, especially if you're going through a tricky time with your...health." His gaze flicks briefly away from her face at that, toward his desktop screen, like it's not polite to look at her. "As with any team player in the office, we have to be sure that no one person is underperforming. Do you see what I mean?"

"No," she says bluntly. "Do you mean I *have* been underperforming?"

"Well, no," he says, pulling at his collar. "But we have to consider the possibility that if something were to happen again, it's the whole company that would—"

"Liam," she interrupts. "You can stop now." Because she finally thinks she knows what he's getting at. She's not sure if she wants to laugh or scream at him. Mostly, she realizes, she doesn't care. Oh, she cares about the *principle* of it, but she doesn't care what he thinks of her. "I get it," she says with a sigh. "You don't want anyone letting the side down."

He heaves a relieved sigh. "Exactly. I'm glad we could—"

She holds up a finger to stop him. He stares at it, almost comically shocked. "But I am pulling my weight, aren't I? Or at least as much as most people here." She lets out a laugh that sounds incredibly bitter. "You're making out like you're doing this for me, to make sure *I'm* okay, that I feel supported, that you tick all the bloody HR boxes. But really, you're assuming that because I had a panic attack at work, once, because I show signs of having issues with my mental health, and because I've had some sick leave recently, I *might* underperform—that's it, isn't it? You don't want somebody with mental health problems on your team in case it leads to fewer accounts, or more work for you, or whatever the hell it is you care about."

"Now, Lissa, I think that's a little—"

"I've worked at this company for years. *Years*," she repeats, getting to her feet. She's not really sure what she's planning on doing, but suddenly she finds she doesn't want to sit there opposite him and his stupid beard. "And do you know what, Liam, I might not be some marketing genius, but the job isn't exactly hard, and the clients like me, and I've never drastically fucked up. But you don't care about any of that, do you? All you see when you look at me now is that one panic attack. You didn't even ask why I've been off sick—you just assumed."

"We missed budget this tax year," he says bluntly. "We can't have it happen again. We need everyone to be a—"

"Oh for God's sake." She throws her hands into the air. "Then fire Gary, who watches Netflix at his desk for, I kid you not, at least half of the working day. Or Emily, who expenses all her lunches regardless of whether she's working. But no, instead you decide to go for me, on the off chance that I might lose it again, is that right?" She takes a breath, her heart beating faster, a surge of adrenaline firing through her as she realizes what she's about to do.

She takes a step toward the desk so she's looking down at him. "Well, you don't have to fire me. Because I quit." She turns on her heel at that, walks straight out the glass door.

"You'll have to write a letter of—" But she lets it slam shut behind her, blocking the sound of his voice.

She strides through the office as quickly as she can, head down, slightly concerned he might come after her. She looks up only as she passes Darcy's desk, jerking her head in a way that Darcy immediately understands.

She's shaking as she presses the button for the lift, Darcy appearing at her side just as the doors open.

"What happened?" Darcy hisses as they step inside. "Are you okay?"

Lissa grabs her forearm, feeling the need to emphasize her next words. "Darcy, I quit."

Darcy's face immediately breaks into a grin. "Thank fuck for that."

Lissa laughs, slightly hysterically. Then she shakes her head. "Shit, Darcy, what am I going to *do*?"

"Anything!" Darcy hugs her as they reach the ground floor, then pulls her out of the lift. "I'm so proud of you."

"For quitting my job? Interesting sentiment." Lissa glances at the ceiling above her, bites her lip. "I'm not actually sure I can just storm out like this."

"What are they going to do, fire you?"

"Good point." She runs her gaze over Darcy's face. "What about you?"

"In general or..."

"You don't want to be here forever either."

Darcy shrugs. "I won't be. I've nearly got enough saved to go traveling for a few months, then who knows?" She smiles slyly. "Maybe I'll even take Aaron with me."

Lissa frowns. "Who is... Your date?!" Darcy is nodding. Lissa laughs, pulling a hand through her hair. "You have one date and you're going *traveling* with him?"

"Well, to be fair, I haven't actually told him this yet, but I always said I'll know when I know, didn't I? And I'm pretty sure I know. So now I just have to work on convincing him of that too."

Lissa reaches for Darcy's hand, squeezes it. "If he's smart, he'll already be convinced."

Darcy twirls her other hand in the air. "Well exactly. Come on, let's go get a celebratory coffee."

"Ah... should *you* skive off work in the middle of the day?"

"Sure. Liam's not out to get *me*, remember?"

They walk to the nearest coffee shop, order two cappuccinos and take a seat by the window.

"Can I ask how the funeral went?" Darcy asks in a quiet voice.

Lissa scrubs her hands over her face. "It was... I mean, the ceremony was beautiful. And Ash... He's definitely not *okay*, but..." She breaks off, looking at Darcy. "He's leaving," she whispers. She's been trying not to say it out loud. Trying not to think it. Trying not to remember his expression right before he turned away from her.

I love you, Lissa. I just thought you should know that.

And she just stood there staring.

"Leaving?" Darcy asks with a frown.

"Bath," Lissa explains, trying to keep her voice totally normal. "He only ever moved back here for his dad."

Darcy picks up her coffee, studies Lissa over the rim of the cup. "I'm guessing you didn't ask him to stay."

"I couldn't, Darce. I..." She trails off, bites her lip. Looks out the window at the golden hue of the city, then back at her friend. And takes a breath. "Okay. I'm going to tell you something mad. And just to be clear, I *know* it's mad, okay? But I need someone to talk to about it."

"Okay," Darcy says. "Shoot."

When she's done, Darcy considers her for a solid minute without speaking. "You really believe it," she says eventually.

Lissa lets out a shaky laugh. "Yeah. I really do. Do you think I'm crazy?"

"Nah." Darcy waves a hand in the air, then cocks her head. "Okay, maybe a little. But I love you anyway."

Lissa snort-laughs and feels something like relief course through her. It doesn't really matter if Darcy believes it. She's okay with *Lissa* believing it, and that's what counts.

"Maybe it's not about the fact that you keep dying in the past," Darcy says musingly. "Maybe it's about the universe offering up the chance to get it right one day."

It's a nice thought, Lissa concedes. "How do I know, though," she murmurs, "that I'm not making the same mistakes? That it's not just going to happen all over again?"

"Well, I suppose you don't. Or I guess it's like with anything else—the only way we stop making mistakes is to learn from them. And the only way to learn is to look at why the mistakes happened in the first place—which might mean looking at the parts of yourself you don't want to face up to."

Lissa considers her. "Anyone ever tell you you're pretty wise?"

"Oh, all the time. Dr. D, remember?"

"I thought that was your supervillain alter ego."

"Well, supervillains are usually wise, aren't they?"

"I mean, no, not notoriously."

And just like that, despite what Lissa has told her, they are on even ground, the way they always have been.

Darcy checks her phone, makes a face. "Shit, I better go back to the office."

"Do you think I should come too?"

"No. I think you should skive off for the day, come back tomorrow with an actual letter of resignation, then work out your notice like a grown-up. But today—why bother poking Liam with a stick?"

Lissa cocks her head. "I'm the stick in this scenario?"

In answer to that, Darcy hugs her goodbye. A few minutes later, a chocolate chip cookie arrives at Lissa's table.

The barista shrugs when Lissa looks confused. "It's from your friend," he says. "She said to say congrats."

Lissa smiles as she breaks off a corner of it, pops it into her mouth. She gets out her phone, turning it over in her hand. She feels surprisingly calm, all things considered. Which she's pretty sure is a sign she made the right choice.

The first person she wants to call right now, to tell him that she quit, is Ash. But she can't. She doesn't want to screw him around—and he wants to leave, doesn't he? Maybe that's what needs to happen. Maybe she needs to do some soul-searching herself, before she can be in the right place to start anything with him, soulmate or no. Is that what Saskia meant when she talked about timing?

Failing Ash, she wants to talk it all through with Mia, but they still haven't really fixed things. So she calls her mum instead.

"Lissa." Her mum sounds surprised—she supposes they don't really call each other like this.

"Hi, Mum."

"Is something wrong?"

"No," Lissa says quickly. "No, I just . . . I quit my job."

"Oh." There's a stilted pause. "I, umm . . ."

"It's a good thing," Lissa prompts.

"Oh—well great! Good for you!"

Lissa wants to laugh at the over-the-top enthusiasm, but she doesn't, because she knows it's a sign her mum is trying. "Yeah. So I was thinking . . . I might move somewhere else for a bit." She says it in a rush, before she's had time to talk herself out of it. But once it's out, she knows that that's what she wants to do. That's what she *needs* to do. She's just never been brave enough to admit it to herself.

"Somewhere else?" She can almost hear the frown in her mum's voice.

"Yeah. Maybe I could even go and volunteer abroad, just for a bit." She's thinking as she's speaking—but again, why shouldn't she do that? She needs to get away from this city, needs to learn to be her own person. And maybe Ash isn't who she's supposed to spend her life with—maybe *that's* what the universe is trying to tell her—but one thing's for sure, he's helped her to see that she wants more from life than she's currently getting. She's loved volunteering at the charity shop, after all, so why not move somewhere else entirely, immerse herself in volunteering, take the time to figure out where to go from there?

"Oh," her mum says. "Well…"

"I don't have to go," Lissa says quickly, already back-tracking.

"No, you should. Or at least, you shouldn't stay for me." Her mum sighs. "I don't want to be the reason you're trapped here—not anymore."

Lissa thinks of Mia, of how Mia has also felt stuck here—because of her.

No one asked you to sit watching.

She winces at the memory, but she supposes the same could be said of her mum—no one asked Lissa to sit by, watching her descent. It was implied, sure, but maybe she could have broken free if she'd really tried. If she'd been brave enough.

"I won't go until late September," she continues. She doesn't say it explicitly, but she'll wait until after Chloe's anniversary. Just in case.

"Oh. Yes. I mean..." Her mum trails off. Perhaps she doesn't want to think about it. Perhaps she doesn't want to address how she usually gets that day. Or maybe she's hoping it will be better this year, what with all the therapy. And maybe it will, Lissa thinks. Maybe there's hope for the both of them.

"I'm thinking of selling the house," her mum says, on a rush of breath.

Lissa feels a little jolt. "You are?"

"Mm. I've been painting, trying to get it, you know, a bit more up to date." Lissa thinks of the paint samples she and Mia saw, smiles just a little. "I think," her mum continues slowly, "that maybe I've been here too long?"

"I think that's a nice idea," Lissa says gently. And then, feeling the need to tread carefully, she adds, "But you should do what feels right for you."

"I don't think I'll go far. I just...I think I need to try to...let go."

Lissa feels her throat tighten a bit. "Yeah," she agrees. "Maybe."

"And if I change my mind," her mum goes on, sounding more upbeat now, "it's not like house sales happen quickly, is it? Not from what I can remember, in any case." There's a pause, then, "I'm glad you're having this fresh start, Lissa." The Fool, in her first tarot reading. Starting out on a new life. Has she come to that point in her future? "I know I haven't always been the best mother, but I do want you to be happy, you know."

"I know," Lissa says quietly, although she hasn't known it, not until now.

When they hang up, Lissa takes a breath, squares her shoulders and finishes the last of her cookie. This is it. A choice, something different. And for the first time since that night in Cornwall, she feels she might finally be making the right one.

Chapter Thirty-One

Lissa presses her phone to her ear as she paces around the living room in her flat. The windows are open wide, and she can smell barbecue smoke from one of the neighbors' gardens.

"Enough," she says without preamble. "Enough, Mia. I hate this. I hate not talking to you. I miss you. I know you need some space from me, and I've tried to respect that, but we need to talk about it, okay? I'm leaving my flat in two minutes and I'm coming to Bristol. I think you might be on your way back from London, so I'm going to sit outside your place until you get home, and I thought I should warn you before I leave in case...Wait."

She frowns in the direction of the front door, where someone is thumping. "That's someone at the door. So I'm going to answer it, and *then* I'm going to come to yours. If you really, really don't want me to, then you've got about forty-five minutes to let me know. Okay?"

She hangs up as she stomps down her corridor, needing to keep up the momentum. But when she opens the door, she stares in shock. Because it is Mia. With her red hair and her freckles and wearing if not exactly the same, then a very similar pair of dungarees to the last time they saw each other.

Lissa holds up her phone. "I was just talking to you."

Mia cocks her head. "Huh. You'd have thought I would have heard."

"Talking to your voicemail," Lissa corrects.

"Ah."

There is a beat of awkward quiet between them. Lissa clears her throat. "What are you...?"

Mia gestures vaguely in the air. "I'm here to kiss and make up. If you'll let me."

Lissa laughs a little. "*Let* you? I was just calling you to warn you that I'm on my way to apologize."

"Trust you to warn someone about that." Then Mia sighs. "I suppose we think too similarly after all these years."

Lissa snorts quietly at the suggestion. She doubts Mia would believe in past lives if they literally walked up to her and set fire to those dungarees. But right now, that's not important. So she steps forward, wraps her arms around her cousin and breathes in her scent.

"I'm sorry," she murmurs. "I'm so, so sorry. I should have said that weeks ago. And I should have known why you stuck around. I should have noticed what you were doing for me."

"I should have talked to you about it," Mia mumbles against her shoulder. "I shouldn't have just assumed you knew how I was feeling without telling you." She breaks away, holds Lissa at arm's length. "But enough with the shoulds, okay? Let's think of what we could do in the future instead."

"You know," Lissa says with a small smirk, "you sound a lot like the psychic I went to see."

Mia wrinkles her noise. "Yeah. You never told me much about that."

Lissa steps aside to let her into her flat. "I figured you wouldn't want to know."

"Was it useful?" Mia asks.

"Yes. I actually think it was." Lissa glances at her. "Though apparently I've still got to make all my own choices."

Mia sighs. "Damn. Sounds like a lot of effort."

"Well, quite. So, want a glass of wine?" Lissa asks.

"Love one," Mia says. There it is—olive branch extended and accepted. And they'll be okay, Lissa thinks. Because of course they will.

"Only one," Lissa says. "I'm picking Elsie up from town today."

"They're finally loosening the reins, huh?"

"Yeah." She opens the fridge, gets out a bottle of Sauvignon. "Though I suppose you can't really blame them, all things considered."

"Suppose not, no," Mia concedes.

They sit on the sofa, Mia curling her legs underneath her. "So, I have something to tell you."

"Good," Lissa says, nodding. "Me too. But you first."

Mia sets her wine down on the coffee table. "I think I'm going to do it. Go to New York."

Lissa scans her cousin's face. "For Lottie?"

Mia bites her lip. "Well, for me too, I guess. And for my parents. But yes, she's a big part of it. I want to go, stay there for a few months. See if it could be anything real between us."

Lissa reaches out to take her hand. "That's brilliant, Mia."

"It is?"

"Of course it is!"

Mia blows out a breath. "Okay. Okay, good." She pauses, biting her lip. "Maybe you could visit? Just for a weekend or something? It's close enough for that, you know."

Lissa nods slowly. "I'd love that. But..."

Mia pauses in the action of picking up her wineglass. "But?"

"Well. I'm actually thinking of taking a little break from Bath myself."

Lissa could swear that Mia's jaw literally drops. "Are you fucking kidding me?"

"No. Although I would *love* to take a picture of your face right now." Mia snaps her mouth shut, and Lissa laughs. And God, it feels so good to be here with her cousin like this. "I quit my job."

"You *what*?"

"I know. And I think I've actually got a plan. I've been googling, and there's this charity that runs camps for kids who've experienced loss. They're looking for camp leaders, and I thought maybe I'd be okay at that."

Mia's eyes seem a little bright. "You'll be *great* at it, Bissa."

Lissa isn't sure, but she won't know until she tries, will she? She can't shake the memory of Rosy from the charity shop holding on to that bear to lay on her baby brother's grave. Okay, being a camp leader isn't going to change the world. But it's something to help children like Rosy. And maybe, for now, something is enough.

She takes Mia's hand in hers, squeezes. "I'm happy for you, you know, Mia. About Lottie. I'm going to miss you, but I really, really hope it works out the way you want it to. However that ends up looking."

Mia pulls Lissa into another hug. When she breaks away, her gaze darts over Lissa's face. "And what are you going to do about Ash?"

And just like that, she's back there.

I love you. I just thought you should know that.

"I don't know," she murmurs. She needs to make a choice. She needs to either tell him how she feels, or walk away forever. She finishes the rest of that thought out loud. "I just... How are you supposed to know if the choice you're making is the right one?"

Mia smiles, brushes Lissa's hair back from her face. "I don't think we can ever know that. But for what it's worth, I think you're doing the right thing." Lissa frowns, and Mia shakes her head. "I just mean the moving abroad thing. I think focusing on yourself, doing something cool like that—it'll be great for you, Bissa. And it's a lot harder to do if you're thinking of someone else too, isn't it?"

Lissa nods slowly. But the truth is, she's not sure what came first. Does she want to move abroad for herself?

Or is she doing it to run away from him? It just feels so jumbled in her brain.

Mia seems to sense her uncertainty. "Maybe if it's meant to be for you and Ash, you'll get another shot at it in the future, once you've had the chance to live a little first."

Lissa smiles, because Mia has no idea just how many shots she and Ash have had. But she holds on to the last card from her reading. Temperance. Timing. So maybe her cousin is right—maybe one day the timing will be right for them.

"So then I said to Jess..." Elsie enters into a long and detailed story about a fight between a friendship group at school, and Lissa nods along, trying to follow—which is easier said than done given that there seems to be a new name introduced every couple of seconds. Still, it makes her smile that Elsie so willingly hands over details of her life now. The way to a teenager's heart is definitely through giving them lifts. Possibly buying booze when they're old enough, though she'll cross that bridge when she comes to it.

"Anyway," Elsie concludes, "Jess says she isn't going to go to Kirsty's party without me, so I guess we'll see." She makes a skeptical face, one eyebrow crooking up.

Lissa laughs as she flicks the indicator to turn right. Elsie flushes and drops the eyebrow.

"Too much?" she asks. "This girl on the netball team can do it and I thought it looked cool."

Lissa laughs again. "I love it." She pauses, then, "Chloe learned to do it when she was little. Spent hours in front of the mirror practicing, and it really wound me up because I couldn't do it." It pops into her head, a snippet of a memory she hadn't realized was there.

"Really? That's cool." Elsie looks out the window. "I wish I could have known her." Then she purses her lips, Lissa catching sight of it in the reflection. "Actually, though, that would never be possible, because if she hadn't died I'd probably never have been born, right?"

"Maybe," Lissa concedes. No way to know, is there? But Elsie is right to some degree—if their dad had never left to be with Nicole, Elsie wouldn't have been born. So yes, she lost a sister. But she gained one too. And there's something that feels full circle about that.

"You still on the netball team then?" she says, remembering the conversation all those months ago when Elsie claimed not to even *like* netball.

"Yeah. It's okay. I think Mum cares about it more than I do. But they've been a bit better recently, letting me do stuff, so I figure I'll keep doing it for her for now."

Lissa nods slowly. "Well, as long as you're not *only* doing it for her. I'm sure she'd understand if you quit."

Elsie only shrugs. Lissa isn't quite well versed enough in her sister's shrug language to tell what it means yet.

She taps one finger on her steering wheel. "So look, there's something I need to talk to you about."

Elsie gives her an almost horrified look. "Do *not* tell me Mum put the sex-talk crap onto you."

"What? No! Jesus. Although..." Lissa frowns over at her. "Do you *want* to have the sex talk?"

Elsie wrinkles her nose. "No. I'll let you know when I do."

"Okay. Deal. In the meantime, though…" Lissa fills her in on what she told Mia and her mum—that she's planning on leaving the country for a bit to volunteer abroad.

Elsie contemplate this for a moment, then grins. "Reckon Mum and Dad would let me visit?"

Lissa finds herself grinning too. "I definitely think we can work on it."

Elsie waves goodbye to Lissa when they reach her house. As Lissa is putting the car into reverse to turn around, Nicole comes out, in a long green skirt and blouse, and gestures for her to wait. Lissa winds her window down.

Nicole bends her head when she reaches the car. "Want to come in?" she asks.

"Sorry, I can't. I'm meeting a friend for a drink." Darcy wants to hear all about her plans—and then, Lissa thinks, she'll have told everyone and there will be no going back.

Well. Nearly everyone.

"Another time, though," she promises.

Nicole nods, but stays where she is. She fiddles with a bracelet on her wrist—gold and expensive-looking. "I wanted to say thank you," she says, stopping her fiddling and meeting Lissa's gaze.

"Of course," Lissa says easily. "It's not that far to drive."

Nicole nods again. "I…It's nice to see you hanging out." She hesitates, then drops her voice a fraction. "We never wanted to push it, because we didn't want it to feel like Elsie was, I don't know, a replacement." It's a harsh word and they both wince.

"I don't think that," Lissa says carefully. She used to, though, she realizes. Not directed at Elsie herself, more at her dad, but still. A replacement family.

"Well, anyway," Nicole continues, "it's sort of why I kept my distance a little. And watching you the last few months . . . I wanted to say sorry, for not trying harder."

Lissa frowns. "What do you mean?"

Nicole gestures to the passenger seat and Lissa nods. When her stepmum hops in, she cuts the engine.

"It's just," Nicole says, twisting the bracelet again, "I felt guilty for taking your dad away after you'd already been through so much. And I wish, looking back, that I'd stepped in more. It's none of my business, your relationship with your mum," she goes on carefully, "but I could see when you were younger that you might have needed someone to talk to. But I was pregnant with Elsie, and we worried about what that would mean to you. Your dad was terrified about having another child, and I just . . ." She swallows. "I could have done more."

Lissa takes a moment to process that. The fact that her dad was terrified as much as anything else. "You couldn't have," she says eventually. She doesn't think she would have accepted help even if Nicole had tried to give it. And her mum certainly wouldn't have.

"I could have tried," Nicole insists.

Lissa thinks of Ash, asking if she ever tried to get to know Nicole. "We both could have," she says.

Nicole pushes a hand through her perfectly styled hair. "I've been a little protective of Elsie." Said like an admission. "Your dad...Well, it's been hard to know what the right thing to do is." Lissa can see it now. The death of a child lingering over them all.

"You don't have to explain anything to me," she says. "But for what it's worth, I think you're doing a good job." Elsie seems happy and healthy, and willing to let Lissa in after years of a strained relationship. And that, as far as she is concerned, suggests good parenting.

Nicole smiles. "Thank you for saying that."

"I mean it. She's pretty great."

"Yes. She is." She pauses. "Your dad...I know he doesn't talk about it much, but he still holds Chloe in his heart. I just thought maybe you'd like to know that."

Lissa swallows, nods. Nicole reaches for her hand, and Lissa lets her take it, feeling the pressure of Nicole's wedding band on her skin. "And I hope you know too that you'll always have a place in this family."

Lissa squeezes Nicole's hand back. "Yeah," she says. "I think I'm starting to."

A new start, she thinks. And hope on the horizon.

Chapter Thirty-Two

It takes her a moment when she wakes to realize what day it is. Because for the first time in as long as she can remember, she doesn't start the day being dragged from a nightmare, doesn't feel the water pulling her under in her sleep. Maybe because she knows now that the nightmares were never about Chloe.

The sky is heavy with unshed rain as she heads up the hill to her mum's house. An ominous sign, maybe, but she's feeling weirdly positive. Like maybe this is the year it can be different. That they can celebrate Chloe—or at least finally take steps to put what happened behind them.

It's only when she reaches her mum's street, the trees along the verge showing the first signs of turning russet with autumn, that the nerves begin in her stomach.

She pushes the front door open tentatively, the way she always does.

"Mum?" But already she can smell it, a kind of sourness inside the house. Her stomach rolls.

And there she is, in the living room. Standing by a fire she's lit, even though it's warm outside, throwing photos into the flames. Lissa watches one curl in on itself, a smiling face turning black with soot.

She moves quickly across the room, grabs her mum's hand before she can throw the next one in. "Mum, no," she says, holding tight when Esme tries to shake her off. She's still in her nightgown. A nightgown that holds a whiff of that same sour smell.

"You'll regret this," Lissa continues, forcing the photos out of her mum's grip. She doesn't look at them. She doesn't think she wants to know which parts of her life her mum is turning to ash.

Esme blinks at her. "What are you doing here?"

"I told you I'd be here." Lissa's voice is gentle, though her insides are screaming at her. Telling her what an idiot she is to have expected anything different.

She leads her mum to the sofa, sits her down. Esme reaches for a glass of clear, strong-smelling liquid on the coffee table, and Lissa immediately takes it from her. Her mum says nothing, just stares up at her out of red-rimmed eyes.

Lissa feels her heart twist. She wishes she could walk away. Knows she never will. "I'll make you some breakfast," she says, turning away and taking the glass with her.

But her mum reaches out to take her arm, her fingers clammy on Lissa's skin. "It's our fault, Alyssa," she whispers, her voice hoarse. "It will always be our fault."

Some things, Lissa supposes, will never change.

The rain starts as she gets back to her road, light droplets spotting her face. Because of it, she's looking down, so she doesn't see him until she's nearly on top of him. He's heading toward her, away from her flat, his eyes also downcast, wearing a leather jacket that she thinks, bizarrely, will be damaged if the rain gets worse. He looks up as they nearly collide, his gaze catching hers. And her heart stutters.

A corner of his mouth crooks up. "Hey."

"Hey." Her voice is barely a whisper.

His gaze briefly moves to a car over the other side of the road. She follows the direction and sees the suitcase, obvious in the back seat. And she knows.

"You're leaving?" She didn't mean it to come out so high-pitched. She knew this was coming, after all. She's had time to prepare, had time to make a different choice. And she hasn't. Still that doesn't stop the leaden weight in her gut.

He nods. "I said I'd come and say goodbye." He smiles a little. "Fitting, I guess." She glances at him in question, and he shrugs. "It was exactly a year ago that we met, technically."

A year, she thinks. And multiple lifetimes. She takes a careful step toward him, tilts her face up. The rain is getting heavier, dampening her hair.

"Where will you go?" she asks. "Brazil?"

A noncommittal shrug. "Going to spend a few weeks in Spain with a friend. But then, yeah, I think so. I'll see what comes in work-wise and go from there." But it's said without the usual sense of freedom, almost sounding a little bitter.

Trying to swallow down her emotion—because she doesn't want to inflict that on him—she closes the distance between them and hugs him, breathing in his scent for the last time. His arms come around her, like he can't help himself, and she squeezes her eyes shut, resting her head on his chest. She feels his fingers flexing on her back. She wants to tell him that she's leaving too. That she's quit her job, that she's going to try something new. But she can't get the words out.

"So, past lives, huh?" he says as he pulls back. She wonders if he just doesn't know what else to say. She managed to stop the tears earlier, at her mum's house, but now she's crying as she nods. "Well then," he says, reaching out to tuck a strand of her hair behind her ear. "Maybe we'll meet again, in another one." But not in this one—because he won't come back. He has no reason to. Not anymore.

She tries for a smile. "You think?"

"Maybe. Maybe that will be our chance to get it right." She doesn't know if he actually believes that or whether he is humoring her, but it makes her think of what Mia said. And about what Saskia said—about having patience. About the timing needing to be right.

He hesitates, then kisses the top of her head—a fleeting, tender gesture. "I'll see you, Liss."

With that, he's moving away from her, back turned in a sudden and complete full stop. She watches him walk across the road, the rain soaking through to her skin. And she knows, in that instant, that she can't do it. She can't stand by while he walks away—can't lose him, not again. Chloe lost her life on this day all those years ago, and as such, the day has always held meaning for her. But maybe that's okay, because it's a reminder to take chances, to live her life.

It's a question of timing. But who's to say the timing isn't right now? As Saskia said, all you can ever do is make the best possible choice in the moment. And this is the choice she wants to make right now.

She takes a step after him. "Wait."

He stops like he was listening out for her voice. Turns back. Something like hope flickers over his face. It's that that makes her sure. The hope. Because like her, he's had so much tragedy in his life, and she doesn't want to be another point of darkness. She wants to be the light.

There is a lump in her throat as she moves toward him, and he mimics her, so that they're in the middle of the road, a line of cars either side of them.

"I love you," she murmurs. She can't remember the last time she said the words out loud. It feels terrifying. Exhilarating.

For one heart-stopping moment he says nothing, staring at her. Then a corner of his mouth pulls up. "Yeah?"

"Yes." Her voice is steady, certain. "I'm sorry I didn't say it sooner."

The smile spreads a little. "Better late than never." But he doesn't reach for her. Instead he stays still, watching. Because, she supposes, that doesn't necessarily change anything.

She swallows. She's the one who has to take the chance

here. Who has to take the leap of faith. "I love you," she says again. And now she closes the distance between them, framing his face with her hands. Her voice grows a little smaller. "And I don't want you to leave me."

He reaches for her waist, pulls her to him. Beneath her sodden jumper, her skin heats at his touch. "I don't want to leave you either. I don't want to leave at all. I want to stay put—with you."

Her heart rate spikes at the low, gravelly sound of his voice, and she places her hand on his chest to steady herself. "Then let's do that, okay?"

"Okay." And then he's kissing her and she's kissing him back, and there is no fear or hesitation, only the taste of him and the pull of something deep inside her. A car horn sounds, too close, and someone whoops.

Lissa is laughing as the kiss breaks off, as Ash pulls her to the side of the road so the car can pass, tires throwing up water from the tarmac. She laughs again as he lifts her on top of the bonnet of his car to keep kissing her. The rain beats down on their heads—she can feel it as she fists her hands in his hair.

When they finally stop, they are both breathless.

"I hate to say it," Ash says against her mouth, "but I reckon we need to make a break for it." Another car passes, splashing in a newly formed puddle. He cocks his head, his hands resting on her thighs. "Your place?"

"No," she says, jumping down from the bonnet. "Let's go somewhere." He considers her, then concedes with a nod, fishing out keys and unlocking the car.

Inside, it's all steamed up. She shivers, partly from the cold, her wet clothes clinging to her. Partly from something else entirely.

He flicks an eyebrow as he looks at her. "Where shall we go?"

"Anywhere!" She can feel excitement bubbling over. It's got to be right. This has got to be the choice she was supposed to make. "Let's go to Spain."

He gives her a skeptical look. "You don't have any clothes." He starts the engine, pulls out. Away from Bath, and toward the motorway.

She makes a *pff* sound. "I'll buy some. Or Brazil," she says, gripping his hand on the gearstick. "I'll come with you." She can do the camp another time, can't she? She can figure out the rest of her life later.

His lip quirks. God, she fucking loves this man. "How about we go to the beach?"

"Sure," she agrees with a nod. She lets go of his hand, pushes her fingers through her hair. "Let's just go *somewhere*." Because she needs to do something; she needs to celebrate this. "Let's go and have sex on the beach."

He snorts. "You know, I tried that once. Not all it's cracked up to be." But his gaze slides to hers, and something inside her fizzes. He takes her hand where it rests on her lap, links his fingers with hers.

"You know I love you, right?" he murmurs.

She looks at him, fingers gripping tight. "I have *always* loved you." She feels it, right down to her soul. And she knows in that moment that the past doesn't matter, because he is the person she's supposed to be with. He is everything. Her past and her future.

She looks back down to their joined hands, smiling.

It's only when she looks up that she sees.

Headlights coming toward them through the dark cloud, the rain.

It doesn't register at first, like things are moving in slow motion. A second to realize what's happened. To see the lorry skidding on the wet road, across the single carriageway and over to their side.

It's going to hit them. It's obvious, in that moment. It's going to hit them, and there's nothing Ash can do about it. He has already snatched his hand from her grip. He is already turning the steering wheel. He glances at her, his eyes dark and terrified. Not for himself. But for *her*.

And she sees what he's going to do. He's already doing it, already turning so that he's the one who will take the impact. So that the lorry, sounding its horn now, like that could possibly help, will hit him first.

She sees one more thing in that instant between life and death. She sees it from the way he shakes his head, like he's shaking away a memory. From the way his eyes flash—wide, bright.

He remembers. He remembers what they were to each other. He remembers that this has happened before—his death, over and over, because of her. A loop destined to repeat.

Her ears are ringing, pulse spiking. It's happening again. And she sees it now, the other times it's happened, almost exactly like this. Drowning, a gunshot, a car. Different deaths, but the same moment, just before. A moment where she has to choose him—or choose something else. Like the art school she didn't go to because of him. Not because he asked her not to go, but because she couldn't stand to lose him. Maybe because of what happened with Chloe, because she can't bear to lose another person. It's connected, like Saskia said.

She chooses him instead of following her own path. He doesn't have these flashbacks, because it's not him making the wrong choice—it's her.

And now it's all happening again. This realization happens in the time it takes to take a breath. Like she is briefly suspended, looking down at the scene.

She can't change the past. She never could. And it's not punishment—it's like Darcy said. The universe is offering her a chance, each time, to get it right. To try and forgive herself for what happened to her sister and move on. To choose herself, in this moment, and not him.

She nearly did it this time. So in the second before the lorry hits, she takes Ash's hand, grabs the steering wheel to steady it. There will be another chance, she's sure of it. This will not be the end.

She smiles at him, bright and sure, as he turns to her in horror.

"I love you," she says. Right before the moment of impact.

Chapter Thirty-Three

Thirty years later

Theo moves up the escalator and through the crowds at Paddington station, listening to his dad's voice coming through his AirPods, telling him about a party he's arranging for when Theo gets home to Dublin.

"Well, more of a get-together really," his dad is saying. "But everyone has said they'll be here. Which is good, given I wouldn't be able to go *there*, so to speak." A subtle dig at himself, Theo knows. It's the main reason he's moving back to Ireland. He hasn't been in the same place much since his mum died when he was a teenager. But he's watched as his dad has become more and more introverted, and maybe it's time to try and help with that before it's too late. And maybe it'll be nice to be in one place for a while. He never thought he'd say that— and maybe it's the old cliché about approaching thirty and wondering what direction you want the next thirty years of your life to take, but he feels like something is telling him to stay put. After all, you can be a music producer from anywhere, can't you?

"I'll be there, Dad," he says firmly.

"Well, good. Because all your shite is already here, and what will I do with it if you don't come home?"

Theo laughs. "I'll call you tomorrow when I'm off the plane at Dublin, okay?"

He hangs up, looking up at the departures boards. It's hot, jackets hooked over suitcase handles, people fanning themselves as they wait for their train. A second wave of summer in mid-September. He always feels weird this time of year. Like there's an important date coming up that he can't remember—someone's birthday he's forgotten. He's never been able to figure out why.

His train to Bristol is on time. If he's quick, he can grab a pasty beforehand. He could've flown straight to Dublin from London, but he has a friend in Bristol and thought, why not?

He scans the other destinations. It's weird—he's always been drawn to certain places. New York, Paris, Bath. And all right, those are places everyone wants to visit, so you could probably argue it's just that. It doesn't feel like that, though. It feels like he has some connection to them. He went to Bath for the first time a few years ago, was sure he recognized the place, even though his dad insisted they'd never been to that part of England before.

Beside him, two women are hugging goodbye, one about his age, one older.

"Maybe I shouldn't go," the younger one says as she pulls back.

"You're going," says the older one firmly. "You've spent too long pandering to my needs. Now it's your turn."

The younger one bites her lip, then nods, giving the other woman one more hug before turning and walking right past Theo, pulling a massive suitcase. She drops something a few feet away but doesn't seem to notice, just keeps striding on, determined. The older woman is already leaving the station, back held ramrod-straight.

Theo bends to pick up whatever it is she's dropped. Her passport. "Hey, wait!"

She doesn't hear him over the announcement of the next train to leave, the general chatter around them. He jogs after her, carrying only a rucksack, and taps her on the shoulder. She jumps so violently she nearly topples over her suitcase.

He holds up both hands. "Sorry. You dropped this." He holds out her passport. She stares at it for a moment, then shakes her head, laughing a little at herself. She reaches to take it, and the tips of her fingers brush his.

"Thanks, hero," she says. "Would be hard to get on a plane without it." Her voice resonates around his brain for a moment, like the echo of something he remembers.

Hey, hero.

He shakes it off. "Yeah. Maybe not impossible, but only if you're, like, James Bond."

"Well, sure, then I could sneak into the bit under the plane. What's it called, where they put all the suitcases?" She frowns. He's kind of fascinated by the little lines that form between her eyebrows. "Actually, though, if I'm James Bond, I probably have my own plane, don't I?"

"Probably," he agrees. He should just let her go—she obviously has somewhere she needs to be. Instead, he feels a slightly irrational desire to keep her here, talking to him. "Question, though—you do know this isn't an airport, right?"

She smiles, and he feels a spark of something inside, like he's glad that he's made this stranger smile. "I'm on the way to Heathrow," she says.

"Ah." There's a pause, and then, because she's still there, looking at his face a little curiously, he holds out a hand. "Theo," he says. He briefly imagines his mum, when she was alive, laughing at him for being so formal.

"Ally," she says, offering him another smile as she takes his hand. The weight of her hand feels familiar in his, and they both hold on longer than necessary.

"So this may be a little weird," he says as they break apart, "but I don't suppose you have time for a coffee, do you?"

She bites her lip, glances at the departures board. Then she sighs, shakes her head.

"Sorry," he says quickly, feeling stupid for asking. He's not even sure why he did—*he* has somewhere to be, too. And what exactly is he hoping a coffee will turn into? They live in different places—they're never going to see each other again. "Of course you don't."

"No, it's just, I really do have a plane to catch. And given it's not a private jet, I can't ask it to wait for me." She holds up her passport. "Thanks, though. You really are my hero."

He can't help watching her as she walks away. She reminds him of someone, though he can't think who. It's the way she moves, he thinks. The way she smiles. He shakes his head, snorting to himself for being an idiot, and starts toward his own platform.

He risks one more glance back, over his shoulder. And sees her glancing back at him too. Their gazes meet, hold. Then she lifts a hand in a final goodbye. Turns away. And is gone.

Chapter Thirty-Four

Ally can't quite shake the thought of the stranger from the train station as she arrives at the airport. She'd wanted, so much, to say yes to coffee—and today of all days should be a reminder to take life by the horns. But her mum had come with her to the station—had actually *come with her*—and hadn't brought up the date once. So she couldn't just abandon her plan on a whim, all because of a weird spark she'd felt when she looked at him.

She can't even explain *why* she'd felt that spark. It was to do with his eyes. Not the color or anything like that, but the way he looked at her. The way one corner of his mouth quirked up, the gesture strangely familiar.

If she'd said yes, though, she'd have missed her plane. And she knows, if she thinks logically, that rather than trying to live up to a filmic meet-cute, the plane is where she needs to be. Because she *did* it. The thing she's been striving toward since choosing her A levels at school— she's now finally on her way.

Still. She can't quite let it go. The image of him

standing there, watching her as she walked away. A weird sense of loss—like she's leaving something behind.

"Ow!" She's not looking where she's going as she heads out of security—which maybe explains the massive fuck-off spike that impales itself into her toe. Or okay, not quite *into*. But it bloody feels like it.

"Ow," she says again, practically hopping when the stiletto is removed, accompanied by a woman's "Shit, sorry!"

Ally whimpers in pain and hops to the side, so that countless other people can move out of security and toward duty-free. She thinks she can feel blood coating her sock inside her trainer. She perches on a bench, reaching to pull off the shoe she literally just put on again.

"I'm so sorry." She looks up to see a woman—fifties, sixties maybe?—peering down at her. "I didn't see you there."

She glances down at the woman's feet. Fucking red stilettos. Who wears those to an airport?

She ignores the woman, continuing the removal of her shoe, then her sock. It might be broken, she thinks. *Of course it's bloody broken.* Don't you break a bone in your toe every time you step down too hard or something?

It might be *seriously* broken, though.

Get a fucking grip, Ally.

"Are you okay?" the woman is asking.

Ally is too busy inspecting the injured toe to reply. It already looks bruised—though there is no blood, so she was clearly imagining that.

"I wasn't looking where I was going," the woman says unnecessarily, still hovering over her. She makes a face at the sight of the bruise. Then she clicks her fingers. "Here," she says, fumbling in her handbag, "I went to Boots just before we came through. I have a plaster." She pulls out a box, keeps fumbling. "And does it hurt? I have paracetamol. A bandage, maybe?"

Ally raises her eyebrows. "Handy, aren't you?"

"Oh sure," the woman says mildly. "Just call me Dr. D."

Ally frowns. "Like a supervillain?"

The woman stops rooting in her bag and stares at her. It's such an odd look that Ally immediately wonders if she's somehow offended her. Though to be fair, she's the one who drove a stiletto through Ally's foot, not the other way around.

"What?" Ally asks.

"Nothing. Sorry." The woman hands over the pack of plasters.

Because it feels impolite not to, Ally takes it, pulls out a toe-sized one. "Thanks." She offers the pack back, but the woman shakes her head.

"Keep it. You never know when someone else might be wielding a lethal shoe around you."

Ally snorts and slips the plasters into her own bag— again, because it seems easier not to argue.

"Are you accosting strangers now, love?" A man with salt-and-pepper hair and a kind smile approaches them.

"Well, my shoe is." The woman looks back to Ally. "Are you sure you're—"

"I'm fine," Ally says firmly, slipping her shoe back on and putting weight on her foot. She's proud of herself, actually. This is something that not so long ago might have caused a panic attack. Turns out therapy actually *is* helpful.

"This is Aaron," the woman is saying. "My husband."

"Hi, Aaron. I'm Ally. Your wife's shoe took issue with my toe."

"Or maybe, to be fair, your toe took issue with my shoe. After all, a shoe is inanimate."

Ally cocks her head. "Whereas a toe can think for itself?"

The woman snorts. "I'm Darcy."

Ally smiles. "Nice to meet you, Darcy. I think."

They gather their stuff—and of course they are all heading the same way, into duty-free, meaning it's that awkward kind of situation where unless one of you thinks of an excuse quickly enough, you end up walking together.

"So where are you off to?" Ally asks out of politeness.

"Oh, we're going to see one of my best friends, Mia, and her wife, Lottie. They live in New York and it's our turn to go to them. We always get together at this time of year." Aaron squeezes Darcy's hand, and the two of them exchange a look. It's not much, but Ally recognizes that look. So, they lost someone too.

"What about you?" Darcy asks.

"I'm actually starting a new job in Massachusetts." A combination of nerves and excitement pulses through her gut as she says it.

"*Are* you? Well congratulations. You know, they say that

when a shoe impales your foot before you start a new job, you're bound to be promoted within the year."

Ally snorts again. "Do they actually say that, though?"

Darcy shrugs. "Probably. Makes more sense than the bird-shit thing, doesn't it?"

Aaron gives a cough that sounds like "debatable," and Ally laughs. She likes them, she decides.

"So what's the job?" Darcy asks.

"I'm working as a kind of... counselor at this kids' camp." *Counselor* for want of a better word, because she's not qualified. Yet.

"Like a holiday camp?" Darcy asks.

"Sort of. It's for kids who have experienced grief of some kind. The camp does all these activities, and there are sessions aimed at dealing with bereavement. We give the parents advice if they want it, but it's also a chance for the parents to have a break and... What?" Because Darcy is looking at her a little strangely.

"Nothing," Darcy says again, smoothing out her expression. "Sorry. It's just... you're giving me déjà vu. So. Massachusetts." They pass one of the restaurants on the upper floor of the airport, head toward the escalators.

"They do them all over the place," Ally says. "I applied to loads and this one said yes." And it feels good, to be moving somewhere completely different. She wants to be away from everything that has defined her for all these years, and she is finally being brave enough to do exactly that.

"Any particular reason you applied for the job?" It's asked with just a *touch* too much innocence—something

Darcy's husband seems to clock too, from the look he gives her.

She could just say no. But her sister is on her mind today—and this friendly couple have lost someone too. "My sister died when I was little," she says as they get on the escalator—and by now she's perfected the art of not quite looking at people as she says this, adopting the right tone so as not to make them too uncomfortable. "It was an accident, but I..." She shakes her head, smiles brightly. "Anyway. You don't need my life story." But it's why she wants this job—why she's so nervous. Because she knows what it's like to be a child unable to process grief, unable to turn to the adults around you because they can't deal with theirs ether. Blaming yourself for what happened.

Abruptly, at the bottom of the escalator, Darcy turns to her and takes both her hands. It happens so suddenly that Ally doesn't have time to move out of the way to avoid it, and behind them, someone gives a loud, disapproving tut as they have to navigate around them.

"Can I ask you some questions?" Darcy says, gaze scarily intense.

"Er... I guess?" Ally tries to gently extract her hands, but Darcy holds firm. She glances around for the nearest security guard—the woman doesn't exactly seem dangerous, but you never know.

"They're going to seem a bit random," Darcy caveats.

"Okay..."

"Are you afraid of water?"

Ally starts, and her hands still. "I actually used to be." She frowns. "Well, I still am, I suppose. I've been working on it." And the dreams that have never made sense, where she wakes with her lungs burning, choking on water that was never there, have lessened.

Darcy nods like that proves a point. "Do you believe in past lives?"

"Ah..." Okay, we're back to crazy. "I guess I've never really thought about it."

Darcy purses her lips. Ally can see Aaron looking at his wife curiously, but he doesn't intervene. "Okay," Darcy says. "One more thing." She takes a breath. "Is there anyone on the scene at the moment—romantically, I mean?"

"Umm...no?" She doesn't mean it as a question, she just thinks it's a bit of an invasion of privacy. She *was* in a relationship, but she broke it off recently, figuring out, with the help of her therapist, that she needed to sort her own shit out before she could commit to someone else. And then the job came along. The last person to ask her out was approximately two hours ago—and she walked away from him.

"Okay. Good." Darcy lets go of her hands, only to cup her face. Seriously—has this woman been drinking or something? A nervous flier? "You make sure you choose yourself, okay? Fix whatever needs to be fixed, come to terms with whatever you need to come to terms with. Do all that first, okay?"

Ally frowns at her—at this very strange advice—and Darcy drops her hands.

"Darce, I think you're scaring her," Aaron says, laying a hand on his wife's arm. "Come to think of it, you're scaring me too."

Darcy waves him away. "She'll get it, if I'm right. If I'm wrong, no one's got anything to lose, have they?"

"Ah..." Ally still isn't following. Another person glares at them as they wheel past a small suitcase—bottom of an escalator not the ideal place to stand, apparently.

"Just," Darcy insists, "don't choose love until you're definitely ready to."

That is pretty much the opposite of the usual rhetoric, but Ally gives a nod-shrug, wanting Darcy to stop the alarmingly intense stuff. "Sure. Okay."

"Are you trying to tell me something here?" Aaron pipes up. Then he turns to Ally. "Sorry, she's not usually like this. Or actually, maybe sometimes, but only with people we know."

"Ally doesn't mind, do you, Ally?" Darcy says breezily. Ally doesn't really feel she can say no to this, so stays silent. "Right." Darcy starts to walk again. "I think we should get a drink. Ally, you like gin and tonic, don't you?"

"I do," Ally agrees—then realizes, too late, that this looks like she's agreeing to said drink.

Darcy gives Aaron a pointed look. Aaron huffs. "That doesn't prove anything. Most of the bloody country likes gin."

"You don't," Darcy says. She steers them toward a bar in a way that leaves little room for argument.

Ally tries to think of a reason not to join them. But her flight isn't for an hour, and she knows that if left to her own devices, the nerves will mount. Besides, she weirdly quite likes this woman. Like she reminds her of a childhood friend. So she doesn't argue as Darcy finds them a table, orders a round of drinks.

And she has this feeling, just for a moment. A rush of certainty, punching through her gut. Like right now this is exactly where she's supposed to be.

Chapter Thirty-Five

Fifteen years later

Out on the cliffs, a safe distance away from the edge, Ally wraps her arms around little Harry, who has launched himself at her in a goodbye. She feels her eyes spark and her throat tighten. You'd think it would become easier after years of doing this, but some of the kids just get to her.

The parents are saying thank you, his mum looking a little less tired than when she dropped him off. Harry promises to come back next year, and Ally promises she'll be right here.

She waves them off as they get into their car, the sea breeze tugging at her hair. She loves it out here on the Cornish coastline, with the sound of the waves a constant backdrop, and the feeling like you're on the edge of the world. It's why she decided to set up her camps here. She spent years learning what worked and what didn't, getting the right qualifications, continuing with her own therapy so that she felt she was a safe pair of hands for the parents to put their trust in. And it's hard sometimes. Really bloody hard. To see the way grief and loss can tear families apart—to see some of these kids come through the doors, dull behind the eyes. But it is the best possible job you could hope for, and at the end of every camp, she feels this brilliant sense of achievement, of *rightness*.

Her one and only full-time employee comes out from the house at Ally's back, the rest of the camp workers already heading to the nearest pub. Mostly the kids stay outdoors, in tents, but the house is useful for evening activities and for any kids who are nervous.

"You did great, as always," Elsie says, patting Ally's shoulder. Ally turns to her, smiles. Elsie's curly silver hair ripples slightly in the wind. She's a good fifteen years or so older than Ally. When Ally advertised for a second-in-command, she thought it would attract someone younger, someone who would only stick around temporarily, a step on the career ladder. But Elsie saw the job advertised while she was living in Bath, and decided it was time for a late career change. And she's stuck.

"You heading for a swim?" Ally asks. It's late in the day, the sun already starting its descent, but Elsie is a keen cold-water swimmer, having taken it up since moving to Cornwall.

"Not tonight. Better first thing. And I'm beat," Elsie says, stretching. "Worth it, though," she adds with a smile.

Ally smiles back. "They always are." And Elsie gets it, because she lost a sister herself. "Your kids still coming down tomorrow?"

Elsie snorts. "Hardly call them kids anymore. But yes. You'll come for dinner?"

"I will," Ally promises. She's never had kids of her own. She's had a handful of relationships over the years, one that lasted more than a decade. But none of them ever quite felt like the real thing. She supposes the timing was never right, and she feels okay about that. Some things just aren't meant to be.

"I know I say it every time," Elsie says, "but they'd be proud, you know." They. Her sister. Her mother. It started because of her sister, but really, it's been more for Ally herself. In order to help the people she runs the camps for, she's had to accept that it wasn't her fault. That some things you can't ever change, no matter how much you wish you could. That you might be able to learn and grow from the past, but you can never alter it. That is part of what she tries to help the kids with—to let go of guilt and blame. She doesn't want it to define other people the way it defined her for so long.

Her mum, though, could never fully accept the past. She tried, but there was a part of her that always felt guilty, and that still blamed them both. And Ally has learned to accept that, too. Because you can try to process your own feelings, control your own actions, but you can't control other people's. In the end, though, before she died, Ally thinks that despite all that, her mother was proud.

"See you tomorrow then?" Elsie says, squeezing her shoulder.

"You will. Bye, Else." Ally gives the older woman a hug, breathing in the scent that has always felt comforting to her—like coming home.

She locks up the house, even though there's little need, given that their nearest neighbor is the cottage that is almost falling into the ocean, one that hasn't been inhabited in years as far she knows. With her swimming costume on under her clothes, just in case, she heads for a walk over the cliffs. She's got in the habit of doing this at the end of every camp, walking along the shoreline, getting to know the ocean's moods while she takes some time for herself. Today it's warm and sunny, sweat pricking her neck beneath her hair. She loved it here the first time she saw it. It had been raining, sky gray, with a storm brewing above the sea on the horizon. But she still loved it. Still knew it was where she needed to be.

Up ahead there's a man walking toward her, close to the edge. It's rare, but not super unusual, to see someone out here—mostly the tourists stick to the more well-known spots.

She lifts her hand in friendly greeting as she gets closer. He's about the same age as her, she thinks, early forties maybe. His arms and face are tanned, and when he smiles, it's the type of smile that makes you want to return it. He walks with the ease of someone used to hiking for miles— or maybe someone used to pounding the treadmill. From the tan, she'd guess the former.

He's almost past her when he stops, turns. And frowns at her. "I know you," he states, completely apropos of nothing.

She comes to a stop too, raising her eyebrows. "I don't think so," she says, offering a smile of apology.

His gaze flickers over her face. "I do," he insists. He

has an Irish accent, she realizes. "I just don't know where from…"

She peers at him a little closer, taking in the strong jawline, the graze of stubble. The green eyes, giving way to amber at their center. She realizes she can feel it too— that jolt of recognition. She can't think *where* she knows a random Irishman from, but her gut tells her she does.

It hits them both seemingly in the same moment, and she laughs. "Are you actually kidding me? Paddington?"

"Yes!" He stares at her. "Wow." He lets out a low whistle. "Can't believe you remembered."

She laughs again. "I can't believe I remembered either." But she can see him now, almost exactly fifteen years ago, handing over her passport. His gaze locked on hers as she turned to glance back. "Small world, huh? Well, clearly we've both aged well, if we're instantly recognizable."

He grins. "I'll take that as a compliment."

"You should," she says, and he grins again.

"So was it worth blowing me off?" he asks.

She rolls her eyes, running with the joke like they are old friends, like they've known each other years rather than seconds. "I had a plane to catch, remember? And yes, it was worth it." Because if she'd stayed to talk to him, she might not be where she is now.

"So you live here?" He gestures around to the cliffs, the grass spreading in one direction, ocean the other.

"Yep," she says easily. "I've got a cave just down the way."

He nods seriously. "Can't beat a good cave."

She snorts a little. "I run these camps," she starts.

"The bereavement camps?" he says immediately. "Or, sorry, I know that's not actually what you call them, but...those camps?"

She raises her eyebrows. "Yeah."

He shrugs in answer to her silent question. "I've seen some of your activities since I've been here. Team-building and stuff? Drawing? And netball. Swear I saw a bunch of kids doing netball."

"That's part of it," she agrees. The netball was Elsie's addition. She'd insisted that years of being on the netball team at school had to be worth something. The drawing, of course, was all Ally. She'd felt over the years that art had helped her, and she wanted to incorporate it somehow. Some of the kids just like painting a pretty picture, but with others, she can see the way it really helps them to get out their feelings.

"They look cool," says the man—Theo, she even remembers his name.

She smiles. "They are cool. So you live here too?"

"Nah, just visiting. Well, a prolonged visit. I lost my dad a while back," he admits.

"I'm sorry," she says, in that automatic way.

"No, it's okay. I mean, it's never okay, is it? But he had a good life. He went through a rough period, but he came through it and it was...Sorry, you don't need to know all this." She wants to know, though. It doesn't really make sense, but she wants to hear this stranger's story. "Anyway, I saw this cottage right on the cliff, and I thought, well, why not."

Her eyebrows shoot up. "As in, the only cottage around here? The one practically falling into the ocean?"

"That's the one. And it's not fallen in *yet*."

"I love that place," she admits. "Well, to be fair, I've never been inside. But I love the idea of it. Although maybe not the idea of falling off the cliff while making coffee one day."

He laughs. "Well, I always did like living on the edge."

They're walking together now—before, they were going in opposite directions, but somehow they've fallen into step beside one another.

"So what do you do?" she asks him.

"I'm a music producer." But he follows it up with a frown.

"You don't like it?"

"No, sorry—it's just I *was* a music producer, until a few years ago. Apparently I can't shake it."

"Ah. How come you stopped?"

He shrugs. "Lost the love of music, I guess. That's why I went into it, but it ended up feeling, I don't know, distant?"

Ally nods, because somehow this makes perfect sense to her. "What do you do now? Play in a band?" She says it as a joke, but she has an image then of him standing on a stage, singing in a jazz band. She blinks it away, not sure where it came from.

"Nah," he says. "I took a bit of time out after my dad, but I'm actually retraining to be a teacher. A music teacher," he adds, slightly unnecessarily.

"That's cool," she says.

"Is it?"

"Well I guess I would say that, given my job. But for what it's worth, I think sharing your love of something with other people can help you rekindle the love for it yourself."

His eyes are very intense on her face as he nods his agreement at that. "Right. That's exactly it. I suppose I just needed to figure out how to be happy staying in one place before I could commit to teaching other people, though." He shakes his head. "Sorry. Too much information again."

"Not at all," she disagrees—and means it. "I know what that's like. I mean, not the staying-in-one-place thing— I've always been good at that—but needing to figure stuff out."

When they get to a point on the cliff where a ledge sticks out, Theo steps up to the edge, peering down.

"Some people jump off that," Ally says conversationally. It's never seemed wise to her, but she's seen the daredevil types leaping into the water, trusting it as a safe spot where they won't hit their heads on the rocks. Some of the kids have asked her if they can do it too—it's stopped her coming anywhere near here with them.

"Hmm," Theo says, still looking down. She can see it briefly, then. Him jumping. Her screaming for him. What is *wrong* with her? He glances back at her. "Maybe we better walk down instead."

They wind their way down to the beach together,

lapsing into a silence that doesn't feel awkward at all. The sun is setting, its orange glow reflected in the water.

"God, it's so beautiful here," Theo murmurs.

"I know," Ally says, matching his tone. "You never really get used to it."

Theo looks at her. "Is it weird if I go for a swim now?"

She waves a hand in the air. "Nah. Go for it."

He strips his T-shirt off, revealing an impressively muscled chest. She feels a fizz of something down her spine—something she hasn't felt in a long time—and looks away out of politeness.

He moves toward the water, and she's about to settle herself down to watch the world go by when he glances over his shoulder. "You coming?"

She hesitates for the briefest of moments. Then she shrugs. "Why not?" She pulls off her dress, thankful that she put her swimming costume on. She watches the way his gaze slides down to her legs before quickly snapping away—exactly the reaction she just had to him. That fizzing inside her intensifies.

She follows him into the sea, laughs as the cold comes up around them.

"Shit," he hisses. "I forgot how bracing the sea in England can be."

There is a moment of stillness between them. A moment where they just look at each other, waist-deep in the ocean. She feels a tug inside her—something more than attraction, deeper than that. And she feels certain that they've been here before. On this shoreline, by this ocean. She can see the way he looked at her in a cottage overlooking the pebbly beach. Can remember the taste of him when she kissed him.

A corner of his mouth crooks up into a playful smile. "Race you?"

She laughs again. It's one of her greatest achievements in life. That she can take these random moments and laugh along with them. "To where?"

He's already off, striking out in a powerful front crawl. "Anywhere!" he calls back over his shoulder.

She follows him, swimming in a way she only managed to learn well into adulthood. It's almost hard to imagine now that she used to be scared of water. She never quite figured out where that fear came from—her therapist said some fears are innate. A psychic she went to see told her it might be from a past life.

When they are out deeper than they can stand, Theo turns to face her, treading water. Her hands move in small circles, keeping her afloat, and she feels the brush of his fingertips against hers as he does the same. It's amazing how her whole body tightens at that fleeting contact.

"Want to head back to the beach?" he asks, sunlight glistening off the droplets of water clinging to his hair.

With his eyes holding hers the way they do, the question feels like more than that.

"Sure," she says as casually as she can, even as her nerves are spiking with something like excitement.

He sets the pace back to the shoreline, and she matches him stroke for stroke. As she does, she has a brief and total sense of certainty. That she has met him before—not just at the train station, but before that. That she has known him before, that he is important.

No, this is not the first time they have met. But maybe it will be the last.

Acknowledgments

When I first had the idea for this novel, I had no idea how complicated it would be to write. It has been my hardest book to write to date—and because of that, I'm really proud that it's got to this point. However, I definitely could not have done it alone.

As always, thank you to my incredibly hard-working, talented and kind agent, Sarah Hornsley, who had to read a very early (and terrible) draft of this novel, and who helped me have the courage to start over again. This year has been quite the roller coaster, and I don't know what I would have done without you.

Thank you to my UK editor, Sarah Hodgson, for believing in this idea when it was just a few sentences and for your patience and understanding while I tried to wrestle this book into shape. Thank you, too, for your creative and passionate publishing over the last few years. Both Sarah and my U.S. editor, Alex Logan, deserve huge thanks for helping to shape this novel into what it is now with some smart and insightful notes. Enormous thanks to both of you for all you have done.

Any author will attest to the fact that it takes a village to bring a book to life. Huge thanks to Jane Selley for a smart and compassionate copyedit. In the UK, thank you to Mayura Uthayakumaran for helping to keep me on track and for all your support. In marketing and publicity, thanks to Kate Straker, Felice McKeown and Sophie Walker for your creative ideas, hard work and general brilliance. Thank you to Emma Heyworth-Dunn for all your work behind the scenes and to Liz Hatherell for a careful proofread. In the U.S., huge thanks to Alli Rosenthal for spreading the word, to Anjuli Johnson in production, and Daniela Medina for your creative vision.

I always knew that there would be a tarot reading in this novel, given the speculative nature of it and to help Lissa figure out what's happening to her and why. I had never had my tarot read before this point, though I've always been interested in it. As such, as part of the research for this novel I had my own tarot reading done—thank you to Jessia Williams, who did a fabulous reading for me and not only helped me understand the process, but gave me some useful guidance in my own life, too. Huge thanks too to my friend and now co-author Katie Brown, who answered many questions about tarot, and helped me design Lissa's reading to be what it needed to be!

Lastly thank you to you, reader, if you have got to this point. Thank you for picking the book up, and for choosing to spend time with Lissa and Ash.

YOUR
BOOK
CLUB
RESOURCE

Visit **GCPClubCar.com** to sign up for the GCP Club Car newsletter, featuring exclusive promotions, info on other Club Car titles, and more.

Find us on
social media: **@ReadForeverPub**

Reading Group Guide

Dear Reader,

Thank you so much for taking the time to read *Over and Over*—and I really hope you've enjoyed spending time with Lissa and Ash!

It took me a while to get to grips with this novel. For a while, all I had was the vague idea—two soulmates who seemed destined to keep meeting each other over the course of many lifetimes but whose stories always ended in tragedy. I loved the idea of questioning whether they are being offered multiple chances to be together or chances to choose *not* to be with each other. It became a novel about trying not to repeat the mistakes of the past—something we all are guilty of from time to time, but for Lissa (and Ash), this plays out in a much more dramatic way.

One thing that took more time than I'd thought

it would was researching the past lives Lissa has been through. I think I lacked confidence here, and the process has really made me appreciate the amazing work of historical novelists! I knew I wanted to show some snippets of her past lives, and in the first incarnation of the novel, I actually tried to write this chronologically, beginning in the 1920s, then the 1950s, before moving to a more recent timeline. I wrote around 40,000 words this way—but all the time I was writing, I knew it wasn't quite working. I wasn't connecting with the characters, and the voice was all wrong—and I think a big part of that is because I was so hung up on getting the historical context right that it was taking away from the more important character elements. I was so relieved when my agent agreed it wasn't working—I trashed the whole lot, changed the characters' names, and went back to the drawing board with pen and paper.

Once I'd decided to write the novel mainly in the present with flashbacks to the past lives, the whole thing came together. I was still so glad I'd done the historical research, but it meant I wasn't getting bogged down by it. It meant I could focus on Lissa and Ash and their story, rather than feeling overwhelmed by the structure of the whole thing. I should have known that from the beginning, really—character always comes first for me.

As part of the research for the novel, I had my own tarot reading done. I knew I wanted Lissa to have some advice from a tarot reader, and I realized I had never done this myself (despite having been assigned to the fortune-telling hut for my school fair when I was about twelve). I am not a huge believer in this (just like Lissa when she first seeks out Saskia), but I found it so interesting—more so than I would have thought. It almost felt like a form of counseling at times, and, having spoken to a friend who is very into her tarot, I think a big part of it for some people is the time and space to grapple with things that might be bothering them in the present, rather than using it to predict the future. That said, I have to admit that the tarot reader got something pretty big to do with my career very spot-on. I still haven't totally decided if I'm a skeptic or a believer, but it's certainly something that will stay with me!

Whether you are a skeptic or a believer in tarot or reincarnation, I hope you've enjoyed spending time with Lissa and Ash. The story took longer to write than my previous two novels, but as a result it's one that feels very special, and I know these characters will live in my head for quite some time to come.

If you did enjoy the story, I'd always love to hear from you. I'm on Instagram at @beckyhunterbooks.

Becky x

Discussion Questions

1. For much of the novel, Lissa blames herself for what happened to her sister, Chloe. Do you think she was right to?
2. Lissa's mother, Esme, seems to also blame Lissa for Chloe's death. Can you understand why? Would you have done anything differently in Lissa's or Esme's situation?
3. Do you think Esme came to terms with what happened to Chloe by the end of the novel?
4. Lissa's father tried to move on from the past in a very different way. Do you think that his way was healthier?
5. Lissa's relationship with Elsie is something that develops throughout the novel. At the beginning, Lissa is struggling to form a sisterly relationship with Elsie. Could you see why?
6. Why do you think Lissa keeps choosing to be with Ash rather than following her own path? Why do you think it was important that she didn't choose him in the final life?

7. Do you think Lissa learned by the end of the novel what she needed to in order for Ash and her to finally have a chance at a happy ending?

8. Do you think it's only Lissa who changed over the course of the novel or did Ash have things he needed to learn, too?

9. Have you ever had a tarot reading, and if so, how was the experience?

10. Do you believe in reincarnation or past lives? If not, can you imagine a situation where you would change your mind?

About the Author

Becky Hunter lived and worked in London for several years before moving to Mozambique to volunteer with horses and try her hand at writing. A few years, a few destinations, and a few jobs later she had the idea that would become her acclaimed debut novel, *One Moment*.

Alongside writing, she now works as a freelance editor and publicist, splitting her time between Bristol and London.

For further updates follow Becky on X @Bookish_Becky and on Instagram as @beckyhunterbooks.